FRENCH HOLIDAY

SARAH READY

CROWN

ALSO BY SARAH READY

Stand Alone Romances:

The Fall in Love Checklist

Hero Ever After

Once Upon an Island

Josh and Gemma Make a Baby

Josh and Gemma the Second Time Around

French Holiday

The Space Between

Soul Mates in Romeo Romance Series:

Chasing Romeo

Love Not at First Sight

Romance by the Book

Love, Artifacts, and You

Married by Sunday

My Better Life

Scrooging Christmas

Stand Alone Novella:

Love Letters

Find these books and more by Sarah Ready at:

www.sarahready.com/romance-books

ONE (CRUMBLING) FRENCH CASTLE. TWO ENEMIES-AT-FIRST-SIGHT. THE HOLIDAY OF A LIFETIME.

Merry DeLuca has a problem—a big problem. Her sister just married her best friend and the only man she's ever loved. Her life is rapidly spiraling down the drain and she doesn't have an escape plan.

So when Merry is offered a three-month holiday living in a romantic castle in the French countryside she leaps at the chance. Merry knows her French holiday will fix everything—there will be mouthwatering pastries, delicious (meaningless) flirtations, and languid strolls through vineyards at sunset. Her holiday will be perfect.

At least, Merry believes that until she arrives and finds Noah Wright—the best man at her sister's wedding and the worst man she's ever known—staying in *her* castle.

Famous travel documentarian by day and arrogant devil by night, Noah refuses to leave the castle. Which means that Merry and Noah are stuck together in France, in a crumbling castle, in a holiday where nothing goes right. Not for Merry and not for Noah.

So they strike a truce—they'll live as cohabitating friends for three-months, and then they'll amicably part ways, never to see each other again.

But the thing about friendship? Sometimes secrets are uncovered. Mysteries revealed. Hearts laid bare. And friendship can start to feel a lot like caring. A lot like love. It can even make you wish that the holiday never has to end.

French Holiday

SARAH READY

CROWN

W.W. CROWN BOOKS
An imprint of Swift & Lewis Publishing LLC
www.wwcrown.com

This book is a work of fiction. All the characters and situations in this book are fictitious. Any resemblance to situations or persons living or dead is purely coincidental. Any reference to historical events, real people, or real locations are used fictitiously.

Library of Congress Control Number: 2022915335
ISBN: 978-1-954007-47-5 (eBook)
ISBN: 978-1-954007-48-2 (pbk)
ISBN: 978-1-954007-49-9 (large print)
ISBN: 978-1-954007-50-5 (hbk)
ISBN: 978-1-954007-51-2 (audiobook)

French Holiday

YOU CAN DO THIS. COME ON, MERRY, *YOU CAN DO THIS*.

It's only thirty-seven steps—I counted them yesterday —down a pink peony-trimmed, silk-runner-laid aisle.

That's not scary.

It's not hard.

It's easy.

You've been walking since you were eleven months old. Mom always exclaimed, "You didn't come out walking Merry, you came out running!"

So. There.

You can do this.

It'll be perfectly painless. There's Leo at the front of the church, looking exactly the same as he did yesterday, and the day before yesterday, and a year ago.

Except today, he's in a black tuxedo, with a single white orchid pinned to his chest. I gave the orchid to him, its subtle cinnamon fragrance drifting between us, as I promised him that I was happy.

Because of course I am. *Of course* I am.

And he looks happy. Some grooms are nervous, they'll have sweat beading their foreheads, or their eyes will dart nervously from the aisle to the priest and back again, and some will look downright bilious.

But not Leo.

His shoulders are back, his chin is up, and when he sees me staring over the jam-packed pews, he flashes me a bright smile and winks.

Dang it.

I quickly take a step back into the safety of the shadowed vestibule.

Oh no. *Oh no.*

Can he tell? Does he know? No. He doesn't know.

"You don't like weddings, do you?" Kimmy Fescue asks in her nasally accent, sending a sidelong glance my way.

"What makes you say that?" I ask breezily, smiling brightly at the dim stone church, the soft organ music, and the overwhelming, schizophrenic scent of spicy cologne and the floral perfume of two hundred people mixing together in a small, humid space.

Kimmy looks pointedly at my hands, and I realize that my knuckles are bone white, and I'm gripping my floral-tape-wrapped bouquet of waxy orchids and dizzily fragrant lily of the valley so tightly that I've cut off circulation. I'm not actually certain I can relax my grip— even if I wanted to—so she has a point. I lift a shoulder in acknowledgment.

She leans closer, the puce color of her bridesmaid dress making her look anemic in the gray light. "Do you want to know the secret to surviving weddings?"

I open my eyes wide and take a step closer to hear her

whisper. Of course I do. I mean, I'm not desperate. Obviously. But I'd like to hear the secret.

Kimmy is my second-cousin. She grew up in Long Island, had sex when she was fifteen to get "the virginity problem" out of the way, and then went on to enrapture my sister Angela and me with salacious tales of teenage sex and scandal for the next five years.

We lost touch when she became a dental hygienist and moved to Cleveland. But now, here she is. Back for the wedding.

"What?" I ask, certain she'll have the best advice.

It's just like when we were kids, tucked in our sleeping bags in the living room, Kimmy sharing life wisdom like exercises for increasing your breast size (didn't work), how to use hardboiled eggs to practice Frenching (I always ended up eating the egg), and where to find the best knock-off Louis Vuitton purses (sketchy basement apartment, side street in Forest Hills, never went).

She glances over her shoulder, her long fake lashes brushing her round cheeks as she glances at the three groomsmen, all in black tuxedos.

Then she looks back at me, a prurient glint in her eye. "Before the wedding begins, you choose a guy. One of the groomsmen."

"Choose a guy?"

"Yeah. You choose a guy. Then at the reception, drink all the champagne you want, eat all the cake you can, and then have mind-blowing, no holds barred, on the floor, against the wall, in the hallway, in the coat closet, in the bathroom if you're into that...do it a few times, at least three—"

"Three times?"

Kimmy nods, then reaches into her cleavage and pulls out a tube of lipstick. She twists it, the bright, flaming red shining as she smooths it over her lips. "You want some?" She holds the tube out to me.

I shake my head. "No. I'll swell up." I gesture vaguely at my lips.

"Ohhh right. The beetle allergy."

She means carmine.

Not that most people realize it, but a lot of red dye is made from crushed up insects called cochineal. Unfortunately, I'm allergic and whenever I use lipstick with carmine, my mouth gets covered in hives.

It's gross.

Kimmy shrugs, caps the lipstick and shoves the tube back between her breasts. "Anyway. I'm gunning for the tall one, Reggie. He looks like he has stamina. I hear he played basketball in college."

She wiggles her eyebrows.

I wince. Kimmy doesn't know Reggie, but I do. He's a friend, just like the other groomsman is my friend. We're a group. Me, Leo, Reggie, and John. There's no way I'm going to get down and dirty with any of them.

Obviously.

And then, well, there's Noah.

So. No.

Kimmy takes in my expression. "I know, I know, it sounds crazy. But trust me. This is the twelfth bridesmaid dress I've had to wear."

She plucks at the puce-colored silk and draws her lips down in a frown. "By far it's also the most hideous. Listen, everybody knows being a bridesmaid sucks. You get all depressed. Oh, woe is me, I haven't found the love of my life, I'm not the one getting chained in matrimony. Boo hoo. Sob sob. The only way to solve that depression spiral is to drink a tanker of champagne and gorge yourself on a sexy stranger. Trust me, it'll fix you right up."

She nods at my white-knuckled grip on my bouquet.

"Okay." I give a tight smile. I'm not going to gorge myself on a sexy stranger. Perhaps Kimmy doesn't have as good of advice as I remember.

Except for the champagne bit. Maybe I'll drink loads of champagne.

The door to the choir room shuts with a hard snick, and I turn to see Vick, the third bridesmaid, lifting my sister's train.

"Beautiful," I say, smiling, even though I saw Angela only three minutes ago, when I helped her touch up her makeup and gave her a pep talk. But now her veil is down and she looks really, truly like a bride.

I ignore the tightening in my chest. Because suddenly, the ridiculousness of Kimmy's advice, the distraction, all that's gone, and I can't breathe.

It's like a giant green anaconda is squeezing my chest and there's no more air. I can't breathe. I can't...no, that's ridiculous. Of course I can breathe. It's easy. Just suck in a breath.

There. Better.

That tightening is nothing. There's no anaconda. No squeezing. It's heartburn, I'm sure, from the four coffees I've already had today. Getting up at four in the morning to help with hair, flowers, and make-up will do that to you.

There. See.

Breathing.

"Do you think Leo will like it?" Angela asks anxiously for the seventieth time today. And she's asking me, because as everyone knows, I'm Leo's best friend. His buddy, his pal, his BFF, his "one of the guys," his...whatever.

I walk forward and straighten her veil. Then I look into her large, brown eyes—the only feature we have in common—and say cheerily, "He won't like it. He'll love it. He loves you, doesn't he? So how could he not? You're gorgeous."

Looking at her nervous expression, like she's asking for something from me, I'm reminded of when we were kids. I was three when she was born, ready to be a big sister. My parents say that when I met her at the hospital I looked at her blonde fuzzy hair and pink face, and I said, "She looks like a baby angel." So they named her Angela.

She was beautiful from the minute she was born. Not like most babies who take a bit to look like anything other than a wrinkled up alien/peanut. No, she was Gerber baby gorgeous.

For the first years of her life, everyone cooed at her, blew kisses, and random shopkeepers would always offer stickers, or balloons, or extra scoops of ice cream. I was never jealous. I was proud. Everyone loved my sister, but none of them got to love her as much as I did.

I always gave her the biggest piece of cake. I let her go first on the swing. If I wanted to watch a travel documentary but she wanted to see MTV, we watched MTV.

When I was twelve, I babysat Kyle Simmons for an entire summer. He put gum in my hair, wiped his boogers on me, and refused to do anything but play Crazy Eights, over and over and over. But I saved up enough money to buy the bike I'd been lusting after.

I wheeled it home, so happy, so impressed that I had a ten speed with hand brakes and shiny red paint, that at first I didn't see Angela hopping up and down and laughing and then hugging me. It was the day before her birthday, and she thought I'd bought it for her. As a surprise.

I gave her the bike.

For some reason, I'm thinking about that bike now. She discarded it after two months of riding it. It's long forgotten in a dusty corner of our childhood garage, chucked behind the flattened cardboard boxes and cockroach traps.

Angela blinks and waves a hand in front of her face. "Leo does love me, doesn't he?"

Yes.

Yes, he does.

The pastor hurries over, dressed in her formal gear. She has chin-length gray hair, round glasses, and a demeanor that makes you feel like you should be whispering, and probably apologizing for something, although I'm not certain for what.

"All ready, ladies?" she asks.

Of course I'm ready. There's no reason I wouldn't be. There's no reason to feel upset. In fact, I wasn't upset at all. That was an anomaly.

I can do this.

Easy peasy.

The organ shifts into the song I know leads up to the bridal march.

Now that I think on it, I never noticed before how much the bridal march sounds like a funeral dirge. The chords are just the same, a slow, pushing force inexorably plodding forward.

"Yes, we're ready," Angela trills, smiling at us three bridesmaids, lined up in our puce dresses. "Aren't we?"

Kimmy smirks at me, nods knowingly at the groomsmen lining up on the other side of the vestibule, and then gives me a lurid wink.

"Merry? All ready?" Angela asks.

"Absolutely," I tell my sister, the woman who's about to walk down the aisle and marry the love of my life. "Never been readier," I say, which of course is a big, fat, red bike-shaped lie.

2

THIRTY-SEVEN STEPS.

That's all.

Kimmy and Reggie, Vick and John are gliding down the aisle. All two hundred guests stand and face the back of the church.

There's Uncle Diego and Aunt Bertie—and wow, how is that hat staying on her head? It has a birdhouse, two stuffed turtle doves, and a bunch of grapes, that's...hmm.

There's a whole row full of our cousins, and the Marlands, our neighbors from when we were kids. And there's my godmother, Jupiter Mountlake.

Leo's parents are at the front, his mom looks fabulous in a peach flapper dress. And then, well, there's our parents. Angela was worried. I told her I'd take care of it.

I didn't.

Mom promised she'd wear the powder blue floral dress, even though she said it made her look like an overstuffed chintz armchair shoved into a corner.

Mom lied.

She's in a floor-length, sleeveless, satin, *white* gown and a wide-brimmed black hat with a *veil*. She lifts her hand when she sees me coming out of the vestibule, wiggles her bejeweled fingers, and raises her eyebrows in a smirk, that I know from twenty-eight years of being her daughter means, *what can I say, if you've got it, flaunt it.*

Angela never loses her temper. She's impervious to our mom's deranged need to always be the center of attention, but this time...

I imagine Angela swaying down the aisle, smiling sweetly at our friends and family, cheeks rosy, a joyful tear in her eye, everyone sighing at the twenty yards of handstitched lace and three hundred and seventeen freshwater pearls sewn into her wedding dress and then...she sees Mom.

"Mother! You dare!" she'll shriek. "You dare!"

And then she'll beat Mom with her white rose, calla lily, and peony bouquet, silky petals flying everywhere. The wedding march will become a surprised clunking of discordant notes. Aunt Bertie will lose her hat. My dad will finally cross the DMZ that was drawn twenty years ago shortly after their divorce and yank Mom and Angela apart.

For his trouble, my mom will crush him with her hat. "You want a younger wife!" she'll yell. "Well, how do you like this Botox?!" Then she'll kick him where she's dreamed of kicking him for decades.

And that will be the end of the wedding. All because I couldn't keep my mind off Leo, and on my mom where it should've been.

I glare at my mom and she puts her hand down and swiftly turns away to stare at the pastor waiting for us.

Right.

Well.

Vick and John are a quarter way down the aisle. Against my better judgment I look at Leo. He's...he looks so happy.

"Smile."

I flinch.

Ugh. I forgot about Noah.

Which is difficult since he's standing next to me and my arm rests on the worsted wool of his tuxedo. The fabric is smooth and warm under my hand and his heat comes through like the sun warming my skin.

Noah's arm is tense, the muscles of his forearm and bicep are tight. If he were anyone else, I'd say he's nervous. But since it's Noah, I know he's tense because he doesn't like being touched—especially by me—and he'd like to get these thirty-seven steps over with.

Well, get in line, buddy.

"I am smiling," I say through gritted teeth, nodding and faux smiling at my Uncle Diego.

Noah turns and studies my expression, ignoring the fact that we're supposed to be counting Vick's steps, so that we can proceed with the wedding march exactly twenty-one steps in.

"It's a wedding, not a funeral," he says in that arrogant way he has. "You look like someone died."

Embarrassed heat suffuses me.

I forget to count Vick's steps.

Noah suddenly pulls me forward, down the aisle, and I trip over my feet. He takes a moment to steady me with a condescending smile and a look in his eyes that says, *smile, and for goodness sake, pull yourself together.*

I loathe him.

I loathe Noah Wright.

Trust me, the antipathy is mutual.

It all started four years ago.

I'd finally landed a job as a human resources assistant (after graduating I'd worked at an all-you-can-eat pasta place while I schlepped résumés around the corporate merry-go-round for years...yes, years).

I moved to a furnished studio apartment closer to my office (supposedly temporary, but I'm still there four years later), and realized I had no friends in the area.

Then, like manna from heaven, I saw Leo open a bodega door for a stooped grandma wearing a babushka. He was going in to shop, but when he saw her struggling with her sack of groceries, he gallantly carried it for her across the street and up to her apartment.

After that, I kept my eyes open for him. He lived in a long, railroad-style, subdivided brownstone, with a tiny patch of grass at the front.

On Saturdays he mowed his front lawn, and then went on and mowed the lawn of his neighbor, a retired taxi driver with crippling arthritis. I'm not a stalker, I found out about his neighbor after we became friends.

But two weeks after I moved, when I went home to visit my dad and stepmom for the obligatory ritual of Sunday brunch, Dad made a point of saying in a loud, shocked voice, "My word, Merry. Are those crow's feet? You look old. You need to find a husband before it's too late."

I told my mom about it in a fit of pique.

She was my dad's first wife. Discarded when she hit thirty for a younger model. He's married down four times now. They keep getting younger. But once they hit that fateful number twenty-nine, the divorce papers are paraded out.

Apparently, my advanced age of twenty-four was concerning for him. My mom though—for once in her life—agreed with him.

"You do, Merry. You look old. And you can't look old, because if my daughter looks old, then what does that say about me?"

Anyway.

It didn't matter. I'd found the man I was going to marry and his name was Leo Fernandes.

Sure enough, one week later, when I was kicking a soccer ball around in the park, he approached me and asked if I wanted to play a pick-up game with him and his friends, Reggie and John.

Our circle was made. Our friendship was formed. Every once in a while I thought I should tell Leo how I felt, but I had time, I had plenty of time.

Why rush love? It should be given time to grow.

Every once in a while, Leo would mention his best friend from childhood, Noah Wright.

Yes. *The* Noah Wright.

Famed travel documentarian, world-class photographer, videographer, erudite travel writer, loved by millions of women around the world.

His smile is enough to send grandmas into convulsions, his insight and wisdom enough to touch the heart of the most hardened cynic. His passion for travel, history, and the sense of place is enough to make anyone imagine how he'd react to traveling over...a woman. At least, that's what the comments online say.

Obviously I looked.

Leo talked about Noah enough for me to be curious about his best friend. Besides, if I was friends with Leo, then I'd have to be friends with Noah, his other best friend.

"You'll love him," Leo said. "You guys will get along so well," he promised. "He's the nicest guy you'll ever meet," he assured.

In my naiveté I believed him.

I believed the documentaries that showed Noah's thoughtful expression, his passionate, resonate voice detailing a romantic seaside vista, or expounding the mysteries of a Neolithic earthen henge.

I believed Noah's artistic photographs, because only a beautiful person could catch beauty like that, right? I believed his blogs and his books, written with such care.

I believed that his art matched his insides. I believed, just like millions of others, that his strong jaw (ugh, can't believe I'm saying that), his glossy, thick black hair (tempting women's fingers everywhere), his soulful (nooooo) blue-gray eyes, and the freckles sprinkled across his cheeks (falsely promising cheerfulness and innocence) meant he was a good person.

Nay appearance! Thou art deceitful!

Or something like that.

Anyway, I finally met Noah two months ago, after Angela and Leo's whirlwind engagement. I'd invited Leo over to my place, I was finally, finally going to tell him how I felt.

Then Angela called, she was home from grad school, a newly minted physical therapist. Her car had a flat, could I please come and bring the jack? She knew I could change a tire. Dad made sure of it. I couldn't leave my sister stranded on side of the road, could I? Leo came.

When he saw Angela...well, I knew.

Whatever we'd had, whatever our friendship was...it didn't hold a candle to what he was feeling for my sister.

But that's how everyone reacted when they first met Angela. She's beautiful. She's angelic. She *glows*. I've seen plenty of guys bowled over by her, usually they recover in a week or two.

Not Leo.

He changed her tire.

He drove with her to her apartment to make sure she made it to her new place okay.

He called me the next day to say they were getting married.

Married.

Because...love.

Noah flew in the next week. Supposedly to make sure Angela was good enough for Leo or some crap like that.

I walked in on Leo and Noah arguing in the coat room of Papa Gallo's restaurant. They were late, my mom, Angela and I were already seated, waiting to meet Noah. I was coming to see if he'd arrived.

"I'm only saying, this is sudden—"

"It's not though. I know Merry, she's the best kind of person. Her sister is just like her, but more. Better. So much better. I love her."

I took a step back, feeling dizzy, my ears burning. This is why you don't listen in on conversations.

"Leo—"

"Noah. I was thinking, you and Merry, you'd be great together, you should—"

"No. Stop. I don't want your pity leftovers. Leave it. You've told me enough about her over the years for me to know that I'm not interested. I'm here about you. Are you sure about this? One hundred percent certain?"

I slowly, so slowly backed away, my cheeks flaming, my heart pounding, my feet scraping over the tile floor, the smell of garlic biting at me, mixing with rosemary and the shameful taste of mortification.

Unfortunately, I wasn't fast enough to avoid Noah spotting my retreat. His eyes, as dark as blue flame, caught me. They widened, ran over me like a hot coal, and then narrowed on my face.

His gaze was as solid as a touch, hot and uncomfortable, like he could pull open my chest, see all the way inside me, down into the depths of my heart, and he didn't like what he found.

Not one bit.

I fought the urge to push back my snarled, shoulder-length brown hair, or pat at the perspiration on my forehead, beading from sitting next to the furnace-hot, apple wood smoking, brick oven.

I even fought the urge to straighten my dress, a baggy, suddenly conspicuously unflattering, khaki A-line that I'd worn to work.

But why should I be uncomfortable? Noah Wright should be the uncomfortable one, after what I'd heard him say.

But no.

I'd been caught.

He knew exactly who I was.

An eavesdropper, by accident or not.

And he wasn't impressed.

Well, I wasn't impressed either.

He may look like a god, have a travel show, books on library shelves, and photographs in museums. Indeed, he may be able to make women weep with one look from his smoky eyes, but women are smart. Very, very smart. And if a man looks like a god, but acts like a jerk, then they can laugh in his face. Because we are independent. Smart. Willing to go beyond looks and drill down to character. For instance, Leo has a wonderful character.

No. Don't think about Leo. He's marrying your sister.

Anyway. I was willing to give Noah another chance. Even three or four chances.

But every time I was forced to be within fifty feet of him, Noah made sure that I knew he was *not impressed*.

On our second meeting at Leo's parents' house, I gave him a bottle of red wine from France as an overture of friendship. I found the bottle in the trash, unopened.

The third time we met, I sweetly offered to drive him back to his hotel. I could be nice. I could *try*. He looked at me like he'd rather sit in a barrel full of oozing pus-filled slugs, and practically ran out of the restaurant to hail a cab.

The fourth time, when we were discussing wedding details at Leo's, with the whole wedding party there, Leo said, "And Noah, as best man, you'll walk down the aisle with Merry."

No one noticed but me, but when Leo said that, Noah went very still, and the corners of his mouth turned down. He didn't look at me, but I could feel all his attention focused on me, like he was touching me and repulsed by what he felt.

I cornered him when he came out of the bathroom.

"What is your problem?" I hissed.

"What?" he pretended surprise.

"What did I ever do to you?"

I admit, this was three glasses of wine in, and all my tactful HR mediation training was out the window.

"I don't know what you're talking about," he said

stiffly, and then he edged past me, making sure not to touch me, even though the hall is about twenty-six inches wide and he's six foot two at least, well-muscled, and me, I'm not petite.

But I wasn't going to be denied, so I whisper-hissed, "I'm talking about your blatant dislike of me. What did I ever do?"

He stopped walking. His shoulders stiffened, and I think, for a minute, he stopped breathing.

Then, he turned slightly to the side, although his face was still buried in shadow and he said what I never, ever wanted anyone to say out loud, "He's in love with your sister. Let it go."

I was too stunned to say anything more as he stalked off. And that is when I decided that Noah and I would never, ever, ever be friends.

From then on we resided in Loathingville, the incorporated town of mutual antipathy.

So.

"Smile," he says again, dragging me down the wedding aisle.

I bare my teeth even wider.

"Go to hell," I say through gritted teeth.

He flashes one of his rare grins and leans toward me. The falsely tempting scent of him, fresh shaving soap mixed with warm skin, washes over me. "Planning on joining me?"

I consider stepping on his toe.

He *knows* I'm already there. Would the point of my stiletto do too much damage? Could he still walk if I "accidentally" shoved my spiked heel into his big toe?

I'm seriously considering accidental maiming when everyone lets out a breathless sigh, my aunt's face lights up with awe, and I know without a doubt that Angela has started down the aisle.

I stare straight ahead, pasting on a bright, bright smile.

I don't look at Leo.

Noah leans down and whispers, "Good job. Save a dance for me."

No.

No way.

No how.

What Kimmy said about surviving weddings flashes through my mind and I wonder, is that Noah's survival plan too? Is he...

No.

As we pull apart, he sends me a wry look.

Maybe he is.

Well, that's a heck no. A strong heck no.

The wedding vows begin.

I grip my flowers.

3

CHAMPAGNE IS DELICIOUS.

I've had two, no three, no...hmmm, well, it's delicious.

The cool perspiration from the glass runs over my fingers and I take another sip, letting the sparkling effervescence nibble at my tongue.

I lean back in the folding chair, one of eight at my empty table, and stare out at the dance floor, where a conga line dance-off is underway. Dinner wasn't half-bad. I sat at the bridal table, next to Noah, where his pointed glances and stiff demeanor distracted me enough that I barely noticed every time the glasses were clanked for another bride and groom kiss-off.

Dinner's over. The cake is cut. The toasts are done. The father-daughter dance is complete and the real party has begun.

I take another sip and tug at my dress. The built-in corset is digging into my ribs.

If Angela had asked, "Merry, do you want your tits to

look fabulous, or do you want to be comfortable?" I would've voted for comfortable. One hundred percent.

I stare down at my gloriously lifted breasts, like two soft pillows mounded high, and scowl. They look perky and happy, like they enjoy being on display. I imagine they got that exhibitionist tendency from my mother.

Oh well.

I whisper at them, "Nobody asked you. Simmer down."

Okay, maybe I've actually had four glasses of champagne.

I take another sip and watch the prism light of the disco ball splash across the dance floor.

My sister and Leo are waltzing to a heavy bass pop song. I smile wryly and let the thumping music vibrate over me. Maybe I'll head back to my room. Angela, in her bridal wisdom, booked the reception in the ballroom of a hotel, so after we get all boozy and exhausted we can stumble back to our rooms and sleep it off.

Bed sounds nice.

But no, it's only eight o'clock. Leaving early would look odd. Although...I don't see Kimmy or Reggie anywhere.

Huh.

My eye catches Noah. He's at the bar, surrounded by wedding guests but still managing to look separate from everyone. Apart.

Not that he doesn't chat everyone up. I've watched dozens of women, from age five to eighty-five, come up to him and tell him how much they love his work. He smiles, thanks them, and gives them an autograph, or takes a selfie, or shakes a hand. You'd think, being constantly surrounded by people, he'd look a part of things, but somehow, he doesn't.

There's something about him that doesn't fit.

I just can't put my finger on it.

Maybe it's that even though people are constantly talking to him, no one is ever talking with him.

I shake my head. No. I have to stop giving deeper meanings to people and things. Sometimes, an arrogant, stand-offish, prickly man is exactly that and nothing more.

Suddenly, Noah turns his face toward me and catches me staring.

He lifts an eyebrow.

I flush. It's the champagne.

Usually, when I'm caught staring I quickly avert my eyes, pretend I wasn't. But I'm too fuddled to bother.

I keep staring.

Oh. Jeez.

He's walking this way. His long-legged stride cuts through the dancing guests, the tipsy couples, and the laughing groups. He has a very distinct stride. It's one without any time for nonsense or wandering, it's the stride of a person who knows exactly where they want to be and exactly how to get there.

I stare boldly at him, tilting my chin up when he stops next to my table, a near empty glass of whisky in his hand. After tonight, I won't ever have to see him again, except maybe at the random Christmas party or christening.

There's a tightening in my chest at the thought of christenings, but that's years away. Plenty of time to adjust to that future.

The point is, this'll be nearly the last time I'll ever have to see him. That makes me feel magnanimous, like I can forgive, forget, and put behind us all the antipathy. I can be gracious.

"Have a seat." I gesture at the empty chair next to me, where he sat during dinner. The table is now cleared, except for our bouquets, sparkly confetti, and half-eaten plates of cake and empty cups.

For a second I think he's going to refuse. He looks behind him at the exit, as if he has many, many better things he could be doing. But then he shakes himself off, like he's flinging off droplets of water, and sinks to the chair next to me.

He sets his whisky glass on the white tablecloth and then leans toward me, his leg brushing against mine, his forearm, nearly coming in contact with my own. I lift my eyebrows, curious as to what he has to say.

He tilts his chin and says in a low voice that somehow resonates over the DJ's music, "Bit of advice. You shouldn't be so obvious."

I flinch. What the heck?

Okay, I take it back, I'm not feeling magnanimous. "I don't know what you're what talking about."

He shrugs and looks out over the dance floor, his eyes landing on Leo and Angela.

When he turns back to me he almost looks pitying, which sucks. "Look. If you're going to insist on being in unrequited love—"

"I am not!"

"With Leo—"

"Stop it!"

"—then you can't be so obvious. The way you stare,

with sunshine and rainbows in your eyes, the way you sigh, all breathy and sad, a blind *and* deaf man would be able to pick up on it."

"I don't know what you're talking about." I scathingly repeat his statement from months ago.

He lifts a shoulder in a shrug, like he couldn't care less whether I admitted to it or not.

"It's not my business—"

"You're right."

"—but unrequited love is probably the worst thing you could do to yourself."

Okay, I have to disagree. "The heart doesn't choose who to love or when to love, and it can't choose when to stop. *Not* that I'm saying I'm in unrequited love. That would be self-sabotaging."

Noah's lips curl into a knowing smile. "Well. Not that I'm saying you're in unrequited love—"

"You just did."

"—but if you were, then you might want to be less obvious. For instance, instead of staring at the object of your affection like a hungry dog begging for a bone—"

"I'm a dog now?"

"And sighing every time he smiles, and blushing whenever he looks at you, and doing everything and anything he asks, like a well-trained—"

"Dog?"

He gives me a flat look. "You might want to try and improve upon the art of unrequited love."

Gah. Is this how he lectures in his videos on the history of Rome? Did I miss his condescending tone? Fine. Whatever. "And how do you suggest doing that?"

He lifts his glass and takes a swallow of whisky, his

throat working, his Adam's apple bobbing. His neck is long and I never noticed quite how appealing the shadow of stubble on his...no.

Too much champagne. Bad champagne.

"You can't let it show," he says in a low, melodious voice that draws me in like an unsuspecting bird flying toward a clear windowpane.

I catch the peaty, butterscotch scent of whisky, taste it on my tongue, as if I'd shared his glass. The throb of the music wraps around us, and I lean closer to him, our mouths nearly touching.

"First, stop staring. Stop the longing looks. Stop looking, period."

I'm caught by his eyes, stare at him.

"Fine. Easy," I say. As easy as scaling the Matterhorn.

His eyes crinkle at the corners. "Next, stop sighing, stop smiling dreamily. Stop, period. If necessary, think of something you dislike." He considers for a moment, then says, "For instance, loud chewing, slow walkers, group texts with too many people, email round robins—"

"People who clip their nails on the subway," I add, nodding, then getting into the spirit of it, "cold, wet socks. Loud talking during movies. Being told to calm down."

He grins at me, a quick flash of his teeth. I struggle to repress my answering smile, but can't quite manage it.

"That's it," he says. "Imagine those things every time you get the urge to plaster that dreamy smile on your face."

Hmm.

"Last, if you have to do something for him, if you are *compelled*..."

I nod quickly. I've been compelled.

Two weeks ago I bought Leo tickets to the New York City FC game (Angela doesn't like soccer), because I knew it'd make him happy. I mean it wasn't just for him, John and Reggie came too, but okay yes, it was, essentially, for him.

"Then for goodness sake," Noah leans closer, articulating his words to make his point, "do it in secret. Haven't you ever read any books? You can paint the walls of your room the color of his eyes, you can save his future child's life from an evil wizard, you can give him your fortune upon your death—"

"These are examples from books?"

He lifts his eyebrows.

Note to self, read more books on unrequited love. Or, better yet, find the movie adaptions.

"You can do romantic, grand things. But they can never know."

"Never?" I ask unthinkingly, taken aback by the force of his gaze.

"Never," he agrees.

Well, isn't that a bummer.

Except he's right, isn't he? If Leo realized, or Angela... it would destroy everything. I don't want to hurt my sister. I don't want to hurt my best friend. I want them to be happy.

So.

Then I think of something which should've been obvious before. "How long have you been in unrequited love?"

He lets out a surprised huff and then, gloriously, his mouth twists into a self-deprecating smile. He looks at the ceiling, tallying up, then says, "Too long."

Well.

Okay.

No wonder he has so much advice to give.

I stare at him and he shrugs, as if to say, *what are you going to do?*

Exactly.

Then he leans back in his chair, and as he does, the intimate bubble surrounding us bursts. The music grows loud again, pressing against me, my champagne has grown warm, and the pain from the bones of the corset digging into my ribs is sharp and painful.

Still, it's early, and I can't leave the party yet.

So I ask on a whim, feeling wistful. "Do you want to dance?"

He frowns and shakes his head. "No."

"But you said—"

"I changed my mind."

"Rude."

He's back to being arrogant and cold again, I can see it in his face. He's separating himself, pulling into that apart, aloof space.

"I have no idea how you and Leo became friends. He's so outgoing and friendly and you're..."

Noah gives me another flat look, which is starting to give me a tickly, fizzy feeling similar to the way I imagine bubbles in champagne feel as they float to the surface.

"You should try to be nicer. More people will like you."

"Lots of people like me," he says arrogantly.

I shake my head. "No. They like *Noah Wright*, they don't like *you*."

At that, his mouth spreads into a wide smile. It's there, then gone.

"Let's have another drink." Suddenly, flying on the

wings of that smile, I'm feeling optimistic, I'm feeling light, I'm feeling that maybe everything will work out, maybe...maybe...

"Good idea," he agrees.

4

THERE'S A SOCK IN MY MOUTH. IT'S MUZZY, FUZZY, SUCKING all the liquid and...no, wait, that's just my mouth. Why, why did I drink so much champagne?

My head spins and pounds in a jolting tilt-a-whirl rhythm. I think about opening my eyes and immediately discard the idea. Prying them open is as appealing as Monday morning meetings without coffee. There's a shaft of light pouring over my face from the hotel room window, baking my eyelids in morning red. I let out a soft moan.

At least the bed is comfortable. The sheets are soft and smooth, they're silky, maybe Egyptian cotton, at least five hundred count, no skimping here. The mattress is pillowed and I'm warm beneath the feathered down comforter. Maybe I can sleep my hangover away. That'd be nice.

I snuggle back down into the bed, burying my head under the pillow to block out the light. There's a lavender spray on the sheets, mixing with the smell of champagne, and peat-smoked whisky. Maybe I moved on to whisky after the champagne? But the only taste in my mouth is the chalky, dry, sweet/bitter tinge of too much champagne. I moan and crush the feather pillow against my head, the sheets slip over my bare skin and I realize I have to pee. Bad.

Bad, bad.

Which means I have to open my eyes. I have to get up.

I stretch my legs over the sheets, the softness gliding over my skin and bare back, and then...

Then...

There's a noise.

A soft, deep exhale.

What. The. Crap.

I freeze.

Petrified.

There's someone here.

There's someone in bed with me.

My heart pounds in my chest, in tandem with the jackhammering in my head, and I hold tense and still, like a rabbit spotted by an eagle in an open field. If I don't move, then they won't realize I'm here.

No. Wait.

That doesn't make sense.

I listen closely. My bed partner lets out a long, sleep-filled sigh, their even breathing filling the silence. Now that I'm paying attention, it's obvious that I'm not alone. The mattress tilts slightly toward the middle, the weight of another person like a gravitational force, pulling me closer. There are more smells, sweat and soap, not just the scent of champagne, whisky, and lavender.

If I stretch my legs just a few inches, I know

instinctually, that I'll run my bare skin against someone else. They're *that* close.

I can feel body heat billowing under the covers. I tend toward cold, usually wearing socks at night. My bed is never this toasty. It'd only be this toasty if I was sharing with someone else. Someone hot.

I think of my hand on Noah's arm as we walked down the aisle. He's hot-blooded. He's warm.

No.

No no no no no no.

No.

Slowly, carefully, I push the pillow off my face and crack open my eyes, squinting into the harsh daylight. Then I quietly and cautiously turn my head, just a bit, just the tiniest bit so I can see who...

Oh. No.

It's Noah.

Of course it's Noah.

Mortification prickles over my skin, itchy hot.

I remember now. There's flashes of us toasting, drink after drink. Conversations about love (we agreed, it's a terrible state), travel (where I'd go, where he's been), and life goals (me: to help people find fulfillment. Him: okay, I don't remember that part).

And then...I'm inviting myself to his room and we're drinking, and laughing, and then...I remember, I told him he had a nice smile and I stood on my tiptoes and kissed him, there was tongue, lots and lots of tongue and then I said, let's do it, let's have no-holds-barred sex against the wall, and in the closet, and in the bathroom, and the hall and...that's it.

I never believed I'd actually forget what happened if I got too drunk.

Now I know.

Champagne is the devil's brew.

It's bad enough that I can't get over Leo, now I've gone and slept with his best friend.

Except, maybe I haven't?

I perk up, feeling slightly better. I don't remember doing it. I wouldn't *really* do it. Surely, I wouldn't. And if I don't remember it, and I wouldn't do it, then it didn't happen.

Logic.

I narrow my eyes and study Noah. He has dark morning stubble shadowing his face. He looks softer in sleep, his hard jaw not as set, his brow unwrinkled. Even his wavy black hair falls over his forehead more casually. And those freckles, the ones that falsely proclaim boyish innocence, well, when he's relaxed in sleep, that promise almost seems true. Even his lips, which are most often firm or turned in an arrogant smile, are soft, slightly open, the lower lip full and tempting. I avert my eyes and look at the rest of him.

Well, at least what's not covered by the comforter.

Because...

The question is—is Noah naked too?

That's the question, isn't it?

Okay. Neck. That's bare. Obviously.

Shoulders. Yup. They're nice shoulders, no one can deny that.

His chest, it's defined, very defined. And there's the top of a tattoo peeking out from the covers, just over his heart, but I can't make out the design. So, he sleeps shirtless. Big deal. Most guys do. Right?

The question is—did we do it—or did we not?

Slowly, I pinch the top of the comforter and lift it an

inch, then another, and another. I suck in a sharp breath and drop it.

Wow. Okay. Wow.

Yes.

He's naked.

But still, that doesn't mean...I'm naked, he's naked, one plus one doesn't necessarily make two.

Not always.

Aaaaand condom.

That's a condom.

There's a condom at the bottom of the comforter.

Why? Why, Merry, why?

Kimmy did not have good advice! When have you ever followed through with her advice? Why did you have to start now?

Okay. Calm down. Breathe. Relax.

It's no big deal.

Noah and I had sex. I propositioned, he accepted. Fine.

But, honestly, there is no way that I want to face this right now. Not feeling the way I do, not with my chest aching and broken from yesterday's wedding (hangovers are the best time for honesty), not when Noah and I really don't have anything in common, not even mutual like.

I can't face this.

So, I do something I'm not proud of, but I'm not *not* proud of either.

I gingerly slip off the comforter, the rustling sheets overly loud, and tiptoe out of the bed, my feet sinking into the plush carpet. I lean down, ignoring the pounding in my skull, and the pinching in my bladder, and grab my puce bridesmaid's dress. Quiet, ever so quietly, I slip the dress over my head. Then I frantically scan the room, searching for my shoes. Ah. There, by the closet.

I tiptoe over and grab them, then wince when I see another condom lying next to the closet.

Bed. Closet.

Against my will I look toward the open bathroom door, the red light of the smoke alarm illuminating the space, and yes indeed, there's another condom on the bathroom floor.

It's mortifying.

It's...well, I mean, I almost wish I could remember. I've never had sex three times in a night before. Bed. Closet. Bathroom.

I slip my shoes on and wonder if we completed Kimmy's survival quest and I'll find another condom in the hallway outside of the door.

Ah.

No.

It's actually inside the room in the hallway by the door. Apparently, from its location, we did it *against* the door.

Well. There you go. Not three times. Four times.

I close my eyes and take a steadying breath. Back in the room, Noah lets out another soft sleep noise. My skin prickles almost like his mouth is on me, his lips moving over me.

Not to state the obvious, but Noah and I aren't exactly couple material. We aren't the love-at-first-sight type, the friends-to-lovers type, or even the hate-to-love type, we're just...a mistake. A terrible, one-night mistake.

I'll go on with my life, my job, my...whatever. And he'll go back to his life. Traveling, filming, and making women crazed with lust.

And we'll both go back to our unfortunate states of unrequited love.

Without each other.

In fact, this is like a bad dream I'd like to forget.

Oh wait. I already have.

With that happy thought, I open the door and flee to my own hotel room. With luck, I'll never, ever, ever see Noah Wright again.

5

AFTER A SHOWER, BRUSHING MY TEETH, DRINKING ABOUT A
gallon of water, and throwing on comfy jeans and a top, I
head to the hotel lobby in search of coffee and dry toast.

The cavernous hotel lobby is quiet this morning, and
the hush seems strange compared to the revelry of last
night. I squint at the bright fluorescent light reflecting off
the marble floors and try to remember where the
breakfast buffet is. But then at the bar across the lobby I
see my godmother Jupiter waving at me.

"Meredith! Morning!"

I lift my hand and smile at her enthusiasm. When I
reach her, I'm glad to see the bartender has laid out a
French press full of hot black coffee and a stainless steel
toast rack full of lightly toasted bread.

"You are my favorite person," I tell her, while I slide
onto the leather-topped barstool next to her. The
welcoming scent of Arabica roast wafts between us.

Jupiter scans my outfit, my messy bun, and the bags
under my eyes, and then shakes her finger at me with

mirth. "Merry! Tell me, how many dubious decisions have you made today?"

I avert my eyes while I grab for the coffee, trying desperately not to picture Noah's long limbs sprawled across the bed, his cheek resting on the pillow.

"None," I say, pouring the steaming, delicious-smelling coffee into my mug.

Jupiter tsks. "Shame. I try to make at least three dubious choices before breakfast every single day."

I nod in agreement. Jupiter was my mom's best friend freshman year of college. While my mom went on to graduate, then marry and have babies, Jupiter dropped out and went to model for artists in Paris. There are portraits and nudes of her at the Tate in London and the Museum of Modern Art in Paris.

She says since her parents gave her the name Jupiter, she may as well live up to it. Her skin is pearly translucent, her hair so blonde it's nearly white, she's tall and sharp-angled, shockingly beautiful and has the wonderful habit of showing up out of the blue and showering me with inappropriate and exotic presents, like a hookah pipe when I was eleven and a pink silk negligée when I was fifteen. Unfortunately I didn't get to keep either.

I once asked her if she liked being a model for famous and temperamental modern artists and she said, "I like being a nude model, because the artists only think about the art. I dislike sitting for portraits, because then the artist is only thinking about me being nude."

I'd been considering sitting nude for evening art classes to help pay my college tuition, but Jupiter said it wouldn't work, because I wasn't able to sit still and I wasn't unusual looking enough.

Jupiter scrapes marmalade over her toast and studies me with quiet intensity. I take a sip of coffee and let it scald my tongue, relishing the bitter taste.

Finally, Jupiter says, "Well. You look better than you did yesterday what with your grabby sister breaking your heart."

I choke on my coffee and then cough, hitting my chest. "What? What's that?"

Does everyone know?

Jupiter rolls her eyes and takes a bite of her toast, the orange marmalade smell drifting to me, making me slightly queasy.

"Your sister has always wanted everything you have. I'm not surprised it came to this."

I press my hand to my stomach. That's not true. Angela isn't like that. Jupiter doesn't understand. She didn't live in our house, didn't grow up like we did, she just blew through for an exciting visit every year or two.

"Where are you off to next?" I ask, directing the conversation away from Angela. I don't feel like arguing with Jupiter.

Her arched eyebrow lets me know that she knows exactly what I'm doing, but she answers anyway.

"France. I have a gorgeous castle there, a seventeenth century chateau. Very romantic. There are nude cupids painted in the bathroom, gold gilt ceilings, and a porcelain toilet that's a replica of the Louvre. I bought it as a flight plan, but..." She shrugs and trails off vaguely.

I try a bite of toast, the dry sourdough bread tastes of salt and poppy seeds and crumbles against my tongue. "What's a flight plan?"

"Oh, you know. A flight plan."

I shake my head. I don't know.

Jupiter gives me a surprised look. "Every woman should have a flight plan."

She looks around the lobby, like she expects someone is listening in, then she says in a low voice, "For when your life is in a trash compactor, and the walls are closing in. Merry! You have to climb out. You're allowed to escape if your life is in a trash compactor." She shrugs and then takes a delicate sip of coffee.

"Is your life in a trash compactor?" I ask hesitantly.

Jupiter waves her hands. "No. No. But haven't you noticed? Women are always told, chin up! Don't complain! Be quiet! Don't ever ask for more. If your life is hard, too bad, that's your lot! Stay with the terrible husband, stick with the horrible job, keep trudging along until you die." She shudders. "No one ever tells women that it's okay to leave. It's okay to get out!"

I shift uncomfortably on the small leather stool and the legs creak beneath me. "Well, I've never had that problem. I like my life."

"Hmm." Jupiter nods, but I can see she doesn't quite believe me.

I do like my life. Except...I wonder what it will look like with Leo and Angela at our family Sunday brunches. Holidays. My friend group no longer a circle. My best friend not my best friend anymore.

But where would I go? And is it really so bad that I'd want to leave?

Yes, a small voice whispers.

I shift in my seat. No.

"Do you know what your problem is, Merry?" Jupiter asks.

I stiffen. "No."

"You've always believed you're the ugly duckling who

never became the swan. You think everyone gets to have magic except for you."

That's not fair. First of all, it's hard not to feel like an ugly duckling when your sister looks the way she does and your mom still turns the heads of twenty-year-olds.

Second, of course I believe in magic. I've loved Leo for years, haven't I? I've always believed we'd end up together, I...

"I'm happy, Jupiter. I like my life. No flight plan needed."

Jupiter reaches over and pats my arm in a motherly manner. "Of course."

Then she pushes the pot of marmalade at me. "Have some vitamin C. It cures hangovers."

6

MONDAY MORNING I'M BACK IN THE OFFICE. SUNDAY PASSED quickly after I had breakfast with Jupiter. After a mid-morning brunch we all gathered in the parking lot and waved Leo and Angela off, on their way to Cabo for a weeklong honeymoon. Noah was conspicuously absent, for which I will be forever grateful.

After the send-off I went home, got into flannel pajamas and spent the rest of the day watching travel documentaries on the Blue Grotto and the Gardens of Augustus, and eating a gallon of chocolate ice cream with marshmallows and hot fudge.

Now, I feel great and I'm ready to start a wonderful week at my wonderful job doing what I love best. I look up when my boss Malcom Wen knocks on my cubicle wall.

"Morning, did you have a good..." I trail off, the smile slipping from my face when I see Malcom's expression.

"Meredith, can I see you in my office?" he asks in that quiet manner he has.

I nod quickly, not able to speak past the constriction in my throat. There are times in life when no words are needed, and this is one of them.

I'm about to get fired. Malcolm may as well have been wearing a blinking neon sign on his forehead. I've seen him give separation packages to enough employees to know what the drawn expression and tightness around his eyes means.

Malcom is the director of HR, my direct boss, and the one who hired me years ago. He has two grown daughters, his wife loves to knit, and he enjoys sharing photos of his rustic fishing cabin in upstate. He's a really nice, soft-spoken man, and I guess if I have to get fired, it's best that it comes from him.

～

I DIDN'T GET FIRED.

Instead, the walls of the metaphorical trash compactor closed in tighter and tighter over the work week. The reason Malcom had his drawn, firing face on was because there's a company-wide culling. A thirty-percent reduction in the workforce, and we in HR are in charge of letting everyone go.

Today is Thursday. I've already told fifty-five people—friends, co-workers, acquaintances—that they no longer have a job. I've watched them walk down the hallway, escorted by security, to sit in the eight-by-eight, gray-walled conference room, where I deliver the news in exact, perfunctory words.

Can your heart break fifty-five times in four days?

I stare into the mirror in the long beige-tiled bathroom and grip the edge of the porcelain sink. My skin is pale, there's perspiration lining my forehead, and my collared shirt is buttoned too tight. I undo the top button, feeling the need to breathe in the bathroom bleach-tinged air.

My bloodshot eyes blink at my reflection and I grip the cold sink harder.

Merry.

You can do this. You can *do this.*

I only have a few minutes before I have to get back to the conference room of doom. Pull it together. *Smile.*

I stretch my lips, and then because that looks garish, I show my teeth in a fake grin. That reminds me of Noah, telling me to smile at the wedding, which surprisingly, makes me smile for real.

Behind me, a toilet flushes in one of the stalls and I jump. I hadn't realized anyone was in here with me. My smile slips a bit, but not fully, as Linda from accounting shoves the stall door open. When she sees me her eyes narrow behind her glasses and my smile slips more.

"Hi. How are you?" I try to smile again, then turn on the sink and hold my hands under the automatic soap dispenser, its whir kicking out foamy pink soap.

Linda turns on the faucet of the neighboring sink with a hard jerk and glares at me as soap falls onto her hands. In the past, she's always been pleasant. She has a pair of dachshunds that she loves and a bumper sticker that says, *My dog is smarter than your honor student.*

"I don't know how you can live with yourself," she says, smacking her hands together under the running water.

My heart kicks frantically around my chest and I press my lips together.

She turns her faucet off with jerky movements. "Tony

has two boys in college. Judy's husband has stage four cancer. Lucinda is getting married in three months. Alan has a baby on the way." She jabs her finger at me as she tells me everything I already know.

What am I supposed to say? I know? It's my job? I'm just doing what I'm told? I'm not the one who chose to fire them, I'm only delivering the news?

None of these make it better or easier. They're my friends too. They're people I care about. I never realized before this week that people can love a company, can love working there, and believe in its mission, they can give their lives to that company, but a company doesn't care back. *It doesn't care.*

I've come to dread every day. I've come to dread waking up, coming to work, walking down the hallway, everyone averting their eyes when they see me. Now I know why executioners always wore a black cloth over their heads. Even if I'm not the ax, I've come to personify it.

Linda is waiting for my answer, a look of disgust on her face.

"If I don't do it, someone else will," I say in a shaky voice.

Mainly, Arseny, the mean-spirited, sour-faced, recent college grad, who enjoys recounting the tears people shed when let go. Yesterday he said, *"Did you see how Roberto was crying when the security guards escorted him out? I wish I'd recorded it."*

Or Olivia, awkward and blunt, to the point of rudeness, her empathy is as high as a pumice stone scraping at callouses.

That's what has kept me going these past four days. Everyone on the list is going to be let go, whether I do it or not. But if I don't, then it'll be Arseny or Olivia delivering the news. And just like when I thought I was going to get fired and was glad it would be Malcom, I want to give my co-workers a bit of dignity, a bit of humanity when they are being tossed aside and told they're unnecessary, unneeded.

So when I feel like I can't do it anymore, when I feel like if I have to watch another person struggle not to cry, or struggle to suppress the fear about what will happen to their family, I tell myself *you can do it, Merry, you can do this*, it's better you tell them than someone else.

But it makes me feel dirty. I never wanted to be an ax. I never thought I'd be used this way. That was naïve of me, really. What did I think would happen when I went into HR? That it would be all hearts and roses?

I want it to stop. But it won't stop. I can't stop it. I can't make it stop. I just have to keep going.

Linda shakes her head, yanks a paper towel from the dispenser and says caustically, "Well, *Merry*. At least if I'm on the chopping block, give me the courtesy of advising me in advance. Poor Priya didn't even get to clear her desk. The picture of her baby is still there."

Linda stalks from the bathroom, the door swinging shut behind her, creaking and groaning as it scrapes over the tiles.

Then, silence.

I glance down at my watch.

My break is over.

FRIDAY AT THREE O'CLOCK I HAND IN MY RESIGNATION.

7

Two weeks later...

Papa Gallo's restaurant is jammed to the rafters with Friday night eaters, hoping to shed the stress of the work week with eggplant parmesan, fried calamari, pasta al Pomodoro and basket after basket of oven-warmed complimentary bread.

As generations of carb-worshippers have known, there's nothing quite like fresh baked bread dipped in olive oil to soothe the weary soul.

At least, that's what I tell myself as I drag my third piece of crusty French bread through olive oil sprinkled with rosemary and cracked pepper.

I keep my eyes on the oil, watching the bread sop it up, and avoid looking at Leo and Angela, cuddling in the booth seat across from me. They're back from their honeymoon and have that wondrously happy, deliriously in love, I-can't-believe-we-were-so-lucky-to-find-each-other look going on.

Angela called as soon as they were back, wanting to show their pictures of Cabo and give me the straw hat, Tamarindo candy, and hand-painted salt and pepper shaker they'd picked up for me while there.

The souvenirs sit on the table between us, amongst the bread basket, bottle of chianti, and plates of pasta letting out garlic and tomato smells.

Angela leans into Leo's side and he brushes a kiss at the corner of her mouth. I keep my head down for another count of three and then look up, smiling brightly.

Mom told Angela I quit my job, but I brushed it off as wanting to move up and move on. I promised both Mom and Angela that I already had many, many interview offers (lie) and lots of prospects (bigger lie), and that I knew exactly what I was doing (biggest lie).

Frankly, I'm floundering, and even the hesitantly approached thought of applying for another job in HR yanks me into sweating, queasy panic. But what else am I meant to do? What other skills do I even have? And can I work for another corporation again? No. I don't think so.

"So, Merry..." Angela leans forward, raising her voice to be heard over the raucous restaurant noise and the sounds of the bar TVs tuned to the night's game.

I nod and scoot closer to hear her, the vinyl booth sticking to my legs and pulling at my skin. Angela smiles at me and looks just like she used to on Christmas mornings when we were little, running down the stairs, about to see the tree, loaded with presents.

"We actually asked you here because we have something to ask you."

Ask me?

Maybe they're buying a new house and they need help moving.

Or maybe they want to take another trip and need me to water their plants.

Or maybe they need HR-type advice, since that's my expertise, or maybe—

"Will you be our baby's godmother?"

I blink.

Blink again.

My mind stalls out, like a car run out of gas, sputtering and then stopping. Angela smiles at me with unconcealed joy, and Leo has that grin on his face that he gets when he's just scored a game-winning point in soccer and knows he's unstoppable.

They're both watching me, waiting for my answer.

I blink again, and then the loud din of the restaurant roars back in, the sharp tinge of rosemary rushes back, and the room comes back into focus. My mind starts up again, the tires spinning, whirring at a thousand miles an hour.

Angela's smile starts to fade and she tilts her head, looking uncertain.

"Merry?"

I swallow, then, "You're pregnant. You're...you're pregnant!"

I jump out of the booth, tripping over my own feet and pull Angela out of her seat, throwing my arms around her.

She jumps up and down and laughs. "I am! Isn't it wonderful? A honeymoon baby!"

I nod and squeeze her tight. Then Leo is there and I'm hugging him too. He's slapping my back and laughing, and I'm pushing away from him, smiling, smiling, smiling big.

"Merry, why are you crying?" Angela looks at me with shocked dismay. "What's wrong?"

I wipe at my face, shoving the tears aside and say, "It's just...I'm happy. I'm just so happy. I'm so, so happy."

I smile and quickly wipe at my face. The hot tears falling.

Angela nods and reaches out and takes my hands. "Me too."

"It's amazing, isn't it? You'll be the godmother then?" Leo asks, leaning back on his heels and grinning at me, his smile full of delight.

"An aunt and a godmother," Angela says, squeezing my hands.

I cling to her fingers, my little sister, who I love.

"Of course I will. I'd be honored."

We sit down, toast the baby with glasses full of chianti, and as I swallow the cherry-tart, tongue-stinging wine, I remember Jupiter's words—*you're allowed to get out, Merry. When the walls are closing in, you're allowed to leave. For goodness sakes, Merry, you don't have to stay. You're allowed to go.*

8

IT'S TEN O'CLOCK AT NIGHT WHEN I CALL JUPITER.

I'm pacing in my living room, ten steps to the window and ten steps back to where the beige carpet meets kitchen linoleum. She picks up on the fifth ring.

"Tell me more about flight plans," I say, skipping the hello. Jupiter doesn't do hellos or goodbyes.

"Ah! I'm so glad you called. I have a situation, and you, my dear goddaughter, are the solution." I hear the clink of ice in a glass and the low volume of a television in the background. Then Jupiter is walking from the room, the sounds fading, a door shutting.

"What situation?" I ask, my flight plan question momentarily forgotten.

"Oh no. It's nothing dire. It's good. All good things. I've met an artist. Fifteen years younger than me, amazing in bed, absolutely worships me. We're holed up in Albuquerque at this roadside motel with one of those quarter-slot vibrating beds."

"Umm." I'm not sure how I'm going to help her in this situation. "You need me in Albuquerque?"

She lets out a high, tinkling laugh. "Never! I'm inspiring a young artist, Merry. I'm his *muse*. It's my calling in life, as you know. We'll be here at least six weeks, perhaps more."

Ah. Aha.

Jupiter has found another struggling artist to inspire. That explains the contented joy in her voice. She's never happier than when she's helping an unknown artist reach the depths of their talent, then once they're known/successful/inspired, she moves on and finds another.

"I'm glad," I tell her. "But what does that have to do with me?"

I turn from the kitchen and pace back the length of my living room, the thin carpet giving beneath my feet, the swish of my jean shorts filling the space.

"France!" she finally says.

I shake my head, "France?"

Then I remember. Jupiter was going to stay at her castle in France. The castle she bought as a flight plan. The romantic, seventeenth century, fairy-tale castle in the French countryside.

"You will go to France instead of me! It's perfect. I've been meaning to go. I need to check on it, make certain it's still standing. Although it's lasted hundreds of years, but still..." She lets out a husky laugh. "You know what I mean. I worry about it, over there in France all alone."

"I...Jupiter?"

"Yes?"

"Are you asking me to stay in your French castle?"

"Oh, would you? That's wonderful! Thank you, Merry! Brilliant idea."

I stop walking and chew on my lip, the tart taste of the chianti from dinner coming back to me.

I only wanted to chat with Jupiter about flight plans, ask her about whether it really was okay to just...step away, give yourself some space. And now, here she is, offering up a castle in France.

It's like one of those movies, where a down-on-her-luck American woman goes to Europe, lives in a romantic country house, has lots of amorous adventures involving food, wine, and attractive men, and then finds herself along the way.

There's lots of soft-focus camera work, landscape panoramas, and saturated colors. For a second, I let myself imagine my life in soft focus, with inspirational orchestral music and sweeping landscapes. I could be that woman.

No, I *am* that woman.

I'm down on my luck.

I'm worn down.

And now I'm being offered a stay at a castle in France, where, in this script in my head, I'll wear a white linen dress and walk through rows of grapes at a winery as the wind blows through my hair. I'll meet a sexy French man named Pierre, and he'll dance with me, the castle in the background, soft music playing, then he'll French kiss me. There will be magic. Lots of magic. And I'll finally, finally transform from the ugly duckling to the swan. For once in my life, I'll find magic.

"Yes," I say, swept away by my imaginings. "I'll do it."

I'll do it?

I nod to myself.

I'll do it.

"Fabulous. I'll send you the details. Stay as long as you like. A week, a month, three months."

Suddenly, my heart feels as if it has lodged itself in my throat, beating frantically. I just...I just agreed to a flight plan.

I'm pushing the emergency eject button, and I'm about to catapult out of my life.

"I'm going to France. I'm going to stay for three months," I decide, thinking out loud.

Jupiter laughs, I hear her young artist calling her name, his voice rich and tempting.

"Alas, duty calls," she says gleefully, and then she hangs up. Like I said, Jupiter's not big on goodbyes.

I drop my phone to the kitchen counter, and hurry to my couch, sinking into the cushions. Then I take the night to book flights, order a suitcase (I never travel), buy online a slew of flowy, ruffled dresses worthy of a romantic French melodrama, and check to make sure that my emergency savings and "someday" house down payment fund will cover three frugal months in France.

I ignore the twisting of my stomach and the rapid beating of my heart. It's the same feeling you get when you're climbing up the highest hill on a rollercoaster and you know that a wild ride is coming. There's fear, anticipation, and excitement. But mostly, there's relief.

I've never in my entire life wanted to leave myself behind so much.

I'm going to France to live in a castle and fall in temporary love with a sexy French man.

I can forget about Leo. I can forget about Angela. I can forget about my one-night mistake. I can forget about my job and all the people I made cry. I can forget about my mom and my dad. I can forget about being a godmother. I can forget about myself.

In France, I won't be one-of-the-guys, platonic friend, big-sister, dutiful daughter, HR assistant Merry. I'll be adventurous, romantic, mysterious Meredith DeLuca. A woman ready to accept all the magic that life has to offer.

9

FRANCE!

I'm in France.

The taxi, a BMW sedan that smells like tobacco, perfume, and leather, rumbles over the country road, an impossibly narrow, winding lane, nestled by lush green slopes and gray-stoned cottages, each one a postcard picture waiting to be captured.

My window is open and the earthy, mountain-stream and apple-orchard-scented air furls around me opening up a brand new world.

France is a revelation.

The air smells different here. Each lungful is a bouquet that cascades through your lungs and fills your cells with spinning, flowering delight. I'm drunk on the air.

The colors are different too. I never realized how pale and washed-out my life was.

The green in France isn't the green of New York, no, it's a vibrant, fertile green, ripe and expectant. Just looking at the green of the fields and the forests passing outside the taxi window makes me want to slip off my shoes and stroll languorously through the soft carpeted grass.

Then there's blue. Who ever said blue was the color of sadness? It's not. The blue in France is the jewel-toned serenade of Lac d'Annecy, tempting you to dive beneath the velvet waters as it brushes over your skin and kisses you breathless.

And red? The red in France is the red clay tiled roof of a chateau on a verdant slope, promising romance like the pouting lips of a woman sipping wine.

See?

The air is different.

The colors are different.

The sounds are different.

As soon as I stepped off the plane, into the airport, I was greeted with a language of song and romance. Even something as simple as "Passport, please," in French pet my ears and made me want to lean forward to hear more.

The people look different too. The children are smartly dressed, chubby cheeked, and beautifully mischievous. The men wear form-fitting clothes and have a flirtatious sparkle in their eyes that makes me think, perhaps I can have magic. The women are sleek, aware of their own power, and impossibly chic. I think, perhaps, I grew up on a different planet, in a different universe. Because no one here is anything like they were back in New York.

And I love it.

Two hours in France, and I love it already.

The chocolate croissant (pain au chocolat) that I

grabbed from the airport kiosk was one of the best things I've ever eaten.

In New York, a baked good from an airport kiosk would taste like rubber shoe soles and dirty cardboard, but apparently in France, even the lowest of the low serves ambrosia. The pastry melted on my tongue, the sweet butter flavor cascaded through my mouth, the bitter-sweet chocolate made me moan, so much so that a man in a black leather coat did a double-take. But oh, oh was it delicious.

I bought a second croissant for the taxi ride.

And here we are, pulling around the bend, and up ahead is Jupiter's castle.

Chateau de Mountlake, she called it, renaming it after herself.

There's a castle at Disneyland, Sleeping Beauty's castle, with gleaming spires reaching to the sky, round turrets as romantic as a towering wedding cake, and glistening walls that call to the princessy dreams of every ten-year-old girl in the world.

That castle has *nothing* on Chateau de Mountlake.

I take in a quick, heart-pattering breath. I think I'm in love.

The chateau sits proudly on a rocky slab overlooking the turquoise mountain waters of Lac d'Annecy. As the taxi pulls to a stop at the end of the lane, the sun peaks from behind a flitting cloud, and when the shadows pass, the beige stone of the chateau walls sparkle like a thousand diamonds lit from within.

My mouth curves with an awe-filled smile.

There are five turrets.

Five.

Each turret has a narrow window at the top, and the

towers are adorned with russet-red spires. I can imagine flags snapping in the wind two hundred years ago, seen for miles and miles. The center of the chateau is rectangular, it looks to be three or four stories tall, a hundred feet across, with a stately arched entrance. There are leaves, grapes, flowers and apples carved into the stone around the entryway, and a wide cobblestone path leads up to the front door.

The driver, an older, apple-cheeked man from Provence, turns and frowns at me.

"Okay? Here?" he asks skeptically in his thick French accent.

We already ascertained that I speak extremely limited French. Mainly, even with my translation guide, I can only seem to remember, "Bonjour," "comme ci, comme ça" and "voulez-vous coucher avec moi ce soir?"

The last one, I will never, ever, ever say out loud in France. Probably.

"Yes. This is it. Thank you!" I say, holding out the money to pay his fare. I can barely contain my excitement. It's perfect. It's beautiful. And I get to stay here.

The driver frowns at me, the edges of his long bushy mustache brushing his chin. "Not here." He shakes his head and winces at the chateau. He does a *no, not good* chopping motion with his hand.

But of course it's good. The chateau looks just like it did in Jupiter's picture, *only better*. I hold up the photo I printed out and the address written on the bottom and smile at him reassuringly.

"It's good. We're here."

He keeps frowning, but I'm already hopping out of the car, ready for my suitcase. The sun caresses my face, the birds in the thick leafy trees surrounding the castle pipe out a welcome, and I can smell the old, heavy scent of centuries of history in the chateau's stone walls.

The driver tugs my suitcase from the trunk, dropping it to the cobblestone pathway.

"Thank you so much," then remembering, I add, "Merci."

He sighs, and repeats the word, "Merci," making it sound completely different than I did.

Then after I pay him, he hands me his business card with his phone number beneath his name.

"You telephone," he says, nodding determinedly.

Apparently, he's really not impressed with the chateau. Perhaps he doesn't think a lone woman should stay by herself in a castle with *five* turrets. No worries. I have a big metal key that looks about three hundred years old and I know how to lock doors. Although I doubt I'll have any visitors or trespassers.

Annecy, according to the guidebooks is a tranquil medieval town filled with half-timber homes, flower-filled stone bridges, and cobblestone pedestrian streets. It's perched on the shores of Lake Annecy and surrounded by the snowy crystal peaks of the Alps. I'm kilometers away from the town, across the lake, in my own fairy-tale.

I wave the driver off, and he leaves with a final shake of his head. As the rumble of the engine fades and is replaced by the buzzing of honeybees hovering over a patch of wild strawberry flowers, I take a deep breath and spin in a circle, my face thrown up to the sky. I'm in France.

France!

When I'm nearly too dizzy to stand, I grab my suitcase

and pull it over the bumpy stones toward the chateau. The base of the chateau is surrounded by rocks, cobblestone, and grass. Jupiter mentioned in her email that there was a small walled garden near the eastern wall with herbs like chamomile, yarrow, and lavender, and some vegetables like cucumber. In fact, she also said that the best way to fight jet-lag was by taking off your shoes, stripping down to your skivvies, and laying in the grass, with fresh cucumber slices on your eyes, and the sun bathing you.

I let out a yawn, my jaw cracking, as I remember that I barely slept on the plane, I've been up for a day and a half straight, and I could really use a jet-lag cure.

I look around, don't see anyone except for a little brown bird hopping around in the shade, poking at the grass, and decide I'll grab a cucumber and try Jupiter's cure before exploring the chateau.

The garden is just where she said it'd be. It's overgrown, which is to be expected, the chamomile is a huge, fragrant mass, the lavender has gone wild, and the cucumber vines stretch every which way for what seems like miles, with cucumbers the size of baseball bats.

I slip off my shoes and press my toes into the shade-cooled grass. It tickles my toes as I breathe in the floral perfumed air. Then I bend down and pick a large, glossy skinned cucumber, and drop it in the oversized pocket of my baggy traveling pants. It barely fits, poking out in an oddly phallic manner.

I stifle a laugh and then look down at my pink painted toenails and wiggle them happily. I feel so free. Jupiter was right. I'm a thousand miles away from all my worries —Leo, Angela, my job, even my one-night mistake with

Noah. It's all fading away. Yes, Jupiter was right. This is exactly what I needed.

"Is that a cucumber—"

I let out a startled shriek at the low, amused drawl of a man and jerk my head up.

He...

He...

He lifts his arrogant eyebrows at the cucumber in my pocket, an ironic smile twisting his lips, a devilish light in his stone-cold eyes.

"—or are you just really happy to see me?"

10

Noah Wright is in France.

At Jupiter's chateau.

Standing ten feet away from me.

He shouldn't be here. He can't be here. *Why is he here?*

It only takes me a millisecond to realize the answer to that question.

The sun backlights him, shading his expression, falling in yellow ribbons over his skin. And boy is there a lot of skin. Because he's only in a pair of shorts, slung low over his hips. There's the flat line of his muscled stomach, the trail of hair leading down to his shorts, the tattoo of, now that I can see it, some sort of landscape, on his bare chest.

Noah's here. He's practically undressed.

His eyes sweep over me from my bare feet to my knotted post-airplane-trip hair, and he gives me an arrogant smirk.

After the wedding, at the too-long brunch, I overheard Reggie and John talking. They were discussing

Noah, how they envied him, because apparently, as man-legend goes, he's like the sailors of old, with a woman in every port. Apparently he's a sex god or, more likely, a crazed sex maniac.

"Couldn't stay away from me, Merry?"

His words crash over me and I realize that I didn't actually leave anything behind in New York. It's all still here, in the horrible form of Noah Wright.

Stalker.

Super creeper stalker.

Evidently, us having lots of drunk mistake sex at the wedding makes him think he can drop into my life any time he wants and get some more.

Not okay!

My blood rushes into my ears and my heart leaps to my throat. Fight or flight kicks in, and my mind lands on fight.

I pull the oversized cucumber from my pocket and brandish it at him like a club.

"Get out!" I wave the cucumber violently at him. "Get!"

His face twists into a startled expression and then he steps toward me, reaching, and I do what any sensible person would do, I smack him over the head with my elongated cucumber.

"Ow! Merry!"

He grabs for my arm, so I hit him again, swinging like Babe Ruth batting for a home run. Noah throws his arms over his head. The cucumber hits his forearm, snapping on impact. The fleshy bits of the cucumber burst, spraying juice and seed across his skin and onto my face.

But the cucumber isn't finished yet, there's still a good three inches left. And as a former boyfriend once boasted, three inches is plenty long enough to get the job done.

I whack at Noah's arms, beating him with the fleshy green mass, turning it to pulp.

"Creepy stalker. I won't have sex with you. I'm not interested!"

I punctuate each word with a hard thrust of my cucumber.

"Creepy!" Thwack.

"Creeper!" Whack.

"Creep!" Smack.

"Get out of my castle! Leo would be ashamed. What are you doing here? Super creep!"

The cucumber is pulverized, Noah stumbles back, a look of horror on his face. "Are you demented? What is wrong with you?"

I slap the final juicy cucumber splooge against his bare chest and pull in a shuddering breath, the sweet scent of hammered cucumber fanning up to me.

I point my finger at him, sticky liquid dripping from my hand. "Go away. Go bother some other woman. In some other country. One who's *interested*."

Noah's jaw drops open. It's not often you get to see someone who is utterly speechless and whose mouth is open and moving but no sound is coming out.

He looks shocked.

Stunned.

Dumbfounded.

I stare at him, breathing heavily, outrage slowly shifting toward hesitancy, a funny, prickly sensation starting up, hinting that maybe, just maybe, I read the situation wrong.

Noah shakes his head, wipes seeds and cucumber chunks from his face, and then snaps his mouth shut.

A heated blush rushes over my skin, stinging like an ice cold hand shoved into hot water.

The piping birds and the buzzing bees fill the awkward silence, looming between us like the high stone walls of the chateau.

Finally, he speaks.

"Merry," he says, that arrogant, terse tone back.

I cross my arms over my chest, dig my bare feet into the cool, plush grass, and lift my chin, ignoring the cucumber juice dripping down my face.

"Yes, Noah?"

He seems to be struggling with what to say. He looks at the sky, shakes his head, looks back to me, shakes his head again, then finally, with careful, measured articulation says, "What am I doing here?"

I nod. Exactly. What is he doing here?

He narrows his eyes. "The better question is, what the hell are *you* doing here?"

11

OKAY.

So I was wrong.

Noah Wright is not a super-duper creepy creeper stalker. In actual fact he's here to write a non-fiction book on the chateaus of the region and to scout filming locations for his next travel documentary.

So my initial reaction was completely off-base. Noah still may be a sex god/sex maniac, but he isn't interested in being one with me.

We have a cold-war-type truce right now, where I won't hammer him with any more cucumbers, and he won't give me any more scathing scowls. I trudge behind him, pulling my wheeled suitcase over the grass and cobblestones, while he stalks to the stone arched entrance.

I don't know how he manages to look arrogant while shirtless and covered in slime, but he does. He crosses his arms and frowns down at me, blocking the door to the chateau.

Apparently, at the wedding, Jupiter mentioned to Noah that she had a chateau in France. And *apparently*, two weeks ago Noah paid her five thousand dollars to stay here while researching and writing his book.

It seems that he decided to stay here long before the idea of coming to France was even a glimmer in my mind.

But still. "You can't stay here."

I cross my arms over my chest too and nod as if it's all decided.

"I'm staying here. Jupiter is my godmother, she asked me to stay here as the..." I grasp for a word. "Chatelaine."

He scoffs. "Chatelaine?"

I nod. "Yes. I'm here for..." I trail off again, it's really none of Noah's business what I'm here for. The point is... "You should stay at a hotel in Annecy. Or at a different chateau. Aren't there hundreds in France? And isn't that what you do?"

I start warming up to my argument. "Aren't you a travel guide? That means you should explore lots of historic houses, lots of hotels, a different one every night. In fact, me showing up is a favor to you, because now you'll realize that staying in one place is bad for your book and your career. See?"

I wipe my hands together, as if it's all settled, and then hold my right hand out to shake goodbye, "Nice seeing you. Enjoy France."

I keep my hand out, even when it grows awkward.

After ten seconds of staring at my extended palm, Noah says, "No."

I drop my hand. "No what?"

I shift on the cobblestone, I'm still barefoot and the stone is cold from the shade of the high walls. I'm aching to get inside and explore, find my bedroom, discover the gold gilt ceilings, the gorgeous murals, and the toilet that looks like the Louvre. It's going to be magical. All I have to do is fix this one little wrinkle.

"No. I'm not going. You can go."

I grip my suitcase handle and inch backward toward the tall wooden planked door. I shake my head. No. No way. There's no way I'm leaving.

This is my chateau.

It was love at first sight.

There was sunshine and birds singing when I arrived. *Love.*

I lift my chin. "Absolutely not. I'm staying here for three months. I'm on leave from work, my apartment is sublet. Plus, I put this location on the passport entry form at the airport as my main address, it'd be *criminal* to stay anywhere else."

Noah lifts an eyebrow as if he can't quite believe what I'm saying. "I paid to stay here. I have a contract. You..."— he frowns—"are sponging off a friend."

"Godmother!"

"I have more right than you do to stay here. Therefore, you can leave."

Okay. Hmmm. He has a point.

In fact, if this were one of the many employee disputes I mediated in HR, he'd likely win the argument. I let out a long breath and try not to panic. If I can't stay here, what would I do? Where would I go? This chateau is my flight plan. It's my magic.

Maybe if Noah understands how much it means to me?

"Look, Noah," I begin hesitantly, peering up at him.

He tilts his head and pastes a patient expression on his face. I avoid looking at the way his biceps ripple, instead I focus on his face, which only makes me remember the kissing. The kissing with lots and lots of tongue.

And of course, the reason for all that kissing.

The wedding.

I press my hand against the flat, grained wood of the chateau door for support. Its warmth seeps into me, like a whispered welcome.

"Look. Noah. Maybe you can't understand, because you already live a life full of adventure, and travel, and magic..."

His eyebrows go up, brushing against the long dark hair falling over his forehead.

I continue, "But for me, this is my first time. I've never gotten to experience anything like this."

Noah's expression softens and I think perhaps I'm getting to him.

"So please, please, don't ruin it."

At that, the softness vanishes, like a cloud passing over the sun, and he's back to his usual stone-cold self. "You can stay here if you like, I won't demand you leave, but stay out of my way. I'm going to be busy working."

I flinch. "But...I..."

He shakes his head. "I know. I get it. You watched a bunch of romance movies about Americans abroad, and you're expecting a starry-eyed stroll in a field of lavender—"

"I am not!" A vineyard is far from a field of lavender.

"—and a romantic chateau with a cast of characters from the local village who are charmingly sweet," he says *sweet* with ironic emphasis. "And I bet you're planning on meeting some amorous Frenchman named..."—he looks at the sky, considering—"Jean-Paul."

"Pierre," I snap.

He almost smiles, the edges of his lips twitching, but then he continues, "Pierre. Who will carry you far away from your old life of unrequited—"

"Don't say it."

"—love. With kisses and sex in slow motion while you stare longingly into each other's eyes."

I flush at that description, because, hmmmm.

"But take it from someone who knows. Even if you travel all the way across the world, you can't leave your problems behind. They're packed up inside you, like the clothes in your suitcase."

He points at my suitcase, and I automatically shove it behind me, the wheels scraping over the cobblestone.

"You don't know anything," I tell him frostily. "I'm just here for a vacation."

He shakes his head, like he's disappointed in me for not being honest.

"Fine. Just as long as you realize, there is no Pierre. There is no magic, romantic chateau. And there is no happily ever after."

Did I really have sex with this man four times in one night?

I scowl at him. "It's amazing all your legions of viewers haven't realized what a cold, cynical, unromantic hardass you are. You sure do have them all fooled. They think you believe in all those passionate historic tales you tell. When you stare so dreamily at a seaside village and quote rapturously some historical poem, they think you believe what you're saying. What a joke."

The corners of Noah's eyes crinkle with a smile. "Merry. You've watched my show. I don't know what to say."

Ha.

By his smile it looks like he has plenty to say.

"So. We're sharing the chateau?" I ask, my heart thumping in my chest. "You stay on your side. I stay on mine. No need to interact."

After all, the chateau is huge. It has *five* turrets.

We'll barely see each other.

Noah gives a rusty laugh. It sounds out of practice, and unused, like a door that's been shut for a long time and is only now creaking open.

Then, he reaches around me, grabs the iron handle, and shoves the heavy front door open. The wood scrapes over the rough stone floor, and dust motes fly toward us, mixing with the heavy, history-laden smell of the inside of the chateau.

"There's only one problem with that plan," he says.

I step beside him, staring at the interior, completely dumbstruck.

"Just one?"

He laughs again and the sound rolls over me and echoes through the dark, stone-walled interior.

"Yes. The problem is, there's only one bed."

Huh. Well.

I really, really don't think that's the only problem.

Not at all.

"Welcome to the magic," he says, throwing an arm out to the empty, dilapidated, filthy, cavernous room, and I realize immediately that he's speaking with a massive dose of irony.

Because the only magic here would be if the chateau's actually habitable.

Jupiter.

What. The. Heck.

12

I CALL JUPITER, AND ONLY WHEN SHE PICKS UP WITH A sleep-slurred voice do I remember that in Albuquerque it's half-past middle of the night.

"Merry? What's wrong?"

"I'm sorry, I forgot about the time change—"

"Ah. You made it! Magnificent. Isn't it wonderful? The joys of France!" Her voice sheds all sleep and regains her usual husky lilt.

I peek through the chateau's front door at the decade's worth of dust and grime coating the stone walls and floor of the main hall. I slipped out because the thick stone walls make getting reception impossible.

"About that..." How do I phrase this delicately? "The chateau is a ruin, Jupiter. It's a filthy, falling down ruin."

Okay, scratch delicately.

There's the sound of a man's voice on her end of the line, and a smile in her voice when she asks, "Is it? I've never been. I got *quite* the bargain when I purchased it."

It's like that scene in the movies when the record

scratches and all movement stops. I suddenly realize I flew halfway around the world to live in a chateau on the word of my godmother and *she's never even been here.*

"What about the gold gilt ceilings, the murals, the toilet that is a replica of the Louvre?"

"Well, Merry, those things *were* in the sales description."

Her voice has gone terse, and I realize that Jupiter has lost her patience. When she gives gifts, be they hookahs for an eleven-year-old, or stays in crumbling castles for a desperate twenty-eight-year-old, she expects full-on, ebullient gratitude.

No wonder my parents always feared Jupiter's gifts.

She's about to hang up, I'm sure of it, but I have one more thing to ask. "Umm, Jupiter? Did you rent the chateau to Noah Wright? Did you know he'd be here?"

"Who?"

There's a deep man-laugh on her end of the line, and I get the feeling some artistic inspiration is about to happen.

"Noah Wright," I annunciate. "The travel documentarian. The best man at Angela's wedding."

I glance back at the interior of the chateau, wondering if Noah's listening in on my conversation. But no, he seems completely engrossed in wandering the perimeter of the main hall, poking at a pile of mounded stones and rubble and shaking his head when a gray moth flies out of the mound, up to the yellow light of the window.

"Ohhh. Noah. Yes. I'd wondered why I received that deposit in my bank account. I'd completely forgotten. Of course he's staying at the chateau. He needed the inspiration. Poor boy."

Oh no.

My chest tightens at the thought of Noah needing *inspiration*.

But then, what does it matter to me?

I narrow my eyes at Noah staring up at the vast wooden beams spanning the ceiling at least forty, maybe fifty feet up. His hands are in his pockets, his neck tilted back, his wavy dark hair brushing the collar of his newly donned shirt. He has a thoughtful, pensive expression. Dust motes fly around him, highlighted in the beam of light flowing through the narrow windows, making dust, of all things, look like glitter and sparkling light.

"Okay..." I say, scraping my foot over the rough cobblestone. "But...what am I supposed to do?"

Jupiter lets out a throaty laugh. "You're in France. In a castle. Get inspired. Live!"

At that, Jupiter hangs up. I stand for another thirty seconds, the phone pressed to my ear, staring at the dirty, crumbling interior.

I put the phone back into my pocket when Noah makes his way across the long, rubble-strewn hall.

"What did she say?" he asks, eying my expression.

I imagine I look bilious.

Apparently Noah only arrived a few hours before I did, he's as new to this as I am, which makes me wonder again, why doesn't he just leave? He has sponsors, contacts, resorts and hotels that I'm sure would bend over backwards to have him stay with them and pay for his room, room service, *and* let him take the comfy plush bathrobe on his way out the door.

So why is he so determined to stay?

"She said she's never been here. She didn't know it was in disrepair."

He nods like it's all completely fine, but still, I have to ask, "Are you sure? You really can leave, you know. Jupiter will give you your money back."

As quick as sunlight flicking through tree leaves, his face goes hard. He turns and walks back into the chateau, throwing over his shoulder, "I'm going to look around. Coming?"

I hurry after him.

13

I'VE DECIDED THAT THE CHATEAU IS LIKE A BEAUTIFULLY wrapped Christmas present.

From the outside it looks amazing. It's wrapped in shiny silver snowflake paper with a bright red bow and sits temptingly under the scented green boughs of a balsam fir tree. You lust after the present, you dream about it, you imagine all the amazing things that could be inside such a beautiful package. And then, finally, on Christmas morning after weeks of expectation and excitement you tear open the package and it's...white cotton crew socks.

Or, you know, a cheap toothbrush, a purple velour mini bath towel, or talc-free foot powder (all gifts I've received).

So.

That's the chateau.

No wonder the taxi driver gave me his business card and said, "You, telephone."

But I'm not going to telephone. I'm going to stay right here.

I've been thinking about what Jupiter said to me at the wedding, and I think she's right. Ever since I was little I've considered myself the ugly duckling that never became the swan. Magic was something that happened to other people. I never even *tried* for what I wanted because I figured I'd fail. Well, this chateau is an ugly duckling too. In fact, it's a hideous, one-eyed, molting duckling.

So guess what? I'm going to love it.

I said it was love at first sight, didn't I? I'm not going to change my mind just because the inside needs a tiny, itty-bitty bit of TLC.

Okay. A lot of TLC.

"What do you think this room is?" I ask Noah, pushing the squeaking thick wooden door inward.

"Bedroom," he says tersely.

And he's right. I step inside, catching my breath at the only piece of intact furniture I've seen so far.

It's a French oak four-poster bed with a moth-eaten burgundy and gold striped canopy. The bed is short, like the ones you see in museums or historic houses, when the average adult was many inches shorter than today. The mattress is lumpy and covered in an old, dingy quilted bedspread. But still, it's beautiful. The columns are ornately carved, matching the vines and flowers on the arched entry, and the wood, even dulled with age, is still smooth and regal. I move closer and let out a happy breath.

There's a large stone fireplace in the far wall with blackened scorch marks on the stone from years of fires warming the room in winter. There are three narrow windows, with wavy, antique glass that distorts the green forests outside, making it look as though I'm peering up at the world through moving water.

"This is perfect," I say, imagining centuries of lords and ladies who must've slept in this room. I can practically see a lord on his knees pledging his troth to a lady in a long, gold, beribboned gown, à la Marie Antoinette.

"I can sleep here," I say, nodding happily. "You can take some blankets and sleep in another room. There's plenty of space."

I turn to Noah, but at his expression my smile slips from my face.

He leans against the doorframe, the casual stance at odds with his expression. "Or *you* could take some blankets and sleep in another room."

I scowl at him. "That's ridiculous. I'm a woman. You're a man. The chivalrous thing to do is let me sleep in the bed, while you sleep on the floor."

Noah shakes his head. "I'm not chivalrous. You sleep on the floor."

I'm sputtering, trying to come up with a response while he turns and walks from the room. I hurry after him, down the narrow, dark, dusty hall. There's another bedroom (no bed), a chapel (kneeling stone and stone cross), and a small room with a stone window seat looking out over the turquoise shaded lake (very romantic).

We've already seen it all, so Noah heads toward the winding stairs that lead up the turret.

"Excuse me," I say, my voice dampening when it hits the tight stone walls of the circular stairs.

"Yes?" He takes the stone steps two at a time, they're

smooth and slope gently toward the middle, worn down by hundreds of years of treading feet.

I rest my hands on either wall, the winding staircase is narrow, dark, and the steps are not precisely even. And, really, based on the rest of the chateau, I don't trust that they're entirely safe.

"Do you think...it's safe?" I ask, abandoning my bed argument for a moment.

Noah pauses in his climb, looks over his shoulder and quirks an eyebrow. "Probably not."

He gives a slight smile and my heart trips over itself, like it's tumbling down the steps.

"I'll stay here then," I say.

He nods and continues up, his footsteps scuffing as he climbs around and around and around. I lean forward trying to hear whether he's fallen, or tripped, or stopped walking.

"Okay?" I call.

I wait for a moment, stretching forward, the damp stone smell clinging to me, the cold of the walls seeping into my fingers.

Finally, he calls, "Merry, come see this."

I hurry up the steps, their pie-shape curves and uneven spacing causing me to stumble as I round the final loop and find myself in a small circular room. Noah grins at me, the smile I remember him having on camera, right before he launches into a rhapsodic description of the gorgeous scenery.

"Wow," I say, spinning slowly in a circle.

The room is only about eight feet across, perfectly round, with slit windows spaced evenly in the stone, lighting the room, so beams of light cross over each other like a sun-woven piece of macramé.

The air is fresh, swirling through, and it smells like the blue mountain breeze and the green of outside. The little room has the quiet, awe-filled feel of a jewel-toned copse of trees in the forest or a medieval chapel with stained glass windows. It's...beautiful.

I walk to a window slit—it spans only a few inches wide—and peer out at the lush trees and the blue-green water, and far in the distance, the timber and stone buildings of Annecy.

"This might be my favorite room," I venture.

"I don't know. I like the great hall. The statue's nice." Noah smirks at me.

In the main hall, which is a massive, cavernous rectangular room, chilled from the stone walls, and only lit by two small windows, there's a fireplace with a huge stone mantel, and carved above the mantel, there's a giant, winged, apple-cheeked, curly-haired cupid. The cupid has a wicked grin and leering eyes, as if he's derived enormous enjoyment from watching the dinner parties and revelry of the past few hundred years.

"I bet you did."

Noah's smirk turns to a quick grin.

I take one last look over the sloping forested hills and start back down the stairs, squishing my hands against the damp walls for extra safety. Honestly, it's a bit sketchy walking down a dark, twisty, stone-carved staircase.

This turret, out of the five, is the only one that was climbable. The stairs of the rest are in ruins, crumbled and unstable. I thought the chateau was huge. From the outside, it looks like it is, but with all the disrepair, there really isn't much livable space.

The kitchen is a long room in the basement. It has a curved brick ceiling and brick floors. There's an iron cookstove, at least a hundred years old. The kind you fill with wood, start a fire, and then cook in an iron pot on top. There's a big, black iron cauldron in a large, open fireplace and an iron spit for roasting meats. And there's a ceramic tub for bathing in. Probably because the kitchen has the only water faucet in the entire chateau. It's an old spigot that splashes cold water into a wide porcelain sink.

Believe it not, the bathroom has a toilet but not a bathtub, shower, or sink. But just as Jupiter promised, the toilet is magnificent. It's ceramic, modeled to look like the Louvre, with its stone columns and stately mansion-like appearance. When you've done your business, you pull on a metal chain, and the toilet flushes, opening the hand-painted pipe covering depicting an unimpressed Mona Lisa letting the waste flush away.

Noah said there's evidence of remodeling in the late 1800s, with shoddy dropped ceiling panels in some rooms, a gilded chandelier covered in cobwebs, and faded gaudy wallpaper peeling from faux-paneling in two of the bedrooms. But apparently, there wasn't enough money to bring in more modern plumbing.

Regardless, that's the whole of the chateau.

A massive main hall, with stone walls climbing high, heavy wooden beams spanning the ceiling, and a leering cupid watching over it all. No furniture, just piles of stone, dirt, and in one corner a wad of clothes from decades ago, where I imagine a wanderer slept for a stay. There's the kitchen. A wine cellar, which I didn't go into because the jungle of cobwebs was *extreme*. And the three bedrooms, bathroom, and the turret room. That's it.

Not quite the palatial expanse I was imagining when I told Noah he could stay on his side and I could stay on mine. In fact, I'm not sure how we're going to avoid each other.

Especially since...

"I'm not sleeping on the floor," I tell him as I enter the dim light of the great hall.

He stops too, looking at the pile of discarded clothes in the corner.

"Look. The way I see it..." I trail off when he turns and lifts an eyebrow.

I clear my throat and continue, "The way I see it is, we can share the bed until a new mattress can be delivered."

"Share," he says flatly.

I nod, thinking back to waking up next to him in the fluffy, warm bed at the hotel.

"I mean, we've done it before." I immediately regret saying that when he winces and looks away from me.

Apparently, he regrets the One-Night Mistake as much as I do. Yes, I've started thinking of it in capital letters.

"What I mean is, we're adults, we can sleep in a bed together without getting the wrong idea, without it *meaning anything*. Right?"

He looks back at me and frowns, his eyebrows drawing low. "What are you talking about? It didn't *mean anything* the first time."

Oh.

Aha.

Okay.

I clear my throat, swallow down a heaping dose of embarrassment, and push on. "Right. Good. Not for me either. So. We can draw a line down the middle of the bed, like the thick walls of the chateau, and neither of us will cross it."

He stares at me a long moment, his expression unreadable, outside the wind picks up and whistles down the chimney, blowing dust around.

Finally, Noah shifts, scraping up some dirt, and says, "I have work to do. I'm going to the gatehouse."

Wait. There's a gatehouse?

Also.

Food.

"Are you hungry?" I call after his retreating figure.

"I put a baguette and some brie in the kitchen. You can have it," he calls over his shoulder. Then he's gone, the door closing behind him.

Okay. Even though Noah can be arrogant, surly, rude, and frankly, pretty horrible about the One-Night Mistake situation, he also can be *wonderful.*

I hurry to the kitchen, my stomach growling.

Food. Then bed.

I'll be asleep long before Noah comes to bed, and I'll be so exhausted that I won't even notice him next to me.

14

I wake up to Noah brushing his fingers over my neck. His touch is light, barely there, and feels like a feather running down my neck to my collarbone.

Disbelief and outrage pulls me out of sleep faster than any alarm clock could.

"Stay on your side of the bed!" I hiss. It's supposed to be a wall! A bed wall!

My first instinct was right after all. Noah is a creepy creeper creep who wants to have *inspiration* sex marathons on a lumpy antique bed in a castle ruin.

I can hear his breathing, feel the heat radiating off him, the old mattress sags toward him. The night is so dark that the room is an impenetrable inky black. I can't see a thing. But I can hear Noah. I can smell him. He must've washed in the kitchen because he actually smells like expensive hand-milled soap. But that's not the point. The point is, I can also *feel* him.

"Stop touching me!" I say, louder this time.

His warm finger strokes my neck, runs over my chin, and tickles my ear. Gah. What the heck?

"Noah!"

He makes a sleep noise, then, "Huh, what? Merry? What?"

Oh. Okay. I see. He was asleep, he didn't realize that he was stroking his finger teasingly over my skin. That he *still* is.

He's one of those sleep touchers. The type that gravitates toward another person while slumbering. The cuddle, spoon, and touch without even realizing it type. In fact, I've been told that I'm a sleep toucher.

"What is it?" Noah asks, his voice thick and sleep rusty, wrapping around me in the quilted darkness.

"Can you stop stroking my neck please?" I ask politely. Patiently.

Noah stills. I can *feel* his utter stillness. Except, not his finger which is now snuffling my hair. Wait...fingers don't snuffle.

"Merry?"

"Yes?" The hair on the back of my neck stands on end. *Don't move. Don't move.*

"I'm not touching you."

"No?"

"No."

Slowly, ever so slowly, I reach my hand up to my neck. When I hit a furry, soft, warm body, I jerk my hand away with a start. There's a squeak. What is squeaking?

"What is it?" Noah asks.

"A...it's..." Oh thank goodness. "It's a kitten."

I reach my finger up and gently pet the fine, warm, baby soft fur. "It's just a little kitten."

The kitten is still now, it's body held rigid, probably

terrified that I'm going to hurt it. So I do my best to soothe it, rubbing my finger over its back.

"Don't worry, wittle kitty. You're so cute. Don't be scared. I won't hurt you."

There's another squeak and then Noah lifts himself on his forearm and bends closer.

"Merry?"

"Shhh. Don't scare it."

"Merry," he says firmly.

"What?" I whisper hiss, keeping a soothing hand on the fuzzy baby.

"That's not a kitten."

"What?"

"That's *not* a kitten."

Then I see exactly what he means because kittens don't have such pointed noses, or scrabbly claws, or long, narrow, *unfurry* tails.

"R-r-r-rat!" I shriek.

I fling the covers back and jump up, kicking and hitting and swinging and...a rat, a rat, a rat. A huge, fat, hairy rat was snuffling my neck!

"Get it off! Get it off!" I shriek, kicking at the bed. The rat is scrambling around, it's claws run over my bare feet, then back again.

Noah sweeps his hands over the mattress, trying to shoo the rat away. But it doesn't work, the rat darts toward me again. It's disoriented. I'm disoriented!

"Make it go away!" Its claws rip over my feet again and I can't take it anymore. I throw myself at Noah, jump onto him, and climb him, like King Kong climbing the Empire State Building.

He grunts at the impact, catches me by the hips, and manages to stay upright for a moment, but then his feet catch on the tangled blankets and he falls backwards, me on top of him.

You'd think it'd be okay, because we're on a bed.

The only thing is, the bed is lumpy, it's unstable, it's a mattress made of wool from about a gazillion years ago, and the frame is old dry oak. It's not meant to withstand this sort of abuse.

Vigorous honeymoon sex. Maybe. Rat-induced melees. Not so much.

So me jumping around, kicking, shaking, and then me jumping at Noah and him tumbling backwards onto the bed from my surprise lunge, means only one thing.

The bed groans, shudders, and then collapses in a violent paroxysm.

The thunderous crack of the bedframe splitting, the howl of the wood splintering, and the ferocious rush of dust as the mattress smashes to the floor is deafening. The air is knocked out of my lungs at the jarring impact of the mattress hitting the stone floor, Noah hitting the mattress, and me hitting Noah.

I lie there stunned and try to pull in a breath and calm my frenzied heart.

Under me, Noah's chest is bare, his skin is smooth and warm, and my fingers are pressed to his pounding heart. He drags in a lungful of air. He's shaking, shuddering really, and all I can think is, *oh god, he's crying, I've broken him.*

I grab his face, afraid to move off of him. Don't they say that you aren't supposed to move the injured person? Does that mean I can't move too?

"Are you okay? Is something broken? Did I puncture your spleen? Can you speak?"

He makes a choking noise.

Oh no. I've come to France for magic and instead I've killed a man by crushing him in my bed.

"Please. Say something," I beg. What will I tell Leo? That his best friend died under me in bed? "Noah. Please."

I rub my hands over his chest, trying to find where he's hurt. He's still shaking, but at my hands venturing over him he stills.

"Tell me," I say.

Finally, he coughs, then, "Wittle kitty?"

Then he starts shuddering and shaking again, and I realize he isn't hurt or dying, he's *laughing*.

I jump off him. "You fiend. I thought your spleen had exploded! I thought you were dying! I was worried about you."

He's laughing even harder now. I can barely believe it. His laugh echoes around the stone room, filling the space with his mirth. I've never heard him laugh so much, not in all the months I've known him.

I cross my arms over my chest and frown, not that he can see me, since it's pitch dark, but still. "I'm glad someone finds rats funny."

I can tell he's trying to restrain himself, the sound of his laugh is muffled, probably by him pressing his lips together.

"We better not get the plague." I glare at his dark shape.

"We won't get the plague."

I shake my head. "That's what they all say."

Not many people know this, but the plague is still around, every year in the U.S. at least seven people come down with it. No joke. I once had an employee try to use it as an excuse to miss a month of work. I didn't believe him so I looked it up. Turns out, the plague is real, but his excuse wasn't. He just wanted paid sick leave so he could go deep sea fishing for a month. That was the first time I ever saw Malcom's "I have to fire someone" face. At that thought, my hysteria vanishes, like it'd never been.

"I don't think I can sleep anymore." I climb off the bed, gingerly stepping on the cold stone floor, my feet scraping wood chunks. I don't exactly want to move, because I'm terrified that somehow I'm going to step on a fat, furry, unsuspecting rat.

Noah sighs, then says, "It's the middle of the night. You should sleep or you'll never adjust to the time change. Trust me."

I hesitate, then admit, "I don't know if I can. Rats... freak me out."

He shifts and I can barely make him out moving on the bed, making up the comforter again, making room for me. "I'll stay awake. You sleep."

My heart melts just a little bit. "I thought you weren't chivalrous?"

"I'm not. You roll around so much in your sleep it's impossible to rest anyway." He says this in a disgruntled, grumpy tone.

I smile as I climb back into the collapsed bed, burrowing into the comforter and the lumpy mattress.

"But what will you do, if not sleep?" I ask, smothering a yawn. "Don't you need to adjust to the time change too?"

"I have work to do," he says, leaning back against the wall, his warmth filling the space between us. "Stop talking. I'm trying to think."

"About what?" I ask, because I'm definitely still freaked out about rats and the quiet makes me nervous.

I guess he can tell because he starts to talk in that low, languorous voice he uses in his travel films, when he's sharing all the stories about some magical, faraway place.

I close my eyes, and his words drift over me, as though from a million light years away, the faded shine of a flickering star.

"...architecture used for...love...limestone from the Loire   Valley...separated   from   her... paintings...inspiration..."

I fall asleep.

15

I WAKE UP ALONE.

The bed is even more destroyed than I realized. The mattress is on the floor, the wood frame surrounds it like the fractured pieces of a jigsaw puzzle. The posts collapsed and split as well, the canopy leans against the window wall. Frankly, I'm amazed we weren't crushed or impaled.

Sunlight streams into the room and even though the bed is a disaster and my fairy-tale chateau is a disaster, I had such a solid night's sleep, lulled by Noah's voice, that I'm feeling incredibly optimistic.

I decide that even though Noah's here, he's not half-bad.

For instance, he could've made a big deal about the cucumber pounding.

He didn't.

He could've been weird about the sex spree at the wedding.

He wasn't.

He could make my life miserable by telling Leo and Angela about my feelings.

He hasn't.

He even could've demanded that I leave the chateau and...he didn't.

So I'm going to readjust my former opinion.

I once loathed Noah Wright.

I thought he loathed me.

But after our shared rat experience and his chivalrous behavior last night, I'm going to say that we've moved from the town of Loathingville into Friendville.

Hmmm.

Maybe not Friendville, maybe Acquaintanceville?

No, that's not quite right either.

Oh jeez.

Not acquaintances. Not friends. Not lovers. Definitely not lovers.

What is this kind of relationship even called?

Chateau-mates?

I shake my head and slip out of the lumpy bed, rustling the sheets. It still smells like Noah's hand-milled soap. Outside, the birds are singing their morning song, and the wavy lines of the windows show a bright blue sky.

The stone floor is cold, and I decide to start a list.

My mission for today is shopping.

I'll go to town. I'm going to buy French bread, French cheese, French wine, and then I'm going to make a French meal in the French kitchen.

I'll order a new (cheap) mattress, sheets, blankets, pillows, a table and chairs, battery-powered lanterns, and newly added to the list, a bedside rug.

Humming happily, I slip into a fresh outfit, one of my

lacy, flitty, romantic dresses, a rose pink knee-length slipdress with mother-of-pearl buttons and a tucked waist. Then, I finger comb my hair and smile as I put it in a French braid, pulling out wispy tendrils as I go. When I'm dressed I feel even more optimistic. I look the part!

I pull out a compact mirror and put on my organic *clear* lip gloss. Smacking my lips and batting my lashes, I say, "Meredith DeLuca, you are a woman to whom magical things happen. You are a swan. You live in a castle. Within a week, a sexy Frenchman named Pierre will be madly in love with you."

I smile at my reflection, letting the affirmation sink in.

I once attended a one-day business leadership seminar at a Holiday Inn, where we had to spend the entire day saying affirmations into a handheld mirror. The presenter was a partially bald middle-aged man who said that affirmations had helped his hair grow back. Before the affirmations he was completely bald.

So anyway, after that seminar, I've always used affirmations. Especially, *you can do this*. Which, come to think of it, hasn't ever been very helpful. Because I've never wanted to do what I'm telling myself to do. But I guess that's life.

Now I'm using affirmations to bring magic and you know…to forget about…everything.

I smile wider, staring into my eyes, "Pierre. Sexy times." And because I liked the sound of it, "Slow-motion sex with Pierre. Magic. *You can do this.*"

There's the harsh, scraping sound of a male throat clearing. My gaze flies to the doorway, and there's Noah, staring at me with a flat expression. I jump, then snap my compact mirror shut and shove it behind my back.

"Good morning!" I widen my eyes and give him a bright smile.

Noah's brow lowers and then he looks from my wispy braided hair to my lady-of-the-castle dress and then back to my smiling face. He doesn't say good morning back. In fact, the purple bruising under his eyes suggests that he didn't sleep at all and that this definitely isn't a good morning.

"Did you, ahhh...." Hear what I said? I want to ask. But it's clear he did by his clouded expression. "Have coffee yet?"

The deep shade of his eyes makes me shift nervously. His expression reminds me of how he looked at me when he saw me for the first time in Papa Gallo's restaurant, when he thought I was an eavesdropper and he found me lacking.

Well.

Whatever.

We're almost-friends. Aren't we?

I smile at him. "I wanted to tell you, thank you for last night. And for...everything. For agreeing to share the chateau, for keeping away the rats, oh, and for the baguette and brie yesterday, it was delicious, and also, for not being upset that I beat you with a cucumber and called you a super..."

I'm babbling. His expression, the dark heat coming off him, the fact that we shared a bed, that I fell asleep to his voice, that he heard me say I wanted slow-motion sex with a non-existent man named Pierre, and the fact that I can't define our relationship, it's all making me babble.

"Creepy creeper creep," he says slowly.

"What?"

"You beat me with a cucumber and called me a creepy creeper creep."

I wait to see if the edge of his mouth twitches in an almost-smile, but no, his mouth is a hard flat line.

"Right. Yes." I nod slowly, feeling as if I'm suddenly on uneven footing, walking up the tilting spiral stairs of the turret in the pitch dark.

Gosh. He must really need some coffee. He is horribly cranky in the mornings.

Then I remember. We're almost-friends now. It's fine. Who cares about cranky. Not me.

I shrug carelessly. "Well. Thank you. I think we're going to have a lot of fun together. I'm really glad. I was worried, because I thought...well, you know. Awkward post-wedding stuff. But it's not awkward, it's going to be pretty magical."

I sweep my arms around the room, trying to encompass the *magic*, even though right now, it's just a destroyed bed and stone walls. You have to have vision to see the magic, but I'm sure he does, considering.

"Right," he says flatly. "Fun." Then he says, "Magic," like you'd say the words *moist kumquat*. Like it feels gross on his tongue.

"Well..." I flush, lowering my arms. "You know what I mean by magic."

If you could take a marble statue and turn it into a man, Noah would be it. For a moment, I almost want to poke him to see if he's as hard as he looks.

"I don't," he says stiffly.

And then I remember my mirror affirmation. *Pierre. Sexy-times. Slow-motion sex with Pierre. Magic.*

I'm about to correct him, tell him I was speaking in metaphor, when he says, "I'm not here for a summer romance montage. This is my job. This is my life. I'm working. I'm not here for fun, for magic, or friendship."

He walks past me, his shoes striking against the stone floor, wood bits cracking under him, then he reaches into his suitcase, pulls out a book, gives me a hard look, then stalks from the room.

Okay.

What in the name of cranky morning people was that?

I slip on my flats and rush after him, hurrying down the winding stairs, only catching him as he's leaving the front hall. I suppose he's heading toward the gatehouse.

The bright morning light and the mountain flower summer air makes me blink and shake my head to clear it as I leave the dark, history-scented air of the chateau. Noah's striding across the cobblestone.

"Noah," I call.

He pauses, his shadow long over the rocks. "Yes?"

I hurry over the little path, still, stupidly, clutching my compact mirror. I swallow, suddenly unsure exactly why I ran after him, the cool fingers of the wind tangle in my hair, and I breathe in the mix of stone and grass. The breeze rustles the nearby leaves of the trees, and I tilt my chin up, looking into his eyes.

When I was taking on-the-job training, assertiveness and directness were always key to working relationships. Clearly I didn't use that tactic in my personal life, but it's better late than never.

"I thought, after last night, we were becoming friends? Was I mistaken?"

He stares at me a moment, taking in the tendrils of hair blowing across my cheeks, slipping free from my braid. He frowns. "I know you're here to cut loose of Leo. I commend you for that. But I'm not going to be your rebound. I'm not interested in being the man you use to get over another."

My breath catches in my throat, my windpipe narrowing. Is that what he thinks?

"I won't be your Pierre," he says, confirming that that is *exactly* what he thinks.

He's angry because he thinks he found me, Snow White wicked stepmother style, sharing all my evil plans with my mirror.

I sputter, coughing, my cheeks burning. "I...I never asked you to be Pierre."

At his expression I know he's remembering the night of the wedding. *Let's have sex,* I said. *Let's do it in the closet,* I said, *in the bathroom, in the hall. Let's do it against the wall,* I said.

Well.

I scowl at him. "Let me be clear—"

"Clear is good."

"I *am* looking for magic and romance."

He lifts an eyebrow, as if to say, *see?*

"I am." I nod forcefully. "But you are the last person I'd ever turn to for magic or romance. It's just not gonna happen."

Excluding the wedding night, obviously. That was an extreme situation.

Noah doesn't believe me. He crosses his arms over his chest.

"Ever," I state. "Just so we're clear."

He stares at me, an intent look on his face, then finally his expression shifts and he says, "We're clear. As long as you remember, I'm not a Pierre. In fact, that movie-induced hallucination doesn't exist. There is no vacation fling to help you get over..."

He trails off at the rumble of a car crunching over the gravel of the drive. He turns toward the sound and I follow his movement, my eyes widening at the sight, not of a car, but of a sleek motorcycle pulling to a stop at the edge of the drive.

A tall, beautifully proportioned man climbs off, his legs clad in tight jeans and boots, a black leather jacket hugging his broad shoulders. He walks toward us, his stride confident and long. As he nears, a shaft of sunlight spills over him, the birds pick up their song again, and a soft floral-scented breeze rolls over us.

When he's only a few feet away, he pulls his helmet from his head, and it's like the unveiling of Michelangelo's David. This man is perfection.

He has shoulder-length, sandy brown hair streaked with gold, a sharp jaw, high cheekbones and full, smiling lips, a broad forehead, and wide, blue-green eyes the color of Lac d'Annecy. His gaze is teasing and flirtatious as he takes in my rose-hued dress and my wide-eyed stare.

"Madame," he says, his voice rich and melodious, wrapping around me like a satin sheet. He holds out his hand, and I lift mine in response, heat tickling my skin.

Who is this man?

He takes my hand and gives it a long, gentle squeeze.

From the corner of my eye I see Noah glower at the two of us, a frown marring his forehead, his eyes narrowing on the man. He clears his throat.

The man keeps ahold of my hand a moment longer, a small smile and a mischievous glint in his eyes. Then as if it pains him, he slowly drops my hand.

"I heard," he says, with the musical sounds of French tinting his English, "I had a new American neighbor. A beautiful woman. I thought I should stop by, no? And see if she required my assistance?"

Holy smoking hotness.

"And why would you do that?" Noah asks, his voice terse.

The man looks at Noah as if he's surprised to find him standing here. He gives Noah a gallic shrug and then turns back to me with a wink.

"Because I'm your neighbor. Monsieur Pierre Thierry. You may call me Pierre."

16

THE SLOPING HILLS, FULL OF EVERGREENS AND CRAGGY rocks, swaddle the bright turquoise lake as we fly over the snaking roads. I cling to Pierre's waist, my arms wrapped tightly around his warmth, feeling free and wild, the motorcycle rumbling between my legs as the speed of the bike gives us wings.

I've never ridden on a motorcycle before. I've never agreed to take a ride with a total stranger to a strange city before. I've never done anything like this in my life. And it feels wonderful.

The bright red roofs, white stone buildings, the canals and arched bridges of Annecy grow closer. Above us a group of paragliders sail through the air stealing a view of the Alps, the chateaus and cathedrals, and Annecy—the Venice of the Alps—with sailboats, tour boats, paddle boats and row boats looking like colorful plastic toys bobbing in a bathtub.

The wind tugs at my dress, pulling on it as Pierre rounds another curve, taking us down, down, closer to old town. I cling tighter to him as the bike tilts, rounding a bend, and grasp the warm leather of his coat in my hands.

My thighs are tense, I'm pressed close to Pierre, and I think I finally understand the appeal of having a powerful bike between your legs and a man to cling to. My helmet muffles the noise and the wind, and it smells, surprisingly, like crisp apples. Which, of course, makes me hungry.

While Noah sent a disbelieving look at Pierre, I seized the opportunity to tell him I was in dire need of groceries and a new mattress, among other things. I asked if he knew of anywhere I could find these items.

"*But of course,*" he said. And then, "*I'll take you there, if you like.*" Then he looked again at Noah and said, "*Unless...your husband?*"

All that time Noah had been staring at Pierre with an intense, almost aggressive watchfulness. I almost thought that he was jealous, which would be ridiculous, but then Noah said, "*I know who you are.*"

It turns out, Pierre owns Thierry Galerie in Annecy, a modern art gallery that showcases French artists.

Noah said, "*Your Gallery put on a Thomas Arnout exhibit last year if I remember correctly.*" Then he lifted an eyebrow at me and said, "*Well, have fun.*"

Fun...like it was all settled and I was going to hop on Pierre's motorcycle, ride off into the sunset and have...*fun.*

Yes, that kind of fun.

I amend my opinion again. Noah Wright sucks.

But now that I'm gripping Pierre's leather jacket, my chest pressed to his back, the motorcycle rumbling beneath us, and Annecy coming close, I decide not to let Noah bother me.

This is what I'm here for.

Like Jupiter said, I need to stop believing I'm a duckling and become a swan.

I let the motorcycle's vibration roll over me and soothe the rough edges and cuts still aching inside, just below my surface.

17

"DO YOU ALWAYS HELP YOUR NEIGHBORS LIKE THIS?" I ASK Pierre as I eye a towering stack of freshly baked brown rolls and artisan breads.

In my arms I have a sack full of local cheeses, raclette, chevrotin, cured ham, pickled onions, earth-scented potatoes, and two long crusty baguettes that stick out of the bag's top.

Pierre's eyes dance with humor. After only an hour of knowing him, I can say that he enjoys flirting more than almost any other activity in life. How do I know that? Because he told me.

He said there is nothing more pleasurable than flirting with a beautiful woman.

I looked down at my feet when he said that, a flush bright on my cheeks. When I looked back up, Pierre was still smiling at me, laughter in his eyes.

That's when I knew he was exactly who I needed. There's no chance that Pierre will fall in love with me and no chance that I'll fall in love with him. We'd just made an eye-contact-pact to have fun.

The good kind of fun. Not the sexy-time kind of fun.

Pierre takes the sack from me and hoists it on a shoulder, then takes my arm in his, guiding me through the thick crowd of the market.

"Yes. I do. Don't they say *love your neighbor*?" His lips curl into a smile and the small lines at the edges of his eyes crinkle.

A laugh is startled from me at his overt smarminess. Pierre gives me a surprised look, and then he shrugs, as if to say, *I am who I am*.

"I don't think they meant it that way," I say teasingly, having the best time I've had in ages.

"No?"

I shake my head, "No."

"Je suis bouche bée! All these years, I misunderstood," Pierre says with mock horror.

I get the feeling he throws in random French phrases to poke fun at me. Because when I told him the only French I knew was from the candlestick character in *Beauty and the Beast* and from the movie *Moulin Rouge*, he laughed like this was the funniest thing he'd ever heard.

Ahead, roasted chickens spin on a rotisserie set against a stone wall. Their herby smell makes my stomach growl. Under a red awning, a market booth is stacked full of jams, honey, and syrups. Past that is a white awning-covered booth filled with pastries, croissants, and heavenly scented doughy cakes.

We're in the historic market, it's full of people, tourists and locals alike, all weaving around the booths, walking on cobblestone streets in the narrow confines of two- and three-story stone buildings painted red, goldenrod, and creamy white. The centuries-old street wends like a meandering river, wrapping this way and that, spilling out at adorable picture perfect stone buildings with little turrets, red-spired roofs, and vibrant red flowers overflowing from iron containers. It seems that all roads lead to the water. There's a reason Annecy is called the Venice of France, and now I understand why.

There are canals here, green-blue-tinted canals, the water edging stone walkways, with old stone buildings, cafés and shops lining the water. Narrow, shiny wooden boats, and white and red wide-bottomed boats move lazily through the water, the guides shuttling tourists past historic sights and under arched bridges.

And the bridges, oh the bridges, they're narrow, they're wide, they're stone, they're iron, they're cobblestone, they're teeming with flowers, they're scenic, they're functional, they're...bridges. I could walk across them all day long, stopping at a market booth in the middle of one, stopping to take a picture in another, stopping for the view in the final.

Pierre and I pause on one now. I lean over the iron railing and look down at the candy corn orange, canary yellow, pastel pink, and mint green historic houses reflected in the rippling waters. It's lunch now, a café across the way is serving meals along the canal, and the scent of melting cheese, warm bread, and grilling steak reaches me.

My stomach growls again and Pierre, gallant Pierre, says, "Would you like to eat?"

"Would I?" I grin at him.

He takes me to a little grassy park at the edge of the lake, where families and couples lounge on brightly colored blankets in the grass. There are blue and white umbrellas lining the shore, and little orange paddle boats you can rent if you want to enjoy the breeze on the water.

We choose a shaded spot under a leafy tree and I settle down on the lawn. The grass is cushioned and full, and it smells like summer. The cool blades tickle my bare legs, and I tuck my dress around my knees.

Pierre sets my sack of groceries down and then opens up a take-out bag of food that he grabbed at a small shop on the way to the park.

"What is it?" I ask, intrigued at the to-go box, plates, and plastic silverware he's pulling from the bag.

"Tartiflette." He says this in a proud, flourishing sort of way, then he opens the container, and my eyes nearly roll back in my head from the delicious smell.

He takes a long spoon and scoops the tartiflette onto my plate. My mouth starts to water at the scent of velvety cheese and crispy bacon.

Pierre smiles at my expression. "A Savoyard recipe. Potatoes, lardons"—he points to the bits that I think are bacon—"shallots, and Reblochon."

I reach for a fork and don't wait for any other explanation. The soft potatoes are silken on my tongue. The lardon is a crisp, delicious smoky bacon. The shallots give a tangy, heavenly taste, and the Reblochon, that must be French for cheese of the gods.

I close my eyes and give a soft moan. I'm never leaving. I'm going to stay right here, in the grass, next to this beautiful lake, eating this melted cheese ambrosia, forever.

"This is the best thing I've ever put in my mouth," I say happily, opening my eyes and reaching for another bite.

Pierre watches me with a sort of shell-shocked expression.

"I'm in love," he says.

I laugh, delighted by the day. "Thank you for bringing me to town."

I turn my concentration to the meal, and soon, so does Pierre, taking hefty bites of the tartiflette and washing it down with a bottle of alpine water.

"Have you lived here your whole life?" I ask, after minutes of silence while I devoured my meal.

"No. I studied in Paris and I lived in New York for two years."

I glance at him, surprised. "I'm from New York. Did you like it?"

"Well enough. But I missed my home and I had..." He pauses and narrows his eyes at the lake, looking up, toward where Jupiter's chateau sits, hidden in the pine trees. "Obligations. Duty."

"Family?" I sketch my hand over the grass, its prickly texture reminding me of my own family.

Pierre nods. "In a way."

I lean back on my forearms, lounging in the grass, and let the contentedness of a belly full of cheesy potatoes and a lazy afternoon spent in the sun spread over me. "Do you like living here?"

I watch a white and blue day sailer skiff over the water, its sail puffing in the wind. I realize that I think France is magical, but if you lived here most of your life you might not see it the same way. Sort of like how New Yorkers become jaded and never look up in awe at the towering skyscrapers.

"I like it," Pierre says slowly. "I'll like it better when

I..." He pauses, and a wrinkle forms between his eyebrows. "Coup de foudre."

He looks at me almost sheepishly, a vastly different expression than his usual flirtatious one.

"What does that mean?"

He shrugs. "A lightning strike."

"A lightning strike?" I ask, confused.

Pierre nods. "Americans say this too. When you fall madly in love at first sight."

Oh.

Ohhhh.

"What? That didn't happen with me?" I tease.

Pierre grins. "Did it not?"

I brush the grass blades off my skirt and start to gather my plate and silverware. "You know, I don't think that love at first sight ever works out. I wouldn't wish for it if I were you."

Pierre gives me a studied look and then reaches to collect his plate as well, putting it back in the take-out bag.

"We will be friends," he says finally. "For as long as you stay in Annecy."

I smile at him. "Deal."

18

Pierre pulls the motorcycle to a stop, cutting the rumbling of the engine. I slip off the bike, the linen of my dress rubbing over my thighs, and take off my helmet. Pierre pulls my sack of groceries from a leather saddlebag and sets it gently in my arms.

"Thank you again," I say, smiling at the charming way his hair sticks up after he pulled off his helmet.

"Friday?" His eyes crinkle as he says this.

I have my groceries, but I ordered more for delivery, as well as cleaning supplies, and a new mattress and linens. I told him that on Friday I'm packing a picnic, taking myself off to a vineyard, and he's invited.

"Friday," I agree.

Then Pierre leans forward, grips my shoulders loosely, and places a kiss on both my cheeks. His cool mouth brushes over my skin, and his stubble stings my cheek. He smells like cold wind, gasoline and flirtation.

He smiles jauntily, hops on his bike, kicks a roar from

it, and then speeds down the drive. I lift my hand to my cheek, touching my skin, and frown after him.

If this were a movie, this would be the beginning of a romantic interlude.

One where the sexy man teaches me about flirting, and kissing, and savoring life. There'd be wine, and chocolate, and allusions to sex. In fact, that's what I came for, isn't it? To have a soft-focus romance so I could forget about losing my best friend, the future I'd always dreamed of, and my career.

But somehow, instead of believing that the universe is lining up to deliver this dream, I feel like I'm being pranked.

I slowly look around at the evergreens, carpeting the grass in cool afternoon shade, and at the sloping mountain terrain rolling down to the lake, expecting that any second, someone is going to jump out and shout, "Just kidding!"

But maybe that's just me believing that wonderful things can't happen to me. Maybe the niggling feeling that Pierre can't possibly be as funny, and kind, and sweet as he appears is just my subconscious trying to prevent me from accepting good things.

For instance, Leo was just as kind as he appeared the first time I saw him. For four years he stayed *kind*. I close my eyes and drop my hand from my cheek. Never mind. Don't dwell on Leo. Dwell on Pierre. He's flirtatious, he's helpful, he wants to be friends.

Onward, Merry.

You're here for a reason.

Like Jupiter said. *Live. Get inspired.*

I open my eyes again and take a breath of the fresh,

invigorating air. Behind me, the chateau is waiting, ready for a major dose of cleaning.

I'M SINGING ALONG LOUDLY TO MY CLEANING PLAYLIST, swiping cobwebs from the ceiling of the bedroom when my phone rings.

I'm surprised out of my song, by the fact that I can actually get reception anywhere in the chateau, much less the bedroom.

"Angela. Bonjour!" I try out my newly accented bonjour and wipe at my forehead, smearing dust and sweat across my face.

Cleaning a filthy chateau is hard work. There's lots of sneezing, watering eyes, and thick layers of grime that frankly, probably need an industrial power washer to remove. But as the afternoon light wanes, I can't help but smile. I'm making the chateau beautiful. At this rate, it'll only take another...ten years for it to look good.

I grin.

"Merry, why haven't you called? You landed yesterday. I still can't believe you just up and left for France. No one believes it. No one. You never do anything like this, I mean, the most exciting trip you ever let yourself take was hopping the ferry to Staten Island, and you had to plan that weeks in advance. Even Leo can't believe it."

I sink against the wall, pressing my shoulder into the cold stone, and peer out the window, spying Annecy across the lake. Even though it was only yesterday I arrived, it had felt like my life was a million light years away. Now it's all back again.

My stomach twists itself into a tight knot and the

delicious tartiflette that filled me up churns uncomfortably.

Angela couldn't believe it when I told her I was moving to France for three months. At first she thought I was joking, then she was concerned that I was having a quarter-life crisis because I'm single and jobless. She said it wasn't like me. She was worried.

What could I say? *Actually Angela, I'm in love with your husband and my crying when I learned you're having a baby made me hate myself.*

Instead I told her I wanted some adventure before I moved on to my next big career advancement. One last hurrah before I settle into life.

So, anyway.

"I'm fine. It's fine. I mean..." I pause, looking over the room with all the wood shards swept into a pile in the corner. Then I think to ask, "Did you know Noah would be here?"

She makes a tongue-clicking sound, the one she makes when she's thinking. "Noah Wright?"

"Yes. Noah. He's staying at the chateau for research."

Suddenly I remember how Noah was standing in the doorway while I chatted with my mirror, so I tiptoe over to the door and look both ways down the dark hall. No Noah in sight.

"Bad luck, Mer. I know he gets on your nerves."

I'm about to deny that when she says, "I forgot, he was asking for your number after the wedding."

I pull back into the room. "He was?"

Holy crap. We slept together. He wanted my number. He...

"Why?" I ask quickly.

"I don't know. He talked to Leo before we left for

Cabo, luckily I was there too, and I gave Leo the no-go sign when he asked."

My stomach which was twisty before, becomes a knotted mess. "Oh. Thanks. I mean, thank you. That was good."

I don't sound convincing. My mind is spinning. What did he want? Did he *like* me?

"Sorry I forgot to mention it. You know how it is. I guess it didn't matter in the long run though. Since he's there with you. How's that going?" she asks dryly.

I never realized that my antipathy for Noah was so obvious that Angela picked up on it. I thought I hid it well.

"It's fine. We don't really interact." Except at night. "It's a big place." Except for the one bed. "And you know, he does his thing. I do mine." I don't want to talk any more about Noah, so I ask before thinking, "How are you? How's life?"

There's a short silence, then Angela gives a loaded sigh, and all of my internal warning signals go on high alert.

"Here's the thing," Angela says.

"Okay?" I say in a small voice. My hand shakes on my phone, it actually shakes. I pace back to the wall and hold on more tightly, quelling my reaction.

"I woke up this morning and Leo was there, next to me in bed, just looking at me."

I nod, realize she can't see me, and say, "Okay?"

I start to pace, walking to the wood pile and then to the door.

"I said, 'What are you doing?' and he smiled and said, 'Looking at my beautiful wife.' I mean, seriously? Seriously? Who stares at someone while they sleep?"

My eyes are wide and I'm looking around the room like a solution will present itself. "I mean, most people would think that's romantic. Right?"

For instance, if I woke up next to Leo and he was looking down at me, I'd probably be ecstatic, then we'd have amazing morning sex.

"You wouldn't understand. You've never been married. Mer, when they say tie the knot, I didn't think it was literal. I go to the kitchen, he's there asking me if he can make me something to eat. I sit on the couch, he asks if I want a massage. I watch TV, he asks me what I'm thinking. Honestly, I didn't realize getting married would mean that he'd *always* be around. It's too much."

Oh.

Oh no.

It's done. It's over.

He's the red bike.

Leo's the red bike and after a few weeks of marriage she's ready to chuck him behind the shabby cardboard boxes and cockroach traps. She's done with him. The shiny new toy is no longer shiny or new.

I kick the wall, then when my toe connects and a spark of pain travels up my leg I muffle a swear word and hop up and down, muffling my yelp of pain.

"Mer. Are you listening? Leo's *your* friend. What do I do?"

I squish up my eyes and say every swear word I know really loudly in my head, then I take a breath and say, "Did you try telling him that you like space?"

"Yes. He looked like a wounded puppy. But it didn't help, because the next morning is when I woke up to find him staring at me."

I let out another breath. I love Angela. She's my little

sister. We survived our childhood together. She's usually patient, often thoughtful. But sometimes...she has a terrible habit of wanting things and then unwanting them.

"Do you think it could be pregnancy hormones?" I ask hopefully.

She thinks for a moment, then, "Maybe. I guess that could be it."

"Okay. Well..." I pause, trying to think of a way to say this tactfully. "I think marriage is an adjustment. It'll take time, but you'll figure out how to make it work."

Don't hurt Leo, is what I want to say.

Don't throw my best friend in the trash.

"Yeah. I guess so. Anyway, I have to go. I see Leo coming down the sidewalk. He was picking up paint samples for the baby's room. Have fun with Noah."

She hangs up and I resist the very, very strong urge to smash my phone against the wall.

My first urge is to call Leo. Ask him what's going on, find out how he's feeling, get his perspective. But it's not my place. It's not my life. I'm not going to start a triangle of drama. I'm going to stay out of it.

When Angela and Leo got engaged I very quietly and very quickly pulled back. I stopped texting him. Stopped calling. Stopped being so involved. And now, for the most part, Leo and I only talk when I'm visiting Angela. And now that I'm in France we aren't talking at all. I don't expect a call or a text for the whole three months. So that I can get over him.

So just because my sister is red biking him, doesn't mean I'm going to rush over, pull him out of the metaphorical garage and ride him myself.

No way. No how.

No matter how worried I am that he's about to get hurt, I'm going to stay out of it. No matter how *compelled* I feel to do otherwise.

Like Noah said, stop. Just stop.

But honestly, when you love someone, it's really hard to stand back.

19

I CARRY A PLATE OF CRUSTY BREAD, OLIVES, LOCAL CHEESE, apples, grapes, and a bottle of wine out to the gatehouse. From what I can tell, Noah has been out there all afternoon and evening working—not bothering to take a break or even eat.

I cleaned another bedroom after Angela's call, in anticipation of the mattress delivery tomorrow. Then I stripped down and doused myself with cold water in the makeshift tub in the kitchen, scrubbing myself with a cloth and soap until my skin was bright red and pink, free of all the grime and dust.

The gatehouse is on the opposite side of the chateau from the garden. It's made of the same stone as the chateau and is just what you'd imagine when you think gatehouse. There's an arched gateway where the former main entrance to the chateau was, but now the path just leads to the woods. On either side of the gate are two round towers, about fifteen feet high, and over the arch is a rectangular room with large windows looking out over the woods.

The sun is setting, sending golden light and lengthening shadows over the grassy slopes and dark forest. The chateau walls turn a glistening flaxen shade in the falling sunlight.

When the sun leaves, so does our light. Unfortunately the chateau doesn't have electricity. I climb carefully up the gatehouse tower and then knock at the partially closed door.

Inside, I can see Noah has a battery-powered lamp lit, and a wooden table full of books, piles of paper, and his open laptop. He turns when he hears my knock and I push the door wide.

"I come bearing gifts." I hold the paper plate between us, stacked high with bread, cheese, and fruit, and then hold out the wine.

Noah's surprised to see me. Whatever he's working on, he was lost in it. He has that hazy-eyed, faraway sort of look someone has when they're in the middle of a daydream and someone interrupts unexpectedly. He glances at the food and wine, then at my face, blinking.

"Right." He gathers himself. "Right. Thank you. That's..." I expect him to say more, but then he shakes his head and says, "Thank you."

He pushes a few books and notepads to the side of the table and then takes the food and wine, setting it down.

I shrug, suddenly self-conscious.

I'd nearly forgotten how we left things earlier today. Him telling me he didn't want to be my Pierre and then me leaving with the actual Pierre. I glance at the wooden table, it's about six feet long, thick and rustic, and completely covered in papers and books. He really wasn't kidding when he said he was here to work.

"Have you been up here all day?" I ask, curiously looking around the room.

It's a long rectangle with curved spaces at either end, shaped almost like a dumbbell. The stone walls are partially covered with paneling and the floors are stone slabs. There isn't any furniture except for the table and a tall-backed wooden chair that looks about two hundred years old. But I can see why he chose to work here, because the windows are large, the light is brighter than anywhere else, and the room is spacious and relatively clean. Plus, it has a nice, expansive, almost inspiring feel.

Noah takes in the space and the table covered in his work and nods.

"Since you left. I took a break for lunch." He studies me, and I expect him to smirk or make a comment about Pierre, but instead his eyes warm a fraction and he says, "Thanks for thinking of me."

"We have to stick together, us chateau dwellers." I smile and after a moment he smiles back.

"Did you want some too?" he asks politely.

"Thanks. I am hungry." I reach forward for a slice of local sheep's milk cheese, and a slice of local apple, when my hand brushes against his, reaching forward at the same time.

The graze of his hand sends a sharp jolt through me and I pull back quickly. Noah pauses mid-reach, then as if nothing happened, he chooses a slice of baguette and an olive and pops them in his mouth.

Okay. Here's the thing.

I don't understand Noah.

I think I do, but then what I know is completely

flipped upside down, and then when I get my bearings, it's flipped again.

I'm getting the feeling, just like I did at the wedding reception, that no one really knows Noah. Sure, plenty of people know *Noah Wright*, but I'm not sure anyone knows *Noah*. This Noah, the one who's standing next to me, casually taking small bites from a slice of bread, his eyes scanning the open page of a book on contemporary French art, his hair a mess, a small smile at the corner of his lips.

We're quiet, the two of us. Enjoying the bread and cheese, apples, and grapes.

The spray of tart grape juice rushing over my tongue sends a shiver over me, and I glance at Noah from under my eyelashes. He's eyeing the bottle of wine with narrowed eyes.

"Do you have a corkscrew?" he asks suddenly.

Oh!

I slap my hand against my forehead. "Of all the things I bought today." I turn to him. "No."

Then I stare longingly at the white Jacquère wine. "It's too bad. The vendor promised me it tasted like a falling star."

Noah glances at me quickly, when he hears my longing tone, his gaze flicks to my mouth. "You really wanted to try it tonight?"

I nod. I did.

"I know a way, but it's unconventional. Do you trust me?"

I give him a startled glance.

"Not even a little bit," I joke.

Then when he frowns I say, "Go on. Open it up. I'm ready for anything."

Okay, so maybe I spoke in haste, because when I agree, Noah grips his shirt and swiftly pulls it over his head. My mouth goes dry, I'll blame it on the bread. There's his expanse of taut skin, his defined stomach and chest, the tattoo over his heart, the trail of hair that leads down, down...my eyes fly to his face.

"What are you doing?" I ask.

I'm not leaping to conclusions—I remember all too keenly where the cucumber massacre got me—but I am curious. And warm. Very warm.

Noah isn't looking at me. He's folding his shirt into a square, then he grabs the bottle of wine, walks to the wall, puts his shirt against the wall, and then—

"You're going to shatter it!"

"You may want to close your eyes, this isn't for the faint of heart."

But I can't close my eyes.

Noah's there, shirtless, his smooth skin gleaming in the light of the setting sun, his jeans slung low over his hips.

He's holding the wine bottle like a marauder about to smash it against the wall, bathing us in his spoils. Instead, he hits the bottom of the bottle against his shirt, knocking it against the wall. I flinch, waiting for the bottle to shatter. But it doesn't. Noah hits the bottle again, a firm thud, then another. I watch his shoulders, his arms, the line of his back. After the ninth thrust the cork is halfway out of the bottle. He turns, holds the bottle out with a triumphant grin. Then he grips the cork between his fingers and tugs it loose. The bottle makes a sweet sound as the cork bursts free, splashing white wine over his fingers.

"Et voilà!" He flourishes the bottle, and I clap,

cheering for the insanity of thwacking the bottom of a wine bottle against a stone wall to open it.

Noah grins, then presents me with the wine.

I take a long drink, tilting my chin back, slugging down the wine. Not only did I forget a corkscrew, I also forgot cups. But I can't be upset. The vendor was right. This wine tastes just like a shooting star. Or heaven.

It's light, with a hint of pear, spring flowers, and the subtle hint of rocks warming in the sun. I love it. I take another swallow, then pull the bottle away, wiping at my mouth.

"Here. You have to try this."

I hand the bottle to Noah, and after raising an eyebrow, he tilts the bottle toward me in a toast and then takes a long drink. I watch his throat work as he swallows.

A current of want, like a raging river, grabs me so unexpectedly that I almost fall over. My blood feels warm and bubbly, just as effervescent as it did at the reception after four glasses of champagne.

"That is good," he says, his voice casual.

He rolls his shoulders and I watch the muscles on his chest ripple. Which is when I think he realizes that he's standing half-clothed next to me. He hands the bottle back and pulls his shirt over his head.

I take another drink, then, "I bought food today. Cleaning supplies. Houseware stuff. I figured if I'm going to be here for three months, I may as well make it habitable." I hand the bottle back to Noah.

A line between his brows appears. "You should've told me. I would've chipped in. You didn't have to—"

"I wanted to." I look around the gatehouse room, at his laptop on the table. "I got a small generator too, for the electronics. You can use it. It should be here tomorrow with the mattress."

A surprised smile lights his face. "Thank you. That's very generous."

"Any time."

He hands the wine back to me.

I take another drink, building up courage. Then when I can't avoid it any longer, I ask, "I talked to Angela. She said you asked Leo for my number?"

If I wasn't standing so close to him, if I wasn't watching closely, I wouldn't notice the subtle shift, the minor stiffening of his shoulders, the surprised flicker in his eyes, there then gone.

So.

He had.

"I did," he finally says.

I hand the bottle back to him and he takes it with a smile.

"Did you..." I lick my dry lips. It's hard to ask, because Noah already made his stance on our relationship clear, but it's just hanging out there, and I feel like it needs to be cleared up. "Why did you want it?"

Noah grabs a grape and takes a bite off the end. The crunch, the fragrant smell pulls me toward him.

Suddenly, a thought occurs to me. Maybe at the reception when he said he'd been in unrequited love, he meant with me.

Maybe the first time he saw me he fell in love. And then when we had sex at the reception he thought it was something real. Maybe when I left and then he couldn't get my number he felt rejected. Doubly so when I hit him with the cucumber. Maybe his hot and cold behavior is because he's in love with me.

I lean forward.

He swallows the grape and then says blandly, "You forgot your clutch in my room. I wanted to return it."

What?

I shake my head. "My clutch?"

He makes a rectangle shape with his hands. "Little purse thing. Matched your dress. I figured you'd want it back."

My clutch? The one with tissues and clear lip gloss inside and nothing else?

I grab the wine bottle from him and take a long, long drink, trying to clear my head. I just created a fantasy of Noah's unrequited love and all along he just wanted to return my ugly, puce, bridesmaid clutch.

Well, what did I expect? He said that night didn't mean anything. I shove the bottle at him then grab a piece of bread, some cheese, and chew furiously.

Noah watches me cautiously, then says, "I'm sorry. I left it with Leo. I didn't realize it meant so much to you."

He spreads his hands out in apology.

I swallow the bread and frown. "It didn't. I'd completely forgotten about it. It didn't *mean anything*."

He takes this in, then slowly nods. "Okay."

Okay. This isn't going to work. Direct and assertive. That's what's best. It's my new life motto.

So here goes.

"I just thought you may have been asking for my number since we had fun at the reception and then had sex four times in one night."

Noah's chewing on a piece of bread. At my words, he starts to choke. Then he hits his chest, takes the wine, drinks, drinks again, then coughs a bit more.

Finally, he turns to me, his expression stunned. "What did you say?"

I gesture between us and stare at him, "I thought you wanted my number because we had sex—"

"We never had sex." He shakes his head forcefully.

"I was there. I'm pretty sure we had sex."

"Pretty sure? Are you deluded? We never had sex."

Okay. By the look on Noah's face, he's certain we never had sex. But...

"When I woke up, we were both naked, and there were condoms everywhere."

He gives me a look of horror. "Yes. Because you found a box of them in my bathroom, then you kept throwing them around the room, telling me about your second cousin and her brilliant strategy to survive weddings."

Riiiight. Likely story.

Except...

Okay, it is a likely story.

"But we were naked," I argue. "When I woke up we were both in bed, stark naked."

Noah closes his eyes and rubs his face with his hand, like he can't believe he has to relive that night.

"You said you couldn't stand your "puke dress" and then you took it off and yelled, 'freedom' like Braveheart."

"I don't remember that."

He smiles. "Too bad. It was pretty funny."

I narrow my eyes. "Why were you naked?"

He flushes, a red stain covers his cheeks and I raise my eyebrows.

"I forgot you were in my room." He ducks his head.

I straighten. "Excuse me?"

He winces. "After you had your condom tossing fun, and stripped off your dress, you climbed in bed and fell asleep. I went to bed in my clothes, but I usually sleep naked and sometime in the night I woke up, overheated, and I forgot you were there. I took off my clothes and fell back asleep. What?"

He scowls at me, but underneath that scowl there's a whole lot of embarrassment.

Oh my gosh.

All this time.

All this time I thought we'd had crazy, no holds barred sex, and we didn't. Not at all.

"But we kissed," I say, eyeing him skeptically.

"We'd both had a bit too much to drink," he says stiffly.

I notice he sets the wine on the table, like he's afraid we're about to fall into the same trap.

"But I remember asking you to have sex. Why didn't we?"

Noah glowers at me, like I just offended him. "I'm not that guy, Merry."

I give him a surprised look, which deepens his scowl. I'm just surprised. That's exactly the opposite of what Reggie and John claimed.

Noah tilts his chin and focuses on me. "Besides, I know where we stand. We both would've regretted it in the morning."

True.

Very, very true.

I take a piece of bread and bite it, thinking while I chew. "So we never had sex."

It's not a question, just a statement of surprise and acceptance.

But Noah nods in agreement. "We never had sex."

Then he gives me a funny side-eyed look and shakes

his head.

"What?"

His scowl slowly spreads into a grin. "No wonder you came at me with that cucumber."

I restrain an answering smile. "You know, for a second, I almost believed that it was me you'd been in unrequited love with."

His eyes crinkle in humor. "That's a fate I don't wish on anyone."

I shove at him, then grab the wine and take another long swallow.

Then I set the bottle down and ask, "Are you sure we can't be friends? I know you said you aren't here for friendship or fun. But are you sure?"

Noah considers this for a moment, his eyes narrowed on the plate of food. "Are you going to keep harassing me if I say no?"

I nod. "Definitely. We're the only two living here after all."

"Don't you have Pierre?" he asks, watching my reaction from the corner of his eye.

Aha.

I knew he'd mention Pierre.

"Pierre already said he'd be my friend. I'm asking about you." I nudge him with my elbow and he shakes his head at me in mock affront.

"I brought you food." I gesture at the plate and the wine. "And a generator."

Noah considers this for a moment, like he's weighing food against friendship.

"Throw in the new mattress and you can *say* we're friends."

I shove at him and he lets out a deep laugh.

"You're such a jerk. That mattress is mine. I rescind my offer."

He's still laughing, his eyes crinkling. The sound of his laugh fills me with a funny warmth.

I glare at him, ignoring the heat spreading over me.

"I don't want to *say* you're my friend. I want you to *be* my friend," I explain, realizing that this is true. I like Noah. I *like* him. And I want him to like me.

"How about a pillow then? I'll do it for a pillow," he says, his lips curling.

I glare, shaking my head. "How about you do it or I'll push you in the moat."

Okay, there isn't a moat, but there is a very cold lake.

He laughs, lifting his hands in surrender.

"Fine. Fine. Friends. We're friends. No bribes needed."

He knocks his shoulder against mine playfully and grins at me.

It's funny, was it only a few weeks ago that I thought Noah never smiled?

He smiles all the time.

"Good. Friends," I say, holding out my hand for him to shake.

He takes my palm, his grip firm, a tingle traveling up my arm as he squeezes my hand. He gives a nod, his eyes smiling into mine. "Friends."

With warmth coursing through my hand and up into my chest, I dive in and ask, "By the way, why were you such a jerk this morning?"

He lifts his eyebrows and my question is answered. He really did think I was trying to seduce him so I could forget about Leo.

He frowns. "In my experience, it's easier to shut the

door early on. That way there aren't any misunderstandings."

"Right," I agree, letting go of his hand. "Well, it's a good thing that neither of us is interested in anything but friendship."

He gives a short nod, turning back to the wooden table full of his work.

That's right. I'd nearly forgotten. He's interested in work, research, his career.

Not so much friendship.

He turns back to me, the edge of his lips lifting, a spark in his eyes.

Or maybe he is interested in friendship.

"Let's eat," I say. "Let's drink."

Then, belatedly, I remember that we have one more night of sharing a bed, so I say, "Liquid courage for when the rats come to cuddle."

20

EVEN WITH A BELLY HAPPILY FULL OF BREAD, CHEESE AND wine, my limbs heavy and warm, like I'm sinking through the mattress, I still can't sleep. I stare up at the ceiling, feeling as if I'm floating through the darkness, and listen to Noah's soft breathing.

When we finished the bottle of wine and the plate of food, I decided to go to bed. The night was cool already, I was tired with the last remnants of jet lag, and I wanted to lay down and fall into a deep sleep. Noah came in and slipped into the bed only a few minutes after I'd laid down, the sheets rustling and scraping over me, letting the cool night air whisper over my skin.

Noah didn't say anything, maybe he thought I was already asleep, so I didn't say anything either. I lick my lips, the minty taste of toothpaste making my mouth tingle. I stare up at the ceiling, the night so dark that I can only make out shadow and darkness.

My other senses are more acute. The taste of mint, the smell of old wood, stone, and Noah, the heat of him, the scrape of the linen sheets, the soft sounds he makes—his breathing, him shifting on the bed, a quiet sigh, as potent as a touch.

Noah's on his back, and so am I, there's twelve inches between us, and I know if I reach out, my fingers will brush against him. I remember he mentioned he usually sleeps naked. When he climbed into bed, I noticed he was wearing shorts and a t-shirt. I wonder if he'll get hot and forget that I'm in bed too? Will he take them off?

A tingling warmth spreads over me.

It's ridiculous. I'm in France to live, to experience magic, to escape. After three months, I want to walk back into my life with my head high and my heart free. I'm not interested in trading Leo for Noah. Why would I fall from one man who never wanted me right to another?

For some reason it seems like I was born with a heart that can only fall for people who will never want me back. It seems the only reason I'm feeling tingles and sparks and warmth is because Noah has made it clear that he'll never want me.

Am I so certain of rejection that I only let myself fall for people who are sure to reject me? I wince and then kick at the sheets and punch my pillow.

"Can't sleep?" Noah asks, and by the weary note in his voice, I think he's in the same boat.

"I'm worried about the rats," I lie. Because honestly, I wasn't thinking about the rats, I was thinking about the current that charges the air between us, as thick and sparking as pushing your hand through static electricity. I wonder if he feels it too?

I'm guessing not.

"Don't worry. I'll keep you safe." There's humor in his voice. "I put down traps."

"Did you?" I turn my head toward him, even though I can't see him. I feel him shrug.

"Well, I called pest control and they put down traps."

"Hmm." I feel almost bad about that. The rat was soft, and I did think it was a kitten, but…no. "Well, thank you. I guess I'll be able to sleep now."

He grunts and then we both settle back.

Five minutes pass.

My eyes are wide open, the moon has risen and I can see the creamy yellow crescent in the window, just a sliver shining down on us.

I stare at it, counting the gray black clouds that slowly pass over it. Beside me, Noah is still, but he's not asleep. No. I can *feel* him thinking. He has the sort of presence that is full of energy, so that even when he's not moving or speaking, you can still feel him in motion. His mind, his emotions, his everything. No wonder he's always traveling, and working, and doing. Lying next to him feels like lying next to a rushing river, and if I dip my hand in, I'll get swept away too. He has that presence that can just carry people away, which is, I suppose, why his documentaries are so well loved. He carries people away.

Still. All that thinking, mine and his, is making it impossible for me to sleep.

Another ten minutes passes, another fifteen clouds shift over the moon, and I can't take it anymore.

"I can hear you thinking," I tell him.

He makes a surprised sound and turns his face toward me.

"Really?" He shifts his pillow, and the yellow light of the moon barely illuminates the line of his jaw, his sharp cheekbones, and the inky black of his hair. I catch his eyes, a spark, trying to make me out in the dark.

"I'm sorry," he finally says.

I smother a yawn. "It's fine. What are you thinking about? Your book?"

Last night, when he lulled me to sleep, he had so much to say, not that I remember much. Mostly, I just remember the timber of his voice.

"No. I was thinking about you actually."

I nearly sit up in surprise. "Me? Why me?"

The long beats of silence tug at me, causing my skin to itch and the electric current pulsing between us to become taut and almost painful.

Finally, Noah shifts, then clears his throat. "I..."

"Yes?"

"I was wondering why you never told Leo how you felt? If I remember correctly he met you five years ago."

"Four," I correct quickly.

He takes this in, then, "I see."

I flush, wondering what exactly he sees.

"So you had four years. And not once did you think, hey I should let him know, see if this can go somewhere. Not once?"

A flash of anger sparks. It's like Noah is poking at a fresh open wound that hasn't had any time to heal. It's still red and angry, not a scab in sight.

"I didn't want to ruin our friendship," I say, using the excuse that I told myself for years.

"Right." He doesn't believe me.

I purse my lips together, pressing them flat. A cloud passes over the moon, plunging the room back into total darkness. My heart flutters in my chest, an angry painful drumming, and I take in a deep breath, the warm scent of Noah burning my lungs.

"I was going to tell him the night he met Angela," I say, letting out my angry secret.

Noah lets out a hard breath.

"Bad luck that," he says, and although it could come across as dismissive, it actually sounds as if he means it, and he's sorry.

And that he understands.

My throat thickens painfully and I know that even this small amount of sympathy could make me cry, so I say, "It's okay. It wasn't meant to be."

While I wait for his answer, I run my hand over the sheet, its worn fabric tickling my hand. It's warm, that space between us.

"Well?" I finally ask.

Noah makes a small noise of agreement, then says in a low, earnest voice, "If he couldn't see how incredible you are, then he didn't deserve you."

There's a tight, expectant bubble of tension between us. It's as if we're both holding our breath waiting to see what will happen next. The room is silent. The bed is hot and still. I stare, wide-eyed into the darkness.

Then the moon flashes through the window and I see the curve of Noah's lips. He catches my eyes in the sudden light, and I realize that we're closer than I thought. We're turned toward each other, only six inches apart, our heads resting on our pillows, turned like two quotation marks, capturing a sentence between us.

That sentence would have only a single word.

Ha.

Yeah...ha.

The sound of laughter.

His lips lift and his eyes crinkle.

I let out a whoosh of air, breaking the crackling tension.

"How'd I do?" he asks. "Is that what a friend would say?"

I can't help it, a laugh escapes. The tiny trickle of a laugh, catching me unaware, breaks something open.

"No." I wipe at my eyes and try to hold back my laughter. "No, it was terrible. You're awful. Did you read that in an airplane magazine self-help article?"

He smiles at me and shakes his head, his pillow tilting him closer, so that I can smell a hint of the wine we shared on him. "I saw it in an in-flight movie. A bad romance."

I grin at him, my cheeks aching. "I'll say."

I mimic him, dropping my voice low, "If he couldn't see how incredible you are..." I laugh.

My laughter trails off at the look on his face. Then he reaches out and grabs my hand, "Don't."

I pull in a hard breath at the strength of his grip and the heat traveling over me. "Don't what?"

"Don't laugh like you aren't. You may not have been incredible for him, but you're incredible for someone. You're perfect for someone, trust me." He squeezes my hand and I flush, his words dropping over me like kisses pressed into my skin.

"That was better," I say finally. I carefully pull my hand from his, letting go of his warmth. "That was... much better."

He nods and then turns on his back, resting his arms behind his head, elbows out.

"Guess I'm friend material after all," he says with a self-satisfied smile.

I let out a humph, then roll over to my side, trying to

bury myself in the lumpy mattress and the moth-eaten quilt.

"Tired?" he asks quietly.

"No. Not really." It's nearly midnight here, but only dinnertime back home.

Noah lets out a long sigh, and I think I feel exactly the same way.

I lay quietly for a long while, staring at the rough stones of the far wall and the stack of broken wood.

Noah doesn't sleep, I know. Every now and then he turns, or sighs, or pushes down his pillow. And every now and then, one of us stretches or shifts so that our legs brush against each other, or our hands accidentally touch, and every time I jerk back, like I've been burned.

Thirty minutes later I can't take the thick silence any more. I've been turning Noah's question around in my head, flipping it left and right, upside down and inside out, asking myself why. Why didn't I let Leo know?

Didn't Jupiter ask basically the same thing?

Haven't I asked myself this same question a thousand times?

"Do you really want to know why I didn't tell Leo?" I ask quietly, almost hoping that Noah really is asleep, and I'm mistaken.

But he stills, then turns his head toward me.

"If you want to tell me," he says, letting me know that I don't have to say anything if I don't want to.

I let out a long breath and then turn my head toward Noah, sending my hand over the sheets until it's in the middle of the bed, right between us.

"It's because..." I pause, my fingers curling into the rough fabric. "It's because I made a promise that I'd never do that to myself again."

I blink into the darkness, waiting to see Noah's features, but the moon is gone again, and I can't.

"Do what?" he finally asks.

My eyes are hot and I blink, suddenly grateful that I can't see Noah. "The only reason I'm telling you this is because we don't mean anything to each other. After this summer, we won't see each other. Okay? I'm not telling you because we're close. I'm telling you this because we're not close. Understand?"

I feel Noah nod. "Don't worry, Merry. I understand."

Something loosens in my chest.

There's a peculiar truth that sometimes it's easiest to share the most painful things about yourself with people you barely know and won't see again. It's as if the pressure of a secret is too much to share in an intimate relationship. But if you know that relationship will end, then the sharing of yourself has an end too. It makes it safe.

I start to speak. I open up and tell Noah something I've never told anyone else.

"My dad loved me best," I admit. "I mean, he really, really loved me. I was his princess. Everyone else always loved Angela. She got all the attention, the gifts, the praise, the love. My mom loved Angela, the teachers did too, the store clerks, strangers on the street, everyone. But it didn't matter because I was my dad's little girl. I shined from his love."

I think back to it, being five years old, my dad lifting me on his shoulders, the love in his eyes. I felt on top of the world, like nothing could ever hurt me, because I'd always have my dad.

I remember being seven, going shopping for a new Easter dress, the pride in his eyes when I came out in a purple lace-trimmed dress with a bow in my hair, and he called me his best girl.

I remember being eight, playing soccer together in the backyard, him kissing my knee when I scraped it, and saying I was brave for not crying, even though it was bleeding. My dad's love filled me up. So even though I was a shadow of Angela to everyone else, not even worth calling second best, it didn't matter, because I had my dad.

"What happened?" Noah asks.

I close my eyes. "The usual. I was nine. My parents got divorced. My mom got full custody of Angela and me. The day my dad left he told me that if he could take me with him, he would. That he loved me, and he wished we could be together, because I was his best girl, and it broke his heart to leave me, but I had to stay with my mom."

I swallow back the sharp pain in my throat and continue on. "I hated it. I made it hard on my mom. I was angry. I yelled at her, talked back, told her she ruined my life. I said dad wanted me and why'd she have to go and be horrible. It didn't go over well. My mom said if dad had wanted me, he would've taken me with him."

I'm surprised when Noah reaches over and touches my hand. He doesn't take ahold of my fingers, instead, he just rests his hand on top of mine. I turn my face into my pillow, take a breath, then turn back to him.

"I decided to prove my mom wrong. I packed my backpack with fruit gummies, granola bars, and juice boxes and I headed across town to the address I knew my dad was at."

"Brave kid," Noah says.

"Mhmm. It doesn't take much bravery when you're certain of someone's love." I shrug. "Anyway, I got there.

Found my dad. Told him I'd come to live with him. That since he loved me, it could be the two of us together. Turns out, it wouldn't be just the two of us. For years, he'd been having an affair. She had two kids already, a girl my age with shiny hair and a purple dress just like mine, and a boy, with a soccer ball, waiting to play in the backyard. My dad didn't want me. Not really. He took me outside, told me I had to stay with mom, that he was starting again with a chance for happiness, and since I was his best girl he knew I'd understand. I didn't. I only knew that I'd been sure of his love, and it wasn't real. I'd taken a chance, and I'd failed."

Noah's fingers drift over the back of my hand, moving in a slow comforting circle.

"Angela found me a block away from home, hunched behind a bush, crying over an empty juice box. Mom had been looking for me for hours. When I got back I never told anyone where I'd been, and as far as I know, my dad never told my mom. He never mentioned me coming by. We only saw him when he came to visit on birthdays and Christmas. He'd bring a present and usually a new girlfriend or wife, a year or two younger than the last. But he never mentioned loving me ever again. And I realized, asking him about it, asking him to love me, that's what ruined it. I promised myself then that I'd never do that again. If I loved someone I'd wait for them to tell me first, I wouldn't chase after them."

I press back into my pillow and stare up at the ceiling. Noah's fingers still on mine and I'm surprised when he doesn't pull away.

"But you were going to tell Leo?"

"The night he met Angela," I agree.

"And the next day they were engaged."

There's no need to agree. Everyone knows the details of Leo and Angela's whirlwind romance. But for once the sharp stab of pain I get when I think about it isn't quite so consuming.

I smile wryly. "I probably wouldn't have told him. I would've chickened out." I'm almost certain of it. "Besides, I don't think you can get a clearer sign than... coup de foudre."

"What did you say?"

"Coup de foudre? Am I saying that right?"

Noah pulls his hand away and the rustle of sheets is loud as he shifts away. "I thought you didn't speak French."

"Pierre taught me the phrase." I admit awkwardly. "It means a lightning strike. You know, love at first sight?"

The silence between us grows charged and I want to kick myself for bringing up Pierre and love at first sight. Now he'll want to know why Pierre taught me that phrase and he'll want to know what we got up to.

But he doesn't say anything. Not for a long, awkward minute. So finally, to break the awkwardness, I ask, "Have you ever experienced it?"

"What?" he says harshly, his voice gruff.

"Love at first sight."

"No," he says quickly, really more quickly and firmly than necessary.

Then he says more gently, "You?"

I think about the first time I saw Leo, how I believed it was love at first sight, but I'm not so sure anymore.

"No. Me neither."

I feel his body relax into the mattress, hear him let out a long breath. I close my eyes, finally tired enough to fall asleep. But as I'm settling down into the blankets, I remember one thing.

"But what about your unrequited love? That wasn't love at first sight?"

"Go to sleep." He sounds tired suddenly, and annoyed, but there's a smile in his voice too.

"Wasn't it?" I pester.

"Close your eyes."

"She must be someone really special for the great Noah Wright to love her."

"Count some sheep."

"Does she know you love her? Or are you a hypocrite telling me to put myself out there and you've never—"

"Goodnight, Merry." He's holding back a laugh, I can tell.

I grin at the ceiling. "Goodnight, Noah. Don't let the bed bugs bite."

"Or the rats."

At that I close my eyes, and sooner than I thought possible, I fall asleep.

21

I WAKE UP, MY ARMS AND LEGS TANGLED AROUND NOAH like the ivy twisting over the eastern tower of the chateau.

The stone is absolutely covered by thick green ivy, and Noah is absolutely covered by me. I'm so tangled up in him that I'm not sure I can extract myself without waking him. My face is turned into his chest, my nose pressed into the hollow of his neck. The pulse at his throat beats steadily under my lips and the warm smell of him fills me.

I squeeze my eyes tight and try to stay loose and still as my mind wakes. So, it's confirmed. I'm a sleep toucher. A sleep snuggler. I'm like a vine, unconsciously moving toward the nearest tree and wrapping myself around... goodness, speaking of trees.

Okay.

This happens.

When men sleep, they sometimes wake up ready. For example, I had a boyfriend during college named Troy, and like clockwork, every morning at 6:43 he woke up, raring to go. The whole time we dated I never needed an alarm. It went like this, 6:43 wake up; 6:43 to 6:47 I come, he comes, we're done. Honestly, he was fast but proficient. 6:48 shower, dress. 7:00 grab the bus to campus. 7:45 I'm at my desk, ready for my 8:00 class. That semester was the only time in four years I was routinely early. It was perfect. I got an A in that morning class.

So, morning wood is a helpful thing. Very helpful.

And natural.

It has nothing to do with my bare legs twined around Noah's and the heat of my skin on his. And the fact that there's an unfurling in my belly—like a dozing cat, lifting its head after a long nap, suddenly alert and ready to pounce—that means nothing.

Beneath me, Noah's breathing shifts and he makes a rumbly sleep noise, his chest vibrating against me. His hands, which were at his side, come up and rest on the cleft between my hips and butt, he pulls me closer, lodging me right up against him.

My *word*.

The feeling inside me perks up, like the cat is twitching its ears, anticipating pouncing and rolling and sex. It's been so long, years, that the sudden throb of lust nearly takes my breath away.

I'm breathing hard, staring at the line of Noah's neck, his dark hair tickling my cheek, the shaft of golden light from sunrise spreading over the bed.

He's still asleep, his lips soft, his breathing even, his fingers curled over my hips.

I'm going to just inch off of him. Just...little by little inch away.

I shift a centimeter to the left, then still, and wait, but he doesn't stir. I slide again, another centimeter. It's a bit like torture, I have to say. But if I go very, very slowly then he'll probably not wake, and he'll never know that I accidentally sleep cuddled him and he unconsciously fondled my butt.

I slide to the right a little more and suddenly Noah's breath hitches and the muscles in his chest and legs ratchet with tension. If before Noah was a warm pillow, now he's a rocky slab.

He's awake.

So there's two ways I can play this. One, scramble away, lightning quick, and pretend this never happened. Or two, slowly roll off him, act like I'm still asleep, then feign waking up and pretend this never happened. Either option gets to the same point, pretending that I never wrapped myself around Noah, my thigh pressing into his, my arms around his chest, my face buried in his shoulder, my breasts pressing into his chest, my lips at his neck, me feeling the very, very hard evidence of Noah *waking up*, with his hands still on my butt.

Okay, after a millisecond of thought I've decided the second option is better. I make a sleep sound and when I do Noah stiffens even more. He jerks his hands off me, like I'm a hot stove. I'm careful not to react, instead I let out a small snore. Then in case I didn't adequately telegraph, *I'm still asleep*, I give another snore. Then I roll off him, fling my arm to the side, and grab the blankets, letting out another sleep moan.

I face away from him, the blankets pulled high, and keep my limbs loose and my breathing steady. *I'm asleep, asleep, I'm asleep. Still asleep.* I keep my face relaxed and I picture myself as an unfortunate invertebrate, boneless and slack. Everything about me conveys sleep, but for good measure I put out another quiet snore.

Next to me Noah's still tense, I can feel him staring at me, like he can't quite believe what he just woke up to. He's quiet for so long that I'm tempted to slit open my eyes to see what he's doing. Is he really just sitting there staring at me?

I think of my phone call with Angela, at her annoyance at Leo for watching her sleep, and I let out a snort. Thankfully I cover it by pretending another snore.

Then Noah shifts and sits up, throwing the blanket off himself. Thank goodness, he's getting up.

"Merry, you are the worst fake sleeper I've ever seen."

My eyes fly open and I flip over, scowling at him. He knew? "You knew?"

He grins down at me, his jaw shaded with morning stubble and his hair sticking up off his forehead. He closes his eyes and lets out a fake snore.

I jump out of bed, then wince at the cold of the stone floor. "Well, I was just trying to save your pride. I didn't want you to be embarrassed."

He lifts an eyebrow.

I scowl at him and head over to my suitcase, tugging out a pair of jeans and a T-shirt. It's another cleaning day.

He climbs out of the bed too, stretching his arms and rolling his shoulders, like he has a crick from me using him as a body pillow. Then he gives me a happy smile.

"Morning, Merry. Sorry you were embarrassed."

"I wasn't!" I shake my head and clutch my outfit to my chest. "I was just worried about you." He nods and although I'm one hundred percent certain he doesn't believe me, I brazen it out. "But since you're not embarrassed and I'm not embarrassed, then..."

Noah watches me silently, waiting for me to finish,

not helping me out by nodding or agreeing or anything. He's just standing there with a faint smile, waiting.

"We're friends," I say.

"Yes."

I like how he says yes, like he's confirming it in a court of law. Assured and certain. It gives me a warm, fuzzy feeling.

I smile at him, "Well, friends would pretend that we never..."

"Fondled each other in our sleep?" he supplies, expression straight. His lips don't twitch, his eyes don't light up, but I get the feeling he's laughing.

"Exactly."

"Right." He nods seriously.

I look at him for a long moment, the morning light filling the room, the chill of the stone seeping into my toes, and I wonder what he's thinking.

Then I remember all that I told him last night, everything that I shared, and I imagine that he's probably thinking that I'm a mess and that he's very glad that we've never done anything more than accidentally sleep together and accidentally fondle each other.

After a long moment of silence, I hold up my clothes and say, "Well, duty calls. Deliveries and cleaning today. You're working?"

He nods. Then his eyes roam to the pile of splintered wood and the dust that I missed in my sweepout yesterday afternoon. "Do you want help?"

He turns back to me and I take him in, rumpled clothes, messy hair, an expression on his face like he's surprised that he asked, but now that he has he doesn't want me to turn him down.

"You'd rather clean than work?" I ask skeptically.

From the peek I had into his working life yesterday I'd think that he wouldn't give up a day of work for anything, much less cleaning.

"No," he says, giving me a cheeky grin.

At least he's honest.

"You don't have to. I'll be fine. I like cleaning."

Strange enough, it's true. I'm one of those rare people who find cleaning meditative. I zen out whenever I start a vacuum. I wave my hand at him.

"I'm fine. Go hermit in your gatehouse. Enjoy the day."

He raises his eyebrows. "Hermit?"

I nod. "Go on."

"Sorry. No can do. I was raised by a single mom. She'd never let me hear the end of it if I didn't help." He gets a stubborn look on his face and I realize that he means it.

He must really love his mom.

I guess I get a soft, aww look on my face, because Noah ruins the moment by saying, "And I want to butter you up, so you let me sleep on the new mattress."

"Get your own," I snap, hiding my grin as I turn and march out of the room.

Behind me, Noah's laugh echoes across the stone, chasing after me.

22

I DO NOT LET NOAH SLEEP WITH ME ON THE NEW MATTRESS, although he doesn't ask either.

Basically, we're both so exhausted from twelve hours of sweeping, dusting, scrubbing, scraping and hauling that we barely talked as we pulled ourselves up the stairs at dusk. I was so tired I could barely force myself to eat even a simple bread and cheese dinner. My thighs burn, my knees ache, my arms are on fire, and my hands are red and chapped. Did I say I liked cleaning? Did I once think it was meditative? I was wrong.

What I'd done before wasn't cleaning, it was pushing around a motor on a stick. Yesterday was cleaning, and cleaning is hell.

Even having Noah working beside me didn't help. We were both too focused on prying up centuries worth of grime to waste energy on chatting. Seriously, it was hard work. I don't think I've ever sweat so much. But the point is, the main bedroom is cleared and cleanish (honestly, how clean can you make a hundreds of years old stone room), the second bedroom is clean(ish) and the kitchen is clean(er).

Anyway.

Today is better.

Today is Friday and Pierre and I are set to explore a local Savoy vineyard. I'm in a flowy white linen dress, with little straps, a low-cut bodice that dips like a heart over my breasts, and a skirt that ruffles and snaps in the breeze like the wings of a dove. It doesn't matter if my legs burn, my arms ache or my hands are raw, because I'm ready to wander rows of grapes, taste delicious wine, and have fun with Pierre.

Because that's what I'm here for.

Pierre is set to arrive any minute and I'm pacing the great hall, trying to keep the dust and gray grime off the white fabric of my dress. Maybe I should wait outside?

Noah is already in the gatehouse, I heard him wander out of bed around seven this morning. He stumbled down to the kitchen and made a French press of coffee and a bowl of granola. Thanks, of course, to yesterday's grocery delivery. After our cleaning spree yesterday we agreed it'd be best to pool our groceries. It was nice, he left half of the coffee for me, next to a clean mug on top of the still-warm stove.

I wonder if he'll miss me when I'm out today. I brush the thought aside. Of course he won't.

There's a soft knock at the door and I rush forward, swinging it wide with a smile on my face.

"Hello, I was wondering..." I trail off, my smile fading.

"Bonjour!" It's not Pierre. It's a woman.

She's holding a large wicker basket out in front of her and it's full of apples, jars of apple jam, apple compote, glass bottles full of sparkling cider, apple juice, and even individually wrapped apple tarts. The basket is nearly half as big as the woman, and I'm so shocked that I reach out and take it from her before she's crushed beneath it.

"Thank you! I'm so pleased to meet you." She leans in and kisses me on both cheeks then tilts back on her heels, her own cheeks blossoming with red.

I stare at her in stunned silence as she hurries past me and spins around the great room, taking everything in. She's like a garden sprite, flitting around, barely taking a moment to land. I'd guess she's barely into her twenties. She's small-framed and a few inches shorter than me. She has freckles, blue eyes and blonde hair that she's braided and wrapped in a crown on her head. As she spins around the great hall, her checkered dress spins like the petals of a daisy. She oohs and ahhs and makes sounds of delight, making her way around the hall.

"What...who..." I clear my throat and awkwardly shift the wicker basket in my arms. It has to weigh at least thirty pounds. Since my arms are burning from yesterday I really need to put it down.

She stops in front of me and smiles. "I hope you like apples."

"I love them." I smile at her. "Thank you...Miss..."

"Camille Petit. And you are Meredith DeLuca."

"Ah. Aha. Yes. Right you are."

She gives me a mischievous smile and I amend my original impression. She's not a garden sprite, she's a troublemaker. But in a good way, I hope.

"Do you mind if I put this in the kitchen?" I heft the basket and when she shakes her head I hurry to drop it off.

When I get back to the hall, Noah is there with Camille.

His hands are in his pockets, he has a charming smile on his face, and I can tell he's full-on in his *Noah Wright* persona. Camille is taking selfies, snapping photo after photo with Noah. I slow down and watch as she shows him the photos, flicking through them and laughing when Noah bends close and says something. It's funny to see Noah like this again. I'd forgotten. In fact, I didn't even realize he was so very different around me until now. Because here he is again, there but apart, together but separate.

I can see it clearly now, when he's around others he winds himself in, taking all of himself up into a tight ball and hiding himself away. He doesn't give any bits of himself away, it's all outward appearances.

He's polite, charming, generous with his time, but he's also aloof in an almost unnoticeable way. I imagine it's what he has to do to protect himself. I'm beginning to realize that Noah is a very private person. An introvert, I'm sure. And if I had to guess, I'd say he's shy.

A warmth spreads over me, a quiet sweetness that feels like the breeze blowing over sun-warmed grass. I don't make a noise, but something must alert him, because Noah looks up, and his eyes find me right away.

I only realize I'm smiling when he smiles back, his charming Noah Wright smile transforming to one that makes me feel like I'm wrapped around him, my legs twined with his, my lips nestled against his neck.

It's a smile just for me.

Crap.

Crappity crap.

Noah Wright.

Do not, I repeat, do not fall for Noah Wright.

I mentally kick myself and turn away when Camille

asks Noah a question and he straightens his expression and looks back to her.

This situation has gone from okay to super-duper not okay in seconds.

I already went over this, I cannot, will not, fall in love with another man who can't love me back. I can't do it. I won't.

"Hello? Meredith?" Pierre steps through the door and I let out a sigh of relief.

Thank goodness.

The sunlight falls over his sandy blonde hair, wreathing him in a golden crown. The hall falls silent, Noah and Camille quieting, and outside the birds start up, as if they are heralding his arrival. He's in his leather jacket, fitted jeans and leather boots, and when he sees me his eyes light up in appreciation.

I flush, and then wave at Noah and Camille.

"Pierre, you remember Noah. This is Camille Petit, she's..."

Oh. Actually, I have no idea who she is. How do you introduce someone who barged into your life only five minutes before?

Pierre seems to realize the trouble I'm in because he smirks at me. Then he turns to Camille and gives her a scowl, almost like a big brother would. "Didn't I tell you to wait at least a week before coming?"

Camille's eyes flash, and then she says something in quick, indignant French. I don't know what she said, but I can interpret tone, and I'm sure she said something along the lines of, *you're not the boss of me, mind your own business.*

Pierre looks between Noah and Camille and narrows

his eyes. Then he lets out a long-suffering sigh. "Does your father know you're here?"

Camille sucks in a sharp breath and then launches into more French.

I watch them. They speak so quickly it's like a tennis match, the words volleying back and forth.

I look at Noah, who is gallantly pretending to not understand a word they're saying, even though I'm fairly certain that he's fluent in French. Didn't I read that in an article about him somewhere?

During one particularly loud exclamation from Camille, which I interpret as, *Pierre you insufferable prig, why don't you ever let me have fun*, Noah winks at me.

I fight a smile and look away, staring at the massive stone hearth and avoiding Noah's sardonic look.

Finally, Camille lets out a long huff and lifts her chin in the air, her nose pointing toward the ceiling. The stone cupid leers down at her.

"Monsieur Wright," she says sweetly.

"Yes, Miss Petit?" It's amazing, but the way he responds with such formal courtesy makes it seem as though we didn't just witness a heated argument. I half expect him to bow. Obviously he doesn't.

Camille holds out her palms in a pretty gesture and says, "Would you be so kind as to come to a vineyard with me today?"

He's stunned. I mean, he covers it well, but clearly that's not what he was expecting her to ask. Pierre lets out a low chuckle.

"She's teasing," he says. "Camille was heading home. Meredith and I will be happy to continue on alone."

"I am not teasing. I love wine. Monsieur Wright loves wine. I saw it in his Bordeaux travel special."

Okay.

Hmm.

Is she...is this garden sprite gunning for Noah?

Is she *interested*?

Camille stares down Pierre, and finally he gives a good-natured shrug, as if they've had arguments like this before and he usually loses.

Noah clears his throat, looking at me. "You and Pierre are going to a vineyard?"

His brows are drawn and he's looking between me and Pierre with a question in his eyes.

"Yes, it's going to be fun." As soon as I say this I realize it was exactly the wrong thing to say.

Noah gives me a flat look, and I know for a fact now that he really, really disapproves of Pierre.

He turns to Camille and gives her his charming Noah Wright smile. "Yes. I'd love to come."

She claps her hands and laughs.

Pierre shakes his head and then holds out his hand, his palm open, "Shall we?"

We shall.

23

Okay.

Even in my wildest, most soft-focused, romantic imaginings, I could never have dreamt up this moment. Pierre gently holds my arm, his warm fingers stroking my bare skin, as we slowly stroll through the rows of grapevines. The narrow rows of grapes hug a verdant slope, the vines and fat leaves, winding around wooden stakes, spilling down toward the blue lake below. The grass squishes beneath my feet, and the gravelly soil crunches. When I brush against a leaf, the green scent of the vine rises to me.

Twenty yards behind us, I can hear Camille laughing as she guides Noah through the grape vines.

"It's so beautiful. Just look at it!" I beam at Pierre and he gives me a kind smile, considering this is probably the tenth time I've said that in the last five minutes.

"I mean it," I tell him, dropping close to the vine to smell a tight cluster of perfectly round, citrine yellow and russet spotted grapes. "Look at these grapes! They're perfect!"

I pluck one from the stem, its round pearly shape, smooth and slick.

"Well, perhaps..." he frowns at the grape in my hand.

I roll it between my fingers, then feeling enlivened by the setting—the breeze rustles my white dress so I look just like the film goddess Marilyn Monroe—I hold the grape between us and smile.

"Perfect," I say.

Then I keep my eyes on Pierre as I slowly peel away the skin of the grape, one thin, slow strip at a time. As I do, the juice runs over my fingers and the bright, tickling scent snaps over us. Pierre watches my fingers work, enthralled with my slow progress. His gaze moves quickly between my fingers and my eyes.

Finally, when the strips lay curling in the grass at our feet, and the juicy grape drips in my fingers, I smile and say again, "Perfect."

Then I sexily pop the grape into my mouth.

Ack.

No!

Ack.

It's an assault on my mouth. The grape isn't sweet, it isn't fruity, it isn't delicious. It's a sour, metallic, astringent ball of gross. My mouth twists, and my tongue is begging me to spit the nasty, squishy, fleshy thing out. I gag. Wave my hand in front of my face.

Pierre's eyes widen.

Mine water.

I can't. I can't swallow it.

We look at each other for a moment, then with my mouth pursing and my eyes watering, Pierre gives a quick tilt of his head and turns to the side, pointing. "See. There is a path to the church. It is scenic, no? A beautiful place for a picnic."

I know what he's doing. He's turned away from me so I can spit this devil fruit out of my mouth. Bless him. While he's talking, I turn aside, cover my mouth and launch the grape into the grass. Then I stick out my tongue and wipe it across the back of my hand, then when that doesn't get rid of the flavor I scrub my mouth on a discreet part of my skirt.

Ick. Yuck.

Horrible.

"Beautiful, no?" Pierre asks, ending his description of the white steepled church at the edge of the slope, and the little red roofed village below.

Quickly, I turn back toward him, pasting a calm, attentive smile on my face. When I do, he turns to me, his eyes dancing with humor.

"Very beautiful," I agree. "Just beautiful."

Then, because I can't help it I wipe at my mouth again.

Pierre watches my hand, the sunlight hitting his eyes so that they gleam like the lake below.

"I must admit." He tilts his head, then smoothly takes my arm again and guides me toward the grassy clearing at the edge of the slope. "Watching you peel that grape was a revelation."

Behind us, Camille laughs, towing Noah along, and then she begins to sing a song in French. The wind brings snatches of the melody and then takes it back again, her voice drifting in and out.

"That wasn't a grape." I shake my head and then shudder.

Pierre gives a gallic shrug. "It was not ripe. And it is not an eating grape. It is a drinking grape."

My cheeks heat. I should've known that.

Still, even though I didn't imagine nasty-tasting grapes in my dreams, I did imagine everything else. The leafy green rows of grapevines, the scent of fruit ripening in the sun, the breeze teasing my hair, the sun painting over my skin, and a man who is attentive and fun.

"You make me wish I brought grapes rather than chocolate for our picnic." Pierre gives me a considering look and I wonder what sort of things he's thinking about.

By the glint in his eyes, I can imagine.

I peeled that grape on a wild impulse, and now I'm not so sure if I should have been quite so femme fatale.

I shrug. It is what it is. Jupiter would laugh it off and say that I was finally living and finally shucking my anti-magic, ugly duckling mindset.

Have fun, she'd say. Live, she'd say. Be inspired!

I nod, then smile at Pierre. "I love chocolate," I reassure him. "It's perfect."

24

WE SIT ON A LARGE CORNFLOWER BLUE AND WHITE LINEN
blanket in the plush grass.

I packed a picnic basket with only enough for two, so
we're eating light. I sit cross-legged, my dress flowing over
my legs, Pierre sits next to me and then Noah and
Camille are on the other side of the spread.

As soon as we sat down, Camille scooted as close as
possible to Noah without actually touching him. If she
could crawl onto his lap without him saying something, I
think she would. There might be enough room for a line
of picnic ants to slip in the space between them, but
maybe not. Noah doesn't seem to notice though. In fact,
he seems oblivious to the big-eyed, head-tilting, lip-
pouting messages Camille is sending his way.

Noah grabs a slice of bread and crumbles it between
his fingers, a pensive expression on his face.

"Let me open the wine," Pierre says, reaching for the
bottle we purchased at the tasting room.

It's another Jacquère. Pierre has a corkscrew. He

spears the tip into the cork and quickly turns it. Instead
of watching Pierre, I quickly look at Noah, remembering
him stripping off his shirt and thrusting the wine bottle
against the wall.

I want Noah to look at me and give his sardonic
raised-eyebrow smile, but Camille is whispering
something in his ear, her hands pressed to the blanket
near his leg, her breast pressed against his arm, and he's
not looking my way.

Oh well. There's no need to feel any disappointment
that he's not looking at me. And there's definitely no need
to feel disappointment that Camille is showing immense
interest in him. Like I said, falling for Noah isn't in the
cards. Even if it means I fall out of love with Leo.

Although, come to think of it, I haven't thought about
Leo in almost three hours. Which means, France is
working.

I give Pierre a beatific smile as he tugs the cork free
with a flourish. When I do, his eyes brighten.

"Wine?" He holds the bottle over my cup.

"Please."

He pours for me, filling my plastic wine glass. Then
he fills a glass for himself. Camille is still whispering to
Noah, pointing out something in the blue-tinted
mountains.

"What will we toast?" Pierre asks, leaning toward me.

Without hesitating I say, "New beginnings."

Pierre frowns, then nods his head. "I thought we
would toast new love, but new beginnings is close
enough."

Hmm.

"Are we toasting love?" Camille asks, turning
toward us.

Noah blinks, as if he's forgotten that Pierre and I are here too. He shakes his head and looks as if he's coming out of a dream. Or a lust stupor. I suppose if France can work for me, then it can work for Noah too. Maybe he'll shuck his bad case of unrequited love as well.

Pierre frowns at Camille, especially when he sees how close she's sitting to Noah. I get the feeling that Pierre thinks of Camille as his little sister.

"We are toasting new beginnings."

"I prefer to toast love," she says, the sun glinting off her crown of golden braids, a challenging spark in her eye.

I get the feeling Pierre is about to argue, so I say, "We can toast love. Love is like a new beginning."

I reach out and pour wine into the two remaining wine glasses, the straw-yellow liquid splashing against the walls and sending up crisp apple and honeyed scents.

I hand the glasses over the food situated between us. There's rustic brown bread, sliced thin. Creamy white pressed cheeses that melt on your tongue and leave a salty-sweet taste. Fresh creamy butter. Brined and salted vegetables. Olives. Sliced pears so tender they disintegrate as soon as they meet your mouth.

"Here," I hand Camille the first glass and then pass the second to Noah. His fingers brush over mine, sending a warm thrum through my blood. I pull back as quickly as I can, then adjust my dress, not looking at anyone while I wait for the feeling to pass.

Pierre moves on the blanket, settling closer to me. Then he says, "To love."

I look up and instead of looking off into the distance at the lush vineyard and majestic mountains like I meant to, I look into Noah's eyes. My chest clenches and my fingers shake on the thin wineglass stem. Instead of looking away, Noah holds onto my gaze, the edge of his mouth lifting. He must be remembering all our conversations about love, how it's a terrible state.

"What do you think of love?" Camille asks Noah, and when she does, I break eye contact, even though he doesn't look away.

Finally, he clears his throat and then shrugs. "I think it's an unfortunate state to be in."

"No!" cries Camille. "That's not true. Love is the most fortunate of states. Everyone should be so lucky as to be in love."

Noah makes a noncommittal noise. "Love makes fools of even the wisest men."

Well. That's a serious assertation. And really cynical to be honest.

"Not true," Camille says, and I notice that her cheeks have gone pink. "Love builds nations. Look at Napoleon and his Joséphine!"

Errrr. Maybe that's not the best example. But Camille's going with it.

"Napoleon's love for Joséphine is not—" I guess Noah is thinking what I'm thinking, but Camille interrupts.

"Love transforms," she exclaims. "Look at the greatest love story ever written, *La Belle et la Bête*, by Gabrielle-Suzanne Barbot de Villeneuve, is that not the height of love? Making a king from a beast?"

She turns to me for support, as if I understood that rapid-fire argument.

"Is that not so, Meredith?"

I glance quickly around the picnic, as if I can somehow magically translate what she just said.

"Err. Well..." Am I about to agree to something along

the lines of Napoleon waging war across Europe as the height of romanticism?

Pierre leans close and says in a low, humor-filled voice, "*La Belle et la Bête* is Beauty and the Beast."

Oh. Ah ha!

"Yes," I say enthusiastically. "Exactly. *Beauty and the Beast*. I agree. Love."

Now that I've agreed, Camille is off again.

"And there is *The Hunchback of Notre Dame*, and of course, Notre Dame itself. And this pear?" She picks up a slice of the fruit. "Was it not grown with love? Of course it was. Love is the most fortunate state, even for fruit."

She thrusts the slice into her mouth. Her bright pink lips close around the pear, and she makes a happy sound.

"Camille's family has an orchard," Pierre says.

Well that would explain the wicker basket full of apples and jams and juices. When she's swallowed the pear she notices me watching her and gives a brilliant smile, I can't help but smile back. She's so effervescent.

"What do you think? Do you agree with Camille?" Pierre asks, then he takes a sip of his wine.

Camille nods her head, as if of course I'm going to agree with her. But Noah, knowing a lot more about me, goes still, and even though he's looking over the picnic spread, and inspecting the plate of vegetables, I know he's waiting for my response.

So, instead of responding right away, I carefully consider my answer. I spin the cool plastic wine stem between my pointer and thumb and frown as the wine swirls. A bee buzzes past, its hum tickling my ear, as it heads toward the fragrant grapevines.

"I think..." I clear my throat and when everyone looks at me I flush.

Pierre nods encouragingly. "Yes?"

"I think that love can bring about the best in us."

"You see," Camille says, clapping her hands. "Meredith agrees."

"But?" Noah asks, lifting an eyebrow. He has that sardonic look that I was waiting for earlier, the one that tells me he knows what I'm thinking.

"But..." I nod. "Love can also bring out the worst. It can hurt. Quite badly. Sometimes, I think life would be easier if people didn't love so much."

Camille shakes her head forcefully. "No. That is the beauty of it," Camille argues. "No one can know the height of love unless they know the depth. It is the agony of love that brings the ecstasy."

I never before realized that a person could actually have a bosom heaving with passion, but that describes Camille perfectly.

Pierre leans forward and places his chin on his fist. He eyes Camille as if he's never seen her before.

"A rose is not as beautiful if there isn't the threat of thorns," Camille concludes.

I'd like to agree, but it's hard, because in my experience the thorns hurt more than the flower is worth.

"I, for one, disagree. For example, a carnation is just as lovely as a rose, but you don't risk injury." Noah shrugs, then reaches forward and takes a slice of bread and a bit of cheese. I watch his hands as he handles the bread, taking it to his mouth.

His bottom lip is fuller than I realized, and there's a small, barely noticeable divot, right at...I realize I'm staring so I quickly turn back to Pierre and say, "What do you think? Everyone else answered. What do you think of love?"

Pierre leans back on his forearms, stretching out, and lets out a sigh. "I'm more philosophical. I think love comes in many forms."

I nod.

"What forms?" Camille asks. Then she reaches out, grabs the plate of pears and offers it to Noah.

I turn back to Pierre. He frowns out at the white church, and the little house next door, with the cobblestone base, the whitewashed walls, and the rustic wooden shutters. "Love can be one of a child for his parents. Or a parent for their child."

"That's not what we are discussing," Camille says.

Pierre shrugs. "It is a type of love. Children need their parents' love. Parents are compelled to love their children."

I look down at the food and pretend to take my time choosing a slice of bread. I don't want to chance seeing the pity I know will be in Noah's gaze. But when I look back up, Noah isn't looking at me, he's studying Pierre with a hard look in his eye and a tightness to his jaw. I don't know that I've ever seen him look at someone with so much intense...dislike? No, not dislike. I can't quite put my finger on it. But really, Noah doesn't need to scowl at Pierre for my sake.

"Go on," I say.

Pierre tosses an olive in his mouth, completely oblivious to Noah's study and Camille's frown.

He chews and then says, "There is also the love of familiarity. Siblings, friendship, affection. For instance, this house." He gestures at the little whitewashed cottage with the brown wooden shutters and cobblestone base. "It is an ugly home."

I make a noise of protest. I wouldn't call it ugly, I'd call it charming. Yes, there may be weeds, and disrepair, and dirt, but it's *charming*.

"I have seen that home nearly every day of my life—when I drive by this vineyard. I would say that I love that home, I have affection for it because it is familiar. The same with Camille." Pierre gestures at Camille and she stiffens.

"Pardon?" She lifts her chin and looks down at Pierre, her sprite-like demeanor shifting to ice.

He shrugs and waves her pique away. "I have known you since you were born. We are neighbors. You have always been here. Like that house. You are familiar."

"I am an ugly house?" Her nose quivers, and although I don't really know Camille, even I can tell that she's not happy with Pierre.

"Like a sister," Pierre says.

"It must be nice to have grown up together," I venture.

"I wouldn't say grow up. I am ten years older. Camille was still a child when I left home."

"Yes," she agrees. "A child, with childish ideas." Then she sends me a mischievous grin. "I will always be young, it is my...joie de vivre. Pierre is not so fond of it. Don't let him fool you, he has a..." She grasps in the air as if searching for the word and then snaps her fingers, "Withered vine."

Noah chokes on the wine he was swallowing and I cover my mouth when I realize what he thinks Camille is referring to.

"My vine is not withered," Pierre says, outraged. "It was once. Only once. How did you even hear..." He quiets at the confused look on Camille's face.

He tries to backtrack, but it's too late, because Camille realizes what he's admitted to.

"Pierre! It is not only your soul, it is something else that cannot feel love."

"I am waiting for le coup de foudre," he says through gritted teeth.

Camille scoffs. "And that is your last form of love? There is nothing else? You cannot have love that grows? Like a vine from a seed? Strong because it takes time to grow?"

Camille's lips tighten, then she turns to Noah and puts her hand on his arm. He's still frowning at Pierre, so when Camille touches him he startles.

"Monsieur Wright, would you like to walk with me?"

Noah glances at me quickly, but what does he expect me to say?

"Of course," he finally says, giving her his best Noah Wright smile. And faster than I can blink they're up and walking across the grass toward the little white church.

I pick up a pear slice and nibble at it as Pierre watches them go with a frown wrinkling his forehead.

"Do you think Camille and Noah..." He tilts his head and studies them. Camille has her arm through Noah's and she's leaning into him, talking excitedly. Noah leans his head closer to her. My shoulders drop.

"Maybe. He is single. And she seems to like him."

He frowns after them. "Do you think Camille wants me to stop acting as an overprotective older brother?"

I hide a smile. "What possibly gave you that idea?"

Pierre isn't fooled. He grins at me. "I see. She's grown. Sometimes I can only see her as a twelve-year-old, getting into trouble, climbing the apple trees. I sometimes forget that she's a woman." He shakes his head. "The ecstasy of love?"

I smile at him. "It sounds like it could be painful."

"Yes. But so would a lightning strike be, no?"

"I think so."

Pierre reaches out and takes my hand, rubbing his fingers over my skin. Then he lifts it and presses his lips against my palm. I resist the urge to look behind me to see what Camille and Noah are doing. Instead, I swallow the sharp taste of the wine and the sugary taste of the pear, and watch Pierre.

Slowly, he lifts his mouth from my hand. "Friendship is a form of love."

"Is it?"

He nods. "Perhaps, if you agree, we might kiss and see if a storm occurs. I like you, Meredith. You are beautiful. You are kind. You are fun." He watches me, an almost shy expression on his face. "If you like, we can see if there could be love."

He reaches up and presses his fingers into my jawline.

Pierre is going to kiss me.

He leans forward.

The breeze blows, sending the perfume of the vineyard over us, and I wait for the soft focus, the orchestral music, the swelling of my heart.

I close my eyes, expecting the press of his lips over mine.

This is good. This is fine. This is...

"May we have some chocolate?" Camille says loudly.

My eyes fly open and I jerk away from Pierre. I look up at Camille and Noah, sitting back down on the picnic blanket.

Camille doesn't seem to realize she just interrupted a moment, but Noah is looking at me with raised eyebrows.

Camille doesn't wait for Pierre to answer. She opens

the box and offers one to Noah, takes two for herself then thrusts the box at Pierre.

"Have one," she urges.

Pierre takes one, gives me a good-natured shrug, and then picks out a chocolate. I'm trying very hard not to look at Noah because he keeps looking between Pierre and me with a question in his eyes that I'm not ready to answer.

"Chocolate?" Pierre asks.

"Sure." I nod, and then instead of handing me the box, Pierre holds his piece up to my mouth, offering for me to take it from him.

Both Camille and Noah, who were having a discussion about their favorite desserts, stop to watch. Okay. This is awkward. Super awkward.

I'm not going to nibble from his hands. So I reach up and grab the chocolate and quickly bite into it. The chocolate is actually really melted from the sun, and so it oozes over my lips. Luckily, it's good. So I don't mind that I have what probably looks like chocolate lipstick.

While I chew Noah and Camille turn back to their discussion and Pierre gives me a laughing smile. I shake my head at him.

"We haven't kissed yet," I whisper to him.

"I predict we will before we leave here." He has a confident smile on his face.

"Probably," I agree, flushing.

My lips have a prickly tingling sensation. I lick them and reach for another chocolate, biting through the shell to the ganache. The chocolate spills over my lips again and Pierre watches my mouth.

As he watches me my lips grow hot, little sparks and needle pricks flowing over them. I'd like to think that it's the anticipation of Pierre's kiss. But it's not. It's really not. I know exactly what this feeling is.

I look over at the box of chocolates, and sure enough, the chocolate shells are swirled with a bright red decorative paint. Carmine. Which means in a few seconds to a few minutes my lips are going to be covered in hives.

I dive for my napkin and scrub at my lips. Even go as far as to dip the cloth in the wine and try to wipe away the food paint. But it's too late. I know from years of this reaction that, while nothing life-threatening will happen, for the next few hours I'm going to have horrendously itchy, mosquito bite-looking bumps all over my mouth.

"Merry?" Noah asks, watching me carefully as I scrub at my mouth. "Are you okay?"

"You don't like chocolate?" Pierre asks.

"Can I talk to you?" I say to Noah, gesturing at a row of grapevines not far away.

He tilts his head in question then nods and walks with me to the grapes about twenty feet from the others.

"Are they reacting?" I ask, gesturing at my lips.

"What?" he stares at my mouth.

"I'm allergic to carmine. Are there hives? Are my lips swelling?"

Noah's eyes widen and he grabs my hand, gripping tightly. "Do you need to go to the hospital? Should I call emergency services? Do you need—"

"No. No." I cut him off. "It's fine. It's only dermatological. I just need you to tell me if my lips are getting bumps."

Noah's shoulders relax, he lets out a relieved breath, and then I think he realizes he's cutting off circulation to my hand, because he quickly lets go. Then he leans forward and peers at my mouth.

"Yeah. There are...actually, there are quite a few."

"How many is quite a few?" I ask. Although I can guess. My lips are stinging and itching and I feel like I was bitten by a swarm of mosquitos.

"Maybe...twenty?" He winces.

"It looks gross, doesn't it?"

I know it does. Bumpy, red, hive-covered lips are not pretty.

"No," he says without hesitation.

"It doesn't?"

He lifts a shoulder. "Not to me."

"So not to you, but maybe to someone else?"

He scowls. "I can't speak for Pierre."

I pull my phone out of my pocket and take a quick shot of my lips. What I see makes me squeak in protest.

"Noah. Will you help me?"

His eyes light with a question. "With what?"

"I don't want Pierre to see my lips like this."

"Why not?" His voice is flat and disapproving.

"Because we were about to kiss," I say impatiently.

Noah's jaw hardens. "If he won't kiss you after seeing you like this, then he doesn't deserve to kiss you at all."

I frown at him and take him by the arms, squeezing. "Please, Noah." And because he looks like he might soften I say again, "Please."

He seems to be having an internal struggle, but finally he nods, "Okay."

And that's how, within two minutes, Noah manages to get us packed up and back in the car with the excuse that he has lactose intolerance and extreme intestinal trouble. While clutching his abdomen and groaning he claims we must leave *immediately* and I have to go too since…no reason. But he was so convincing that Pierre and Camille didn't suspect a thing. Even though I kept my hand over my mouth the entire time. Who could notice that when Noah kept groaning, "The cheese! The cheese! Why France, why?!"

Noah glances over at me, steering around a curve in the road. "Do you need to go to a pharmacy?"

I shake my head. "I have an antihistamine in my suitcase."

He nods. "Okay."

My lips itch and sting, and I know I look frightful, but for some reason, having Noah see me like this doesn't make me embarrassed or make me want to hide until the hives go away.

"Thank you for that," I say as he pulls up the slope toward the chateau.

"You're welcome." He glances at me quickly and the corner of his lips tugs into a smile. "By the way, I stand by what I said."

"What?"

"If you can't let him see you like this, then—"

"He thinks I'm beautiful," I interrupt. "He wants to kiss me. He won't think that anymore if he sees this. And he won't want to kiss me either."

Noah frowns as he pulls into the chateau drive, the car rumbling over the gravel. Ahead, the chateau rises from the grassy, rocky ledge. Noah steers to the circle in front of the entrance and pulls his rental car to a stop. The car is quiet when he shuts off the engine, and suddenly the sting in my lips is nothing compared to the tight stinging sensation moving between us in the small car.

"Merry," he starts.

But I shake my head. "You don't have to do the friend thing. You don't have to tell me I'm beautiful just as I am, or that he doesn't deserve to kiss me."

"I wasn't. I'm not. I only want to say that if a person doesn't like you when you strip everything away and show them who you are, bumps and all"—he nods at my lips—"then they aren't the one. And if you can't show them who you are, bumps and all, then you already know they aren't the one."

I reach up and touch my lips, they sting beneath my fingers. "I wasn't talking about love. I was only talking about kissing."

Noah's gaze drifts to my fingers and to my mouth and I get the feeling he's imagining that kiss. Not the one I'd have with Pierre, but the one we shared after the wedding.

There was heat, and his tongue thrusting into my mouth, and his hands stroking down my arms, and over my back, he tugged me against him, and I threaded my hands around his neck as he nibbled my lips.

That was a *kiss*.

He leans towards me, spanning the few tight inches between us. I drop my hand as his eyes darken and we move only inches apart. The air crackles and I can taste the sweetness of wine and expectation on my tongue. I wonder if it will hurt when he kisses me, or if his lips rubbing on mine will feel like sweet relief.

Yes.

Yes please.

Suddenly Noah leans back, leaving the space between us cold. He jerks open the car door and the lake breeze and the sound of chirping birds fills the car, sweeping out the crackling expectation.

His expression is conflicted as he drags a hand through his black hair. I wonder if he's thinking about the girl he loves. Thankfully, I wasn't thinking about Leo. In fact, he's barely been on my mind at all today.

But that thought dampens my mood, because I remember clearly Noah's crisp words. *I will not be your way to get over Leo. I will not be your rebound affair.*

And really, it's not fair to do that to him, is it?

I clear my throat. "Thanks again," I say brightly. "I'm going to go find that medicine."

"Right." Noah nods, his eyes darting to and then away from my lips. "Right. Let me know if you need anything. If I can help."

I open my door and breathe in the evergreen scent of the alpine trees.

"I'll be fine," I promise.

At least my lips will be. I can't say the same for anything else.

I hurry off before either of us can say anything more, rushing into the dim interior of the great hall. As I push open the heavy door, Cupid leers at me from the mantle.

"What are you looking at?" I ask, hurrying past him and up the stairs.

My footsteps echo as I run up the turret's stone steps.

What am I doing?

I'm getting over one unrequited love to fall right into another, but this time when I fall in love I'll probably break my leg.

But isn't breaking your leg supposed to be good luck?

Wait.

No.

No no no no no.

Next time I see Pierre, I'm doubling down. We'll kiss. We'll laugh. We'll have fun.

It'll be amazing.

All I have to do is put my mind over my heart.

Come on, Merry, you can do this.

25

THE NEXT MORNING, I STROLL INTO THE KITCHEN IN A PINK floral dress with ribbons, and a bounce in my step. My lips are back to normal, it's a beautiful blue sky day, and I'm feeling as light as a red balloon floating in a clear sky.

"Good morning." I smile happily at Noah.

He's kneeling by the iron cookstove, striking a match for the fire. When I say "morning" he turns, nods, then goes back to concentrating on the stove. Then, almost as if he only now remembers what happened yesterday he turns back to me.

"You're better," he says, smiling.

I nod, pucker my lips at him, then grin when he shakes his head.

I wander farther into the kitchen. The arched brick ceiling, the iron stove, the old sink, it's like a time capsule. "I'm really glad you knew how to use this thing."

The fire is lit and burning now and Noah closes the door. In fifteen minutes or so the top will be burning hot, and the water reservoir will have lots of hot water for coffee.

"I didn't actually." He brushes his hands on his jeans and stands up.

"What do you call this?" I gesture at the burning stove, the pot of oatmeal on top, and the coffee press filled with grinds. Last night, he even made a dinner of fish caught from the lake, new potatoes, and cream sauce, all on this monstrous, Victorian-era wood cookstove. I didn't even have to badger him to share. When he saw me morosely slicing a baguette for dinner, he hid a smile, took down another plate, and shared his meal.

"Do you want to know a secret?"

I lean forward at the small smile playing over his mouth. There's a hint of wood smoke tickling my nose.

I nod. "Yes."

"Six years ago I was stranded in a small Mexican village. A little old lady took me in. She had a stove just like this. As part of my payment for room and board, she made me cook for her twelve sons and thirty-seven grandchildren. It was cooking trial by fire."

My jaw drops as I look between Noah and the cookstove. "Are you serious?"

He grins. "No."

I scoff and shove his shoulder.

"I watched a video tutorial," he admits.

"Oh. Huh." We both stand there and contemplate the old black stove. The heat has kicked up and I can feel it radiating off the stove in waves.

"To be honest, I'm surprised it worked."

I nod. Me too. The bed broke, the pipes don't work, the plaster's cracked, the stairs are crumbling, but the iron stove is still kicking. Amazing.

The oatmeal on top of the stove bubbles, letting out sighs and pops, and a homey, morning smell.

"I feel like I'm in a Victorian penny novel," I say, reaching for a wooden spoon to stir the oatmeal with.

"Is it a gothic piece?" Noah asks, eyeing me with interest.

"What would that mean?"

He considers this, rubbing a hand over his dark morning stubble. "First off, you'd have to be a single, young woman in an unfortunate circumstance. Family troubles, financial troubles, job troubles."

"Meh." I shrug.

He smiles. "The young woman relocates to an old dilapidated mansion with at least one tower room. The house is usually perched on a cliffside."

"Alright."

He nods. "In the mansion there's always a dark, brooding, misunderstood gentleman who the heroine thinks did some terrible deed."

Dark. Check. Brooding. Check-ish. Terrible deed? No.

I shake my head. "Not getting that vibe."

Noah lifts an eyebrow. "And there's a mystery. Something terrible happened in the past at the mansion, and the heroine has to solve it and save the hero."

"Do you read these books?" I frown at Noah. "I mean first, you're telling me about all the novels that have unrequited love in them, and now you're telling me the basic plotline for gothic romances."

The side of Noah's mouth kicks up into a smile. "Don't you read?"

"I watch movies."

"Well then when I get back next week, we'll watch *Rebecca* or *Jane Eyre*."

I nudge him with my arm, smiling, "You want to watch a...wait a minute, where are you going?"

Noah takes the wooden spoon from my hand and stirs the bubbling oatmeal. After he knocks the spoon against the edge of the pot, he says, "I have a few locations I need to visit."

Oh. Right. His documentary. "I keep forgetting you're here to work."

He drops the spoon, turns to the counter, and pulls a bag of brown sugar out of a tin.

"Where are you going to go?" I ask, when I realize he isn't going to elaborate. And then, when I realize that I'll be here all alone, "And when will you be back?"

When I arrived and the taxi driver dropped me off, I didn't have any worries about staying alone. Now, well, I'm not exactly worried, but there is a tight, lonely knot working its way into my chest.

Noah sprinkles brown sugar into the pot, clumps of sugar falling through his fingers. He concentrates on evenly coating the boiling oats with sugar, then with a satisfied nod, he says distractedly, "I'm researching a painter. He did quite a few landscapes of chateaus. I want to see if I can find more pieces."

I remember the books spread out on his wooden table in the gatehouse, and even the story he told me while I drifted off the night the bed broke.

"Do you always feature artists in your work?"

Noah snaps the lid closed on the sugar tin. "Not always."

His answer is short, but by the way he avoids my eyes and keeps his face turned away and his hands busy, I think he's not telling me the whole story.

"Is this my mystery?" I joke.

Noah looks up quickly. The shadows of the kitchen and the light from the fire flicker over him, highlighting the intensity in his eyes.

"What?"

"My gothic mystery? Is this the one I'm supposed to solve?"

I thought I was making a funny joke, but Noah's mouth flattens into a hard line. "There's no mystery. He painted French chateaus and then he stopped."

I frown at Noah. For there not being a mystery he seems awfully irritated with me.

He moves to pour steaming water into the coffee press, and as the water hisses I shift uncomfortably.

"So why do you have to leave to research the paintings? Can't you do that from here?" My voice sounds as hollow as the wide, tube-like kitchen.

I suppose that's really what this is about. I don't want Noah to leave for a week. After only a few days I've gotten exceedingly comfortable with the idea that he and I will be living here for three months—together.

Noah sets down the water pot and slowly turns to me. Whatever he sees on my face has his expression softening.

"Sorry, Merry. I'm cranky before coffee."

"Oh. That's okay." I nod. Didn't I already say as much the other day?

He reaches around me and pulls two mugs from the wooden shelf, brushing my arm as he does. The mugs clatter as he sets them on the counter.

"His work is displayed in galleries and in public exhibits at some of the chateaus he painted. I'm going to the locations to see everything in person. It'll be hours of driving, overnight stays, I'll probably be gone a week or so. I didn't think. You'll be alright by yourself? I figured you wanted me gone." He gives me a quick grin, then pours two cups of coffee, the steam and rich smells drifting up.

I almost ask, *can I come with you?* But that would be crazy. Besides, I'm supposed to be pulling back from Noah, not pushing closer.

"I'll be fine. Thank you," I say, grabbing the mug and taking a sip. Hot. That's hot. I wince as the nutty coffee scalds my tongue.

Noah lifts an eyebrow. "Fine?"

"Great. Splendid. Amazing. Like you said, I wanted the chateau to myself."

He looks unconvinced.

I point at the oatmeal. "I'm only disappointed because who will work the behemoth if you're not here?"

Noah cracks a smile. "Ah. Now I see. You're only concerned about your stomach."

"And the rats."

He nods. "And the bats, I suppose."

"There are bats?" I look at the kitchen ceiling as if they're currently hanging upside down from the brick arches.

Noah looks sheepish. "Sorry. I thought you'd seen them. Forget I said anything."

I scoff. "Fine. I'm not scared of bats," I lie. Then brazenly, I say, "As long as there aren't any cockroaches I'll be fine."

Noah turns away so quickly to stir the oatmeal that my senses go on high alert. "Noah."

"Yes?" he doesn't turn around.

"Did you see any cockroaches?"

He glances at me from the side of his eye. "Alive?"

"You saw dead ones?"

"Have some oatmeal." He thrusts a bowl toward me, full of piping hot sugar-covered oatmeal.

I stare at him, and he stares back, an expression of pure innocence on his face. Then, "You're from New York, how can you be scared of cockroaches?"

I let out a loud huff. "That's exactly why! I've seen them. I know them. They're sadistic. They haunt you, only coming out in the dark. They're as big as a fist, as smart as a cat, as fast as a blade, as indestructible as...as..."

I'm getting worked up. Me and cockroaches, we don't get along. Not since I woke up one night when I was five, with one scratching at my mouth. I shudder and Noah steps forward.

"Do you want to come with me? On my trip?" he asks, and I can tell he wasn't thinking of inviting me, but he looks so concerned about my fear of cockroaches that he's actually asking. Which is...sweet. Really, really sweet.

But if there's one thing that I'm scared of more than cockroaches, it's falling into another hopeless love story.

"I'll be fine," I tell him.

Then when he doesn't look convinced I say, "Just lend me one of your big, fat books. I'll keep it by my bed and use it to crush them if they come near."

I smile at the affronted look on his face.

"You'd use a book as a cockroach swatter?"

"Errr...maybe?"

He shakes his head and then lets out a low, rumbling laugh. "Merry, what am I going to do with you?"

A flood of warmth flows through me, and I realize that my body took his question in a completely different direction than he intended. My limbs go languid and my insides feel warm and fizzy, and a thousand suggestions of what he can do are flashing through my head.

I clear my throat. "I'll be fine. Have fun on your trip."

Noah gives me a questioning look, but then shrugs and takes a bite of his oatmeal. After that we eat our breakfast in silence.

And even when he loads his suitcase into his rental car and says a quick goodbye, I'm careful to keep it light and not let on that I'm going to miss him. That even before he's out of sight, I already do.

26

NOAH'S GONE. WHICH MEANS THE CHATEAU DECIDES IT'S the perfect time to show me exactly what it can do.

Saturday I walk into the bedroom and find a fat, shiny, twitchy-antennaed cockroach scuttling on the wall. I scream, pick up a heavy hardback book—sorry Noah!— and slam it against the wall.

Again and again and again, missing the cockroach by a hair each time.

The cockroach survives but the wall doesn't. After the third hit with Noah's tome, the centuries old plaster cracks, like thin ice on a winter pond, and then half the wall crumbles, the plaster collapsing in a giant heap.

I stand, stunned, while a pile of rubble avalanches around me, kicking up a cloud of gray dust that would do a volcanic eruption proud. It smells musty, dusty, and as the cockroach scuttles into the cracks I sneeze, and then sneeze again. Wiping at my watering eyes I turn and take in the damage. Unfortunately, the bed, the old woolly mattress that Noah sleeps on, is covered in a thick layer of debris.

Sunday, I scrub and sweep the plaster massacre, and then go to take a bath. The pipe, my lone, sweet water pipe? When I turn it on full blast, it sprays my face, the ceiling, the walls, it sprays everywhere. The only way to get it to stop? Turn it to a slow, leaky trickle.

Monday, a violent storm hits the mountain. The winds howl through the narrow halls and the round turrets, screaming through the chateau like a haunting.

I huddle in my new bed, with the covers pulled over my head. The light from my phone glows as I scroll through old photos of me and Leo. Before when I looked at these I saw me and Leo, a pair.

Now, looking at them, I see what the reality was. A girl, hopelessly in love, and a guy, completely uninterested. It's clear as day.

My smile in the photos is radiant. I lean toward him like a plant twining toward the sun. And Leo, he looks happy, but distracted, or impartial, or...heck I'll call it like it is, he's the same in all the photos whether he's next to me, or Reggie, or John.

The magic I'd spent years imagining? It was never there.

A bolt of lightning spears jagged across the sky at the same time a roar of thunder shakes the chateau. I jump and cover my ears, dropping my phone.

"Lightning? Really?" I yell, feeling shaken and embarrassed. "Why don't you hit me? Huh? Why haven't you ever hit me?" And then, instead of fizzling off and moving on, the storm does just what I ask.

A bolt of lightning strikes the turret. The flash blinds me, and I swear sparks fly. I stare, wide-eyed out the window, shivering and shaking. Because when I asked for a lightning bolt, I was asking for a metaphor. Not to actually be hit by lightning. I wrap the blanket tightly around my shoulders and shiver myself to sleep.

Tuesday, when I step outside, the cucumber patch is a ruin, and the shingles on the turret are singed and blackened.

Wednesday, only five days after Noah left, I wake up expecting the worst. Instead, Pierre texts and asks if I'd like to have a dinner.

I say yes.

27

"OKAY. THERE'S ONLY ONE WAY TO PLAY THIS AND YOU HAVE to do it right. You have one chance. Don't mess it up," Angela says firmly.

"Why only one chance?" I pace in front of the arched entry, the grass tickling my bare feet.

"Merry! Listen to me and listen closely."

"Okay?" I tilt my head and wish that I had a notepad to write this down. Sometimes Angela has really excellent advice, but usually I forget it when I'm supposed to be using it.

"You said this guy is coming for dinner?"

"Yes. Tonight. At the chateau."

Angela called to tell me about how for the past week she's been hugging the toilet non-stop. Morning sickness joy. When she asked me how I was, I told her about my upcoming date with Pierre.

Here's the thing, Angela has always had luck with men. She only has to look at them and they fall over themselves to do whatever she wants. Me? Well. Not so much.

"And he's expressed interest?"

"Mhmm," I confirm, thinking about how Pierre talks about love and kissing.

"Then tonight is the battlefield."

Ugh.

"Why is this a battle?"

"Love is a battle!"

Oh jeez. Sometimes I think Angela took my mom's views on love a little too seriously.

Love is a battle is one of my mom's favorite quotes. Usually she says it when toasting a new relationship. Inevitably these relationships always end in blow ups and fireworks. She saves the silent, epic, decades-long, cold war battle for my dad. Either way, I've never thought that it was a healthy perspective.

"It'll be fine. I was thinking about going on a bike ride with him and packing a picnic. It would be really cute to—"

"Stop."

"But—"

"Merry. Stop."

I stop.

"I'm going to share something with you. When a sexy man asks you to dinner, you don't mess around with bikes and picnics and *cute*. No. You lay out a plan. A battle plan."

I freeze. My toes dig into the sun-warmed grass and I look around the lawn, at the stone path, the dark green woods, the glistening beige stone of the entry. Is she joking? I'm expecting to hear a laugh sounding on the wind, above the noise of the chirping woodland birds.

"I'm not following," I finally say.

"I know. You're not the strategic type. That's why you have me. Write this down."

"What?"

She laughs and then I hear a glass tinkling and running water. Hmmm. Cold water from a working faucet sounds really nice. Maybe a slice of lemon. My mouth waters at the thought. Ice water. Mmmm.

"Do you have pen and paper?"

"Oh. Right. Yes."

I don't. Obviously.

But Noah does in the gatehouse. I hurry across the lawn and then up the steps, taking them two at a time.

"Are you still there?" I ask, hoping that the thick stone hasn't blocked reception.

At Noah's makeshift office, I shuffle through his books and papers, stirring up the scent of parchment and old book binding, until I find a clean sheet of paper and a pen.

"Ready."

"Good. First, you need to prep the field."

"Prep the field," I repeat, writing this down word for word.

"That means shower, shave, wax, pluck, lotion, perfume, make-up—but not too much make-up—hair, lingerie, push-up bra, and a dress that shows cleavage, lots of cleavage. Got it? Did you write all that down?"

I scrawl the word cleavage on the paper and underline it three times, pressing firmly. "Yup."

I look around the room, expecting for some reason to see Noah here, giving me his sardonic smile, an eyebrow raised. In fact, the shadow of him is still here, probably because I can smell a hint of evergreen drifting in through the cracks in the stone walls, which reminds me of the clean, crisp scent he has when he's lying next to me in bed.

I shake my head, knocking Noah's sardonic smile away, and forcibly underline cleavage again.

"Good," Angela continues, "Then you need to set the stage. Write that down."

I write *set the stage* on the paper. "Got it."

"Usually I like the damsel in distress routine. That always works."

I write *damsel in*...then I stop, midway through the *n*, and say, "What do you mean?"

Angela clicks her tongue impatiently. "You know. Men like to solve problems. So I like to give them problems to solve. Like, I lost my contact lens and I need help finding it. That one is nice, because when I bend over they can see my breasts."

The hair on my arms rises from a sudden chill. Is she saying what I think she's saying?

"What else?"

"Oh you know. I'm lost. I have a flat tire. That sort of thing."

"Uh huh."

The night she met Leo flashes into my mind with crystal clear clarity. She battle-fielded him. She damsel-in-distressed him. I thought it was love at first sight, but was it actually love at first battle?

Was it?

"Is that what you did to Leo?" I ask, unable to hold in my suspicions.

"What?" Angela lets out an uncomfortable laugh. "No. Nooo. That was happenstance. He was there. I was there..." She trails off.

I realize I'm gripping the pen so hard that it's possible it might snap in half. I take a breath and loosen my fist.

"Anyway, Merry. You've prepped the field. You've set the stage. Manufacture some sort of problem. Then once he saves you and feels all manly, that's when you give him *the look*."

"What look?" I snap.

"You know, *the look*." She lowers her voice meaningfully.

I scowl at the piece of paper. Then I scowl at the wooden table covered in Noah's notes and books. Sure, I know the look. It's the one Angela has had since the day she was born. The one that I don't have.

"I don't have the look."

"Everyone has the look."

"I don't."

"You do."

"I'm telling you, I don't."

"Merry, I promise you. If you prep the field and set the stage, all you have to do is give him *the look*, and he'll be falling all over himself to do whatever you want."

I throw the pen down and it skitters across the table and clatters to the floor.

"Like marry me?" I ask angrily. My chest heaves as I draw in a burning breath. "Do you think if I gave him the look, he'd ask me to marry him?"

There's silence from the other end of the phone.

I take in a sharp breath, the air biting at my lungs.

Finally, Angela says, "Are you angry with me?"

"No," I say automatically. Then, since that's a lie, and I remember that my new motto is directness and honesty I say, "Actually, yes."

"Why?"

I stalk across the stone floor and look out the window, glaring at the treetops and the bright sun sparkling over the diamond-studded lake. Okay, so directness is my new motto, but maybe I'm not ready to be fully direct.

"No. I'm not mad. I'm just stressed. It's a lot to think about. You know, I've never been the best at first dates. Or dating. It's not easy. Love."

Angela lets out a long sigh. "Mom and Dad really messed us up, didn't they?"

She sounds sad, and small, and a lot like my little sister, who would always climb into my bed at night whenever she had a bad dream and press her cold feet into my calves and wrap her arms around my waist, until she fell asleep again.

I lean against the stone wall, its coldness seeping into my skin. I'm chilled and I can taste a flash of fatigue and bitterness, like old turned wine.

Stupid. Stupid past.

"I don't know," I say quietly. "Maybe we messed ourselves up."

I hear Angela set her glass down and then she hurries from the kitchen, her shoes clicking on the tile. "I'm back in the bathroom. Think I might puke."

Actually she does sound really queasy.

I stand straight. "I'm sorry. Do you need to go?"

Water from the faucet runs, and there's splashing. "No. Maybe." Then, "Merry?"

"Yeah?" I walk back to the table and trace my fingers over the paper I was writing on.

"I was thinking. You know how Mom always criticized you when you were little?"

I hold still, my finger stops tracing the words. Angela's never said anything about this before. I didn't realize she'd noticed. Like I said, she doesn't complain about Mom or Dad.

My throat burns when I say, "Yeah?"

"I guess, I always thought, Mom criticizing you so much? It never made you stop loving her. It just made you stop loving yourself."

My throat catches and it seems like the room wobbles. Just a bit.

Because my sister just stuck her finger into the depths of me and hit a spot that I never realized was aching and sore. I press my hand to my chest. Is that it then? Can everyone see my shortcomings clearly except for me?

I don't know what to say. What is there to say?

Yes?

Okay?

I guess so?

Or, no, that's not true, I love myself so much!

But Angela doesn't even know the worst of it. Because when Dad turned me aside and told me to go and not ever come back, that's when I really, truly stopped loving myself. Let's be honest. All those people on the internet, or in self-help books, or on cutesy bookmarks who tell you to love yourself, well of course you want to love yourself, *of course you do*. And when you're a kid, you do. You do. It's a big, brave, giant sort of love.

But then, with each knock, each criticism, each rejection from the people you love and trust—because they're your parents, they're grown-ups, of course you trust them, of course you love them—with each rejection, that big, giant self-love becomes smaller and smaller and smaller, until, I guess, it's almost gone. Or it is gone. Either way. It's hard to find once it's gone.

But that's why I'm here, isn't it?

To find the magic again?

Angela moans. "Really don't feel good. So tired of puking. So, so tired of it."

I clear my throat, wipe at my eyes, and paste a smile on my face. "Cheer up. It's worth it."

"Ugh."

Before she goes, I do want to ask one thing. "Are you and Leo...doing okay?"

She moans, a long drawn-out, painful, I'm-going-to-throw-up sort of moan.

"It's fine. I'm too busy puking for much else. He brings me ginger ale and crackers. It's fine. Except, he brought in falafel for lunch the other day and I nearly threw up from the smell. I had to yell at him. Then the man-smell shampoo he uses, it makes me want to barf. And the mint gum he chews. Gross, I want to vomit. But other than that, yes, it's fine."

"So...you're good? Still wildly in love?"

She moans again. "Love is a battle, Merry. Gosh, I want to curl up and..." She mumbles something that I can't make out. Then, "Sex is not worth this pain. It's not. It's not."

Okay then.

"Okay, feel better. I'm going to go prep the field."

She sniffles, and then, "Don't forget *the look*. But just kiss. No sex. Or, no babies. Gah. Why didn't they tell me about morning sickness? Why didn't I know it wasn't just morning? It's morning, day, night, all the freaking time sickness."

Hmm.

"Okay. I'll let you go."

"No sex! I mean it, Merry!"

"Honestly there is this thing called protection...birth control."

"It's not one hundred percent. You could be me. Don't do it, Merry! Not until they invent the morning-sickness cure."

Okay. Right.

"Alright. I'll let you go. Talk to you later?"

She sniffs again and I hear the toilet flush. "Bye. No wait. I almost forgot. Leo mentioned something about Noah..."

I stiffen, then press the phone closer to my ear. Stupidly my heart flutters, like a trilling bluebird in a cheesy animation. "Okay?"

"Hmm. Nope. Can't remember."

Ugh.

"Is he still there with you?" she asks.

I shake my head, then realizing she can't see me. "No. He's been away for nearly a week, out on some research project."

I frown at the empty gatehouse room, filled with his presence, but absent of him.

"Oh good. That's good. I can't remember but I think it was something about how Noah's really screwed up. Some weird thing from his past. Something he did. Some awful thing. I don't know, I was thinking about French fries dipped in mayonnaise at the time, I wasn't really paying attention. But..." She moans again. "You were right. He's not...ugh. Mayonnaise. Oh no, mayonnaise. Gotta go. Gotta go."

"Wait. What do you me—" I cut off. She's already hung up.

I stare out the window, trying to see farther than the

dark green trees and the azure lake, all the way to the far, far distant sky.

Noah has a deep dark secret?

No wait. That's not what Angela said. She said he has something weird in his past. That he's screwed up. That he did *something*.

Something weird that screwed him up?

Something awful?

Well, I mean, I have something in my past that screwed me up. That isn't a big deal.

Everyone who makes it to adulthood has something that screwed them up.

Curiosity nibbles at me, like the teeth of a hungry mouse, gnawing at the edge of a block of cheese, taking quick, urgent bites. I tap my foot, the sound tattooing across the stone room. Should I call Leo? Should I ask him? Just a quick call. It wouldn't be a big deal.

No.

No.

If Noah wants me to know about his past he'll tell me. And as for Leo, that's done. I'm not calling him.

I shove my phone into my pocket and then slowly turn, taking in the room, the table, all of Noah's research notes.

I run my hand over one of his books, opened to a page showing a painting of a beige turret with a woman leaning over the stone edge, the wind whipping her hair and her dress behind her, so that they look like black wings, willing her to take flight. A golden sun shines down, illuminating the sky and the stone walls, but she's left in shadow. I shiver. In the painting the woman's features are tinged with something like ecstasy. And the hint of wings makes her look as if she's considering leaping off the tower. The painting doesn't show how high the walls are or what lies below. You can't know, if she leaps, whether she'll be safe or whether she'll be broken.

The painting is tinted with a sense of foreboding.

Strangely, the turret looks similar to one of the towers here at Chateau de Mountlake. If it is one, then the woman probably wouldn't survive the leap. I run my finger over the glossy page and trace the caption. It's called *Prendre la fuite*, and then translated in English it says, Escape, or The Flight.

I let out a shaky breath and then turn and hurry down the stairs.

I wonder if that woman was considering her flight plan? Was it as simple as that? Probably not. It was likely some other type of flight.

The painting hangs in my mind, so I close the book in my head and put it aside. That research is for Noah. It doesn't impact me. He's looking at chateaus. Not flight plans. And whatever Leo told Angela about him, that doesn't matter either. So I close that too.

I'm here for magic.

I'm here for...fun.

So.

Onward.

28

I DIDN'T REALIZE QUITE HOW HARD IT WOULD BE TO *shower, shave, pluck, wax, lotion, perfume, make-up, hair, etcetera,* when you only have an old tub in the kitchen and cold water that sprays to the ceiling when turned to anything more than a trickle. Plus, there aren't any mirrors. Just my compact mirror.

But I persevered!

I am an American women in soft focus, with orchestral music and dim lighting!

I splashed cold water over myself, shaved *everything* and only nicked myself seventeen times—shaving with cold water is awful, horrible, bad. Then I slathered myself in the lavender goats milk lotion I picked up from the market, and then did a sexy smoky eye.

Of course, I had to watch a tutorial for that. It took about fifteen minutes...okay, two hours, but why don't they tell you doing a smoky eye is *impossible*?

Then I braided my hair into this complicated crown braid inspired by Camille—another tutorial—it took only an hour, honest. After all that prep, I only had to select sexy lingerie, a push-up bra, and a cleavage-baring dress.

Unfortunately, I didn't bring super-sexy slinky lingerie. I brought beige or white or nude cotton underwear and comfortable t-shirt bras. Apparently, in my frilly dress fantasy, I forgot that the frilly dress sometimes gets *taken off*. I blame my underwear selection on the fact that I like to be comfortable, I like to kick a soccer ball around for fun, I like to clean and keep busy. The point is, I don't have sexy, slinky lingerie for tonight.

No matter. It's not as if Pierre and I are going to have sex.

We're going to kiss.

Maybe.

Probably.

But we're not going to get naked. So there isn't any reason to worry about the underwear situation. Based on that, I chose the white underwear and white t-shirt bra. Then I slipped on my frilliest, sweetest, lilac-colored dress, with romantic little white flowers sprinkled over the fabric.

If I do say so myself, I look kissable.

At least, my three-inch compact mirror tells me I look kissable.

Now, I'm in the kitchen, with the stack of ingredients I bought at the market this afternoon, ready to cook a romantic dinner.

The old oven has a stack of wood burning in the firebox (I pulled a Noah and watched an instruction video! I know the lingo now!), the damper is open, and the water is heating. There's a bit of smoke, it curls up from the stove like circles puffed from a pipe, and the acrid scent tickles my nose. I have a giant aluminum pot on the stove, a lid, and a pair of metal tongs. The water's simmering, almost ready.

I flinch when I look back at the counter, because there, waiting to be cooked, is the lobster. Or Louis as I named him. Which I shouldn't have. You should never name food. But after I bought him, he stared at me with his black, shiny eyes and his twitching antenna and I thought, *you look just like a Louis.*

So.

"I'm sorry," I tell him. "But this is for a good cause."

He's in a thick brown paper bag, the edges rolled down. The bag smells like the fish counter, all briny and weedy and fishy. His (or her? Is he Louise?) umber and copper coloring, I think, will turn bright red after cooking. I don't know though. I've never cooked lobster. I like lobster, I eat it, but, okay, he's staring at me, it's freaking me out.

He's a big one, almost a kilogram, big enough for two people, the vendor assured me. His claws and legs are twitching and scrambling around the sack, making a scratchy, clawing noise, the scritch-scritch sounding like, *don't eat me, don't you dare eat me.*

I close my eyes to block out Louis's accusing glare.

"We have to eat you," I tell him. "Angela texted and said lobster is the only food that guarantees..." I trail off. Obviously Louis/Louise doesn't want to hear about how Angela claims there isn't any food better than lobster for *battle.*

She said the crunching, the sucking, the breaking apart of the flesh, the mess, all the licking was the best way to draw attention to lips and kissing and—

Louis beats himself against the side of the paper bag

and it scoots across the counter. I let out a muffled shriek and jump back. I shove the bag back and hiss, "Stay put. It's fine. It'll only hurt a little bit."

Why. Why oh why.

Maybe I shouldn't do this. Maybe I'll keep Louis as a pet?

A snapping, clacking sound comes from the bag, and I peer over the edge. Louis's legs twitch and he glares balefully. No. I can't keep him as a pet. Clearly, he hates me.

"I'm just going to do this," I tell him. "I'm going to put us both out of our misery. Pierre will be here in thirty minutes. We can't delay any longer."

I pause, looking down at his twitching body and his down-turned mouth. Gosh. Suddenly, for no reason whatsoever, I feel as if I'm back at work, leading a friend and coworker into the conference room to fire them.

They knew what was going to happen. I knew what was going to happen. Yet I still did it. Because it was going to happen one way or another. My eyes sting and I wipe at them, sniffing.

I did it. Didn't I?

Because I felt I had to. Because I wanted to give my coworkers a bit of dignity.

"I'm not crying," I tell Louis.

He clacks a claw in response, snapping his disbelief.

"It's just...you're going to be eaten either way. It's going to happen." My shoulders slump.

Louis doesn't care. His body twitches and he rams against the bag. At the stove, the lid on the pot clatters noisily from the steam escaping. It's time.

In my mind, I remember the conference door clicking shut and Louis's expression reminds me of what I did. I thought I was past this. I thought I'd left it behind. My hands shake as I reach out to grab him.

"We'll do this fast," I say soothingly.

Then, because I'm still thinking about my job, I say, "How about an appreciation speech? Everyone deserves a little something...errr...Louis was a good lobster. He liked the water..."

I wrinkle my forehead and stare down at him. He's stopped moving to listen, his black eyes considering.

"And he liked to...eat? And swim? And"—I hurry to finish—"he enjoyed life. He was a good and decent lobster," I say more firmly, picking up confidence. "Thank you, Louis, for your job. We appreciate you. Thank you."

Gosh.

That was the worst appreciation eulogy ever.

But looking down at Louis, I think he kind of liked it. He's stopped scratching and clawing, and he's just pondering the brown walls of the paper bag.

So there you have it.

"Okay. Easy does it," I tell him, then I gather all my courage, clench my teeth, stiffen my arms and swoop my hand into the bag and grab him round the body.

Ack!

Did I think Louis was peacefully surrendering to his fate?

No. No he's not. He's a vicious lobster demon.

His legs scrabble, his body twists, his head pivots, and his claws snap. I screech and almost drop him, but somehow I manage to keep ahold of him.

"Stop it! Stop it! I gave you a speech!" I shriek.

He claws at me again and the cold, wet, scratchy dampness of his hard skin scratches at my hand, and I swear, he's a centimeter away from taking off a finger.

"Stop it!"

I dart across the stone floor and fling the lid off the pot. It clatters to the ground. The steam rushes high, like a hot geyser, and I throw Louis into the boiling pot, like I'm offering a virgin sacrifice to a frothing volcano in some sadistic fertility ritual.

Except, Louis isn't a virgin, he's a lobster, and I'm not wishing for rain, I'm wishing for magic and—

"Ahh! No! Ahh!"

He's leapt out of the pot onto the counter. And he's livid.

You'd think a boiling water burnt lobster would run away and hide. Escape. But not Louis. He charges at me, his claws snapping. I shriek and grab the metal tongs.

"Stay back!" I swing them at him and clack the metal forks together threateningly. The tongs don't deter him. Louis has a vendetta.

He charges again, lunging at me. I jump back. I'm terrified of a two-pound lobster, and his waving antenna and clacking claws.

I shudder, waving the tongs, and then seeing the lid on the floor, I grab it, and even though it's as hot as a loaf of bread just out of the oven, I hold it in front of me like a shield.

"This is inappropriate," I tell him, brandishing the pot lid. "You are going to be cooked. That's life. Bad things happen. You deal with it. You carry on. You just say, *Louis, you can do this*. And you do it! You just do it. Okay? You just do it."

I glare at him and he glares back. We have a stand-off. And I realize, yes, I'm talking to a lobster, I'm telling him my philosophy on life. And if Jupiter were here, she'd say, *Merry, you're wrong, you don't have to do this, you can jump out of the trash compacter,* or the boiling water, in Louis's case, but...argh...

No.

"You have to do this," I tell Louis, inching toward him, holding my lid out so he doesn't take off a finger. "And so do I."

Angela said that lobsters make magic and I very much want magic.

I drop the tongs and then lunge at Louis, darting my hand in to grab him round the middle. But he's fast. Faster even than a New York City cockroach.

He darts toward me, I shriek, and then he's running across my ingredients. He charges through the huge flat square of soft, creamy, salty European butter, crushing and squishing it. He massacres the plate of fresh thyme and sends the arugula and dandelion greens flying in the air, flapping like green flags in the wind. The cherry tomatoes and tiny onions roll across the counter and rain to the floor, bouncing across the stone. He's rampaging across the counter, laying waste to my dinner plans—just like a man, laying waste to a stupidly naïve girl's heart.

It's like he knows.

Louis knows just what he's doing. The butter is smeared over the counter, the greens are shredded, the tomatoes splattered. It smells like a pulverized salad, with fishy brine mixed in. But Louis isn't done. He glares at me then charges back toward me, ready to wreak havoc on my platter of artisan cheeses, the basket of bread and the glistening apple tarts.

"You wouldn't dare," I breathe.

He would.

He charges.

Brave Louis. Mad Louis.

He's the Napoleon of lobsters and my dinner is all of Europe. I growl at him. Well, guess what, Louis, that pot of boiling water? That's your Waterloo, buddy.

He dashes at the cheese plate. The gooey raclette, the heavenly Reblochon, the hard, golden yellow Beaufort. I spent hours shopping for these cheeses. This food! And he's about to destroy it.

I don't think. I just know I need to stop him. I swing with the tongs, aim for Louis. He darts to the side, sliding over the Reblochon. I miss. Hit the cheese. It splatters with a loud squelch and spurts onto my face. Louis is already off, jumping over the cheese plate, darting back and forth. I swing, hitting and missing, like a messy version of whack-a-mole.

Then Louis jumps from the cheese plate and dashes to the tarts.

I freeze.

He glares at me.

I glare back, staring into his beady black eyes.

Would he?

Will he?

"Don't," I say.

But who am I to ask him not to ruin my dessert? I'm trying to whack him with tongs and toss him in boiling water.

So, he does.

He jumps onto the tarts, and I think, no, *I know*, he's cackling as he pulverizes the pretty little tarts, with their perfectly sliced apples and shiny sugar drizzle.

"Noooo!" I cry, my voice echoing miserably through the brick-walled kitchen.

Then Louis stops, looks at me, and waggles a claw in the air, like he's giving me the middle finger.

I let out a shriek of rage, hold up my tongs, I'm going to—

"Merry?"

I stop.

Whirl around.

My breath whooshes out of me, and all my bravado disintegrates. I drop the tongs, and they clatter to the floor.

Noah stares at me in stunned silence, his eyes wide, his mouth working, but no sound coming out.

Embarrassment creeps over me like the steam curling out of the pot.

Noah wipes his eyes, shakes his head, looks around the kitchen, then, "What...what? Are you okay? I heard..."

I look quickly back at the counter. Louis, the devil, is using the distraction of Noah to slip away. He's retreating, backing toward the edge of the counter so he can leap off and escape to fight another day.

"Hold that thought," I call, then I swing around and dash at Louis. But dang it. The floor, it's covered in goopy cheese splatter and butter. I slip, slide forward, and while I reach out, still determined to catch Louis, he dives off the counter, and I fall, chest first into the tarts.

I hit the counter with my fist and let out a cry of frustration.

"I'll get you next time!" I shout, sounding like a bad TV movie villain.

Behind me I hear Noah trying rather unsuccessfully to restrain a laugh.

Slowly I peel myself from the counter and turn to face Noah.

He's trying very, very hard not to laugh. His lips are

tight, his shoulders are shaking, and his eyes are full of mirth.

"Hi," he says.

I take in a few breaths and survey the damage. Louis scrambled through a large crack in the wall. He's probably terrorizing the local family of rats. The greens look like they were picked up by a tornado and thrown around the kitchen. The cheese and butter are splattered on the walls, the floor, me. In fact, I can taste the creamy, cheesy goodness of the Raclette on my lips. And the tarts. The poor, once-beautiful tarts. Well. Most of them coat my breasts.

I hold up a hand and give a little wave, ignoring the heat in my cheeks. "Hi. You're back."

I try not to think about how happy that makes me feel.

Finally, Noah's stoicism breaks, and he flashes a grin. "You okay?"

I nod. "I'm making lobster."

His eyes roam over the kitchen, then back to me, a hint of laughter still in his eyes. He steps closer to me and I notice that he has purple bags under his eyes that weren't there before, and he's rumpled and unshaven.

I think his trip must not have gone as well as he hoped, because there's a tension around his mouth, even with his smile. When he's close enough for me to remember how he feels when he's near—like viscous heat and crackling tension—I say, "I missed you."

Then when his eyes widen, I realize exactly what I just admitted, and I try not to kick myself.

"I mean..." I gesture around the kitchen, "I really could've used your help."

He nods as if there wasn't anything strange about me

missing him and that yes, indeed, it can all be chalked up to me needing help with the behemoth stove.

Then he smiles, reaches up and plucks a wilted dandelion leaf from my hair. His eyes crinkle. Then he lifts his other hand and slowly drags his thumb over my upper lip, wiping away the cheese. My heart stutters, then beats wildly, as the heat from his thumb pressing into my lips scalds me from the inside out.

My eyes fly to Noah, wondering if he's feeling the boiling heat that I am, but he's concentrating on my mouth, and although I'd like to say that he looks swept away by the moment, I'd be lying.

I remember those pictures of me and Leo. The ones where I was starry-eyed in love, and where Leo, looking back, was not. So I watch Noah with impartiality, even though my breath is short and my mouth is tingling. I see that his expression is neutral, perhaps amused, but definitely not...dumbstruck, or lightning struck, or...ugh.

I take a quick step back.

I smile at Noah and wipe at my chest, apples and pastry crumbling to the floor.

He gives a jaunty smile and wipes his hands on a towel on the counter. When his back is turned I give myself a quick lecture. Noah does not love you. Noah is in love with someone else. You will not fall in love with him. You will not fall into lust with him (scratch that, too late). You will not play with fire because, like Angela said, he is screwed up. I shake my head. No. I don't care what Angela said. But I do care about not getting hurt. Therefore, do not fall for Noah Wright.

Remember what he said?

I prefer to make things clear at the beginning so there are no misunderstandings.

That thought has the power of a splash of ice-cold water in the face. I'm not interested in being the pathetic unrequited love girl for the rest of my life, hopping from one hopeless love story to another. When Noah turns back around, I've schooled my expression and put my priorities back in place. I know what I need to do.

He smiles at me, and I squash the little leap in my chest like I squashed the apple tarts.

"Why were you cooking?" He brushes at the hair that's fallen over his forehead, and I'm so distracted that I answer without thinking.

"I have a date with Pierre."

His hand pauses and then he drops it to his side, his expression one of stunned amusement. He looks around the kitchen again.

I sigh. "It was going to be lobster in butter herb sauce, local cheeses, and apple tarts." When I say, *apple tarts*, my voice wobbles a bit.

Noah looks at me quickly and frowns. And ugh, I think I might cry. And it's not that I'm sad. I'm not. It's just...

"I'm a mess, aren't I?"

I'm asking about more than the splattered cheese and tarts and the massacred kitchen, and Noah knows it. There's something in his eyes that tells me he knows exactly what I'm asking. Maybe Angela was right, maybe he is screwed up, because only somebody with experience would hear what I'm asking.

He steps forward again, looking down at me, and I get the feeling there must be cheese still on my mouth, because he's staring at my lips again.

"No," he says quietly.

"No?"

"You're perfect." He reaches up and I think he's going to cup my face and kiss me.

Yes. He's going to kiss me.

His fingers scrape my cheek and my eyelashes flutter. But then, instead of dropping his mouth to mine, he smiles, steps back and holds up a slice of apple coated in pastry crumbs.

My hand flies up to my cheek. There are more crumbs there. I'm even more covered in food than I realized. And Pierre is going to be here in less than thirty minutes.

I shake my head. "He'll be here soon and...gah. Look at me."

Noah shrugs. "Like I said, if he doesn't want you even seeing the bumps—"

"Yes. I get it." I put my hands on my hips. "But I spent all day, nearly ten hours, getting ready for tonight. And now. Look!" I gesture at the kitchen and at myself. "Look at me."

His brow furrows.

"I'm looking," he says in a low, careful voice.

My mouth wobbles again.

"I know. It's stupid. I want to make a good impression. But is that so wrong? Pierre sees *Meredith*." I say Meredith with all that the name encompasses. The chic, frilly dress-wearing, carefree woman who is kissed by sexy Frenchman and doesn't spend years longing after a man who doesn't want her. Then I shake my head and gesture at the mess coating my dress. "He sees Meredith. He doesn't see *Merry*."

"I like Merry."

I shake my head. "No you don't. You think you do, but you don't."

Noah gives me a flat look, as if I'm crazy to suggest that I know what he likes or doesn't like.

"I like you." He's daring me to contradict him.

I wave my hand in the air. "Okay, fine. You like me."

He lets out a long sigh.

I scrape my foot over the butter-slick stone, then look back to him, noting the lines between his brow.

I give him a consolatory smile. "You know me, I'm just looking for fun. For magic. Bumps and imperfections don't have any place in magic. Remember when Cinderella went to the ball? Her dress was perfect, it wasn't smeared in cheese and apples. If it had been, the prince wouldn't have kissed her."

I don't know why I'm admitting this to Noah, except, "You know how it is. You said you were all for me getting over my unfortunate state of unrequited love. This is me doing it."

I hold out my hands, palms up.

Noah's jaw tightens, and he looks as if he wants to argue, but then his gaze softens and he nods. "Alright. I'll help you."

The knot of tension in my chest eases and relief flows through me, tasting sweet like fresh apple tarts. "You will?"

"Sure." He runs his hand through his hair and looks around the kitchen. "How much time do you have?"

"Thirty minutes."

Noah's lifts his eyebrow, but then he shrugs and says, "Okay. Go get cleaned up. I've got a few tricks up my sleeve. It'll be fine."

I almost ask him, *what kind of tricks?* But then I realize we only have thirty minutes and I have to scrub off cheese and tart and put on a new dress, comb the arugula from my hair, and reapply my make-up (the smoky eye is *not* happening). So I throw my arms around Noah, give him a quick hug, breathing in his warmth and solidness, then before he can do anything more than stiffen and pull in a sharp breath, I hurry off, leaving him in the mess of the kitchen. I sprint up the round turret stairs buoyed by Noah's promise.

29

I HURRY BACK INTO THE KITCHEN, FACE SCRUBBED AND FREE of make-up, my hair brushed out and put in a simple braid, a new clean, periwinkle blue dress on. It took all of ten minutes, which means the clock is counting down.

Noah's at the wood block counter. He's swept the ruined ingredients into a pile and is using a rag to wipe up the last of the smeared cheese. There's the savory, homey smell of herbs sautéing in butter, combined with a happy sizzling sound coming from the iron skillet on the stove.

He turns and when he sees me his eyes crinkle with the hint of a smile. It hits me right in the chest and then shoots down my legs and trips up my feet. I stumble a bit, then reach out to catch myself on the edge of counter.

I pretend to inspect the bunch of thyme, bruised from my tong beating, then look at Noah and smile brightly. "Hi."

"Hi." He lifts his eyebrows and then nods. "That was fast."

I hold out my hands, "That's me. Fast."

Unless I'm doing a smoky eye and a crown braid, then all bets are off.

Noah's staring at me, a bemused expression on his face, so I reach up and touch my cheek. "Do I still have something on me?"

He blinks, looks away and shakes his head. "No. You're fine."

I let out a relieved breath. "That's good. Because I don't have time for anything better."

At that Noah gives a sharp nod and turns to the stove, shaking the iron skillet. The butter snaps and sizzles, and another puff of buttery herb smell wafts to me.

"So...what are we making?" I step forward and stand next to Noah.

He shakes the pan again and then raises his eyebrow. "You owe me for this, you know that, right?"

I scoff, buoyed by the teasing light in his eyes. "Are you angling for my mattress again?"

He laughs, but then I remember. "So...about that."

He frowns and then moves the butter off the stove. "We're talking about the mattress?"

"Mhmm."

"Can you hand me the eggs?"

On the counter there's a basket full of brown eggs. I was shocked when I realized that in France people leave their eggs on the counter. No refrigeration!

Which is a good thing because we don't have a refrigerator, but it still feels strange. The woman at the market told me—if I understood her correctly—that because the eggs aren't washed (true, they have dried goop and tiny feathers stuck to the shell) that they shouldn't be refrigerated.

That it's perfectly safe! That the American way of washing and refrigerating eggs is...something in French. I don't know. So, anyway. They're on the counter, in a basket, and I am all for it. I pick up the basket and carefully set it next to Noah.

"Thanks." He smiles and grabs an egg.

I watch as he swiftly cracks a dozen eggs into the butter-coated skillet and shakes it briskly. The yolks are bright orange. The eggs mix together and Noah keeps shaking until they swirl around like the stars in Van Gogh's Starry Night.

"Do you want a fork?"

He shakes his head no. "Tell me about the mattress."

"I broke it." I wince.

He stops swirling the eggs and frowns. "You what?"

"See, there was this cockroach."

His frown turns to a grin.

"And it was big. Really big. Like cat-sized." I hold up my hands in the *this big* gesture. "And it was coming at me. So I had to think fast. I grabbed a book."

"You did not."

I purse my lips together. "Okay. I didn't."

"Which book?"

I scratch my chin and think. "One with a cover? And a title?"

He gives me an appalled look, then realizing that he's stopped shaking the eggs, he starts up again.

"Anyway. I used the book to scare the cockroach."

"So it was a horror novel?"

I laugh and we share a grin. "No. It was some sort of giant history book. Four hundred pages or so. I was going to bore the cockroach to death."

"Did you succeed?"

"I didn't."

"But my mattress died?"

"It did."

He thinks this through. I can see him trying to work out how it might have happened, and I see when he finally decides that he can't possibly work it out.

"Basically, I tapped the wall with the book."

"Tapped?"

"Mhmm. And then, the wall, being old—"

"Three hundred and seventeen years," he agrees.

"Collapsed onto your bed."

He drops the skillet back onto the stove and gives me a stunned look.

I nod. "Yeah."

"You killed a wall and my mattress, but the cockroach survived?"

I stare at him. How does he not get this? "Cockroaches *always* survive."

He throws back his head and laughs. It's a delightful, rich, warm, buttery laugh, and I can't help but smile at him.

When he stops he wipes at his eyes and says, "Does this mean I get your bed? You take the floor?"

I put my hands on my hips. "The eggs are overcooking."

He scoffs, then moves to the counter to slide the yellow, fluffy, herby eggs onto a ceramic plate.

As he does, I tell him, "If you'd forgotten, you're chivalrous. You'd never make me sleep on the floor."

He lifts an eyebrow. "Is that what we decided?"

"Yes."

"For this omelet and the bruschetta I'm about to make, you owe me half your mattress."

He stops and holds out his hand for me to shake. I mean, there isn't really any argument here. I destroyed his bed.

"Fine. But only until we get another one. And only if you promise to stay on your side."

He gives me a side glance, because we both know that I'm the sleep snuggler.

"Deal."

We shake.

Then for the next fifteen minutes we work side by side, cutting the baguette, grilling the bread over the curling blue and orange flames, mixing the salvaged tomatoes with salt and olive oil. The heat radiating off the cookstove fire makes my cheeks warm, my skin glisten with perspiration, and my breath short. Or honestly, maybe it's the heat radiating off Noah.

Standing so close to him feels like standing in front of the stove's firebox. Either way, as I brush against Noah, hand him ingredients, drizzle olive oil into the bowl he holds out, I feel a warm flame curling inside me, trying to grow into a blaze.

Five minutes before Pierre is supposed to arrive we have a small feast of omelet, bruschetta, cheese (the Beaufort was spared), and wine.

"So..." I glance around at the miracle Noah pulled off. "We did it."

"We did it," he agrees.

"I'll have a date after all."

He nods. Suddenly, or not suddenly if I'm honest with myself, I wish the date were with him. I wish we could have another night like the one we spent in the gatehouse. Talking and eating and laughing.

We're silent for a moment, then Noah nods and says, "I'll get out of your way. Have fun."

Fun.

I feel my shoulders slump, so I push them up and nod. "Okay. Thank you."

And that is all there is to say about that.

30

PIERRE ISN'T ALONE. HE DIDN'T DO IT ON PURPOSE, BUT somehow, on the way from his house to the chateau, Camille found her way onto his motorcycle.

He gives me a sheepish smile while Camille circles the grassy knoll on the lakeside edge of property. The sloping cliff is a tumbling drop. As she leans forward to look over the edge, the wind whips her hair and she laughs delightedly.

Today she's in cropped navy pants and a white boatneck tee. She has a yellow scarf threaded through her hair and even though she didn't bring any apples, the redness of her cheeks reminds me of the plump, red fruit.

"Dinner parties are always better with friends," Pierre says apologetically.

I can't help but smile at him because he looks so uncomfortable. His hair is messy from the motorcycle helmet and his blue-green eyes are embarrassed.

"They are. We'll have fun," I reassure him. Hopefully we'll have enough food for three.

Pierre makes a noise and I don't know whether he's agreeing or disagreeing. But then he turns all that charm on and says, "You look beautiful. I hope later we can—"

"Thank you for inviting me." Camille pushes next to Pierre and elbows him in the side, cutting him off. "I brought apple tart."

"Oh," I say in surprise, because, well, I didn't invite her, but...apple tart. "No. Thank you."

She waves my thanks away and then casts her gaze over the chateau walls. The shadows from the turrets fall over the green grass, and the late afternoon air smells of wind over water, and sun warming stone.

"Is Noah here?" she asks. Her considering gaze drifts to the arched entrance.

Ah.

Aha.

That's why she came.

I should've known.

"Camille has told her father, her mother, her brothers, her cousins, all the orchard employees—"

"Not all," she says, holding up a finger.

"That she is friends with the famous Noah Wright."

"Hmmm." I give a stiff smile. Is she allowed to claim that? Can she really say that? Did he tell her they were friends?

"Is he here?" she asks again.

Pierre gives me a hopeful look. I imagine if I tell Camille where Noah is, then she'll leave us alone. And then Pierre and I can have a romantic dinner in the garden. Which is what this was all about.

I nod and point to the entrance. "He's inside. But he might be busy, he just..."

Camille doesn't wait to hear more, she's already taken

off. Once she's disappeared through the entrance, Pierre takes a step closer and smiles.

The aloneness of standing on a cliffside, with a chateau above us, a lake below us, and the soft country sounds, fills me with the expectation of a soft-focus moment.

Pierre leans close, his eyes warm.

"Bonjour, Meredith," he says in a warm voice.

My chest tightens. I take a step back, flustered, and smooth my hands over my dress.

"Bonjour," I say quickly.

Then to cover the confusing and conflicting emotions wrestling inside me, I nod toward the chateau. "Dinner's ready. We can eat outside if you want to help me carry it?"

Pierre walks next to me through the dim great hall. Cupid leers down at us as Pierre regales me with how his week has been full of tourists looking for nudes not landscapes, and paintings of bare breasts not beautiful chateaus.

"I understand," he says as we walk into the kitchen, "I appreciate feminine beauty as much as the next person. But I sell landscape art, not portraits. It has been a week of nude fanatics."

I nod. I know a lot about nude art, that being Jupiter's specialty. I know a lot less about landscapes. Maybe Pierre would have something in common with Noah. I wonder if he knows anything about the painting that I saw in Noah's book.

"I saw a painting earlier, it was called *Pren* something...in English it means, Escape or The Flight. Do you know it?"

Pierre frowns and considers my question, "Je ne sais pas."

I frown at him and he amends his statement. "Can you describe it?"

I stop at the kitchen counter and consider what I remember of the painting and try to evoke the feeling it gave me. "It was of a woman. She had long black hair and wore a long white dress."

He nods and gestures for me to continue, an interested smile on his lips. "Sounds intriguing."

"She was standing on top of a tower, it almost looked like the turret here." I look at Pierre to see if any of this rings a bell.

His smile slips and a frown line forms between his eyebrows.

"Here?"

I nod. "Yes. And it looked like she was about to leap. Or not. I don't know." I shrug, then look at Pierre again. "Do you know it?"

His eyes move around the kitchen, landing on the plate of eggs, the bruschetta, the bucket of ice-cold water from the tap, chilling the white wine.

I think maybe he does.

Something about the tilt of his chin and the thoughtful, faraway look in his eyes, as if he's remembering the image of the woman on the tower, makes me think that he's seen it before.

"I think...hmmm...I think you are describing a Thomas Arnout painting. Are you interested in his work?"

I shake my head quickly. "No."

Pierre tilts his head and smiles at me then gestures around the kitchen. "You prepared a feast. Thank you."

"It was nothing." I hide a smile at the thought of how preparing this meal was the opposite of nothing.

Pierre steps forward again. "Before we are joined again by Camille, I thought perhaps you would like to share an appetizer?"

Okay.

So appetizer is definitely code for kiss.

And Pierre has such an earnest expression on his face that I can't help but shove aside the conflicting emotions and say, "Yes please."

He takes my hand in his and squeezes. The light from the cookstove fire plays over us and the smells from Noah's cooking still hang in the air. I touch my tongue to the corner of my lips and Pierre smiles and leans forward.

My heart thuds as he does because I'm about to be kissed. I'm about to be kissed by a gorgeous man in a French chateau while wearing a frilly dress. I'm waiting for the cellos and the violins to start playing.

Pierre's lips are an inch from mine, I can feel his breath as he lets out a shuddering exhale. I close my eyes. This is going to be good. No. It's going to be perfect.

"Ack!" Pierre shouts and yanks back, tugging his hand out of mine. "Gah! What is that?"

My eyes fly open. Pierre is gyrating. That's all I can describe it as. His legs are kicking, his arms are swiping and he looks almost like he's dancing the jitterbug.

"What?"

"Agh!" He shouts again.

And then I see it.

Louis.

He's on Pierre's pant leg, his claws clamped onto the fabric. Louis's snapping at him like a vicious despot defending his territory.

"Ack!" Pierre lets out a bellow. Louis's claws snap.

Then Pierre flings his leg, kicks as hard as he can, and dislodges Louis.

Unfortunately, the dislodging means that he kicks Louis like a soccer ball. I don't duck fast enough. In fact, I don't duck at all. Louis soars through the air, his legs wriggling, his antennae waving, and his mouth gaping. His eyes glom onto me and I know we're thinking the same thing.

You.

Then Louis smacks into my chest with a forceful crack.

His legs wriggle over my breasts and his claws grasp the frilly fabric of my neckline. He clings to me with all his furious might. I can't help it, I shriek. I've never felt anything so repulsive in my life as lobster legs molesting my breasts. His twitching antennae tickle my chest and he makes a shuddering, clicking sound as his thick, hard claws grasp onto to my dress.

He won't let go.

The lobster terror won't get off.

I smack at him. I shake like a petitioner at a prayer meeting and let out a muffled, disgusted shriek.

Then, there's the sound of loud footsteps sprinting down the hall, and Camille rushes into the kitchen, Noah right behind her.

She shouts something. Then she reaches for the bucket of ice cold water, yanks out the wine bottle, and dumps the entire five gallons of water over my head.

The icy water hits me like a slap. Louis, the horrid crustacean, must get as big of a shock as me, because when the water hits, he seizes and then falls to the stone floor. I blink and drag in a breath. Then I shake the freezing water off and wipe my eyes.

I stare, stunned, at Camille.

She holds the bucket in her hand. There's a look of triumph on her face. "The fire is out!"

At that, Louis picks himself up and scurries across the stone floor, back into the dark wall crack and his family of rats.

I shiver and wrap my arms around myself, covering my breasts in my now see-through dress. Gooseflesh rises over me and I shiver again. My hair drips and there's a pool of water collecting around me.

Noah turns from the crack in the wall, a laughing spark in his eyes as he takes me in.

Pierre stares at me in shock.

"There was no fire," I tell Camille, although I get the feeling she knew that.

"No?"

I shake my head. "No."

"You should not yell if there is no fire."

I nod. "Okay."

Pierre shakes his head, moving from shocked to befuddled. "Was that a..."

"Cockroach," I say, "The darn thing won't die."

Noah covers a snort with a cough.

"This is an odd place," Camille says, looking around the kitchen suspiciously.

Yup.

I run upstairs to change. Again.

Luckily, this time around, the meal wasn't ruined.

31

It's hard to stay angry with Camille when the grass is soft, the food is delicious, and the setting sun is sending streaks of warmth over my skin.

After I came downstairs in my third dress of the day, a long floral print peasant dress, we all decided to have a picnic near the cucumber garden.

I lean back against the warm stone wall of the chateau. It holds the day's sun, and I soak in its warmth. The wall is solid and reassuring and the grass tickles my legs. There's a line of ants crawling over the grass, aiming, I'm sure, for the platter of bruschetta, cheese, and omelet.

I'm sprawled on the grass, my face turned toward the sun. I'm considering whether or not I have room for another bit of crusty, savory bread, or if I should save room for Camille's apple tart. Pierre lays on his side, his elbow crooked and his chin resting on his hand. The sun shines on his hair and burnishes him copper and bronze, so that he almost looks like a painting in a gallery. I think

it would be called *Gentleman Picnicking with his Lady.*
Either that or *Aborted Kiss.*

He was smart enough to bring three bottles of wine,
all young, tasting of freshly fallen snow and ripe cherries.

I've kept my attention on Pierre and purposely not on
Noah. I've angled my body toward Pierre, addressed all
my questions to him, and engaged him in small talk and
laughter.

Tell me about your gallery—Annecy, yes—Raclette,
of course—apples, no pears, no apples—no siblings—
simply delicious—art, family business, yes—have more
wine—love chateaus—bruschetta—

And that is how it went, back and forth, round and
round. All the while Pierre and I spoke, drank cherry-
flavored wine, and ate bruschetta, ripe tomato dripping
from my fingers, I kept my face turned away from Camille
and Noah. They were on the other side of the picnic
platter, and Camille had been regaling Noah with stories
about growing up on an orchard for the past half hour.

I can't say for certain, I don't know what he's thinking,
but by his short, quiet answers given once every five or
ten minutes, I'd say that Noah's in need of a rescue. Either
that, or he's so enthralled with Camille he's forgotten how
to speak. I brush my hair and casually turn my head to
peek at him. When I do, I realize that he has taken that
exact moment to look over at me.

Camille is describing how her family once spent three
hours frantically looking for her when she was three after
she'd climbed up into an apple tree, eaten half a dozen
apples, and then fallen asleep. She'd been napping while
they'd been frantic.

Pierre is describing a new artist he's found, one who
paints with rustic realism.

They're both speaking, talking like two bubbling rivers converging, and as they do, Noah and I take a moment to just...look.

Our eyes connect.

I almost feel like we're both floating down those rivers, and we're in separate boats, traveling in opposite directions, and we only have a moment to catch gazes, because soon, inevitably, we'll flow apart.

And even though he doesn't smile, his lips don't pull up, I know that he's telling me something. The edges of his eyes crinkle at the corners, and they light with a spark like he's sharing a joke. He still looks tired, he has those bags under his eyes, and the wear and tear of whatever happened on his trip this past week, but now he also looks happy. And I think, maybe, it's because he's sharing himself with me.

"Do you agree?" Camille asks.

Noah yanks his gaze from mine and the moment is broken. He turns to Camille, gives a short nod, murmurs yes, and then she's off again and he's completely engrossed in the way she waves her hands, moves her lips, and bounces with energetic storytelling fervor.

He doesn't look back at me.

So.

I was mistaken.

There definitely wasn't a moment. There wasn't a shared anything.

But then, right before I'm about to turn back to Pierre and ask him how he found this new rural rustic realist artist, Noah reaches for another piece of bruschetta, and when he does, he glances at me quickly, and winks.

Before I can react he turns back to Camille. But

there's no denying it, there's no mistaking it. Noah winked at me.

My heart catapults into my throat and bounces around, skipping joyfully. And I scold it, thinking, that was a *friend* wink. Stop it. Stop jumping around.

But it doesn't. Not for a good thirty seconds. So I grab my glass of wine and take a long, calming swallow.

"I am desolate," Pierre says, shifting closer to me.

"What? Why?"

"Because," he gives me a self-aware smile, "despite all my attempts, I don't think we are meant to be."

Okay.

Wow.

I bite my lip then move closer and say quietly, "That obvious?"

He makes a small noise and gives a shrug. "We can be friends."

"I thought we were already friends?"

"True."

He leans so close that our noses almost touch. I can see the pinkening of his nose from the sun, and the little flecks of hazel in his eyes. I can smell his aftershave and the hint of cherry from the wine, and I can feel his laughing self-awareness. "There will be no kiss," he says in mock desolation, his lips close to mine.

I smile and brush back my hair, blowing free in the breeze. The light is right. It's soft, golden, the sun's rays just edging against the horizon. The atmosphere is right. There's a fairy-tale castle with turrets, a picnic in the grass, mountains and lakes and the vibrant, swirling colors of the Alps. And there's even music, Camille has her phone out and is playing Noah a song. And me, I'm ready to be kissed. I'm just not ready to be kissed by Pierre.

"No kiss," I agree happily.

And I think my happy tone must surprise him because he lets out a surprised laugh and moves closer so that our noses are touching.

At that Camille claps her hands, and I jump back at the sharp cracking sound.

"On a trop dévié du sujet. Revenons à nos moutons," she says in rapid-fire French, and then I think she sees my blank expression because she holds out her hands and says, "The chateau! You must tell me, how is it living in a haunted chateau?"

The sun slips beneath the mountain and a shadow falls over us. I involuntarily shiver at the mention of hauntings and the ominously timed shadow. I frown at Camille and rub my hands over my goosebumped arms.

"What do you mean haunted?"

Noah sits straighter and tilts his head. "Haunted?"

Ha.

He probably thinks this gives credence to his gothic novel nonsense. I can see his mind whirring. I'm sure that tonight he's going to mention it while we're lying together in bed. I'll never get to sleep.

Pierre shakes his head and gives Camille a warning scowl, which to be honest, only makes me more concerned.

Then Pierre sighs and says reassuringly to me, "There is no ghost. She doesn't exist."

Wait.

Ghost?

She?

Camille said haunted, she didn't say anything about a ghost, or a ghost who is a female.

Camille bounces up and down and then points up at the only flat-topped tower. "Yes there is. She's there!"

I look up quickly, expecting to see a specter leering down at us, her ghostly figure misty and eerily transparent. I even expect her to be tragically young with a mournful expression and some sort of Marie Antoinette dress. Come to think of it, maybe she's even holding her own guillotined head.

I shiver, but no, the tower is the same as it always is. Tall, rectangular stones set apart like gapped teeth, a flat top for pacing, or viewing the mountains. The beige stone is dull now that the sun has set, and the long shadows of the trees play over the surface. But no, there's no ghost.

"There is no ghost," Pierre says firmly. He shakes his head and his hair falls over his forehead. Then he reaches forward and takes the pastry box with the apple tarts. "Dessert, anyone?"

Camille waves his question away and leans forward, her thigh brushing against Noah's. "Have you seen her?"

Noah lifts an eyebrow. "No."

Not to be deterred, Camille turns to me. "And you?"

She looks so hopeful, so caught up in the fact that we're staying in a haunted chateau that I almost hate to disappoint her. But I hate the thought of a haunted chateau even more, so I shrug.

"Sorry. No."

She deflates, her excited expression crumpling. "I thought you would see her. The tragic history of the chateau is legendary. Because it is haunted, no one has lived here for decades."

I glance back at the walls of the chateau, expecting it to seem more sinister, but it's still the same as it was five minutes ago. Well, darker, because the sun is setting, but the same. Except, now that the sun has set, I see the bats Noah warned me about. They're diving out of a boarded up window in the highest turret. Their black, winged shapes, with swiftly beating wings, are performing acrobatics in the sky above us, and their high, sharp squeaks pierce the night air.

I follow the looping circle of their flight, at least five or six of them above us. Then I glance back at Noah and lift an eyebrow in acknowledgement of the bats.

He smiles.

"We don't have to dwell on this," Pierre says, opening the dessert box. "No one wants to hear the story."

But the more Pierre tries to steer the topic away from the ghost, the more curious I become.

It's not as if the chateau is actually haunted. I'm not living in a gothic novel. I'm living in an American-goes-to-France-to-find-magic soft-focus film.

I turn to Camille and give her an encouraging smile. "I want to hear the story."

When she hears this she claps. "Yes! Yes you do."

I glance at Noah to see if he's interested, but instead of catching my eye, he's frowning up at the turret. There's a crease between his eyebrows, as if he's still looking for the ghost.

Pierre hands me a plate with a slice of tart. He shakes his head ruefully as Camille situates herself in the grass. She settles in as if she's a storyteller and we're all gathered around her to hear her wondrous tale.

"It happened thirty years ago," she begins.

"That recent?" I sit up straight. I'm surprised. I

thought we were talking about a ghost from the 1700s, an old, fading, Marie Antionette type ghost.

"Twenty-nine years," Pierre grumbles, and Camille waves her hand at him, shooting him a censorious look.

Noah finally takes his gaze from the turret and turns back to Camille, but he seems distracted, the frown line is still between his brows.

"Do you know who lived here thirty years ago?" Camille asks me.

I shake my head. "I don't know anything."

"Thomas Arnout," Camille says, as if she's pulling a rabbit out of a hat.

I stare at her blankly. The name sounds familiar but... "Okay?"

I look to Noah, maybe he knows the name, but he's cutting himself a piece of the tart and not paying any attention.

"One of France's most prominent artists. Savoy's favorite landscape painter. Don't you know him?"

Oh. Ohhhh. Thomas Arnout.

He's the artist who painted the picture of the woman on the tower. All of sudden, I'm gripped by a chill. As if someone reached out and trailed cold fingers down my spine. I look up at the tower Camille pointed at again. And yes, sure enough, there's no mistaking it. That's the tower from the painting. I can picture the woman there, standing at the edge of the wall, her dress flying out behind her. Her fingers grip the stone, her body is poised between stillness and flight, her face the epitome of ecstatic yearning.

"Do you know him, Noah?" Camille asks, leaning closer to him.

He stiffens. I think he doesn't like her sitting so close,

because he takes his plate of apple tart and leans back, farther away from her.

"Perhaps. I may have heard of him." Noah shrugs casually and takes a bite of the tart.

Pierre makes a disbelieving noise. "Perhaps? Not perhaps. You came to my Arnout exhibit last year. You mentioned him the first day I came to visit Meredith. I remember the opening of the exhibit. You asked many specific questions. You were very"—Pierre frowns, then says—"persistent."

Noah stills and puts down his fork. He scratches his chin in thought, then shrugs casually. "I suppose. I research a lot of artists."

I look between Pierre and Noah. There's an undercurrent here. One that's barely noticeable and that I can't quite grasp, but I know that neither of them is being completely forthcoming. It's as if their words are telling one story, but the unspoken words are telling something else.

But what?

I don't know.

"What does he paint?" I ask Camille, trying to break the tension twining around us, like the shadows fingering across the grass.

"Beautiful chateaus. Gorgeous landscapes," Camille says, her face lightening with enthusiasm. "My favorite painting is of this chateau."

She gestures at the stone wall beside us. "It is far away, there are the mountains, the lake, and far in the distance, the chateau."

She purses her lips together and looks up at the lavender tinted sky, "Whenever I see it, I can taste crisp apples, and I smell mist rolling down the mountain, and I feel homesick, even if I'm already home."

"That's..." Sad? Lovely?

"But that is not his most famous painting."

"It's not?"

She shakes her head no. "His most famous is of the ghost."

The chill is back, trailing down my spine. Goosebumps pop up on my arms and I shiver.

"Arnout was born in Annecy. His parents died in a house fire and he was raised in an orphanage."

"This is all common knowledge," Pierre says, taking a swallow of his wine.

Camille ignores him, engrossed in her tale, "When he turned fifteen, he went to Paris and studied the great artists. He lived on the streets and sold his art to tourists. After years of this, he was noticed by the great collector Jacques Thierry."

I lift my eyebrows at Pierre and he nods, "My father."

"After that, Arnout gained popularity. He traveled the world and painted landscapes in his unique style."

"It is brushstrokes of raw emotion," Pierre confirms. "His paintings are not images, but emotions."

"He painted in many countries. But his most loved paintings are of his chateau period, and most importantly, his paintings in Annecy."

"Why?" I ask.

I look to Noah to see if he knows. After all, he just returned from a week traveling France, seeking out a French painter who specialized in chateaus.

I narrow my eyes on him.

Wait a second.

Noah isn't looking at me. He's busy eating his tart,

dragging his fork over his plate, seemingly engrossed in the thin apple slices and the crumbling pastry crust, licking the sugar from his lips. I'm not fooled. Even though he appears to be consumed by his dessert, all of his attention is on what Camille is saying.

"Because in Annecy, he painted love," Camille says triumphantly. She waves her hand. "Love. He loved Annecy. And he loved the woman in his paintings. She was the only woman he ever painted. The only woman he ever loved."

"The ghost?" I ask, just to be sure.

Camille gives a satisfied nod.

"She isn't a ghost," Pierre says.

The sky is dark now, the lavender has faded to indigo, and a chill is setting into the stones. The grass has lost its sun warmth, and now it itches my legs with cold, tickling spikes. I reach forward and grab my tart, certain that a bit of sweetness will help chase away the dark.

"She is," Camille says. "Thirty years ago, Arnout brought a woman with him to Annecy."

"Okay?"

Camille shrugs, then continues, "They stayed for months in this chateau. People still remember the music coming from the tower. They would dance. Drink wine. He would paint. Dozens of paintings. He was possessed by her."

"This is conjecture." Pierre shrugs, discarding Camille's tale.

"This is legend," she contradicts.

I cut into the tart with the side of my fork, its crust crumbling beneath the pressure. I scoop up the glistening apples and bring them to my mouth. The cinnamon, the glossy sugar, the tart, crisp apple bite at my tongue, and my eyes widen as I sink my teeth into the flaky buttery crust cradling the apples.

That's good.

That's really good.

I glance at Noah. Maybe he wasn't pretending to be engrossed in the tart as a way to avoid talking about Arnout. Because, wow. I'll be distracted by this tart for the next hundred years. I eye the pastry box and calculate if I can have another. Only when I'm satisfied that I can do I take another forkful.

When I let out a small moan, I realize that everyone has gone quiet, and both Pierre and Camille are watching me with identical expectant expressions.

"Hmmm?"

"There was a fire," Camille says, as if she's repeating herself.

I swallow. "At the chateau?"

She nods. "Arnout said it started when a gas lamp overturned."

Of course. If the chateau doesn't have electricity now, it didn't have it thirty years ago.

"They were in the tower." She points at the same tower, the tall, flat spire black against the indigo sky. "The stairs were blocked. The fire consumed the tower. The only way out was to jump."

"No," I say, thinking of the painting's title. *The Flight. The Escape.*

I stare at the tower. It's at least a thirty foot drop to the ground. They jumped? I glance at Noah. Does he know this story? He must if it's common knowledge, but he's staring at Camille with the same tense watchfulness that I'm feeling, so maybe he doesn't know the ending.

"Yes." She nods. "The woman—"

"What was her name?" I ask. It seems horrible to keep calling her *the woman*.

Camille shrugs and brushes at her skirt. "No one knows."

"That is true," Pierre says, frowning at Camille.

"As the fire grew, Arnout knew they could die in the tower, or they could jump. The woman was scared, so he told her to look at him, watch him and they would hold hands and jump together."

I rub at my arms, the sweet apple cinnamon taste turning hot like fire and then cold like ashes. This can't end well.

"All the paintings were destroyed in the fire, sadly," Pierre says with a wistful sigh, and I give him a stunned look. He's thinking about paintings? When two people's lives hang in the balance?

Even Noah, who hasn't given any indication that he cares what happens one way or another, sends Pierre a disbelieving look.

He shrugs. "My father saw them. He claimed there were forty-eight paintings destroyed in the fire."

Camille scowls at Pierre. "You are shriveled."

And even though he doesn't say anything, I remember Pierre snapping, *it was one time*.

"They jumped." Camille looks over her shoulder at the tower, and I picture Arnout and his lady. The golden light in the painting that I thought was the sun must have been the glow of the fire.

There's silence as we all trace the thirty-foot drop from the tower to the grassy knoll below. In the chill, with the bats squeaking above, the wind working through the trees, and the darkness of night encroaching, I swear I can hear the crackling of flames and acrid smell of smoke burning canvas.

"Then what?" I ask, certain she'll tell me that the lady died and that is why the chateau is haunted.

Camille holds out her hands before her, palms up. "Arnout broke his spine. He could not walk for years. He lost his right arm. He could not paint for longer."

I look to the ground at the base of the tower, and wonder, if I walk over there and look closely, will I be able to see the remnant of love and dreams still broken in the grass?

"And the woman?" I ask.

Camille shakes her head. "She disappeared. No one ever saw her again."

"But wasn't she injured?"

"No one saw her," Camille repeats. "Arnout said they jumped together. But no one ever saw her."

"Ever?"

"Never," Camille says. "Except as a ghost. Some people say they see flames or hear music drifting across the lake. And sometimes there is a glow in the shape of a woman, standing on the tower."

I lean toward Camille, drawn in.

"These sightings only happen after three bottles of wine," Pierre says, shaking his head.

But I want to know. "Never? No one ever saw her again? Not even Arnout?"

"No." Camille shakes her head. "And seven years ago, Arnout disappeared as well. No one knows where he is. He painted one final painting. Then he wrote a letter donating his remaining work to Thierry Gallery, and then"—she waves her hands—"poof."

"Poof?"

"Gone."

Pierre sighs, and it's loud enough that I'm pulled back from my imaginings.

I look to Noah. He's staring at the tower again. His face is so covered in shadow that I can't make out his expression, but his shoulders are slumped and he lets out a long, lonely-sounding breath. No wonder he asked Pierre about Arnout. If anyone would know, it would be Pierre.

"So where is he?" I ask Pierre.

Pierre looks back to me—he was studying Noah, frowning at his profile. "Pardon?"

"If Arnout donated his paintings to you, you must know where he is? And the woman?"

His frown deepens and he shakes his head. "No. Sorry. I know nothing."

At that, Noah turns back from the tower and levels a cold look at Pierre. And there's so much emotion in that look that Pierre can't help but notice it. He turns back to Noah and for a moment it's as if they are locked in a struggle, and neither of them is willing to give in.

Camille glances between Noah and Pierre and then lets out a small gasp. "Pierre, you know where Arnout is?"

Pierre scoffs and looks away from Noah, breaking their impasse. He flicks at the crumbs on his pants. "No."

Noah turns away and his face is buried in shadows again.

"But you could solve the mystery," Camille persists. "There are conspiracies," she tells me in an aside. "Some say Thierry Gallery blackmailed Arnout into giving all of his work to them." She waves this away. "Not true. That is obvious."

I watch Noah, the stiff line of his shoulders, the hard

tilt of his jaw. Maybe it isn't so obvious to everyone. Does he believe Pierre blackmailed Arnout? Is his documentary actually an exposé?

"No. Not true," Pierre agrees.

"Some people claim Arnout died seven years ago. Others say he went into hiding because of criminal activity or threats or..."—she shrugs—"too much speculation. Some say he is with his lady, the ghost. But most people agree..."

She stops and looks at me to make sure I'm paying attention. I lean forward. "Agree what?"

"That there are more paintings. Hidden paintings."

I frown, especially because at that, Noah's hands clench into tight fists.

"Why?"

"Because of the postscript in the letter," Pierre says, shrugging.

"What did it say?"

Camille rubs her hands together, and even in the dark I can see the spark in her eyes. "It said, *Mon ange, come find me where we escaped. I will give you the paintings of my heart. Hurry. I am flying away.*"

"What does that mean?" I frown and look between Pierre and Camille.

"*Mon ange* is his angel," she says meaningfully. "He's speaking to the ghost. Don't you think?"

I'm not sure what I think. I turn to Pierre. "Why did he leave everything to you?"

Pierre shrugs. "He felt indebted to my father."

Noah stiffens and at that, Pierre stands abruptly. "Shall we? It's cold."

He holds out his hand for me, and after a small hesitation, I reach up, grasp his warm hand, and stand.

After a moment of surprised silence, Noah stands as well and helps Camille to her feet.

"Is our fun finished then? Have I ruined it with stories of ghosts?" Camille asks.

"No. Of course not. Thank you for the tart," I tell her.

She smiles and nods. "But of course! A tart for a tart."

I frown at her, and Noah does a double take.

"What?"

Camille frowns. "Is that not what you say? Something tasty for a nice woman?"

I honestly can't tell whether or not Camille knows what she's saying. Did she purposely call me a tart?

Or... "I think you mean a sweet for my sweet."

She shakes her head. "No. A tart. I'm certain."

I narrow my eyes. Now I'm sure that she tossed the ice-cold water over me on purpose. She's a wily one, this Camille. She looks innocent, but, nope.

And without a doubt, she's angling for Noah.

At that thought she turns to him and says sweetly, "Will you walk with me to look over the lake? It is beautiful at night."

She moves to take his arm, but he quickly shakes his head. "No. Thank you. I have..." He points vaguely toward the chateau. "Work."

And before she can respond, he tips his head to us, says a quiet goodbye and hurries away. I stare after him, frowning. That was really not anywhere near as smooth as he usually is.

We collect the dishes, the food, swat at the bugs becoming more bold in the dark, and then take everything to the kitchen, stumbling through the darkened chateau.

Then, with Camille hovering nearby, I wish Pierre goodnight and wave them off.

With the rumble of Pierre's motorcycle still echoing down the drive, my phone buzzes. When I look down at the screen a text from Angela flashes.

How is the battle?

I give a wry smile.

Done, it was a quickie, I text.

You had sex?!

Ugh. I didn't realize she'd take it that way, although I should have.

No. Nothing happened.

Kiss?

No.

What happened?

Nothing. Nothing happened. Except Pierre and I agreed we weren't meant to be. And me, myself, and I agreed that Noah is...wonderful.

Pretty freaking wonderful.

Except, after dinner and Camille's story, I'm starting to think that Noah's joke about gothic romances might not be a joke.

What happened here?

What happened with the woman?

And why does Noah care so much?

Because clearly, he does.

I decide to ask Angela, even though I promised myself I wouldn't.

Can you ask Leo what he said about Noah's past?

Why?

I scowl at my phone and then bat at a moth that's been attracted to the glow of the screen.

Just ask him. Please.

She doesn't respond, so either she's asking him, she's puking, or she got distracted and can't be bothered. Either way, I shove my phone in my pocket and head inside to get ready for bed, only to remember that tonight, Noah and I are sleeping together.

32

EXCEPT, WE DON'T.

Noah hasn't come back from wherever he went after the picnic.

I lay awake for a long while, waiting for the text from Angela that never comes, then I toss and turn, watching the moon make its way across the window, until finally it's gone, on to another part of the night sky.

I drift off for a few minutes, catching moon glow dreams that hold snatches of tragic ghosts, psychotic lobsters, and a brooding gothic man locked in a chateau tower. But at a quarter to two, after hours of tossing and turning, I kick at the sheets that have wrapped themselves tightly around my legs, put my feet to the cold stone, and grab the battery-powered lantern.

You'd think with tales of fire, and ghosts, and hauntings I'd be scared to walk around a seventeenth-century chateau, alone, in my nightgown with only a lantern, but I'm not.

Well, I'll amend that. I'm not afraid of ghosts. I am

afraid of cat-sized cockroaches and I'm wary of vengeful lobsters pinching my bare toes. Because of that I hold the lantern out and let the weak yellow light fall in a pool in front of me as I hurry through the hall. My footsteps echo in a scritch-scritch pattern as I pace the length of the hall and down the round stairs of the turret.

Usually this late at night I'm asleep, tucked up under my soft cotton sheets and deep in dreamland, so until now, I've never known how the chateau transforms at night.

The air is thicker, more slumberous and heavy, and I swear, the stone, which usually smells like plaster and dust and earth, now smells like a night garden, laden with pregnant expectancy. During the day, the chateau is filled with the noises of the birds outside, cars passing, wind circling, but now, with all of that silent, it's easy to hear the chateau. The quiet whoosh of feet over stone, the sighing of wings against wooden rafters, the groaning of old pipes, the scrape of my palm against smooth plaster, and finally, when I reach the front door, the rasp of the wooden door brushing over the uneven stone floor.

The moon is there. It's hanging over the gatehouse, like a white grape, not a drinking grape, but an eating grape, round and perfect and ready to be plucked. The breeze tugs at my nightgown and when I rush across the dewy grass, I kick up winged bugs and a grassy, sleepy scent.

With the dark and the quiet, I know exactly where Noah is. The gatehouse window glows, a warm parchment yellow, spilling light over the yard, and there silhouetted in the window, is Noah, bent over his books.

I hurry up the steps and when I thrust open the door, Noah turns at the noise.

You'd think I would anticipate his surprise. I mean, it's only logical that if you're alone in a room at two in the morning, you aren't expecting company. So it's funny that I'm surprised at the stunned look on his face.

He stands, pushes aside his chair and shakes his head, taking me in.

It's then I realize he might not be shocked because I'm in the gatehouse, but because I'm wearing a short white cotton nightgown that is possibly (probably) see-through, my hair is messy and falling down my back, I'm holding a lantern out in front of me, and I look like I've *seen* a ghost or I *am* the ghost.

And why am I here?

There's no reason expect I wanted Noah to come to bed with me.

I flush and drop the lantern to my side. "I was looking for you."

Noah shoves back his chair and takes a step toward me, avoiding looking at my somewhat (completely) see-through nightgown.

He frowns and studies my expression. "Is something wrong?"

Yes, I want to say. *You haven't come to bed, and we joked about sleeping together. I ruined your mattress. We made dinner together and laughed about the mattress. Why haven't you come to bed?*

But obviously I don't say any of that.

Instead, I set down the lantern and walk to his work table.

"I couldn't sleep," I say casually.

"Ah."

He doesn't say anything more, just follows me then watches as I look over his books and documents. I brush my fingers over the old newspapers and journals. There's the large art book, still opened to the same painting, and now that I know what to look for I see that many of the articles are about Arnout.

I rest my finger on a painting of a chateau that I've never seen before, tracing the rounded, grassy hills in the foreground.

"You're looking for him, aren't you?"

Noah doesn't answer, so I take my eyes from the painting and look at him. He's staring at my shoulders, at the thin straps holding my gown up, and my hair falling over my bare skin. My shoulders grow hot under his gaze and a pink flush works itself over my chest, tingling in memory of how it felt when he touched me.

I take a step toward him, luxuriating in the warmth rushing through my veins and the hazy fullness in my blood. It's like I've drunk all those glasses of champagne again and I'm floating. When I stop a foot away and look up at him, I can't deny it anymore. I didn't come out here to ask him why he isn't coming to bed, I came out here to kiss.

Noah's eyes glow like a hot summer blue sky, heating everything they touch. And even though he's tired, and worn, and by the way his hair is mussed, he's frustrated, all of that falls away when he sees the expression on my face.

"Did you need something?" he asks, and then his eyes widen and he flinches, as if he didn't realize what he said could be taken two ways.

The flinch was subtle, involuntary. Which is why, at that flinch, a metaphorical bucket of ice-cold water, just like the one Camille threw on me, douses all that bubbly, floaty, kiss-me glow.

I turn back to the articles to hide my embarrassment. Then seeing the painting of *The Escape,* an idea comes to me. "Do you think, in the letter, Arnout meant for her to come here?"

Noah shakes his head, confused, "What?"

I gesture excitedly at the painting. "He said to meet him where they escaped. This painting is clearly of the tower here. It's called *The Escape.* Where else could he mean?"

Noah frowns at me. "The only problem is, he isn't here."

"Oh. Right." I hadn't thought of that.

"He hasn't been here since the fire." Noah shrugs and joins me staring down at the painting.

"You already thought of that, didn't you?"

"Sure."

"So you are looking for him," I say.

I take in his notes and the laptop open to a copy of a handwritten letter. I'm guessing that must be the letter Arnout left with Pierre.

He nods but doesn't say anything more.

We stand in silence, staring at the table for a good thirty seconds.

The heat coming off him reaches out and curls around me. I sway closer, chilled from the stones on my feet and the cool air of the room. If I can get close enough to him, I think I'll feel deliciously warm.

Finally, I ask, "Why?"

"Why what?"

"Why look for him? Why do you care?"

Noah shakes his head, as if he's protesting the fact that he cares. When he does, I catch the scent of toasted baguettes, fresh thyme and cherry-flavored wine, reminding me that no matter how much he claims otherwise, Noah does care. He helped me make dinner, didn't he? He helped me clean. He rescued me after the chocolate fiasco.

He cares.

"I don't," he says, shaking his head. The lantern plays over his face, casting him half in shadow, and I know for a fact that he's lying.

"You do."

He gives me a flat look, then when I refuse to look away, he scowls and then tiredly rubs at his eyes.

"You care," I tell him. "I saw the way you looked at Pierre."

At that he raises his eyebrow in surprise and I nod at him. "Exactly. You were furious. You don't like him. You think he's hiding something."

"He is hiding something."

"Gotcha." I give a quicksilver smile and Noah scowls.

"Fine. I care." He drags his hand down his face and lets out a tired sigh.

I sidestep closer to him, barely press against his side, just a breath of contact, and ask, "Why?"

Noah makes a small noise in his throat, then leans forward and pushes the papers around the table, looking for something. Finally he uncovers a newspaper clipping. He holds it out to me and I take it, the paper is worn and thin and crinkles in my hand. It's an article in French and there's a painting printed in black and white.

"What is it?" I ask, staring down at the landscape.

"It's his last painting."

The image is only about one inch wide and two inches high. It's hard to make anything out, but there are the mountains and the rolling hills I've become familiar with. I can also make out a sliver of the lake, a smudge to denote the buildings of Annecy, and then, on the edge of the painting there's a stone chateau. In front of the chateau, a man sits alone. High above him, in the tower, is the shadowed face of a woman. Maybe there. Maybe not.

"Le Pont," I say, reading the caption.

"Le Pont," Noah agrees, saying a completely different word than I did.

"What does that mean?" I ask, rubbing my hands across the news ink.

Noah frowns down at the painting, and then he bites at his lower lip in concentration. I have the strongest urge to join him in that nibble.

"The bridge."

My shoulders slump. I thought it would be something more meaningful, some sort of hint, or clue, or revelation. Like Le Pont is the name of a chateau only ten kilometers away and that is where Arnout is!

But no.

"The bridge," I say flatly.

Noah smiles.

"So what's so special about it?" I ask, shaking my head.

"Besides being his last painting?"

I nod.

"Thierry Gallery sold it for two million euros."

I let out a low whistle, and Noah stifles a short laugh, giving me the side-eye.

"That is special," I agree.

"Thierry Gallery has made a lot of money off of Arnout's disappearance."

Okay. That's a serious accusation.

"You think Pierre disappeared Arnout?" I put finger quotes around *disappeared*.

Noah gives me a considering look, then lifts a shoulder. "I think Arnout asked to be found"—he points at the letter displayed on his laptop—"he wants to be found"—he points at the painting—"and he hasn't been found yet. Pierre Thierry is making sure of that."

Okay. This sounds crazy. This sounds like a mad conspiracy theory. Like those theories you read in the comments sections on the internet. Like chapstick actually causes your lips to be chapped. Or the particle accelerator caused two dimensions to collide and that's why some people believe the Monopoly man has a monocle. It's cuckoo.

But didn't Camille say that the region was rife with conspiracies about Arnout's disappearance?

"You think I'm crazy," Noah says, turning away from me.

"No," I begin, then I amend. "Maybe. Okay no. I just think, he asked the lady in the painting to find him. He didn't ask you."

I wince when Noah stiffens, because I guess that came out a little harsh. Who am I to judge? If he wants to research an artist and try to find him then that's his business. In fact, it actually is his business. He's making a documentary about it. At least, I think he is.

"Are you including Arnout in your documentary?" I ask, just to make sure.

He waves his hand at the table. "If I can find him."

Then he runs his hand over his face again, and I'm reminded about how tired he looked when he arrived.

"Were you looking for him this past week?"

He nods. Then, "No luck."

"I mean, maybe he doesn't want to be found. Maybe he only wants to be found by the woman. And there isn't anything sinister about it at all, it's nothing more than a man who got old...how old is he?"

"Eighty."

I nod. "Exactly. He's just an eighty-year-old man who retired and wants some peace and quiet with his lady. And Pierre, who is a nice guy—"

Noah lifts an eyebrow.

"He is. He's just protecting Arnout's privacy. Or he doesn't know anything, like he says."

I feel like I'm mediating an argument between Noah and Pierre, even though Pierre isn't here and Noah doesn't want to be mediated.

"Maybe you could explain to Pierre that you want to include Arnout in your film—"

"He's tight-lipped. He repeats the same thing. *I don't know where he is. I know nothing.*" Noah glares at the painting, frustration rolling off him in waves.

I tap my finger against the wood grain of the table and think. "You could just...forget about it."

Noah swings to me, a surprised look on his face. His thighs brush against mine, causing my whole body to tingle with awareness and my face to go hot.

"Is that a no?"

"He wants to be found."

There's a world of conviction behind Noah's words and again I wonder why.

"But maybe you don't have to be the one to find him," I offer hesitantly.

Standing so close to him, I can feel the tension in his arms and his shoulders. I can see the frustration in the clenching of his jaw. Then he looks at me, and something in him relaxes, and his eyes soften. His lips turn up in a self-deprecating smile.

"Didn't you know, Merry? That's the problem with the world. People always think that someone else will do it. And then someone never does."

Hmmm.

He has a point.

"But why you?"

He moves closer, and if I wanted to I could lean into him and soak up all his warmth. He looks down at me, a wry smile on his lips. "You want to know all my secrets? Tit for tat?"

I blink up at him, fuddled by the way his lips are curving. "What tit?"

He grins. "You told me about your childhood. But only, if I recall, because you didn't like me and we'd never see each other again after this chateau stay."

A slow cold trickle of mortification drips through me and I give an apologetic smile. "I'm sorry?"

He laughs, a happy, freeing sound. "Don't worry. I know where we stand."

"No you don't." I shake my finger at him, feeling flustered and self-conscious.

"Sure I do. You're in love with my best friend and in like with my"—he scrunches his eyebrows together —"worst...help me out here."

"Enemy?" I lift my eyebrows.

"Too harsh. Foe?" he says, then shakes his head, discarding that.

"Nemesis?" I ask.

"Antagonist?"

We grin at each other.

Then he says, "You're in love with my best friend and

in like with my worst foe. And I'm stuck in the past, chasing after something that doesn't exist."

I frown at him, but he continues.

"Which is why you can tell me things you'd never tell anyone else, and I can do the same."

Ah. I see.

Even though I'm getting over, or to be honest, am over Leo, and I know that I don't want Pierre, Noah is still in unrequited love with someone else. I came here to move on, but he didn't.

"Okay," I say, "tell me all your secrets."

He lifts a corner of his mouth and then says, "You look cold. Come here."

He holds open his arms, and since all I've wanted to do since I walked into the gatehouse is stand in his arms, I don't ask questions, I just thrust myself into his chest and bury myself in his warmth.

He lets out a surprised huff and then wraps his arms around me. I nuzzle my cheek into his chest, smell his soap through his merino wool sweater, and feel the steady rhythm of his heart against my face. I close my eyes.

"Okay, tell me."

He sighs, and his hands slowly move over the straps at the back of my nightgown. So slow, so unnoticeable that I could almost think he's not touching me at all, except for the fact that everywhere his fingers light, my skin burns from his touch.

"Just like you," he begins, "my dad wasn't around."

"You were raised by your mom," I say, remembering how the day we cleaned the chateau together he mentioned his mom would be ashamed of him if he didn't help.

He tugs me closer and I let my body relax into him. I rest against him, like he's a warm, lovely bed and he's telling me a nighttime story.

"It wasn't until I was four and went to preschool that I realized other kids had dads at home. So I asked my mom, where's my dad?"

His fingers pause, then after a moment he starts tracing up and down the strap again. With each stroke of his finger my skin grows warmer and warmer, and my muscles relax into him.

"She said, you don't have a dad. And she was so upset when I asked, that even at four I knew not to ask again. When I was eleven I looked at my birth certificate. There was no father listed. But after seven years I'd worked up enough courage to ask her again, where's my dad? You see, I'd built up all these fantasies about him. He was a royal and I was the secret heir to his throne. Don't laugh."

I'm not. I'm not laughing. I shake my head and wrap my arms around him, holding his sweater in my fists. I know better than most how many fantasies a kid can build up in their mind about their parents' love.

"Or I thought, maybe he's an astronaut and he's been on the International Space Station for years. Or he was a prisoner of war and he wanted to come home but couldn't. Or the best of them all, he was my fifth grade teacher, who I really liked and would've loved for my mom to marry."

"I'm sorry," I whisper into his chest, my lips right over his heart.

He's stiff, but when I say this he lets out a breath and his shoulders relax. "Well. You know how it is. After another few years of pestering my mom, she finally broke down and told me. My dad was a nobody. She didn't even know his name. He was just some nameless man that came through town one night and never returned. He didn't know I existed. If he did, he wouldn't care, and I needed to stop asking about him."

I pull in a sharp breath.

"How old were you?"

"Fifteen." He shrugs. "I'd already figured it out. Why else would she be so defensive? Me mentioning my dad was the only thing that ever upset her. But I'd spent my whole life building up this man. I imagined that he was out there wishing he were with me, just as much as I was wishing I was with him."

My breath freezes in my chest.

This.

"You were in unrequited love with your dad?"

I feel him look down at me and when I glance up there's a wry smile on his face. "Figured that out, did you?"

When I asked him how long he'd been in unrequited love, he'd answered, *too long.*

I'd made the same mistake that Camille made and Pierre corrected. There are many different types of love, Pierre had said, one of them being the love a child has for his parent.

"Did you ever find him?" I ask, although I suspect I know the answer.

"No," he says quietly. "Never."

I sigh and lean against him again. I breathe in his warm scent and run my hands over the muscles of his back. The gatehouse has fallen quiet. Even the light of the lamp is quiet, a low, flickering yellow, the battery starting to give way.

My toes are going numb from the chill in the stone, so

carefully I step forward and rest my toes on Noah's leather shoes. He lets out a huff and then shakes his head.

"Come here," he says.

Then he pulls me to the window. There's the stone sill, twelve inches wide and four feet long. The window has condensation collecting at the bottom of the glass. The wavy distortion from the old thick windowpanes displays a night full of swirling stars, wispy gray clouds, and trees that look as if they were finger painted into existence. He sets me on the sill and I perch on the edge. The cold stone penetrates my thin cotton nightgown.

Noah sits next to me. Then he reaches down, grasps my ankles and pulls my calves up onto the stone. He sets my bare feet in his lap. Then he chafes his hands together, warming them, then sets them on my legs, rubbing his hands up and down my calves and over my feet.

"You're like ice," he says, frowning down at his hands tracing over my legs.

"You're like fire," I say, and when he looks at me with his brows drawn in surprise I shrug. "It fit."

He smiles, his eyes scrunching up.

"Sure."

He concentrates on warming me.

Then he gives me a smile and says, "To make a long story short, so you don't freeze to death before I finish, when I saw Arnout's letter I knew exactly what he was saying."

I nod and relax into the delicious scraping of his warm hands over my legs. A liquid heat travels up my calves, across the dip of my knees, up my thighs, and pools in my belly.

"Unrequited love," I say.

"Love," he agrees.

But then I'm pulled from the languor he's working into my skin. "But he's not asking for you. He's asking for her."

Noah's hands pause just beneath my knee. His thumb circles the sensitive spot on the underside.

He asks, "Do you think, sometimes, when you love someone who won't or can't love you back, do you think, maybe, you just want someone, anyone, to care? Just...anyone?"

I tilt my head and consider this. I spent my childhood wishing my dad cared. I spent four years wishing Leo loved me. In the end, did I just want someone to care?

"I care about you," I say suddenly, wanting badly to make this clear.

The corner of Noah's mouth tilts up. "Thanks, Merry."

He doesn't say *I care about you too.*

So instead of letting there be an awkward silence, I add, "I think you may be right. I'm sure that Arnout will like it very much that you care about him enough to make sure he's okay."

Noah's pensive. He looks lost in thought and for a minute he's silent.

Suddenly, I let out a wide, jaw-cracking yawn. I cover it with my hand and try to hide it.

But Noah turns to me and a wide, slow smile spreads over his face. "Tired?"

I shrug. "Maybe."

He lifts an eyebrow. "I just remembered you ruined my mattress. Didn't you promise to share your bed?"

My blood fizzes, like freshly poured champagne, and I look at him with mock confusion. "Did I?"

"No kicking, no snoring, no sheet wrestling," he says with faux seriousness.

"Is 'sheet wrestling' code for something?" I ask, feeling bold.

"Yes. It's code for don't steal the sheets or I won't protect you from cockroaches."

Ha.

I give him one last smile and take in the feel of his hands resting on my calves. Then I swing my legs off the sill and press my feet into the cold stone.

"You know," I say, turning as Noah stands, "in case I didn't mention it, I'm really glad you're here. With me."

Noah studies me for a quiet moment, then he steps forward and takes my arm, just like he did when we were walking down the aisle at the wedding and says, "Me too."

Which isn't exactly *I care about you too, Merry.* But it's close.

33

I BOLT UPRIGHT, FLING THE SHEETS BACK, AND STARE WIDE-eyed at Noah.

Of course, I'm on top of him. My legs straddle his hips. My thighs sink into the heat of him, and my hands are pressed into his bare chest. His muscles tense and I catch a glimpse of the tattoo beneath my spread fingers.

He comes awake with a start.

His eyes widen.

Because, yes.

I'm wrapped around him. Again.

And he's ready for action. Again.

But that's not what has me bolting upright and flinging back the covers.

No.

Honestly, us waking up twined together has become the norm. That's not unusual.

What happened though is. I had a dream. And it's the answer to the mystery.

"I had a dream," I say excitedly, bouncing a bit on top of him.

Noah groans. He shakes his head and his mouth forms a tight line.

"I figured it out. My brilliant subconscious mind figured it all out!" I fling my arms wide and then gesture at the window. Out toward the lake and Annecy.

Noah doesn't look. Instead he winces.

"Don't you want to hear? Aren't you excited?"

"Merry." His voice is morning gravel thick and his mouth turns down at the corners. The soft sunrise light sifting through the windows paints his freckles gold in the cutest picture I've ever seen. But even though the light spills over him and he's in a soft, lavender-scented bed, he looks terribly uncomfortable.

"What's wrong?" I ask, looking around the room.

When I turn back, he nods toward me meaningfully.

My hands press into his chest and my legs grip his middle. My thin white nightgown rides up my thighs, and I don't have any shorts on. It's just me. Pressing into him.

A skin-pricking blush flushes over my chest and up my neck.

Okay.

Yes.

I see the problem.

"Oh. Right." I give a firm, business-like nod. Then with as much decorum as a duchess at an afternoon tea, I lift my thighs and side scoot until I slide off of him and onto my side of the bed.

The cushiony mattress sinks and shifts beneath me. I tuck my calves under my thighs, spreading out my nightgown, so all my bits are covered.

He lets out a tight breath and shakes his head, staring at the ceiling. "What were you saying?"

I bounce a bit again, reminded of why I woke up so excited. "I had a dream."

He nods and his feather pillow makes a crinkling noise as he shifts. "Me too. I was dreaming I was a tree and this strangler vine was wrapping around me."

"Ha ha." I poke him in his bicep and finally he turns and grins at me.

His eyes are warm and intimate.

"I swear," he says, "the man who ends up with you will never get any rest."

My heart, which had been floating in my chest like a happy, buoyant balloon, deflates.

Because.

"I've never had any complaints." I stick my nose in the air.

He scoffs. "I didn't say they'd be unhappy. Just tired."

I stifle a startled laugh. My heart lifts again. "That's what coffee is for."

He covers a smile with his hand and then rubs at his eyes, making a deep, morning, rumbly sound that hits me right between my thighs.

"So. You had a dream?" He stretches and sits up in bed. He's in pajama bottoms and nothing else. The expanse of his bare chest, the lines of his muscles, the trail of hair leading down, it's incredibly distracting.

I blink at him, then when I realize his eyebrows are raised and he's waiting for me to respond, I say, "Yes." Then, shaking out of my stupor, "Yes! I figured it out."

Noah stands and then stretches his arms over his head. I wish he'd stop doing that. It's making it nearly impossible to think. Especially because I know exactly what he feels like under my hands.

Soft.

Firm.

Hot.

Jeez.

I shake my head and jump out of bed. The cold stone floor does exactly what I hoped. The icy cold on my bare feet zaps me out of my lust haze. I hop over to my suitcase and grab a cotton day dress.

"Remember last night?"

"Which part?"

Fair question. I could be asking about Louis the lobster, or Camille's bucket of water, or him holding me on the windowsill. But I'm not.

"The painting you showed me. The one called Le Pont."

"Sure."

He's stopped stretching and is watching me with a curious smile. I notice that he also seems much more rested than yesterday. The purple bruising under his eyes is gone and his shoulders are relaxed. I smile at him, happy that he looks better.

"I dreamed that we were in Annecy."

"You and me?"

"Uh huh." I nod happily. "And we were wearing our wedding outfits. I was in my puce dress"—I wrinkle my nose—"and you were in your tux."

He scratches his chin and I notice the morning stubble lining his jaw. He smiles at me. "Go on."

"We were looking for your dad."

Noah narrows his eyes. "Okay."

"He was a cheesemonger in Annecy. And we needed some raclette for Pierre's wedding."

"Right." Obviously Noah doesn't see where this is going. "Who was Pierre marrying?"

I wave this away. "That's not the point."

"It's not?"

"No. The point is..." I hold up my hands, the day dress I'd grabbed waving like a yellow flag. "We had to cross a bridge to get to your dad's cheese shop. And without the cheese the wedding couldn't happen. Mystery solved!"

Noah stares at my dress, fluttering in a stream of sunshine. There's a line between his eyebrows and his mouth turns down. Then, he says, "So your dream solved the mystery of Thomas Arnout?"

"Exactly!" I beam at him, glad that gets it.

He shakes his head. "I don't get it."

Or not.

"Your dad. The cheese. The wedding. The bridge."

Okay. Now that I say it like that it doesn't make any sense.

Noah smiles at me. "I think this is that moment where coffee would help me a lot."

I smile back.

He looks so cute with his rumpled hair, morning stubble, and that look of befuddled amusement on his face. There's a light pillow crease on his left cheek that I want to run my fingers over. And I bet, if I did, he'd give me another smile, one full of consternation.

And then I wouldn't be able to help it. I'd stand on my tiptoes and I'd give him a kiss. A quick one. Just a touch of my lips to his. Like that first, shallow bite of a peach. When you rub your lips over the soft skin and take the top, fleshy layer in your mouth. The sweet juice coating your lips, the summer flavor teasing your tongue.

Just a touch. A taste.

This image is so real, so compelling that I take a quick step back.

Noah wrinkles his brow. "You don't want coffee?"

I clench the dress in my hand, the linen scratching my fingers.

"No." I shake my head. "We don't have time. We have to go now."

Maybe the breathy urgency in my voice spurs him. I don't know. But Noah takes a step forward and asks, "Go where?"

"Annecy!"

I gesture at the window, at the white mist rolling over the lake, spreading over the shadowed shore of the city.

"Why?" He steps close.

He stares down at me, the heat rolls off of him, and the scent of his shaving soap entices me to lean closer.

"Because," I tell him, "that's where the Lovers' Bridge is. And that is where we'll find Arnout."

34

It's not quite seven. The air rising off the water still has that morning cold bite that lasts even in summer. At least until the sun burns the chill away.

The area around Lovers' Bridge, or le Pont des Amour, is sleepily quiet. The wooden boats clank against the docks they're tied to. The stone walkways lining the canal are empty of pedestrians and only a few birds hop along the grass searching out worms. The iron lamps still glow in the early morning. In the distance, over the lake, the mountains are bathed in sunrise orange, like the trees are on fire and it's spread into the water, spilling toward the bridge.

Noah and I stand in the middle of le Pont des Amour.

In front of us, the lake spreads, with the mountains towering high, and the chateau hiding far off in the trees. Behind us, the canal flows, with stone walkways, gardens, and the promise of romantic wooden boat rides.

But what could be more romantic than the Lovers' Bridge?

The perfect arch of the bridge reflects in the smooth blue-green water. Below us, not even a ripple mars the gold-tinted reflection.

I lean against the thin iron railing and the cold metal digs into my forearms. The black iron has curls and circles and x's, all delicately twined together. On either side of us, the bridge is lined with smooth white stone that dips into the water.

I stand on my tiptoes, lean over the railing, and look down at my distorted reflection. And of course, at Noah standing next to me.

"There's a clue here. I'm certain." I drop back to my feet and walk to the end of the bridge, dragging my hand along the railing.

"You think Arnout's final painting was referencing this bridge?" Noah's right behind me, a warm presence at my side.

"What else?"

He lifts an eyebrow. "I don't know. Any other bridge in the world? Any other bridge in Annecy? A metaphorical bridge?"

I shove my elbow into his side. "Not possible. Think about it. He told the lady to meet him where they escaped. Then, the painting was called the bridge. Where else would he be telling his lover to meet him but at the *Lovers' Bridge*?"

I give him a triumphant grin.

At his still skeptical look my smile slips a bit. "We just have to look around." I glance at the ground, the railing, the stones. "He may have carved something here for her to find. A note. Or a clue."

Noah's brows lower as he considers this. Then he nods. "Alright. Fine. Let's look."

Ha.

He's into my idea.

I walk slowly and carefully study every single surface of the bridge. As we pace the little bridge the sun rises higher, the mist burns completely away, and the street lamps click off.

"Not seeing anything," Noah says, sounding grumpy.

"You're cranky before coffee."

He gives me a surprised look, his hand resting on the railing.

I nod. "I noticed it right away. If we lived together, I'd make sure you had coffee as soon as you woke up. Every day."

Noah's eyes gleam. "We do live together."

I think about our old woodstove. About the insane log-lighting, fire-burning, smoke-sniffling process that it is to make a pot of coffee.

"Hypothetically," I correct. "In a world where I owned an instant coffee maker."

"I don't drink instant coffee."

I grunt. "You would in my hypothetical world."

"Ha."

I grin at him. "You'd be too tired from sleeping with me to care whether it was instant or not."

He tilts his head, gives me a strange look, and then nods. "Fair point."

Suddenly I realize that *sleeping with me* could mean more than sharing a bed. I quickly turn away and continue the search.

While I'm walking down the bridge, scanning for clues, my eyes land on deeply carved letters in the large white stones. "There!"

"What? Where?"

"There!" I point and run to the edge leaning down to get a better look. "I knew we'd find something. It's the clue."

I grin at Noah. He's behind me, as close as he can possibly get without touching me, to get a better view of the letters scraped into the stone.

"What does it say?" I ask, squinting at the writing.

"It's in French."

I nod. "Yes?"

"Si tu pouvais lire dans mon coeur…"

His voice is deep and the way the words dance over his tongue make me straighten and turn toward him. We're so close that when I turn, I press against him. I stumble back a bit, and he reaches forward and steadies me. His fingers spread over my arms, pressing gently into my flesh.

Where his fingers press, a pulsing thrum spreads through me, traveling over me. I sway toward him, my thighs brushing his, my breasts pressing into his chest. I look up and swipe my tongue over my dry lips.

He stares down at me and gives me the same look I remember from the moment before we last kissed. The only time we ever kissed.

A heady, drunken sweetness throbs through me.

"What does it mean?"

He stares at my lips. "If you could read my heart…"

I wrinkle my brow. My breath feels heavy in my lungs. Overhead the wind rustles the leaves and I try to pull in a deep breath. "Is that all?"

He shakes his head.

"What else does it say?"

"Tu verrais la place où je t'ai mise."

His words scrape over me, like fingers stroking my inner thigh, climbing higher, higher.

"Yes?" I tilt my chin, tug on my lip with my teeth. My lips ache. I've never wanted so badly to kiss someone.

Never in my life.

"If you could read my heart, you will see the place I have given you there."

And then that moment I've been waiting for, the one from my dreams…it happens. The sun shines in a golden beam over us. The breeze fans out my dress. The birds chirp and in the distance, a violin plays a high, long note —the beginning chords of a love song.

It's magic.

It's…

Love?

My chest expands.

My head spins.

It's love.

I'm in love with Noah.

If he could read my heart, he would see his name written there.

Oh. My. Word.

I've fallen out of love only to fall in unrequited love again.

But I don't have a moment to worry, to get scared, or to flee. Because Noah's still holding me, and when he breathes the last words, he leans down and closes his mouth over mine.

35

IF I THOUGHT FOR A SECOND THAT THIS WOULD BE A SLOW, languorous, sweet kiss, I would've been wrong. Very, very wrong.

Noah's mouth isn't gentle.

He doesn't coax.

He isn't sweet.

No.

He swears, low and quick, and then his fingers dig into my arms and he crushes my mouth with his own.

His mouth bruises mine.

I gasp at the heated pressure of his mouth, the forceful explosion of need that rushes through me.

I want him. I want him so, so much.

He makes a low, pained sound in his throat.

The noise vibrates over my lips.

He tastes like sunshine washing over a ripe, sweet, juice-laden grape, pressed into sparkling sweet champagne. I drink him, taste his sun-warmed lips, the effervescence bubbling through my veins.

And suddenly I'm flashing back to the hotel room.

We'd kissed like our lives depended on it. Like if our lips disconnected we'd stop breathing. I'd gripped his hair, he'd lifted me by the hips and shoved me against the wall. I'd scratched his shoulders, he'd bitten my tongue, I'd gasped, he'd swore.

He'd said, *Merry, Merry.*

And I'd said, *Yes, more, yes. I want you. I need you.*

And he'd said, *Merry, my Merry.*

He'd said my name like if he stopped saying it then the earth would stop spinning.

"Merry," he breathes again, a plea against my lips.

Then the Lovers' Bridge, the violin music, the sunlight setting fire to the lake, it all vanishes. It's as if it all winks out of existence, and the only thing left is Noah.

Kissing me.

I remember it now. I can't let him go. I can't take my mouth from his. Because if I do, the sun won't rise, the birds won't sing, and the world won't be right.

His fingers press kissing bruises into my arms, urging me closer. I reach up, grasp his shoulders, and hold on tight.

He licks my bottom lip, as if he's running his tongue across warm chocolate melting off a strawberry. Then he takes my bottom lip in his mouth and sucks. And when he does, there's an echo of him taking me in his mouth and sucking me *down there*.

Right *there*.

I can feel him, on every part of me, inside and out.

A noise catches in my throat and he takes it from me.

He thrusts into my mouth and all coherent thought fades.

I've caught fire. The sun has fallen across the bridge.

The bright rays dance over my closed eyes, and it has lit me from within. Or, no. That's Noah. He's lit me from within.

Please, I think I say. Or maybe I kiss it.

Either way, he understands.

He grips my hips, lifts me. Fits my legs around him. Wedges me between his firmness and the metal of the bridge. He's hard against me and I bury myself against him. Lose myself in his mouth. In the feel of him pressed to me.

My dress flutters around my legs. Rides up my thighs.

He tastes like morning.

He tastes like waking up twined together every day.

He tastes like love.

The metal of the bridge digs into my back, his fingers dig into my hips.

And me?

I hang on.

I hang on as an avalanche of want cascades over me.

It's as if all these months we've been dancing around this truth. And all the tension is finally erupting.

"Merry," Noah breathes. And when he does, I can feel him growing impossibly hard.

I don't think. I respond.

I run my tongue over his, taste his sun-warmed taste, and then I run myself along him.

He groans.

Presses me closer.

My breasts rub along his chest. They're full. Heavy. Sensitive.

More.

When I move over him, my whole body lights up even

more. Like I'm the lake and he's the sun pouring liquid fire over me.

"Kiss me," I tell him. "Don't stop."

He doesn't.

I hang on. Ride him. Suck him. Revel in him.

This is beautiful.

This is love.

Love.

At that, I decide I'm through with bridges and kisses on bridges. What I want is a bed. A warm, comfy bed in a French chateau.

"Make love to me," I say against Noah's mouth. "Take me home. Let's make love. All day long."

At that, Noah freezes.

Since I'm clinging to him like a strangler vine on an oak (as he aptly dreamed), I feel every bit of the tension that suddenly grips him.

Then he relaxes. It's only a second that he was tense, but it's enough.

I feel him frown against my mouth, then he slowly pulls away.

My lips were full, warm, feeling slightly bruised and tingly. Now, they sting, chilled as the cool breeze robs them of Noah's warmth.

I press them together as cold mortification trickles through me.

"Or not," I say, smiling at Noah, my lips only wobbling a little.

He watches me, his eyes hazy blue, like the mist over the lake. And I think I see in them as much want as I'm feeling.

But I can't be sure.

When can I ever be sure? Every time I think someone could love me, I'm wrong.

Every time I put myself out on a limb, the limb breaks.

And I fall.

I sigh, keeping my smile in place.

"Too much?" I ask brightly, keeping it light.

Because when it's all said and done, I don't want to lose Noah.

I'd rather be friends than nothing at all.

He gives me a small smile, then slowly lowers me to the ground. I drag over him, and the evidence of how much he wants me is still there. Rubbing along my sensitive spot.

I draw in a shuddering breath.

He pauses. And I think, for a moment, that he's going to lift me back up and start kissing me again.

But instead, he gently sets me to the ground. He makes sure I'm steady and then he steps back.

My legs are wobbly, and even though the stone is firm beneath me, I feel like I'm swaying. I take a moment to right myself.

I clear my throat. Brush my dress back in place. Pat my hair. Smile.

Noah turns to the side for a moment and looks out over the mirror-smooth surface of the lake. When he turns back his eyes are less *I'm going to make love to you in public*, and more, *I like you as a friend*.

So.

Yes.

Too much.

"So. We kissed. Again," I say, choosing the direct route. That's my style now. Take the bull by the horns.

Noah wrinkles his nose and lets out a half-cough, half-laugh. "You could call it that."

"But no sex," I broach. "Because we don't do that." It's a semi-question/semi-statement.

Noah reaches out and takes my hand. He carefully threads his fingers with mine. At the feel of his fingers linking with mine, his gentle squeeze, my heart flips over itself. He pulls me along the bridge, back toward town. "No sex."

I shake myself, yanking out of how much just him holding my hand has electrified me.

I blink up at him.

"Is it because we aren't together?"

I glance up at him to gauge his reaction. But he seems like he's lost in thought, staring at the words carved into the white stone.

"Who do you think wrote that?" I ask, nudging his arm.

"Hmmm?" He looks down at me, his cheeks red. Then, "Oh. Flaubert."

"I'm sorry. Who?"

"It's a famous line from Gustave Flaubert. He wrote *Madame Bovary*."

I sigh. Ah. Okay. "Another book I need to read that I never will."

His eyes crinkle into a smile. "It's a movie too. We can watch it together."

I look up at him quickly as we step off the bridge onto the stone walkway lining the canal. Would that be a date? If we watched a movie together, would we be dating?

Would I watch *Madame Bovary* and then have incredible, slow-motion sex while we stared dreamily into each other's eyes?

I almost snort at the unlikely picture.

First, I don't think Noah will make love in slow motion.

Not judging by how he kisses.

Second.

No.

I don't know why he kissed me. I don't know why he says he likes me. But he's made it pretty clear that I'm not lover/girlfriend/marriage material.

I think about that depressing thought as we walk, my heels click-clacking rhythmically on the stone walkway. His footsteps sound heavy and assured, mine quick, soft, almost as if I'm afraid to make a sound or leave a mark of my passing.

When the silence has lasted long enough, I decide it's time to move on to safer topics.

"I'm sorry my dream was wrong," I venture. "I thought we'd find a clue. I was certain that Arnout meant for the lady to come to the Lovers' Bridge."

Noah nods, not seeming too put-out that our early morning mission failed.

I suppose he hadn't actually put much stock into my dream. Plus he's been looking for Arnout for a long time. He probably expects disappointment.

Down the path, a few morning commuters scuffle along, their long coats blow out behind them, like sails puffed out by the wind. It's almost like a morning sailboat race, the commuters billowing past.

Noah squeezes my hand and pulls me closer as a man with a red veiny nose and wire-framed glasses nearly collides with us.

The warmth of Noah's hand echoes through me.

See. This is nice.

Friendship is nice.

A boatman climbs onto his wooden boat and begins to unravel the coiled rope. He studies us, presumably checking if we might be interested in a romantic boat ride.

I give him a no-thank-you smile, and he turns back to his rope.

Annecy is waking up.

The buttery smell of freshly baked croissants drifts to me on the breeze. My stomach growls loudly.

Noah smothers a smile and glances at me. "Do you want some coffee? Breakfast?"

Okay. Never mind.

Friendship is nice, but I have to know. I can't just let it go.

"Why did you kiss me?"

Noah stops.

Pulls his hand from mine.

Turns to me.

Steps closer so we're facing each other, only inches apart.

"Isn't it obvious?" he asks in a quiet voice.

The shadows from the low morning sun shining through the trees play over his face. The wind flits my dress across my legs, teasingly rustling the skirt. The violin still plays. It's another love song. The colors are vibrant. The sounds are musical. Noah's eyes are an earnest, clear, open blue.

But even with all that, I still can't tell.

"Not to me," I admit. "It's not obvious to me."

He gives me a small smile. The freckles on his cheeks are so endearing I want to reach out and press my finger to each one of them.

"I like you, Merry. I like you a lot."

You'd think my heart would do a happy dance. That I'd spin in a circle, fling my arms wide, and smile.

But you'd think wrong.

Because now that I've realized that I'm in love with Noah. In love deep. Deep. Deep.

Well, being in like?

That's just another way of saying *you're not the one.*

36

THE COFFEE, A CAFÉ AU LAIT, COATS MY TONGUE WITH velvety, milky perfection. I don't think I've ever tasted such a delicious coffee. It's sweet, creamy, yet slightly bitter, like dark chocolate nipping at your tongue. Maybe that's what makes coffee good? The sweet with the bitter.

Although, thinking about that, I feel like Camille with her "love isn't love without beauty and pain" philosophy. And that makes me think of love being like a flower. It grows, it blooms, and then inevitably it withers and dies.

Which, I think, is how my parents look at love. They've been tending their fallow fallout garden for decades now. It's a cold-war post-love dystopian view of the entire process.

I glance at Noah from over the ceramic rim of my white mug. The warm coffee coats my upper lip in a frothy café au lait mustache.

I wonder what he thinks of love.

I mean, I know he told Camille love makes fools of even the wisest men. And also that he knows from experience that unrequited love is a bad idea. But what does he think of love at this moment?

Noah sits across from me at our little marble-top café table. He leans forward in his wicker chair and studiously surveys his croissant as he smears it with glassy, orange-peel-flecked marmalade. Gosh, when Noah concentrates on something, he really does give it his full attention. I watch him scrape his knife over the pastry, perfectly spreading the marmalade in an even layer. The tart tang of the orange rises to me, tickling my nose.

He's so focused. It's engrossing how focused he is. But then he pauses, his knife halfway across the flaky pastry, and looks up at me, a quick, flashing grin on his face.

"What?" he asks.

I set down my coffee cup. It clatters against the marble and I lick the froth from my lip. I ignore the humor that lights his eyes and instead lean forward.

"Do you like croissants?" I ask.

I pick at the corner of my little square apple tart. The edges puff up, curling over to form a small basket, and in the middle there are perfect, thinly sliced apples, shiny with sugar. I put a sliver of pastry on my tongue, and let it melt while I wait for his answer.

"Define *like*," he says.

Ha.

I lean back in my chair and let the breeze ruffle my hair. It's still before eight. I like the anticipation of a new day that seems to fill this part of town. We're sitting on a sidewalk, with people hurrying by to their jobs, or children holding their parents' hands on the way to school, and I feel happy. Morning time is so full of hope. I *like* it.

"Like, as in, does it make you happy?" I ask.

Noah's eyes darken and the edges of his lips curl up. "Yes. I'd say that if I like something, it makes me happy."

My mouth stretches into a wide smile.

Aha.

We're speaking in code.

"And..." My eyes drift over our small round table, landing on his coffee, our pastries, the soft boiled eggs still in their shells, the little jars of yogurt. I finally settle on the coffee. "Do you like café au lait?"

"Yes. A lot." He lifts an eyebrow, and then as if to illustrate his point, he reaches for his cup and takes a sip.

Oh. Darn.

He likes me a lot, and he likes café au lait a lot. Does that mean me and coffee are on the same level?

"Do you like café au lait?" he asks.

And without thinking, I respond, "It's the best thing I've ever tasted."

He laughs. "You say that a lot."

"I mean it a lot."

He nods, then picks up his croissant and takes a large bite, making a happy noise as he does. It sort of reminds me of the noise he made while we were kissing. And that makes a little vibration zing through me, hitting me right in the core.

Okay, yes, Noah likes croissants.

"Do you like traveling?" I ask, realizing that I assume he does but I'm not sure.

He lifts a shoulder. "Sometimes. Not always."

"Did I already ask you this? At the wedding?" We talked about a lot of things at the wedding that I don't remember.

"No." He shakes his head, then wipes his hands on his napkin. He's already finished with his croissant. He ate it with *gusto*. See. No slow motion for Noah. Just devouring.

"Why do you do it then?" I pick up my tart and take a small nibble. The apple is tangy and crisp.

"I'm looking for something." Noah looks over the table at our small feast and then chooses another pastry from the basket. "That's why I began traveling. You know I went to school for film, right?"

I nod. He went to the same university as Leo. He studied in the film program, while Leo went for non-profit management.

"I was going to do nature, you know, those grizzly-in-the-waterfall-about-to-eat-a-leaping-salmon sort of shots?"

I nod at his wry smile.

"Right. I know the one."

"That's what I wanted to do."

Grizzly-bear-gaping-maw shots are a far cry from travel shows.

"What happened?"

He looks down at his breakfast and tears a bit of his croissant off but instead of eating it, he sets it back on his plate. He glances back at me and shrugs.

"My mom got sick. We fought. I ran. All the way across the world. And I kept running. Then I realized I wasn't running, I was looking."

I remember when Noah and I talked at the wedding that I told him I thought my purpose was helping people find fulfillment, but I can't remember what he said.

"Looking for what?" I ask.

At the tightening of his shoulders and the firm line of his mouth, my breath catches and I think he's going to say—

"Love."

My heart flies up into my throat and beats feverishly. "Like, love of a place? A beautiful town?"

I gesture at the cobblestone street, the canal flowing lazily past, and the medieval buildings painted bright colors. The scent of croissants and coffee and the touch of cool lake-fresh air. This is a place to fall in love with.

He lifts a shoulder again, a small movement. "I feel guilty. I've felt guilty for years," he finally says. "To be honest, the things I did, sometimes you don't realize that a relationship can be so fragile. That you can break a relationship and then never get it back. I thought I'd always have love, so when it was gone, I kept looking to get it back."

"So all your traveling, your whole career is a search to get love back?"

Gosh. No wonder he sounds so poetic when he's talking about those seaside villas and quaint mountain villages.

"Something like that." He frowns and then looks out over the sidewalk, toward the canal, and a boatman rowing past. A couple sits in the back of the wooden boat, the woman rests her head on the man's shoulder.

Suddenly, I'm filled with optimism and hope. "Whatever you said or did, I'm sure it isn't irreparable. You shouldn't feel so guilty. Anything can be fixed. Anything can be forgiven. Right? Isn't that the power of love?"

Noah turns back to me and for a moment his eyes flicker with something like a wish upon a star, then they turn dark and shadowed. "That's desperately naïve. It's a stupid, foolish hope. Stupid on the level of unrequited love."

He shrugs, then looks back down at his pastry.

"It's not—"

He looks back up, and I cut off.

"I *like* foolishly hopeful," he says.

I give him a small smile and he smiles back, pulling me in with the warmth in his eyes. "Like, as in café-au-lait-level like? Or as in marmalade-on-a-croissant-level like?"

"How about Merry-DeLuca-level like," he says.

My lips tingle as his eyes drift down to them. Unconsciously I reach up and touch them, brushing my fingers over their fullness.

"Speaking of…"

"Yes?"

"Is this Merry DeLuca level like above café au lait like?"

"Without a doubt."

"And above marmalade croissant like?"

"Exceedingly so."

Hmmm.

That's promising.

That's very, very promising.

"Is Merry DeLuca level like above your like for traveling to your favorite destination?"

His expression stills, then, "What if you are my favorite destination?"

Holy crap.

Holy moly crap.

He just went there.

"As in, an I-like-you destination, or as in, I-want-to-explore-your-body-like-the-cobblestone-streets-of-a-French-village destination?"

"The latter."

I pause. Oh gosh. I can never remember what it means when someone says the latter. Is he talking about the first thing or the second?

No.

Noooo.

"Errr. Um. So the latter? The better option."

"Yes. Not the former," he agrees, his eyes sparking.

"You like exploring French villages," I hazard.

He grins.

I guessed right. Note to self, the latter means the last option.

Which begs the question. "So you like me, a lot, a lot."

He nods.

Then raises his hand, flagging the waiter for the bill.

"I'm sorry," I persist. "Does a lot, a lot sort of encroach on the boundary of possibly…"

I can't say it.

I want to say *love*. Love for crying out loud, love!

But I can't.

My tongue is thick and sticking to the roof of my mouth.

I take a gulp of my café au lait, now cold, and not as delicious, then I swallow and ask, "Have you ever found what you're looking for? Traveling? Have you found it yet?"

Love!

Love!

I take my napkin and grip it in my hand, wadding it into a tight ball under the table.

Noah leans forward and starts to speak. But then the waiter is there, standing at the table, thrusting the bill in between us, speaking French to Noah.

It doesn't matter. As soon as the waiter leaves, Noah will tell me. Or not.

But as they're talking my phone buzzes. I pull it out of my purse and glance at the caller. It's Angela. Which is weird because it's the middle of the night back in New York. I look back to Noah. He's engrossed in a conversation with the waiter—who apparently is a big fan of his— since Noah is autographing a napkin.

I catch his eye, point at my phone, and when he nods, I get up and answer. I walk away from the table toward the canal.

"Hello?"

"Merry? Ugh. I just puked everything I've ever eaten. My life is the worst."

I stop at the edge of the walkway and look down at the green-blue water splashing against the stone wall.

"I'm sorry."

"Ha. Don't give me false pity. That's not why I'm calling."

"Isn't it the middle of the night there?"

I glance up at the sky, squinting at the sun.

"Yes. But as I was puking, I remembered that you wanted me to ask Leo about Noah. So I did. And man, are you going to be glad that I asked. That guy's no good. Really messed up. I have no idea why Leo is friends with him. Noah has the whole world fooled. You really pinned him. Not a good guy."

I quickly look back at Noah. He's still talking to the waiter, his polite, charming, I'm Noah Wright demeanor in place. The sun plays over him, highlighting the freckles on his checks. He looks at me then, as if he can sense my gaze, and flashes me a small smile.

I look away quickly. Guiltily. I pretend to inspect a large pot of purple petunias at the edge of the walkway.

"What does that mean?" I ask in a low voice.

Angela moans, then I hear Leo, his voice a rumbling murmur.

"No!" shouts Angela, "For goodness sake. I don't want tea. I don't want crackers. Do you want me to puke again? Go back to bed."

I hear her kick shut the bathroom door and then, "Morning sickness has turned me into a monster. If our marriage survives this pregnancy I'll be shocked. Ugh."

My chest pinches painfully at that thought, but not as much as it would have a month ago.

"Angela. What do you mean about Noah not being a good guy?"

"Oh. That. It's insane. You were right to never like him. I can't believe he was in my wedding. In fact, I'm kind of creeped out you're staying in the chateau with him. I mean, are you even safe? I asked Leo, he was like, it's fine. Because that's what men say. But I don't think it's fine. Not with his past—"

"Angela, for crying out loud, what about him is so bad?" I swing my hand in frustration, whacking at the petunias.

A passing woman gasps at my outburst and says, "Excusez-moi!"

I wave apologetically at her and turn back toward the canal. "Just...what is it?" I ask more patiently.

Angela sighs, then in a whisper I can barely hear she says, "Merry, he's a murderer."

37

A LARGE GRAY CUMULUS CLOUD AS THICK AS A MOUNTAIN moves across the sun and sends the morning into sinister shadow. I shiver at the sudden chill and rub the goosebumps on my arms. Annecy is no longer a charming, romantic town, it's dark, cold and haunted. Even the trees, which before looked like arms draping lovingly over the canal, now look like skeletal fingers grasping at unsuspecting humans passing below.

"Did you just say..."

"Murderer," Angela confirms.

My mind can't comprehend this. Every time I touch on it the word slips away, as easily as the wind ripping a silk scarf from my neck.

Noah.

Noah Wright?

The Noah Wright?

If what Angela's saying is true then...a stifled laugh chokes off, halfway up my throat. Noah asked if I was living in a gothic novel, and I said, very confidently, no.

Because that would mean that I was a single, young woman in unfortunate circumstances (okay fine), living in a decrepit old mansion (yes), with a brooding man who has a dark secret (no). But that no has now become a...yes?

For the first time in my life I wish I read more. Then I would know what happens at the end of those gothic novels. What does the dark brooding man do? What happens to the young woman? Are they like horror novels? Is the audience yelling at the woman "don't go into that mansion!" because they can all see that there's a man there with a sadistic criminal streak?

"What do you mean exactly?" I ask Angela. "Because that's a serious accusation."

On the other end of the line, Angela makes pained moaning sounds, and I'm fairly certain she's about to be sick again.

"Angela?"

"I'm fine. I'm fine. See, I only know what Leo told me. But when they were at university the police came and took Noah in for questioning. He was the prime suspect." Angela gags and then moans. "Sorry. So gross."

"Suspect in what?" I ask impatiently.

"His mom's disappearance. They had a terrible fight and then right after that she disappeared and—"

A loud noise, like the roaring of the subway rushing down a dark tunnel, that awful, shrieking roar fills my ears and I can't hear what Angela's saying anymore. I can only hear Noah's voice.

We had a fight.

I ran.

I've felt guilty for a very long time.

"Merry? Are you listening to me?"

I shake my head, then ask, "So they found her?"

I'm wondering how Angela leapt from disappearance to murder.

"No," she says in an ominous tone. "No one ever did."

His mom has been missing for years?

"But that doesn't mean—"

"The neighbors heard yelling. And there was blood. And nothing else."

Okay.

Right.

But...

"Merry, you need to find somewhere else to stay. I think—"

A heavy hand closes on my shoulder, tightening.

I let out a startled shriek and jerk away.

When I spin around Noah is there a stunned expression on his face. His hand hangs in the air between us.

My stomach twists.

I've felt guilty for a very long time.

Angela gasps. "Merry, what? Are you okay?"

Noah drops his hand and gives me a confused smile. "You alright?"

I nod and point at my phone. "Mhmm."

"He's there, isn't he?" Angela asks.

"Okay, I'll talk to you later," I say in a chipper voice to Angela.

"No. Don't go. I'm telling you, Merry, you need to find another place to stay. Leo thinks it's fine, but it's not fine."

I smile at Noah, lifting my lips into quite possibly the fakest smile ever. I'm not sure, all I know is that my mouth feels waxy and heavy.

"Uh huh. Yup. Okay. Tell everyone hi for me."

"No, Merry, I'm not done telling you—"

I hang up.

Noah tilts his head, the shadow from the gray clouds making his blue eyes almost black. His smile falls away and his lips turn down. I can't help but stare at his mouth. I was just kissing him, kissing him like my life depended on it.

A hysterical laugh travels up my throat and then chokes off.

"Are you alright?" he asks again, stepping closer.

And then, as he comes near, his warmth closes over me and the goosebumps and the chill fade. My stomach settles and my heartbeat slows.

And even with Angela's dire warnings still portentously closing around me, all I want to do is lean into Noah and take his hand and stroll along the canal.

It's funny, the day lightning strikes and I realize without a doubt that I'm in love, my sister calls to tell me the guy's a psychopath.

At that thought, my phone starts ringing again.

It's Angela.

I hit ignore, and a half second later it starts up again.

I turn it off.

Noah puts his hands in his pockets, his shoulders casually slumped as he watches me battle with my phone.

Once I've shoved it back in my purse, I shrug and say, "Sisters."

"Isn't it the middle of the night there?"

I nod and then look back at our café table. All our dishes are cleared away and the table is wiped clean. Noah holds up a white paper takeaway bag.

"I had everything packed up. I'm sorry, I have to get back to—"

"No. It's not a problem. I was done," I quickly assure him.

He nods, unconvinced, looking as if he wants to ask why I seem so jumpy. I feel like a cat, my back arched, the hair at my neck sticking up on end.

Maybe he can sense this because he reaches out and tucks a strand of my hair behind my ear. When I stiffen, he frowns and pulls away. And I want to kick myself because this is Noah.

"Everything okay back home?" he asks.

"Oh. It's fine. Angela just has morning sickness."

"Ah." Noah makes a sympathetic face. "Sorry."

"Don't worry about it." I wave my hand, casually brushing it away. Then I gesture down the street, toward where we parked. "Ready?"

He gives me a look, uncertain, then nods.

As we walk along the water, my shoulders relax and my stride loosens. The bulky gray cloud, ominous in its gloom, finally moves across the horizon, giving way to the sun. I shift my purse to my other shoulder and look up at Noah.

He seems lost in thought, his brow wrinkled, the edges of his mouth tight.

I wonder, does he suspect what Angela told me?

Or did he think I already knew about his past?

Being Leo's best friend for years, I imagine maybe he thinks I already knew.

Or maybe not. Maybe Leo was sworn to secrecy and no one knows. Because I've never seen a word about it online. You'd think in all those articles and fangirl posts about Noah, someone would mention his murky past. But no. There isn't even a whisper of it.

And I'm struggling, because how do you broach a subject like this?

Oh, hey Noah, you know how you mentioned that fight with your mom? Did you by any chance off her?

Yeah. Not so much.

"Sorry again," Noah says, and I startle.

"What?"

"I'm on a deadline."

What? Did he just emphasize the word *dead?*

"What did you say?"

"Deadline." He frowns at me.

"For your book?" I ask cautiously.

I'm being ridiculous. Deadline is a normal, everyday word.

We pass a gardener. He's bent over, pinching the brown heads of the petunias and forcefully yanking them off.

"Yeah," he nods offhandedly, then, "I never understood deadheading."

He frowns at a gardener bent over a wide ceramic pot overflowing with crimson red petunias.

"*Dead*heading," I repeat slowly.

Noah gives me a funny look. "You know, snapping the heads off flowers." He shrugs. "My mom liked gardening, she always made me deadhead."

Jeez. Jeez.

I bite down on my lip. Now would be a good time to ask about his mom. It's a good opening.

"So..."

"Sorry about being a kill—" A car backfires, covering his words.

But did he just say sorry for being a killer?

"What?" I ask, staring at him in wide-eyed shock.

"Sorry for being a killjoy? For not being able to stay in town longer?" he says again, frowning at me.

Oh. Ohhh.

Noah stops walking, and I pull up short.

We're near the car, on a narrow, cobblestone paved side street.

It's the old, cozy kind of street built hundreds of years ago, before cars and buses needed room to drive. The old stone buildings line the street so snuggly that when people open their front doors, they'll step into the street.

If I couldn't hear the steady engine rumble and the horns of cars in morning traffic, and if I couldn't smell the mixture of diesel and coffee, I'd easily imagine I was in the past, five hundred years ago. Even the wooden doors in the stone buildings are so short, I'd have to stoop to enter the homes.

And here we are, standing together in this curving, narrow, historic side street. All alone. If someone peered at us through the window, they'd probably think we were about to kiss. That's how we're standing. Close. Staring at each other.

I lick my lips. They're dry from nerves.

Noah watches my mouth.

"You'd asked if I'd found what I was looking for," he says, his blue eyes shifting to mine.

I stare up at him, like a bird caught in a snare. "Did I?"

The side of his mouth kicks up. "Before your phone call. You asked if in all my travels I'd found what I was looking for."

"Oh. Right. I did."

I'd been asking, in my horribly roundabout way, whether or not he'd found love.

Preferably with me.

"I'm not good at opening up," he says, vulnerability painting his expression. "But I don't want you to wonder. In case things go wrong, or we never see each other after your holiday, then I want you to know. Yes."

I look up at him. "Yes?"

He smiles and nods. And it's the sweetest, shyest smile I've ever seen. And I decide right then and there, Angela is full of crap. Leo is full of crap.

Whatever happened, I believe in him.

His mom may have disappeared after an argument, but that doesn't mean he had anything to do with it. And obviously the police felt the same way.

I believe in Noah.

And even if my sister or all those gothic novel readers are shouting at me to flee, I don't care. No matter what his secrets are, I believe in his goodness.

At that, I smile, stand on my tiptoes, grip his shoulders for balance, and press a kiss to his lips. I meant for it to be quick, but at the sweet spark that lights in my lower belly, I stay longer, brushing my mouth along his.

Noah reaches out and wraps his hand along my hips, spreading his fingers over me. Caressing me.

When I finally pull away, his eyes look sleepy and hungry at the same time. Like a predator lying in the shade, pretending to nap, but in actuality seconds from pouncing.

"Bonjour," I whisper, liking how the French sounds rolling over my lips. I touch my mouth where the feel of his kiss lingers.

He smiles. "Bonjour, Merry."

I'm about to go in for another kiss when a surprised, happy cry sounds from the end of the street. "Noah! Good morning!"

I turn and there's Camille, her crown braid wrapping around her head, her lips pink. She's wearing navy pants, a striped scoop-neck shirt, and she's pushing a turquoise bicycle down the street.

"Morning," Noah says, surprise in his voice.

Camille pushes her bike between Noah and me. I take a quick step back, not wanting to have my toes run over.

"I was coming to see you today," she says huskily.

"Really?" asks Noah, rocking back on his heels.

She pouts, her lips as reddish pink as ripe apples. At first I think Noah is going to politely disengage, pull me away so we can continue our conversation, but then he asks, "Why were you going to stop by?"

The metal parts of Camille's bike squeak as she pushes it back and forth over the cobblestone. She has a basket in the front, and in it, there's a paper-wrapped bouquet of white roses, and a thin, golden baguette. I swear, she couldn't be cuter if she tried. She even has that fresh, spiced apple scent coming off her. I imagine she bathes in apples.

"Ah yes," she says exultantly, "Because I wanted to tell you my news."

She stops and her eyes spark. She lifts her chin, then with relish she exclaims, "I, Camille Petit, have found the ghost lady of the chateau! She is not dead!"

38

I STAB MY FORK INTO THE ROUND FLAT SLAB OF BRIE ON MY plate and watch it jiggle like a speared jellyfish. The brie vibrates, the creamy yellow-white cheese throwing off its ripe nutty scent. When it stops shuddering I stab it again, then again, poking holes in the cheese that close almost as soon as I tug my fork free.

I'm alone in the kitchen, sitting cross-legged in front of the cold iron stove, the plate of brie in my lap and a stale baguette in a paper bag leaning against the wall next to me. I'm sure Louis, my lobster terror, is lurking somewhere nearby. Surely he wouldn't pass up this opportunity to terrorize me?

Although, according to a quick search online, lobsters can't survive outside of water for longer than thirty-six to forty-eight hours. So sadly my ferocious nemesis is not long for this world.

I think back on how he attacked Pierre. Maybe he isn't my nemesis, but a protector of my virtue?

I stab at the brie again. The kitchen is falling into

shadow, it's late afternoon and the long tube-like room feels as hollow as an empty sausage casing. The fire, when lit, gives the room a cozy, medieval feel, but now it's like a barren shell.

I grip the neck of the open bottle of wine at my thigh —it's more lukewarm than room temperature—and take a long swallow.

After Camille joyously told Noah of her discovery, we went racing off to the grassy park by the lake. The one where Pierre and I had our picnic. There, a woman, "the ghost" stood by the shore of the lake, painting personalized postcards for the tourists. She was stationed next to a bald man who sold crepes from a bicycle cart and a woman who stood with a five-gallon bucket selling white and red carnations.

Camille skipped across the grass, tugging Noah along. He was more alive, more alert than I'd ever seen him. Even more so than when we'd kissed, which was saying something. But as soon as we neared the woman, when we could see her henna-dyed hair, her long freckled arms poking out of a fringed shawl, and the light fuzzy mustache over her lip, I knew without a doubt she wasn't "the ghost."

And so did Noah.

She was nothing like the woman in the painting.

"Yes, I was Arnout's lover. I am the lover he painted," she claimed in a German or maybe Austrian-tinged accent.

Camille beamed. Certain of her discovery.

Noah listened politely, but the light that had momentarily filled his eyes dimmed, and the way he looked over the lake, back toward the chateau, was despairing and distant. Almost as if he'd been told he'd finally reached home, only to realize that home was another thousand miles away.

We left the woman after paying twenty euros for three personalized postcards, signed by Arnout's "one true love."

Noah drove Camille and me back around the lake, up the twisting mountain hills, and Camille, unnoticing of Noah's dampened spirit, asked to see his work.

That was hours ago.

She went into the gatehouse with him.

And she didn't come out.

At least for the hour that I waited, pacing in the cucumber garden like a stupid, jealous, love-sick fool.

I scowl and decide to head outside again. The damp, closed air of the kitchen isn't doing me any favors.

But before going I shove the massacred brie and the stale baguette toward the crack Louis escaped through yesterday. Maybe he'd like a last meal. Or I suppose his friends the rats might. That is, if they aren't all caught in rat traps.

In the garden, I take off my shoes and scrunch my toes in the cool, prickly grass. The garden is shaded from the tall stone tower blocking the afternoon sun. The cucumbers have recovered from the storm. Their vines stretch across the grass, the fat leaves spread wide, and an occasional bright yellow flower spots their reaches. Dozens of long, glossy cucumbers spear the ground.

I squat down in the grass and snap one from the vine. Then I snap the cucumber in half. Its juice sprays across my fingers and releases its clean, sweet smell. I take a nibble, sucking at the flesh, and avoid looking at the gatehouse.

The smell of the cucumber, the taste of it makes me

remember the day I arrived. I didn't want Noah here. In fact, I'd never wanted to see him again. I thought he was an arrogant creep with questionable motives. I thought he never smiled, had no sense of humor, and had fooled the world into thinking he was a good person. I believed he and I had nothing in common.

If Angela had told me before I arrived here that Noah was a murderer, I might...I might have believed her.

How much a few weeks can change.

I think about how last time I was here, in this garden, I called Jupiter. She'd mentioned how Noah needed inspiration, and suddenly I wonder, how much does she know about him? And more, how much does she know about this chateau?

I decide that while I'm waiting for Noah to finish his long afternoon with Camille, I'm going to do a little research of my own.

39

"Merry! Splendid. Please tell me you're wrapped around a gorgeous Frenchman, making passionate love, and you accidentally dialed me while in the throes."

I raise my eyebrows and peer at the obscenely elongated cucumber at my feet. "Hello, Jupiter. Not exactly."

There's no reason to ask her why I'd have a phone with me while making love. What would I be doing? Texting with one hand, caressing with the other?

"Oh well, it's the thought that counts," Jupiter says with some disappointment.

"Still in Albuquerque?" I ask, imagining her holed up with her artist.

Jupiter gives a husky laugh. "No. No. That bird has flown. He only needed a little inspiration. I'm in Kalamazoo. There's a fabulous installation artist here who has fallen on hard times. Not for long though, Merry. Not for long!"

Passion fills Jupiter's voice. It's the particular tone that she has when she's looking at a piece of art she loves or thinking about inspiration. I wonder what Jupiter's life would've been like if she'd never fallen into the art scene. It's impossible to imagine her at home, baking cookies. When I try, I see her in a hot pink, frilly apron, squirting frosting on a sugar cookie, railing at me about the artistic inspiration behind cake decorating. And of course, the particular uses of frosting in bed play.

I kick at the elongated cucumber and decide to get to the thrust of things.

"Jupiter, what do you know about Noah Wright?"

I stop kicking the cucumber and stand still, waiting for her answer. There's silence on her end of the phone, and either I've lost the connection or I've stunned her into silence.

"Who?"

I look up at the sky, beseeching heaven. "The man you leased the chateau to. The one who is staying here with me! The travel documentarian. The man you said needed inspiration! Noah Wright! The best man at Angela's wedding. Remember?"

She sniffs, an affronted sound. "Don't yell at me, Merry. When you yell your face turns a peculiar shade of puce. Always has. By the way, did you know that puce was first made popular by Marie Antoinette? She wore it to court and King Louis said, 'My dear, you are the color of a flea,' although some people say 'the color of flea's blood' but all the same, it's the color of squashed flea blood on linen sheets. It was all the rage after that."

"That's gross."

"So is yelling when I've only just woken up," she says matter-of-factly.

"Good point. I'm sorry. But, Jupiter, I really need to

know. Why did you say Noah needed inspiration and what do you know about him?"

The breeze, bending round the chateau wall, lifts my hair and tickles my cheek. I push it back and pace closer to the stone wall. It blocks the wind.

Jupiter takes a long breath. "I don't know anything about him," she says finally.

"But you said he needed inspiration." I hit my hand against the stones of the wall, they're as hard and as unyielding as Jupiter, giving nothing.

"Oh, he does," she confirms. "It's something in his eyes. You can always see it in their eyes."

"In his eyes?"

"Mhmm. An artist in need of inspiration always has the same look in their eyes. You can't miss it."

Okay.

Well.

Then, because I'm a glutton for punishment, "Did you give it to him?"

"Of course I did! Do you think I'm a miser? Just because he isn't a painter or a sculpture or...really, Merry."

My stomach plummets down to my feet, settles in the grass and rolls around a bit. I feel like I might be sick. Jupiter and Noah.

"So...you and Noah?"

She scoffs. "I sent him to my chateau, didn't I? And then I sent him you."

Oh.

Ohhh.

I sag against the wall, leaning against the hard surface for support. Was Jupiter attempting a fairy godmother moment?

I smile, but then the stone scratches against my back, reminding me of the other reason I'd called.

"About the chateau. Do you know anything about the former owner? Thomas Arnout?"

"The artist?" she asks with interest. "He didn't own the chateau. Jacques Thierry did."

I narrow my eyes, squinting at the lake and Annecy beyond. Isn't Jacques Thierry Pierre's father?

"But I do know Arnout lived in the chateau for years. Created many works there. All lost in the fire, of course. It's quite exciting to own a home where such a renowned artist lived and worked. Did I tell you I got it for a steal? Only a million euro!"

Gah.

She was robbed.

But years ago, one of Jupiter's artists died (a really famous one), and in his will he left her dozens of paintings. She kept the paintings that were sentimental to her, but the rest she auctioned, and that left her with, as she says, more money than she can spend in fifty lifetimes.

"Yes," I say, "but do you know anything about the time he lived here? About the fire? Or about the woman he painted? Where she is? Or where he is? You know lots of people in the art world, maybe you've heard something?"

I wait expectantly. I love Jupiter, I do, but pulling information from her is as easy as catching a fish with your bare hands.

"Oh, I'd forgotten he had a muse. Hmmm. To be honest, I never traveled in that circle. In those days I was in London, then New York, Berlin, now that was fun. Did I ever tell you about Berlin?"

"Yes," I say quickly, because when Jupiter starts to talk

about her nude, an eight-foot-tall likeness painted on the Berlin Wall, she can go on for hours. "But his muse, do you know anything about her? Or about him? He can't have just disappeared."

"But he did! He did, didn't he? Hmmm." I'm losing her. Jupiter isn't at her best in the mornings, and in Kalamazoo it's not even nine o'clock. To Jupiter that's unreasonably early.

I guess she doesn't know anything. I push off the wall.

This was a dead end. Jupiter doesn't know anything about Noah. She doesn't know anything about Arnout.

"Do you know, I do remember something," she says.

I stand straight and grip the phone tighter. "Really?"

"Yes. You know Arnout broke his spine, lost his right arm? That's the death knell for an artist."

"Yes?"

"If ever someone needed inspiration, it was him."

"Okay?"

"So I mentioned it to my friend, the Marquess."

Oh, right, the Marquess. Back in the nineties, Jupiter was the mistress of a Spanish marquess, who was a passionate collector of art.

"And he said, I remember now, 'No, once a man's soul has been given, he cannot give it again. He has no need of inspiration, he has his bridge.'"

I shake my head, not sure I heard right. "His bridge?"

"That's what he said. I thought it was odd, but I didn't pursue it. That was just at the time I found Rafael, and I was distracted for two years, and then...well..."

Rafael is the man who left her his paintings. She never talks about him. I think, of all the people Jupiter has inspired, Rafael may be the only one she ever loved.

But Jupiter doesn't like to dwell on sorrow, she leaves that for other people. So I keep with the topic at hand.

"Do you still talk with the Marquess?"

Because if he knows where the bridge is, then our mystery might be solved.

"No." She gives a husky laugh. "When I knew him in the early nineties, he was nearly one hundred years old. The stories he told. Do you know the turmoil he saw? The changes to the world? It's astounding. Art was his reprieve, his solace. He had romance in his soul, just like a true artist. Without art, a soul becomes a barren desert. Art is rain for the parched earth. Have you heard from your sister?"

"What?" I shake my head at the abrupt topic change.

"I imagine about now she's decided she doesn't want her husband anymore."

"Why would you say that?" I snap, shocked that she's spot on.

"It's easy. I may not create art but I'm still an artist. And to be an artist you have to see people exactly as they are, not as you want them to be. Or more importantly, as they want you to see them. I always told your mother it was wrong to spoil Angela. When children are spoiled nothing can ever satisfy them. They are a great, empty hole, devouring everything. They search for something to satisfy them, but nothing ever does. Like a stomach stretched out, it takes more and more to fill them, until nothing can. Nothing and no one will ever be enough. It's terribly sad. I'm certain she thought that if you loved Leo, then surely he would be enough. Of course, he isn't. He can't be. She has to find that out herself though, poor girl. I'm sure she'll be leaving him soon."

"She's pregnant," I say, my mouth numb. Jupiter

usually flits around, never landing long enough to make much sense. But then, she just cut to the heart of the matter in seconds. Not that she's right. Angela wasn't spoiled. She was just...loved.

Jupiter tsks. "Oh dear. I hope I'm wrong then. But I rarely am."

I glare at the lake, the sun reflecting harshly off the surface. Even though I should look away, I don't, and my eyes start to water.

"She's happy. She'd never leave Leo," I lie, and I'm sure Jupiter can hear it, so I say more firmly, "They're in love. Coup de foudre."

"Hmm."

She's not convinced, and although there's no reason I need to convince her of anything I say, "I didn't love Leo. He was only my friend. It wasn't love. She didn't take anything that wasn't given."

"I know, dear, I know," Jupiter says sadly. Then, "Oh, look at the time! The gallery opens at ten and I'm still in bed. What am I doing?"

And before I can say good luck, or goodbye, or anything more about Angela and Leo, or Noah and Arnout, she's gone.

I swipe at the tears pooling at the corner of my eyes. Then I blink quickly to get rid of the dancing sparks from the blinding reflection off the lake. But even looking away, little sun spots float in my vision, and it's hard to see.

I rub at my eyes, scrubbing the wetness away.

I'm not crying because of Angela and Leo.

I'm not.

It's only...sometimes, even if you want to let the past

go, when you've been clasping onto something so long, it hurts when you finally open your hand.

I don't love Leo.

And now that my hand is open, I'm free to reach out and take the hand that's offered to me. The one I want.

At that, I walk across the shaded grass, through the cucumbers, their summer scent spiraling up to me. I hurry under the shadow of the tower that the lady and Arnout leapt from and come into the sunshine of the drive.

The gatehouse is there, and coming out of the door is Camille.

Her cheeks are red, there's a small smile on her face, and she's touching her lips in a just-been-kissed gesture I know well, because I just did it this morning.

My feet scuff on the stones of the drive as I stumble to a stop.

Camille looks up from her musings.

When she sees me her eyes widen and she smiles.

And I can't help but think she looks like she has a secret.

A delicious, triumphant secret.

40

"HE IS PERFECT, IS HE NOT?" CAMILLE ASKS, HER CHEEKS pink.

This is only the second time that I've ever been alone with Camille. Before, Noah and Pierre have always been near, and so, I'm seeing her in a different light.

In their company she stands differently, smiles differently.

Now, she seems younger, and although I know she's in her early twenties, she looks like a teenager. A giddy, buoyant, starry-eyed, first-love teenager.

I've never been sure how I've felt about Camille. With the water dousing, and the tart comment. But seeing her like this, I can't help but feel sympathetic. Even if she just kissed Noah. Or more.

"I didn't know you were still here," I say, ignoring the "perfect" comment. And ignoring the fact that I paced for an hour, waiting for her to go, before giving up and retreating to the kitchen.

"I'm going now," she says, retrieving her turquoise

bike from where it leans against the gatehouse wall. I hadn't seen it there.

Camille pushes it across the gravel and stone, its wheels crunching the rock, then she pauses next to me.

"I know you want him. But you cannot have him. He was mine first." She's leaning close, her voice low with conviction, her eyes bright.

And I see it.

Right there.

Another victim of unrequited love.

I know exactly what Jupiter means now when she says it's something around the eyes. Right there, in Camille's eyes, I can see it.

"How long?" I ask.

"What?"

"How long have you loved him?"

"Will you leave him alone?" she asks hopefully. "He is happy with you. But he is better with me."

She leans close and I can smell the apple on her, the clinging scent of her family's orchard. Camille smells sweet, she looks sweet, but she's all thorns and determination.

She's very much the opposite of me. In the past, if I wanted something that someone else wanted I would step aside. If I didn't want to do something but it was to help someone else, I would do it, even if it hurt me.

You can do this, I told myself.

It was my motto.

You can do this.

I shake my head no. I can't do this. I won't. I won't leave Noah alone. Not as long as he wants me near.

Camille drops my gaze and runs her fingers over the handlebars of her bike. She strokes the pink ribbons threaded through the wire basket. The roses in her basket have wilted, the edges have already turned brown and curled.

"I was fourteen," she says, keeping her eyes down. "I have loved him for eight years."

Behind us, the chateau stands high, solid. I wonder, how many times in the past centuries has it witnessed a similar scene?

Carefully, gently, I say, "I'm sorry."

Camille looks up, her expression stormy. "There is nothing to be sorry for. Only leave him alone. Let me have him."

I shake my head. "No. I'm his friend. I won't leave him alone. As for letting you have him, that's for him to decide, isn't it?"

Camille grips the handlebars of her bike, her knuckles turning white. "Eight years ago, he was to be married. She broke his heart. I found him in my orchard. His heart was broken and I gave him a piece of mine."

She hits her chest with the flat of her palm, then makes a fist and pulls. When she opens her hand, I look closely, expecting to see her heart there. "I gave him a piece of my heart to heal the break in his. Can't you see? He may be happy with you, but with me, he is alive."

She looks back at the chateau, up to the gatehouse, her lower lip shaking. "I wish he never knew Arnout. I wish he could forget about the lady. I wish..."

I lean forward, waiting for her final wish, but she shakes her head and turns away from the gatehouse, leaving her wish unspoken.

Then all that she's saying sinks in. Eight years ago, Noah was still at university with Leo. As far as I know, Noah has never been engaged.

In fact... "You wish Pierre..." I trail off.

Camille lifts her chin. "I wish Pierre could see me."

I nod.

I understand.

All this time, Camille hasn't been angling for Noah, she's been trying to make Pierre see her. Not as the girl that grew up on the orchard next door, but as the woman who loves him.

And Pierre, he's been looking for a lightning strike, while this whole while he's had a fire that's been burning for him for years.

Camille was touching her mouth in the just-been-kissed gesture because she'd been thinking of Pierre, not because she'd been kissing Noah.

"Okay."

Camille glances at me quickly. "Okay?"

"I can help you."

"You will?" she asks in surprise. "How?"

I smile at her. "Easy. We're going to create lightning."

41

WHEN I WAS IN ELEMENTARY SCHOOL, WE MADE LIGHTNING in science class. It involved an aluminum pie pan, a Styrofoam plate, a wool sweater and a pencil. I can't remember the exact explanation, but it was something about electrons and insulators.

I sent Camille to town to pick up everything she'd need to create a miniature lightning storm. She seemed somewhat (okay, very) skeptical, but she pedaled down the drive with energetic determination.

Tonight, Camille is going to make lightning for Pierre, and that is that.

It's up to them what happens after that.

I climb the steps of the gatehouse, the narrow stone walls hugging me as I climb the winding stairs. The light is faded in the stairway. It's cool and dim, even when the sun beats down bright outside. And as I walk up the stone steps, my feet scuffing on the time-grooved stairs, I feel as if my feet, weathering the stone, are adding to the story of the chateau.

I haven't only fallen in love with Noah. I've also fallen in love with the chateau. For the chateau, it may have been love at first sight, but after that first sight, I've learned to love every flaw, every fault, every worn stone. I love how when the sun rises, the walls turn gold, and glitter, even through the ivy, clinging to the cracks in the stone. I love the damp, stone smell, heavy with history. I love the soothing whispers the stone makes as you walk. I love how the light falls through the windows like a trickling waterfall, barely seen in the cool, dim rooms. I love the broken, groaning pipes, the Louvre toilet, the fire-breathing stove, the crumbling plaster, the leering cupid in the hall, the rats, the bats (not the cockroaches, my love ends with cockroaches), and I love how staying in the chateau makes me feel alive.

As if for the first time in my life, I'm living as me.

As if when I first saw the chateau, it said, "Bonjour Merry," and finally, I woke up and said hello back.

I smooth my hand along the cold, rough stone and come into the gatehouse room.

Noah turns when I enter, a shaft of sunlight falling over him. The tension in my chest that I'd forgotten was there eases and falls away.

His lips lift into a smile. "There you are."

I raise my eyebrows, happy at the sound of his voice. "Were you looking for me?"

"No, just hoping." His eyes warm. His expression reminds me of pulling off my clothes and lying naked in the sun.

I think he must see some of what I'm thinking, because his eyes go from warm to hot.

I take a step forward, farther into the long stone room. It's as sparse as always, the wooden table covered in books and papers, the old chair. The lead glass windows let in wavy, fuzzy light that falls across the bare, stone floor.

When I step forward, Noah meets me, and at his look, I swallow.

He wants me.

But that reminds me of my phone call with Angela, my call with Jupiter, his hours-long sequestering with Camille. All the unanswered questions.

He wants me.

I want him too.

In his look I can see him picking me up, backing me against the stone wall, kissing me until I'm out of breath and desperate.

I can taste him already, the coffee and croissant flavor that I know will be in his kiss. The hint of marmalade and longing.

I take another step forward. Noah reaches out, runs his fingers across the back of my hand.

"I have to ask you a question," I say.

He smiles and nods, his fingers playing over my skin.

"What happened to your mom?"

42

NOAH'S FINGERS STOP, THEN HE PULLS HIS HAND AWAY. His expression shifts from warm as the sun to as unreadable as stone.

The gatehouse, which had been full of sunshine spilling over the floor like threads of gossamer, dims, as a cloud passes across the sun. I hold back a shiver and keep Noah's gaze.

"What do you want to know?" he asks, his voice careful and measured.

I can see it. He's folding up into himself, pulling everything back. Just like at the wedding reception, he's showing his outside but reeling in his inner life and his feelings.

"Don't," I say, holding out my hand, as if I can stop the thread he's tugging on.

He gives a hard swallow and his eyes flicker in acknowledgment. Then his shoulders relax and the hardness at the edge of his mouth softens.

I let out a relieved sigh when I see him opening

back up.

"Do you want to walk?" he asks, nodding at the stairs. "I need some fresh air."

No doubt.

It's been hours he's been holed up here. And no matter how charming the gatehouse is, it's still an old stone room with no breeze and no creature comforts.

I follow him down the stairs and then blink at the sun when I step onto the grassy lawn.

Noah tilts his face up to the sky and takes a deep breath. In the afternoon, the air here always smells heavy, like pine, cucumber vines, and stone. I think it's because the sun has had enough time to warm the earth and saturate the air with all the scents of the chateau. Regardless, it always smells the same, and if I could capture it, like a photo taped in an album, I would.

I'd put it next to a picture of Noah, the shadows and sun playing over him. His wavy hair messy, his jaw unshaven, his eyes closed, his mouth twisted ruefully.

Finally, he opens his eyes and turns his gaze on me.

"Leo finally told you?" He sounds tired, resigned.

"Angela," I say.

He nods, as if it's all the same. Which I suppose it is.

He looks out over the lake, toward Annecy. "When are you leaving?"

Wait.

What?

He thinks I'm going to leave?

Okay. Of course he thinks I'm going to leave.

I imagine, over the years, a whole lot of people have left him once they found out about his past.

Noah isn't looking at me. In fact, he's very carefully keeping his eyes on the crystal lake, the town, the peaked mountains with their deep fanning evergreens. He looks everywhere but at me.

It's fine. I don't need him to look at me. We can just stand next to each other and look in the same direction.

I move closer, reach out, and carefully put my hand in his. When I do, he stiffens. I don't say anything. Neither does he. Slowly he relaxes, threads his fingers with mine.

I'm not leaving.

"Do people usually leave?" I ask quietly, still looking at Annecy. There's a beautiful orange-hued building that stands out against the turquoise blue of the water.

Noah is quiet. The breeze rustles through the leaves and snags at my hair, blowing it across my cheeks.

"No," Noah says. "Leo is the only one who ever knew. But let's be honest"—his voice turns wry—"once there's a suspicion of..." He trails off, finally peers at me, an eyebrow raised.

"Murder," I say, the word acrid on my tongue.

He nods. His eyes are tired and filled with old grief.

Suddenly I realize that old grief just might be harder than new grief. New grief has a brilliance, a jagged, harsh, biting brilliance. But old grief, the jagged edges have curled, the harsh bite has worn down, and now, it's a faded, crumbling creature that is slowly, painfully turning to dust. I can see the echo of that dust in his eyes. It's like a dried, browned rose, decades old, that with a single touch will crumble.

"If people knew, it would be hard for them not to question, doubt, wonder." He shrugs. "It's easier to not say anything. To not get close to people. Then I won't put them in the awkward position of having to end a relationship."

No wonder. Gosh, no wonder.

I remember at the wedding telling him that people liked *Noah Wright* but they didn't like *him*. How much that must have cut him.

"I'm not leaving," I tell him, just in case my death grip on his hand wasn't clear enough. Then I smile. "It was hard enough convincing you to be my friend. Do you think I'd let you go that easily?"

He gives me a surprised smile and I wonder how many times in the past few weeks I've done the opposite of what he thought I'd do.

Then he gives me a searching look, as if he's trying to work out my resolve.

Finally he says, "You should wait until you hear everything before you make that decision."

Hmm.

"One question."

"Okay?"

"In those gothic novels you talk about, with the dark broody man in the decrepit mansion?"

Noah's brow wrinkles and he shakes his head. "Yes?"

"Does the heroine die?"

He gives me a flat look, but the edge of his mouth is twitching. Ha. He's trying not to smile.

"I'm serious," I say, batting a strand of hair out of my face. The wind is picking up and more clouds are gathering. "The answer to this question is of vital importance."

Noah nods. "You want a spoiler?"

"Yes. Do they die?"

He solemnly shakes his head, then says, "Worse."

"What could be worse?"

He tugs on my hand and then starts down the stone path, leading around the chateau, toward the cliff edge.

"You'll have to read them to find out."

I shake my head. "I thought we were watching the movies together." Then I nudge him with my shoulder. "A date."

He smiles at that.

We round the last tower. The mound of grass slopes down from the tower, leading gently to the rocky cliff. The grass, lush behind us, becomes patchy until it gives way completely to the russet-colored rocks that line the edge of the cliff. The rocks dip over the edge, like a stone waterfall. The boulders are the bubbles, falling, falling, until they dip to another grassy, tree-lined bend, all the way down to the edge of the lake.

If this chateau had been built to defend against invading armies it would've been the perfect strategic position. But it was built long after castle warfare. No. It was built at the edge of the cliff not for war, but I think, for love. To be a jewel, perched on top of a sun-bathed cliff, set like a stone in a crown, reigning over Lac d'Annecy. A testament to beauty and love.

"They don't die," he says again as we stop at the edge of the cliff, inches from the sheer drop.

The wind is stronger here, it tugs at my hair and pushes me closer to the edge. My stomach tilts, like a child sweeping down a slide. Exhilarating and frightening at the same time.

"I'm glad," I say. Then, "Tell me."

Noah looks at me, weighs me, and I stand with my chin up, urging him on.

"She was sick," he finally says, and when he does I let out a small breath.

"I remember," I say. He'd told me as much.

He nods, then in mutual agreement we drop to the

rock, sitting with our shoulders pressed together, our hands still linked. He sets our hands in his lap and runs his opposite hand over mine, tracing up and down where our fingers connect.

The rock slab is warmed by the sun, and the heat soaks into my thighs. We hang our legs over the edge and I dig my heels into the surface, needing to feel something solid.

"I went home for a long weekend. To do laundry, get a home-cooked meal. The sort of thing you do when you're at university." He's concentrating on our hands, not looking up.

"As soon as I got home I knew something was wrong. My mom loved a clean house. But there was dust on the side tables. Dirt on the floor. The dishes hadn't been done for at least a week." He looks up and shrugs, shaking his head.

"It sounds ridiculous. How could dirty dishes give foreboding? But they did. When I saw the medicine bottles lined up on the vanity in the bathroom, I wasn't surprised. It's like the dust and the dishes had forewarned me."

He looks away, out over the open air at the drop below us. "This is the first time I've ever talked about this," he says.

I squeeze his hand. "I'm here," I tell him.

It feels as if we're about to jump, to throw ourselves together, off the edge. For years, Noah has been standing here, and now I've joined him.

"I confronted her," he continues, his voice so quiet the whistling wind nearly steals the sound of his words. "She had brain cancer. It was fast. She had six months to live, at most. She described it like a net, meshing into her brain. They couldn't remove it, it was insidious. And already, she'd had it for two months, which left..."

"Four months," I say.

"At most."

A sailboat crawls across the blue water, its bright white sails billowing in the wind. We watch it pass, growing larger as it nears, then smaller as it goes.

"What happened?" I ask.

He shrugs. "I don't know."

I frown. "What do you mean?"

He tilts his head again, and finally I realize what kept Noah apart from others. It's the weight of his past, you can see it on him, in his shoulders, in the way he approaches the world.

"I was so angry she hadn't told me. The way I saw it, she should fight. She should've told me. If I'd known I would've left school. Come home. I would've helped her fight. She said that's exactly why she didn't tell me."

"She didn't want your help?"

"She didn't want me to give up my passion. She said she wouldn't be able to forgive herself if I gave up on what I wanted, just to watch her suffer."

"I'm so sorry."

He shakes his head. "Don't. She didn't want anyone's pity. Not even mine."

"I meant for you," I say. "I'm sorry she said that to you. It wasn't her choice to make."

He nods and I can feel the ache in him. "I would've left school. I would've chosen to stay with her every minute. Every day until the end. She knew that. So she did what she thought was best. That's what parents do, I think."

Thinking about my own parents, I wonder if that's

true. In everything they did, was it really what they thought was best? I imagine it must've been. Even at their most hurtful, they must've been doing the best they knew how.

"Your mom loved you a lot," I say.

"She did," he says simply.

"Did she disappear for you?"

He shakes his head no. "She told me that she was losing her memory, losing her cognitive function. It was a process of the disease. That in a matter of months, maybe weeks, days if she was unlucky, she'd cease to know me, cease to remember. The shock, I can still feel it, as if a wall of ice slid inside me and I couldn't feel anything, could barely understand what she was saying. Then she said, I remember this, I won't ever forget the words, she said, 'I'm going to spend my last days with your father.'"

"What? But..."

Noah nods. "Exactly. The man whose name she didn't know. The man who didn't matter. The man she'd spent the last twenty years convincing me didn't care. She was going to leave home, leave me and take my final months with her and give them to a man who she'd spent twenty years denying. She didn't want me to see the end, she wanted to be with my father."

"But why?" The question is torn from me. It doesn't seem right. It doesn't seem fair.

"Because she loved him. She'd spent decades loving him. She'd never stopped."

I can't imagine. What must this have felt like for him? I try to picture Noah at twenty-one, learning that his past was a lie. That his mom is dying. That his dad is out there, somewhere. And most horrible of all, that his mom doesn't want him to be there at the end.

"So she left?" I ask.

"She left," he confirms. "After a lot of yelling. Angry words I can barely remember but will always regret. There was a bottle of wine, she said it was from near where my father was from. I was so angry I picked it up and threw it, shattering it against the wall. There was red wine and glass everywhere. A shard hit my mom in the leg. Another in her arm. She bled. Quite a bit actually."

"The blood. Angela said the police found blood."

He nods, his mouth twisting. "I've never been able to drink red wine since."

"Where was the wine from?"

He gives me a funny look, his brows lifted. "Savoy. A Mondeuse."

Oh.

Here.

Here.

And me, I naively gave him a bottle of red wine from France when we first met. I was so angry when I found it in the trash, I'd thought...I thought he was a cold, arrogant, horrible person.

"So that's why you threw out the red wine I gave you."

He gives me a surprised look. "I'm sorry. I didn't know you saw that."

"I thought you were terrible." I lean against him, dropping my head to his shoulder. "Probably the same as you felt about me. Mutual antipathy."

"I never thought you were terrible," he says in surprise.

I look up at him, lifting my head from his shoulder. "Yes you did. Remember Papa Gallo? When you first saw me, the way you looked at me, like you thought I was the worst? And you told Leo that you'd heard enough about me over the years to know that you wouldn't like me."

"First of all," he says, "the first time I saw you I thought you were the most beautiful woman I'd ever seen, and if I ever had the chance to talk to you, much less make you smile, I'd be the luckiest man on earth. The second I saw you, I wanted you."

"But..."

"Then I saw the way you were looking at Leo, and I realized who you were and that you were in love with him."

"I wasn't—"

"You were."

I sigh. "I was."

"Leo always had women in love with him. At university anytime a girl talked to me, she was doing it to learn more about Leo, or get closer to Leo, or make Leo jealous."

"Really?"

"I wasn't always the man I am today." He lifts his eyebrows in a way that's full of self-awareness and self-deprecating humor.

"That's hard to believe."

He shrugs. "Anyway, for years Leo told me about you. In offhanded comments or stories, you were always there, on the fringe. I knew in the way he talked that Merry DeLuca, his friend, was just another woman hopelessly in love with him. I'd seen it enough. I didn't begrudge you it, I just didn't want to be a part of it."

"So when you saw me—"

"I didn't know you were Merry DeLuca."

"Until you did."

"Until I did."

"And you liked me?"

"I more than liked you. But you love Leo."

"Loved. Past tense."

He looks over at me, a question in his eyes. "Have you fallen out of unrequited love?"

"I realized it was bad for me."

By the look in his eyes, he'd already known that. It's not been kind to him either. All those years he was imagining his dad, and then his mom went and left him. Alone.

"Merry?"

"Hmmm?"

"What are you thinking about?"

I shrug. "Your parents."

"Ah." He nods. Puts his arm around my shoulder and pulls me close. "Have you figured it out?"

"What?"

"Who they are."

I look over at him, frowning.

Who his parents are...

His dad is from Savoy. His mom loved his dad for decades. *His dad is from Savoy.* For years, Noah has been looking for...

"Your dad is Thomas Arnout? Your mom is the lady?"

I glance quickly back at the chateau, at the tallest tower, as if they'll be standing there, looking down at me, confirming the truth.

Noah makes a small noise of assent.

"But how?" I ask, not understanding how this could be, why this would be.

I mean, of course, the mechanics are easy, man and woman have sex, baby is born. But the rest of it...*what happened*?

"During our fight, I told my mom if she went to my dad, I'd never forgive her. I told her if my dad hadn't wanted us for twenty years, then he wouldn't want us now. Not me. Not her. I was angry. I was stupid."

He shrugs, although the pain in the shrug is there for anyone to see. "Then she told me a story, and it sounded crazy. The things she said weren't anything like the mom I knew. I didn't believe her. I wondered if maybe the brain cancer was already causing confusion. She claimed that my dad was a famous French artist."

"Arnout."

He nods. "She claimed they'd fallen in love and lived in a chateau together. My mom was twenty-five when she visited France. Arnout was in his early fifties. She said it was the best time of her life."

I look back at the chateau, imagining them there.

"I didn't believe her. It didn't make any sense. Why keep any of this from me? Why would she hide this for twenty years? She said a fire destroyed most of Arnout's work. It started after they'd had too much wine and he kicked over a gas lantern in his studio. Turpentine and fire don't mix. They'd nearly died from the smoke and the flames."

He stares out over the sheer drop of the cliff's edge.

"They jumped from the tower to survive," I say for him.

"That's right. He broke his spine, lost his painting arm. My mom was pregnant with me. She thought she'd lost me. She bled. She broke her collarbone. When she went to see Arnout in the hospital he was filled with so much guilt and shame that she knew he would never paint again if she stayed with him. She knew it would take everything in him to recover and learn to paint again with his other hand. If she stayed he would give everything to her and leave nothing for himself. She said that she needed Thomas, but the world needed his art more."

"And he painted again?" I ask, not knowing if the work I saw was from before or after the fire.

"He did. It took years, but he painted again. He traveled the world and became even more acclaimed than before the fire."

"But your mom never saw him again?"

"I don't know. I don't know if she saw him after she left."

"Because she did? She left?"

He swallows, then nods. "I never saw her again after our argument."

I squeeze his hand and try to send all the comfort I can through my grip. "The police thought she'd been killed?"

He shakes his head. "Her boss filed a missing person's report. The neighbors mentioned hearing our argument. They found the broken glass, the blood. Later, they discovered she'd flown to Paris. Until then I was frantic. Terrified. When they told me about the flight, the fear turned to anger. I was so angry. She'd never said goodbye. I never got to say goodbye." He pauses, then, "Or I'm sorry. I've always wished I could tell her I'm sorry."

"She knew. She knew you loved her. I bet that's why she left the way she did. She wanted you to keep making films. Keep being an artist. I didn't know her, but it sounds to me that she wanted you to live your life fully and not worry about her."

In fact, she reminds me a bit of Jupiter.

Jupiter has always lived her life trying to help artists

bring their light into the world. She once told me that artists are like birds, compelled to sing, even when it hurts. She felt it was her job to soothe, to give solace, to take a bit of the pain away, so they could keep going. Inspiration, she calls it.

I wonder if Noah's mom also gave inspiration, in her own way.

"Maybe," Noah says. "But I did worry. Even when enough time passed that I knew she had to be gone, I still worried. I never received any notice. Whenever I try to find her, there's nothing. No record. It's like she disappeared. Just...gone. There's the record of her flight. Her landing. And that's it. After that, no one cares. She's just another person who ran off and left their old life. Case closed."

But not for him.

Never for him.

"What was her name?"

"Yvette."

"Was she French too? Or American?"

"She was from Saint Martin. When she was with Arnout she stayed in France on an expired tourist visa." He shrugs. "That's why no one saw her after the fire. She thought they would send her home. She moved to the US before I was born."

"How long have you been trying to find her?"

Because by searching for his dad, he'll find his mom, or at least what happened to her. Surely?

"Since twenty-six hours after the police let me know she'd flown to Paris. It took those hours for me to sober up and get over my hellacious hangover. Then I used every spare moment to look for her. For Arnout. I graduated. Changed my focus from nature to travel documentaries. I went everywhere he's ever lived or painted. Combed the world. Traced his life. His career."

He shakes his head, fatigue and frustration written in the lines on his forehead.

"You're certain he's your father? You're certain she went to him?"

Noah winces. "I doubted it after the first year. I'd hit dead end after dead end. Arnout had disappeared a few months before my mom did. I began to doubt they'd ever met. Maybe she'd read about him in a newspaper. Made it all up. But then I went back and looked at the letter he'd written for the Thierry Gallery and at his last painting."

"His painting?"

"The one you saw in the newspaper."

I frown, thinking of the grainy black and white image. With the man sitting alone, at a chateau, the ghost of a woman, maybe there, maybe not.

"Does the woman in the painting look like your mom?"

He shakes his head. "Her hair is the same. Long, black. Maybe a bit of similarity in her chin. I don't have photos of her when she was young, and I only remember her as the mom whose lap I sat on, who tucked me in, whose hands soothed me. I can see her as she was when I was an adult. Lines on her cheeks and forehead, round at the middle, from too much happiness, she said, a scar on her wrist, from when I accidently crashed the car into the garage door when I was sixteen and the passenger window broke." He smiles at that. "I didn't know her when she was twenty-five. I don't know what she looked like then. Besides..." He shrugs. "It wasn't the woman that convinced me."

"It wasn't?"

"No."

"What was it then?"

"The name of the painting." He lifts his eyebrows. "I should've seen it right away."

I try to remember the name, then I do. "The bridge?"

Hadn't Jupiter said something about the bridge? That's right. The Marquess had told her that Arnout didn't need her inspiration, he already had his bridge.

"*Le Pont,*" Noah confirms.

"*Le Pont.*" I frown. "But why would that convince you?"

He clasps my hand more tightly. "Because my mom told me she'd named me after the spot she and Arnout fell in love. That she'd written to tell him about me. And his response was a painting."

"*Le Pont?*"

"*Le Pont,*" he confirms. Then so quietly I have to lean closer to hear, he says, "Noah Lepont Wright."

43

THE WIND PULLS AT ME, GROWING COOLER WITH THE encroaching nimbus gray clouds, rolling over Annecy.

Open air extends in front of us, and I feel suddenly as if Noah and I are falling. As if we've leapt off the cliff, and we're falling, falling. Far below us, the lake gleams a silver and cyan patina, a mirror of cloud and sky. I wonder, if we fell and plunged into the cold alpine water, would our lungs freeze?

Because right now, I've lost my breath.

Noah is Arnout's son.

Noah has been searching for Thomas Arnout, because Thomas Arnout is his father. He's been searching for Arnout in an effort to find his mom, who disappeared nearly a decade ago.

While he's traveled the world, creating documentaries of secluded villages, mountain outposts and little-known tropical islands, he's been scouring the earth for his mom. For his dad.

"I've been everywhere," he says. "I've been

everywhere Arnout ever visited. Anywhere they might've escaped to. He told her, *find me where we escaped.*"

"Why didn't he ever contact you?" I ask, wondering if Arnout knows Noah is his son, why hasn't he sought him out?

"I don't know. It's why I think Pierre is hiding something. If my dad knows. If my mom found him. Then...where is he?" He trails off in a shrug. "I've finally come back here. If he's not anywhere else in the world, he has to be here. He has to be."

"Did you tell Pierre that Arnout is your father?"

Noah barks out a humorless laugh, then stands, reaches his hand out and pulls me to my feet. The momentum of rising pushes me into Noah's arms. He makes a noise as I collide into his chest, and then he wraps his arms around me. He pulls me close, away from the edge of the cliff.

The chill wind falls away and I grow warm as I lean into him.

He smiles down at me and brushes my hair off my face, the wind blowing it wildly. "I didn't," he says.

He doesn't seem to want to let me go. It's okay, I feel perfectly wonderful standing in his arms, with his finger trailing over my cheek.

"I think he'd help you if he knew you were Arnout's son."

Noah drops his hand from my face a wry look coming over him. "And what would I tell him? Oh hello, Pierre. The man who left you all his work, the art you've sold for millions, is my father. I don't have any evidence that he is except for the word of my mom, who disappeared years ago and is likely dead. Oh, and my middle name coincidentally matches the name of a painting. Now tell me where he is."

Noah laughs again, but it's without humor. "He'll think I'm after the money or the art. He'll think at best that I'm sadly mistaken and at worst a psychopath. None of this will entice him to share Arnout's whereabouts. If he even knows."

I wince. When he puts it that way. "But Pierre might believe you. He's a good guy. *We can do it*. We can find Arnout together."

Suddenly I realize that the reason *you can do this, Merry* always felt wrong is because I was waiting to say *we can do it*. We. Together.

"We can do it," I say again. "Even if Pierre doesn't believe you, we can do it. I know we can."

Noah sighs, tugs me closer. "Your tenastic optimism has always bordered on delusional."

I put my arms around him and grin at the smile in his eyes. "It's why you like me."

He tilts his head and considers this. "Is that it?"

"Tenastic isn't a word," I say. "Tenacity is, but not tenastic."

He looks me in the eyes and says, straight-faced, "Wrong. You are the epitome of tenastic."

"Ha."

"Stubbornly tenastic. I've added it to the dictionary. Merry DeLuca, tenastic."

I like it that he's made a word for me, I like it a lot, but, I say, "I think you are. You're the tenastic one. You've been looking for your parents for nearly a decade. You could've given up years ago. No one would blame you."

He presses a soft kiss to my lips, there then gone before I can respond. I look up at him in surprise.

"What was that for?"

Not that I didn't like it.

"For seeing me. For understanding. For staying."

"Of course I'm staying," I say with feeling. "I love you, don't I?"

Then I realize what I said.

I stiffen, then look up, a sort of stunned fear growing inside me. I just told Noah I loved him. Out loud. I said it. Even though I promised myself I'd never tell someone I loved them without them saying it first. Without being sure that they loved me back. And while Noah has hinted at it, he's never outright said it.

The sound of the wind groaning over the trees, the shrill call of the hawks soaring on the mounting breeze, even the whistle of the wind through the turret's leaky roof, it's all blazingly loud as I wait for Noah to speak.

My heart thuds, hard, painful beats, a tight fist pounding against my chest.

And all I can think is, *why'd you say that, why'd you say that?*

Noah studies my expression, taking in every emotion that's warring inside me. Love, fear, hope, trepidation, courage, embarrassment, want, need. They're all there. And all I can think is, *please. Please don't hurt me.*

He could so easily hurt me.

More easily than Leo or my dad, or anyone really ever could.

Finally, he reaches up and rubs his thumb across my lips.

And I can tell, he's not going to say *I love you* back.

He isn't saying anything.

So I smile at him, a big, wide shining smile to cover up the shrinking of my heart.

Years of rejection have me adding quickly, "Just add me to your Noah Wright fan club. I heart Noah Wright. Did you see the hot pink t-shirts for sale? Are you in charge of merchandizing? I have to say, twenty-nine dollars is robbery. But there it is. I'm finally a Noah Wright fan. You know...that kind of love. Fangirl love." I nod and press my lips together. "Besides, what kind of friend would I be if I left?"

Idiot.

Idiot.

"Merry..." he says, completely unconvinced with my fangirl spiel. There's a struggle taking place in his expression, the tightness in his jaw, in his arms, holding me.

But this morning he said yes. *Yes*, he'd found what he was looking for. *Yes*, he'd found love.

He unclasps his hands from me, takes a step back.

What was the yes for, if not this?

And because this is France, and even though I'm standing on a cliffside with thunderclouds gathering above, instead of in a vineyard with the sun shining down, this is still my chance. My chance to finally reach out and open my hand.

"You know what, never mind, I'm not in the Noah Wright fan club."

He frowns. "You're not?"

I shake my head. "No."

Noah's frown deepens.

"I'm in *your* fan club." My heart is racing around my chest, but today has been a day of revelations and I think I've come far enough to take this leap. Be brave, Merry.

"Is there a difference?" he asks.

"You know there is."

The edges of his lips lift.

"This morning you said yes. You told me you didn't want me to be confused. When I asked if you'd found love, you said yes."

He nods. "I did."

"Then?"

His eyes shift, become a mirror of the silver cyan of the lake. Deep and fathomless. I fall into them, my body growing warm and languid.

"What is it?" I ask.

"If you could see my heart..."

My own heart expands, growing with hope. "I'd see the place you've made for me there?"

He nods. I watch the shadows and the sun flit over his face, watch the rawness in his expression.

"What are you thinking?" I ask, needing to know.

"You don't want to know."

"I really do."

He gives me a considering look, then nods at the smooth russet-colored rock, speckled with sunlight.

"I've had this fantasy for weeks now," he says, "of you lying on this rock, wearing only your earrings. Nothing else."

My word.

"That sounds..." I stop, catch his eyes with mine, drag my teeth over my lower lip. "In this fantasy, are you there too?"

He swallows. Nods.

"Am I yours? Are you mine?" I ask.

He holds out his hand, palm open.

I put my hand into his, a lightning storm traveling through me when I do. The sparks growing, electrifying my blood.

"I'm yours," he says. "I've been yours from the start."

At that, the clouds finally open, and the rain begins.

I look up, drops falling on my face, cold water running over my skin.

Thunder booms, shaking the air, the sound ricocheting off the chateau.

"I'm yours too. For as long as you want me," I tell him.

And for a moment, I believe that *as long as he wants me* will last forever, but then I remember, for most of the people in my life, forever isn't very long at all.

Then, over the sound of the rain beating down on the rocks, I hear Camille shouting, "Meredith? Bonjour? I am here!"

Noah frowns, wipes the rain from his eyes, "Is that Camille?"

I nod. "She's here for a lightning storm."

44

CAMILLE STANDS ON THE HIGHEST TOWER, THE WIND whipping her dress around her legs, the misty rain creating an ethereal glow. Most of the towers have conical red roofs, spired points like you'd find on Sleeping Beauty's castle.

But the highest tower, the one with the spider web of light shining around the highest room, lets out onto a flat roof edged with stone. It's the type of tower you'd find on a medieval castle, with a defender pacing its length.

Lucky for Camille, it's also the only tower that's still accessible.

She paces the length of the tower now. She's a white figure, stark against the ominously darkening sky.

She's in a lacy white dress, and I'd say she's laying in on a little thick, but the ghost lady of the tower schtick seems to be working for her.

Pierre stares at her from the drive, a look of disbelieving horror on his face.

"When you said she wouldn't come down, I never

believed..." A rumble of thunder cuts him off, and he flinches. Then his face goes pale. "She'll be hit by lightning."

Noah and I glance at each other. After Camille arrived, it took her about three minutes in rapid-fire French to explain all the reasons Noah should help her, or if not help, at least not stand in the way of love.

I thought making lightning from the paper plate and pie pan would be enough, but Camille, being Camille, decided that real lightning combined with fake lighting was even better.

"She'll be killed," Pierre says, shoving his helmet onto his motorcycle, not taking his eyes off the pacing figure of Camille.

"You better go get her then," Noah says, straight-faced, which I know is hard because of the way he laughed after Camille and I shared our plan.

Pierre's eyes flash and his mouth tightens. "I will. My apologies."

Then when another growling rumble sounds, he sprints across the drive, puddles splashing at his passing. He ducks through the front door and disappears into the great hall.

"What are the chances this works?" I ask Noah, staring up at Camille.

She peeks over the edge, sees us looking, and gives a jaunty wave.

I lift my hand and wave back.

"One in a hundred," Noah says.

"Really? You don't have any faith in my lightning plan?"

Noah grabs my hand and tugs me close, shielding me

from the wind. It's misting rain over us in sideways sheets.

"It's a metal pan and a Styrofoam plate. You're making static electricity. It's..." He stops when he sees my glare, my raised eyebrows. "I mean, of course it's going to work. Pierre wants lightning. He'll get lightning."

At another rumble and a sharp gust of wind, Noah gives me a serious look. "But promise me, if you ever want me to kiss you, just ask. Don't set up an elaborate science experiment in a tower."

Hmmm.

"I promise," I say and I can tell he's waiting for me to ask.

Right here. Right now.

But even though I'd really like to stand here and kiss in the rain, I can't, because we have a job to do.

Pierre has burst onto the tower, his figure emerges, and from his stance, the way he advances on Camille, he's blazing mad.

"Look at that," I say, pointing at Pierre.

Noah grunts. "Alright, maybe a fifty percent chance this works," he amends.

Because when Camille rebuffs Pierre, he grabs her wrist and spins her back around. It looks almost as if they're dancing. Tiny, sprite-like Camille, in her soaking wet white dress, and Pierre with his height, his broad shoulders, and his leather jacket. He tugs her to him, shakes her. He shouts. She shouts. Their words are lost in the wind and the rain. She shoves him away. He pulls her close. Another thunderous growl, the earth vibrates, lightning strikes over the lake. Neither Camille nor Pierre notice.

Because—

"One hundred percent," Noah says.

I nod. Because they are kissing. They're kissing a lightning strike kiss. The kind that leads to beds and babies and a lifetime spent together.

Pierre lifts Camille. She wraps her arms and legs around him, and he starts walking toward the trapdoor. He'll carry Camille inside, to safety, never breaking their kiss.

"It's a shame," I say.

"What's that?" Noah tugs me closer, both of us still staring at the tower. The rain gets in my eyes, and I wipe at them.

"I really wanted her to do my experiment for him."

Noah scoffs. Then he nods at the front door. "We better hurry."

We jog across the lawn, the wet grass spongy as we squish through the fresh mud. Another lightning bolt cracks, this one closer, and I slam the front door, just as the rain picks up. It's dark in the great hall. All the sunlight that usually comes through the windows is gone, shielded by the rainclouds. The sound of rain beating against stone echoes loudly around the empty hall.

Because of the storm, the stone smells damp, and even Noah and I smell of summer rain, sharp and crisp. Wet.

I shiver, because without the sun and without Noah's warmth, the cool air forms goosebumps on my wet skin.

Right now would be a nice time to kiss, to be held, to burrow under blankets with someone you love.

But right now we have to race up the tower steps. As Noah and I run across the hall, Cupid leers at us from his perch.

"Mind your own business, you lech." I stick my tongue out at him.

"Are you talking to me?" Noah asks, pulling me up the stairs, our hands slick from the rain, our feet slipping on the stone steps.

"No. Cupid. He's always watching me with his horny eyes."

"The statue?" Noah asks.

"Yeah. He's a lecher. I swear."

We round to the second floor, the stairs twisting, and keep climbing, up to the third floor. At the fourth floor there is the empty stone room. The beautiful room with the window slits and the magical web of light. To me it's the most romantic room in the whole chateau. From there, you can climb the final stairs and open a trap door in the ceiling to come out on the tower roof.

Camille and Pierre are there now.

Camille and I made a plan. A really nice plan. A battle plan, if you were to think of it from Angela's or my mom's perspective. But I prefer to think of it as a lightning plan.

We decided that I'd call Pierre over, frantically telling him that Camille wouldn't come down off the tower and I needed his help.

Check. Done.

Then, when Pierre retrieved her, I would lock them in the tower room. For the night. Together.

To make it cozy and sweet, we stocked the room with my lightning experiment, a picnic basket full of food, a bottle of wine, a pile of pillows and blankets, and candles and matches.

That bit was Camille's idea.

I wasn't entirely convinced. I said if Pierre knocked or protested I was opening the door.

We've made it to the room, Camille and Pierre still haven't come down from the tower.

Another thunderous boom sounds and the tower shakes. I look quickly at Noah and he shrugs. "It's stood for centuries, it'll be fine."

That's not exactly reassuring since it's only *sort of* stood for centuries.

"Let's just check," I say, pointing at the trap door. "Maybe they couldn't get it open."

I walk into the room and Noah follows. He takes the lead and climbs the stairs. The trap door creaks as he swings it open and a blast of rain and wind rushes in, wetting the stone.

Suddenly Noah steps back, giving way to Pierre, stomping down the steps with Camille in his arms.

I look quickly at Noah. He's stuck behind Pierre, trying to pull the trapdoor shut, tugging against the wild gusts of wind.

Pierre hasn't exactly noticed us, he's still kissing Camille. And Camille, I've never seen anyone look so happy. Her cheeks are pink, and she's holding on to him like she's finally gotten everything she's wished for. She turns her head, breaking away from Pierre's kiss as he comes down the stairs, and gives me a brilliant, happy smile.

Since she broke their kiss, Pierre seems to realize where they are. He shakes his head. "We're...I'm...I..."

He's speechless.

"We are going," Camille says. "Au revoir."

I smile. "Au revior!"

That's all it takes.

Pierre nods, clasps Camille tighter in his arms and strides out the door.

Above, Noah finally manages to yank the trap door shut. But as he does, the wind howls through the room and with one final mighty gust the heavy room door slams shut.

With the trapdoor closed and the tower room door shut, the space is suddenly smothered in silence.

I stare at Noah.

He stares back.

"Did we..."

"Just lock ourselves in?" he finishes.

I hurry to the door, tug on the old brass ring handle. The door doesn't budge.

"Yes. Yes we did."

So that part in the plan about locking two people in a room with lightning and wine, tempting them to kiss and make love?

Check.

It's just the wrong couple.

I look at Noah. He has a comical expression on his face. His hair is dripping wet, his eyelashes spiky, and there are raindrops on his skin.

"Maybe this is Cupid paying me back for calling him a lech," I say laughingly.

Noah walks down the stairs, his eyes on my lips. "You know, that's not Cupid."

"It isn't?"

He shakes his head. "No. That's Anteros."

"Who?"

He smiles, steps forward and tucks a lock of wet hair behind my ear. "Anteros. His name is carved beneath him."

Interesting, although not quite as interesting as the way Noah is looking at me.

"He was the Greek god of requited love."

"Really?"

"And the avenger of unrequited love."

Huh.

"All this time, I painted him wrong." I shake my head at the strange twist of having the avenger of unrequited love perched on the mantle downstairs.

I guess Anteros and the chateau he reigns over led me in the right direction.

I reach up and wipe the rain water off of Noah's cheek.

"He's my champion," I say smiling.

Noah pulls me closer. "He is, isn't he?"

I nod. Then with my heart beating in time with the rain I ask, "Would now be a good time to ask you to kiss me?"

45

NOAH'S HANDS TIGHTEN ON ME AND MY BREATH GROWS short at the look in his eyes.

The drumming of the rain against the stone becomes less ferocious and more a melody. The music of the rain is better than a sweeping orchestra. The growing darkness in the room, split suddenly by lightning, is better than soft focus.

My wet dress, sticking coldly against my skin, water pooling around our feet, is more romantic than a white cotton dress flowing in the breeze.

Why?

Because I'm with Noah.

And a dark, stone room, a cold, damp draft, a thunderstorm, it all becomes the stuff of dreams.

I shiver as he rubs his hands down my arms, his touch a mirror of the lightning lighting the sky.

"Now would be a damn good time," he says, his voice as rumbly as the thunder.

I grin at him. "For kissing?"

He rubs my arms again. "You're cold."

"I should probably get out of these wet clothes," I lift my eyebrows and smile. "Luckily, there are blankets. Lots and lots of comfy blankets."

He smiles back. "That is lucky. Very fortunate."

Then he reaches up and strokes his hand over my shoulder, playing with the strap of my dress. A full body flush races over me as fast as a streak of lightning. Was I cold? I'm not cold anymore.

One touch and I'm burning.

Did I imagine that Noah would be a fast, pounding against the wall, legs over my head, kind of lover? That's what his kiss this morning led me to believe.

But I was wrong.

By the way his fingers move across my skin, the soft puffs of his warm breath as he leans close and sets his mouth over the pulse in my neck, I know he is going to take his time. Savor the act, like he's slowly sipping a glass of prized wine.

My word.

The aching slowness. It's excruciating. It's enthralling. My head falls back, I bare my neck to his mouth.

He presses a kiss to my collarbone. To the space where my shoulder and neck meet. Each kiss sinks warmth into me, sizzles through me, lighting spaces inside that I didn't know were dark.

I grab his arms, dig my fingers into him. Make a noise. That's me making that noise, isn't it?

His fingers play with my strap, his index finger, a callous on the pad, scrapes over my shoulder, and that slow, deliberate, butterfly-light touch ignites me.

I reach up, grab his hair, pull his mouth to mine.

His lips are as hot as I imagined they would be. They're scalding. I cry out as we come together.

My cry seems to spur him, because the breath whooshes out of him, a painful sound, and he takes my mouth, sucks at my lip, swallows my noises.

My word.

My word.

Are we about to make love?

I think...

"Merry! Noah! Are you locked in?"

It's Camille. Her voice high and concerned.

"Hell." Noah starts to pull away.

I shake my head and tighten my fingers in his short hair. "Ignore her."

I bite Noah's bottom lip and he groans, sounding pained.

"Merry? Noah? Are you okay?"

It's Pierre.

And bless him, he starts jiggling the brass handle.

Noah swears against my mouth and I whimper as he pulls away.

I'm on fire. Every single inch of my skin is burning. I'm lit up and the only thing that can put out this need is Noah.

My body aches.

Literally aches.

"Go away," I call.

But it's too late, the thick wooden door swings open, and Pierre and Camille stand in the entry.

Our sopping wet, worst-timing-on-earth, unwanted rescuers.

"I knew I heard the door lock!" Camille cries

triumphantly. "You are lucky I told Pierre that we should check."

I clear my throat, casually push my strap back up my shoulder, and press my lips together.

"Very lucky," Noah says dryly.

Pierre looks between the two of us, frowning. Then he focuses on Noah, his eyes narrowed.

You'd think, since he'd just been kissing Camille, he wouldn't mind that Noah and I were (clearly) having a moment.

I'm about to tell him so, when Pierre snaps his fingers and says, "I remember now. I know who you are. You should be in jail."

46

THE HOT COFFEE MUG WARMS MY HANDS AND THE SMELL OF the French roast is soothing. There's something calming about the routine of making coffee that makes even the most bizarre revelations seem normal.

Start the fire. Warm the water. Grind the beans. Pour water over the grinds in a French press. Wait. Press. Pour. Add cream and sugar.

Unless you're Noah. Then, you drink it black.

If I were to judge Pierre's expression, I'd say that he thinks the black matches Noah's soul.

After Pierre's stunned pronouncement, Noah shrugged and said in a casual voice, "Since we're all here, and wet and cold, we may as well have some coffee."

When I told Pierre he didn't know what he was talking about (how many people know about Noah's mom?), Noah shook his head and said, "No. Technically he's right."

Which mollified Pierre enough for us all to walk

silently down the winding stairs to the dark, empty kitchen.

I kept sending Noah questioning looks, which he pretended not to notice. Once, he sent me a reassuring smile, which did not reassure me at all.

But making the coffee, that was a good choice.

I'd like to get out of my soggy, cold clothes. They have that damp chill stickiness that is so uncomfortable, it's hard to think of anything else. But I'm not leaving, not even for the three minutes it'd take me to run upstairs and throw on a new dress.

Because.

The four of us stand close to the fire burning in the old iron stove. A trace of smoke hangs in the air and mixes with the taste of the coffee.

"I think these are illegal," Camille says, pointing at the stove. "Environmental laws." Then she breathes in the steam rising from her cup. "I am thankful. Il fait un froid de canard."

I'd ask what that means, but I'm distracted by the glare Pierre is sending Noah's way. Noah has just finished handing everyone their coffee and is taking a sip from his mug, looking completely unconcerned.

Pierre shifts on his feet, and he seems to have grown in size. All the dislike and frustrated anger rolling off him makes him seem taller and wider. The easy-going Frenchman is gone. In his place is a man readying to fight.

Which is another reason I'm not leaving to take off my wet, itchy clothes.

I take a casual step closer to Noah, prepared to "accidentally" throw my hot coffee on Pierre if necessary.

Noah notices me placing myself between him and

Pierre. His eyes crinkle at the corners, even though he doesn't smile, and he subtly shakes his head, edging back in front of me.

Apparently, he doesn't want my coffee tossing protection.

Not that he needs protecting.

This is Pierre after all.

But he said Noah should be in jail.

To which Noah said *technically* he's right.

But what does technically mean?

The arched ceiling of the kitchen presses down, and shadows from the fire flicker over us, painting eerie pictures. I wonder, was this once the dungeon? No, I'm getting carried away, there was never a dungeon here.

I take a sip of my coffee, letting it scald my tongue. It's so hot I barely notice the flavor. I think the only one enjoying the coffee is Camille. She's drinking it with relish and staring at Pierre over the rim of her mug with an expression that I can only call undiluted joy. The whole, "you belong in jail" thing doesn't seem to have phased her.

Pierre slams his mug down on the counter, the hot coffee splashing over his hand. I flinch. That had to hurt, but he doesn't seem to have noticed. He's too busy staring at Noah.

"Ça suffit! Appelons un chat un chat—" Pierre growls.

"English?" I interrupt. "Please."

Pierre scowls and thrusts a finger at Noah. "You are a criminal. I knew I recognized you. But not until I saw you wet from the rain—the same as that night—did I know for certain."

Pierre stands with his feet wide, his hands clenched.

"Comment est-ce possible?" Camille asks.

She looks at me in concern. I don't think she realizes she spoke French, or that I don't know what she asked, so I can't answer her.

Noah rolls his shoulders and nods. "You're right. It was me."

If possible, Pierre grows even more tense. "Give it back. If you give it back, I won't contact the police."

"Whoa," I say, holding out a hand. "Hang on. Let's slow down. We're all friends here. Right? Friends?"

I move my mug in a let's-make-merry sort of way and smile. If there was ever a time for me to use my mediation training, this would be it.

Pierre looks like he's hanging on to his calm by a fingernail.

And Noah?

I thought he was relaxed, but I was wrong. Under that casual stance, that cool façade? He's coiled tight, gathering himself, ready to strike.

The question is, why?

I know that Noah believes Pierre is hiding something. I know that Pierre (now) claims Noah stole something.

That's a good place to start.

"There's no reason we can't solve this ourselves. Did you know I have years of experience in mediation? I can help." I restrain a shiver from the cold of my clothes and move closer to the fire.

"Ah! Perfect. Meredith will help and we will all be friends," Camille says, smiling widely.

"And then we will go," she adds to Pierre, saying *go* with particular meaning.

For a moment he hesitates. He looks back toward the hall and I think he considers *going* right now. But then his gaze shifts to Noah and he scowls, "Friends is impossible."

"No!" Camille says, stomping a foot. "What did Napoleon say? Impossible n'est pas français!"

She lifts a finger proudly in the air, as if she's leading an army. Camille must really like Napoleon.

"What does that mean?" I ask her.

She smiles at me, "Impossible is not a French word."

Ah.

Good one.

"Right," I agree. "As such, we're all friends here. So I'm going to mediate. Pierre"—I nod to him—"please start at the beginning and tell us what you meant when you said Noah—"

"Is a criminal," he says stiffly.

"Yes...start at the beginning."

He takes a deep breath through his nose, his cheeks are red and with his wet, messy hair, he looks like an angry mountain lion, with his hackles raised.

"Last year, Thierry Gallery had a special Thomas Arnout exhibit."

I nod. "I remember. That's where you and Noah first met."

At least, that's what Noah said when he recognized Pierre the first day Pierre came by the chateau.

Noah lowers his chin and settles back against the counter, his legs stretched out. To anyone, he'd look like he was casually listening, sipping his coffee. To me? He's waiting for something. He's tense, although the tension is hidden.

Pierre looks Noah over, not fooled by his stance. "Yes. Noah introduced himself at the opening. He asked many questions about Thomas Arnout. More questions than even Arnout's most ardent admirers ask. But I dismissed it, because he was a filmmaker, no? Filmmakers, reporters, biographers, they always ask questions. I gave the only answer I have, I do not know where Arnout is. I do not know what happened to him."

Noah makes a disbelieving sound and for a moment he and Pierre stare at each other, waiting for the other to make the first move.

I clear my throat. "Please continue."

Pierre breaks Noah's gaze and looks back to me. "A week later, at the closing of the exhibit, there was a thunderstorm."

"Like this storm," Camille says. "I remember it because my apple trees were hurt."

Pierre glances at her and seeing the sadness on her face he reaches over and takes her hand.

Before I thought Camille had the most feelings, but seeing the expression on Pierre's face, I think his feelings for her run just as deep. It only took a lightning storm for him to realize it.

"So this storm a year ago? What does that have to do with Noah?" I ask.

Pierre looks back to us but doesn't take his hand from Camille's.

"I stayed late, taking down the displays, properly storing the work. It was midnight before I left. On the way, I saw a man in the rain. It was nothing, I was certain. But then something in the way he moved made me turn back. I was five kilometers outside of Annecy when I did. A lightning strike hit the power line. Annecy lost electricity. The streets were dark. The rain blinded me. I stopped in front of the gallery. There was a shadow inside. A man."

He turns to Noah, sends a baleful glare. "You."

Noah dips his chin in acknowledgement.

"I ran inside, heedless of my own safety. Concerned for the art. I grappled with the man. It was dark. Black. He was soaked, his hair long and wet over his face. He shoved me aside. I ran after him, but he was gone. I never knew who it was...until today. When I saw you, rain-covered in the dark."

"What did he steal?" Camille asks.

Noah and Pierre stare at each other again.

Pierre scowls.

Noah lifts an eyebrow.

Finally, Pierre says, "I don't know."

At the same time, Noah says, "Nothing."

Wait. Nothing?

"Nothing," I say, just to be sure.

"Probably nothing," Pierre acknowledges. "My desk was opened. My papers spread out. I had surprised him in the act of—"

"Taking pictures," Noah says.

"For your movie?" Camille asks in a bright, excited voice.

Pierre turns to her, an expression of surprised betrayal on his face. "You're sympathetic to him?"

Camille widens her eyes and bats her lashes. "No. I am sympathetic to you in all things."

Wow.

Okay.

As much as I thought that wouldn't work, Camille has this stuff down, because Pierre is eating out of her hand.

"So that's what happened?" I ask Pierre, "You found Noah in your gallery, taking pictures of...what?"

Pierre frowns. "I don't know. There were many papers on my desk."

Okay. Fair enough. I turn to Noah, "But you know what you were taking pictures of."

He nods and smiles at me, a fond smile, one that you'd give someone that you love. I feel as warm from it as I do from the curling heat of the fire.

"I'd like to know," I say. "If you don't mind telling us?"

Pierre narrows his eyes, "Yes. I also would like to know. Why enter my gallery at night? Break the lock? Why—"

"Thomas Arnout is my father," Noah says.

At that Pierre stops. "Your father?"

Noah nods and pushes away from the counter, standing tall. "Thomas Arnout."

Pierre shakes his head. "That's impossible."

"No." Camille shakes her finger. "Impossible n'est pas français."

"But it is," he says. "It's impossible."

The fire crackles, snapping a log, sending out heat. Noah looks over at the stove at the noise, then back to Pierre.

He says in a low voice, "My mother, Yvette Dubois Wright, is the lady from his paintings. She is the woman on the tower. Before she"—he pauses, swallows, then says —"died."

I reach over and take his hand. He squeezes my fingers, then continues, "Before she died, she told me that Thomas Arnout was my father. She's the lady who jumped from the tower during the fire. I have been looking for Arnout for seven years. And you"—he levels a hard gaze on Pierre—"know where he is."

"You broke into Pierre's gallery to find your father?

And the lady?" Camille asks, with a how-romantic expression in her eyes. She turns on Pierre. "Do you know where Arnout is? You must tell him. Arnout is his father."

Pierre shakes his head, pulls his hand from Camille's and takes a step back. He recedes from the light of the fire. "No."

"You truly don't know where he is?" I ask, disappointed.

Pierre's gaze is covered in shadow when he says, "I mean, no, Arnout is not your father."

"You're so certain?" Noah asks.

"Yes," Pierre says. "Because whatever your mother said, it cannot be true."

Noah cocks his head, a frown marring his forehead.

"Why?" I ask.

"Because the lady," Pierre says, "was Helene Thierry. My mother and I lived here at the chateau with Thomas Arnout when I was a child. My mother is the lady. And my mother is long, long dead. Arnout did not leave me his work out of respect for my father, but out of love for my mother. There is nothing else. Whoever your mother was, she was not the lady. Whoever your father is, he is not Arnout."

47

HOW DO YOU TAKE THE NEWS THAT YOUR FATHER ISN'T WHO you thought he is?

Well, I suppose you take it the same way you did the first time. Seven years ago, Noah thought his dad was a nameless man who his mom spent one night with. His mom shattered that illusion when she told him his dad was Arnout. For years Noah searched for both his mom and his dad. And now it's all shattered again. Because Arnout isn't Noah's father. His dad is back to being that nameless, faceless man.

A bit like Noah right now, actually.

He leans against the stone wall of the tower room, his legs spread out, his face obscured by the heavy rain cloud darkness. It's early evening and the moon and stars are shut out by the storm.

I lay on the nest of blankets, the feathered comfiness softening the stone floor. My head is in Noah's lap, and as he stares silently at the narrow window, he absently strokes his fingers through my hair. His fingers are as warm as the kitchen fire, and I turn toward them, breathing in the smoky coffee smell that lingers on him.

A bolt of lightning illuminates the room, showing me that Noah's mouth is tight, his eyes weary, but thankfully, not defeated.

The clash of thunder follows, echoing like boulders thrown around our small tower room. I stretch my hands up and bury them in the warmth of where his clean, dry shirt meets his abdomen.

Before coming up to the tower room we changed into dry clothes. Shivering, I even put on a cashmere sweater over a long dress. We padded up the steps, me in socks, Noah in jeans, a t-shirt, and bare feet. He's always hot, even in a chilly downpour in a damp stone room.

He hadn't necessarily wanted to come up here. After Pierre and Camille left I don't know that he wanted to do anything. He just stood in the kitchen, staring at the old iron stove crackling with heat, a bleak expression on his face that made my heart ache and made me want to do something, anything to chase that wounded look away.

So I took his hand, told him we weren't going to waste the picnic basket we'd prepared. I told him everything always looked better on a full stomach, and then I pulled him up the stairs.

He didn't protest.

He didn't really say much of anything. Not when we changed and not when we sat down on the floor and I somehow ended up cradled in his lap.

Another bolt of lightning illuminates the room in an electric white, and when it does, Noah looks down at me, his blue eyes reflecting the sparking light. Before the room shifts to black I catch the flicker of a rueful smile on his lips.

"Seven years," he says his voice as gray as the walls.

"Seven years?" I ask, shifting on his lap, looking up at his shadowed face.

"Searching for a lie."

His hand stills in my hair and he lets out a long breath. "Where is she? Where did she go?"

His mom.

If Arnout isn't his father, if his mom didn't go to him, then where did she go?

"Perhaps Pierre is wrong," I venture. "Maybe after he and his mom went back to his dad, then your mom came. Pierre was a kid back then, he can't know everything."

Noah makes a sound, unconvinced. Then he strokes his fingers over my temple, down my jaw, as light as misting rain.

"No. You heard what he said, you were there too."

I did.

Pierre told how his dad had discovered Thomas Arnout and then introduced his work to the world. When Pierre was four, his mom and dad separated. With the divorce papers drawn, Helene started a relationship with Arnout. She and Pierre lived at the chateau with Arnout for nearly a year. Then Pierre caught viral meningitis, and overwhelmed by the illness, by the fragility of life, Pierre's parents reunited.

A year later, the fire ravaged Arnout's work and left him broken. No one had ever seen a woman living there after Helene. There was no lady but Helene. She died a few years later. Then when Pierre was eighteen his father passed. Shortly after, Arnout retired, leaving all of his work to the gallery. Pierre said he, his mother and his father were the only family that Arnout had ever had. There was no one else.

I'm sorry, he'd said, *but the lady is not your mother. Arnout is not your father.*

But do you know where he is? I'd asked. *If Noah could just ask him, just to be sure.*

No. I'm sorry, he'd said.

And that was that.

Even though Noah had told him his mother had flown to France years ago to be with Arnout, that she hadn't been seen since, still Pierre didn't know, couldn't say.

"Do you know what the worst of it is?" he asks.

I shake my head no, causing his hand to rub along my cheek. The steady drum of rain against the tower walls blends with his voice as he speaks.

"The worst isn't not finding my mom, I know she's gone. It's losing Arnout. At first I told myself I only wanted to find him because then I'd find out what happened to my mom. But over the years, that changed. It happened slowly, so slowly that I didn't know I'd built him up until it was too late. He was better than the astronaut dad, bigger than the royal, more real than that prisoner of war I'd dreamed about when I was little. Because he was my actual father. I've spent years building him up in my mind. Imagining what I'd say, what he'd say, making excuses for why he never tried to find me. I'd already forgiven him, because he was my dad. I wanted to believe that when I met him, he'd recognize me and tell me that he loved my mom and that he was proud I was his son."

Noah shifts beneath me and I move my hands over his arms, his legs, his chest, in comforting strokes.

He looks down at me and says, "It feels almost like he's died. Which in a way, I guess he has. Because the man I built up never actually existed."

I sit up then, and in the dark stone room, in the nest of blankets, with the pattering rain, I put my arms around Noah and hold him.

"I'm sorry," I whisper.

"It's okay," he says, sighing into my hair, his breath tickling my skin.

"It's not," I tell him, aching for him.

He takes my arms then, tugs me close so that when I look up, my face is only inches from his. His heart beats against my hand, as steady as the rain.

He looks down at me. "It is Merry. It's okay."

Another lightning strike slashes the sky, mimicking the current charging between us.

"Why?" I ask, leaning closer, our lips nearly touching.

Then even in the dark, I can see his smile. "Because I found what I was looking for. Remember?"

Love.

He found love.

"I remember," I whisper, and my voice is barely discernible over the rain.

His hands stroke over my arms and it's as if his fingers are infused with lightning bolts, everywhere he touches I light up, again and again.

"I'm going to let the past go," he says, his voice intense. "Will you join me?"

In letting the past go?

Gladly.

"Always," I tell him. "Wherever you go. I'll be there too."

He lets out a breath, as if he's been holding it in for years, and he's finally able to exhale.

His fingers brush my jaw, barely light on my lips, pull away. Then he says, "Will you let me make love to you?"

I smile and I feel that smile all over my whole body. "I thought you'd never ask."

48

AT MY WORDS NOAH TAKES MY MOUTH AND SENSATIONS pour over me, like the storm outside is echoing inside me. Rain, thunder, lightning. It's all there, captured in the moment Noah's mouth meets mine.

He makes a sound like the growling of thunder, then threads his hands through my hair, tugs me closer and devours me. Slow. Fast. Slow. No fast.

My hands are everywhere. Touching him. Taking him in. His skin is hot, smooth, except for the hair on his arms and the stubble over his jaw. He's hard, there are so many contours on him. The muscles of his shoulders, his biceps, the thickness of his forearms. I can't stop touching him.

Even while we kiss—as his hands slide down from my hair, work over my neck, down my shoulders, even while he's working magic with the way his hands drag over me, and all I want to do is lie back and beg him to do whatever he wants—even then I can't stop touching him. Because I have to touch him too.

He bites at my lip, sends his mouth over my jaw, to my neck. I throw my head back when he gently bites down on my bare skin. Then his hands push beneath my sweater, his calloused fingers rubbing over my shoulders.

At the touch of his hands on my bare skin, every thought vacates my mind except one. I need him to feel this much pleasure too. I need him to feel what he's doing to me.

I grab the fabric of his t-shirt, pull at it, and when he realizes what I'm doing, he lifts his arms and lets me tug the shirt free. I'm beginning to love lightning, because just as I pull the shirt free, another bolt illuminates the room, and I see the flat muscles, the hard planes, the trail of hair, the tattoo over Noah's heart.

I press my hands against his bare chest, reveling in the silkiness of his skin over hard muscle.

"Let me," Noah says.

He reaches forward, dipping his mouth to my neck as he pulls off my sweater. He pushes the soft fabric down my arms. The cold air rushes over me, leaving goosebumps.

My hands are still exploring his chest, so I feel the exact moment his heart picks up speed. And even with the rustling of clothes, the sound of rain and thunder, I can still hear his shaky exhale as he pushes the straps of my dress down and reveals my breasts.

"Beautiful," he breathes.

Then he brushes his hands over my nipples and they peak, hardening and tightening. I let out a soft noise, because every time he sends his fingers gently over my breasts, I can feel it *everywhere*.

My breath comes in sharp pants as he unclasps my bra, drops it next to my sweater and pushes my dress down over my hips. The look in his eyes...every time the sky lights up, I can see him, and what I see...it's a revelation.

"I used to think about this," I tell him, tugging at his jeans, running my hand under the fabric. "I'd wondered if you made love like you explored a new city."

He gives me a smile, his hands cupping my hips, slowly drawing my thong down my thighs. "Really?"

I swallow, my mouth suddenly dry at the look in his eyes. "I watched the episode where you explored Venice. Finding all the hideaways, the unexplored places, the forgotten treasures. You were so passionately..."

"Thorough," he says.

"Very thorough."

He grins as I kick my thong to the side. I'm bare before him. Wearing nothing except my earrings. The cold damp air drifts over me, making my nipples peak.

"Do you know what the problem with my show is?" he asks, kissing up my legs as he does.

"No." I hold onto his shoulders as he grips my hips.

He gently pushes me back to the feather comforter and the warm pile of blankets. Rubs his thumbs in circles over my hipbones.

"The problem is, they're always *Venice in a Day*, *Paris in a Day*, *Fiji in a Day*. I don't want a day to explore you. I want a lifetime."

As he says that, he sets his mouth to my clit and kisses.

I arch my back, cry out. His mouth sends a jolt through me, my blood electrifying. Another bolt of lightning shoots through the sky, a crash of thunder.

He sucks on me, sends his mouth over me, I arch into him, climb, climb, climb, my body is full of him, full of heat, so full of his love I can't contain it anymore. The storm inside me swells, and I come apart, I come apart in his arms.

It took three long kisses, the whisper of his stubble on my thighs, his mouth on my clit and his fingers at my entrance, and that's all. I was wound so high, so tight, that just his mouth pressing to me had me coming undone.

I thought the only way to make lightning was with a pie pan and a Styrofoam plate. I was wrong. All I need to make lightning is Noah's lips pressed to me, him breathing my name.

I grip his bare shoulders, arch against his mouth. I'm hanging on to him too tightly. I know there'll be bruises, but I can't let go. Wave after wave after wave leaves me mindless, needing him.

Finally I look at him watching me. There's a light in his eyes. I swipe at the tears falling like rain.

"Did you say you want a lifetime?" I ask, reaching out, pulling him up to me so I can feel the weight of him on me.

He rests his forearms over me, presses a knee between my legs. When he dips his head to me, his lips run over mine. "That's how long I'll need to learn everything there is about you. I want to know it all. Every part inside and out. And as you change, over the years, I want to be there to see that too."

I smile up at him with my heart in my eyes, there for him to see.

"Do you know, I think I'll need a lifetime too. If you don't mind? Maybe I'll write a book, just for me. I'll call it *Exploring Noah Wright for a Lifetime*. There'll be chapters."

"About what?" He smiles as I unbutton his jeans and push them down his legs.

"About what you like."

"You," he says, kicking off his jeans.

"Coffee," I say, pushing at his boxers. "Art. Travel. Crumbling chateaus. Gothic romances."

I can see the flash of his grin as another lightning bolt strikes, this time farther off. The storm is moving away, the lightning dimming. But that's okay. We're making our own lightning now.

"You," he says again.

Then I push his boxers down and free him.

My word.

I can't help it. I reach out. I have to touch him.

He sucks in a sharp breath when I wrap my hands around his hard length. His skin is velvet smooth, but there's such hardness there. Such strength.

I shouldn't be surprised, that's one of the things I love about him. His strength. He has so much strength.

But I can be strong too, can't I? He asked me if I'd leave the past behind. If I'd step into a lifetime with him. And even though the words haven't been said, I can say them first.

I can say them and not be afraid. Because my answer is yes.

"I love you," I tell him. "I love you."

He captures the final I love you with his mouth and then he captures my hands, holds them down over my head, and thrusts inside me.

"Say it again," he says, breaking our kiss.

"I love you," I say.

And then he thrusts again and I cry out at the feel of him inside me, at the heat, at the fullness, at the sparks that travel at lightning speed through me.

"I love you," I say again, and each time he thrusts I'm saying it.

I love you, I love you, I love you.

He pistons in and out of me, pulling me higher, higher, until we're high, high on the tower. He clasps my hands. Presses into me. The heat of his skin keeps me warm. His mouth gives me breath. His hands hold me, keep me on earth. Until I can't stay anymore. And I'm so high, there isn't anywhere to go but down.

The thrust of him, the deepness of him inside me, the friction of him against me, I can't hang on anymore. He makes a sharp noise, grips my hands more tightly and says against my mouth, "I love you too."

At that, I clutch his hands, and fall.

I'm falling, falling, falling, and he's falling with me.

Or are we flying?

I don't know. I only know we're doing it together.

"I love you," he says again, his voice deep and urgent. "I love you."

And when he's done loving me, we do it again.

Against the door. In the hall. In the bathroom. And finally, carrying the picnic basket of food down the steps, we make love in the bed.

49

THE SUN RUNS LIKE A STREAM OF WATER ACROSS THE BED, spraying light over my closed eyes.

I let out a soft sleepy moan and stretch my arms and legs, feeling the scrape of the sheets along my skin. It's warm in the bed, comfortable, and I was having the most wonderful dream. My skin is still flushed, my muscles tired and floaty, and I decide now is a good time to roll over and fall back asleep.

I bury my face in my feather pillow and pull in a long, happy breath. My pillow doesn't smell like lavender, like I expected, but coffee and firewood smoke and Noah.

Then there's a sleepy sigh from the other side of the bed. A rustling of the sheets.

I come fully awake.

And I realize for the second time in my life that I'm waking up naked in bed with Noah Wright.

The bed is toasty, deliciously warm. Now that I'm awake I can feel the sensation of him only inches away. If I stretch my legs or my arms, I'll touch him. The steady sound of his deep, still-sleeping breath is the loudest sound in the room.

I open my eyes and blink up at the ceiling, at the cracked plaster walls, the beam of light falling over us, and I smile. I smile and smile and smile. I don't think I've ever smiled so big in my life. My face feels as if it's going to break if I smile any bigger.

Me and Noah Wright.

Merry DeLuca and Noah Wright.

Okay, my face hasn't broken and I'm smiling even more.

Last time I woke up like this I snuck out of the room, praying to never see Noah again.

This time...

I turn and peer at Noah.

He's still asleep. He's a deep sleeper that one. Not much wakes him. Although, I have to say, he did expend a lot of energy last night. Never again will I wonder why he needs such large shoulder and bicep muscles.

Because...yes.

Anyway, this time, I'm not going anywhere.

I shift over the mattress, then burrow against him, tucking my head onto his shoulder. I didn't think he'd wake, but he lets out a soft sigh, turns his face down toward mine, and kisses me.

"You're not sneaking away this time?" he asks with a laugh in his voice.

Ha. So he's remembering the same thing I am.

I sniff. "I didn't sneak away last time. I walked out, at a normal volume and pace, with great dignity. You were just too passed out to notice."

He chuckles and the sound vibrates through me.

Certain parts of me that I thought were too tired to wake up this early perk up and take notice.

"I noticed," he says, dropping another kiss to my jaw. "I just kept my eyes closed. I figured if you were going to go to so much trouble to sneak out, I'd better not spoil it for you."

I scramble up and stare down at him. "You did not!"

He tilts an eyebrow and I realize that yes he did.

"Why didn't you say anything?" I frown at him.

"Did you want me to?"

I pause at that. "Well. No."

He grins, then, "I did try to call you, you know."

"My puce clutch?"

"It was a good excuse."

Oh.

He'd liked me from the very start. It only took me a little while to catch up.

He reaches up and strokes a bit of my hair, wavy and tangled from sleep, and smiles at me.

Suddenly, I feel self-conscious. I push my hair behind my ears and blink down at him, fighting between the urge to go wash my face and fix my hair, and the stronger urge to stay in bed with him for the rest of the morning.

"I'm glad Jupiter leased you her chateau. And I'm glad you were too stubborn to leave," I tell him.

"And I'm glad you decided to stay," he says, a warm light in his eyes.

I like the look he has. I recognize it now as the one that means I love you.

I brush my hand over the tattoo at his heart. In the light of morning, I finally have the opportunity to look closely. It's a landscape, as beautiful and detailed as any painting. It has waving green grass, a wide-limbed shade tree, a small, barely discernible stone cottage.

"What's this of?" I ask.

He looks down at my fingers stroking his chest. "It's nothing."

"No way! You have to tell me. I'm putting it in my Noah Wright guidebook."

Noah laughs. "Alright. Fine."

Then more seriously he says, "It's an ink drawing my mom had. She hung it in every house we ever lived in. She always told this story about it, she said that no matter where I was in the world, that if I kept the picture of that house with me, then I'd always be home. I got this tattoo after she disappeared. Since I travel so much"—he shrugs —"I didn't want to take the actual drawing with me."

My throat tightens at the look in his eyes.

"Home is where the heart is?" I ask, pressing my hand against his heart.

He smiles. "Exactly."

I bend down and press a kiss to his lips. "You have more capacity to love than any person I've ever known. That's one of the things I love about you, you know that?"

He grips me by the hips, his fingers pressing gently into my skin. "Merry? Are you saying you love me?"

"Didn't I tell you enough last night?" I ask, blinking down innocently at him.

"No. Not nearly enough," he growls.

So we take the morning, and I tell him some more.

50

THE FIRE CRACKLES IN THE IRON STOVE, WARMING THE kitchen. Noah's at the stove, shirtless, stirring our late breakfast of scrambled eggs. I'm sipping a cup of coffee, letting the warmth spread through me. I'm trying to decide if it's Noah's low-slung jeans and bare abs that are making me hungry, or the smell of butter, eggs, and toasting bread.

"What are you going to do now?" I ask.

"Buy a kitchen table and chairs," Noah says, smiling back at me as he taps the wooden spoon against the edge of the skillet.

I have to admit a table and chairs will be nice, but that's not what I meant.

"A wooden table," I agree as he turns back to the eggs and pulls the skillet from the stove. "But I actually meant, what are you going to do about Arnout? Didn't your latest project include him? Are you going to give that up?"

Noah slides the eggs onto the plates, next to the

toasted baguette. He concentrates on what he's doing, staying quiet, but I know he's thinking.

Finally he turns back and hands me my plate. "Bon appétit."

"Thank you." I smile at him and set my plate on the counter.

Noah leans next to me and watches the steam rise from the bright sunshine-yellow eggs. "No, I'm not giving up on my project. I'm going to finish my book. Finish research for the film. Then move on to the next project. Nothing changes."

He shrugs and then takes a bite of the eggs. Then after he swallows, he says, "Well, nothing except everything."

"Yeah." I nod and then reach for my breakfast.

I pile eggs on top of the toasted baguette and then take a bite. I close my eyes. The eggs are creamy, the baguette is toasted by the fire and buttered to perfection. Honestly I'm going to miss this horrible stove.

I open my eyes.

Miss it.

Right.

Because in a little while, both Noah and I will be leaving. And then what?

"So you're finished with your search for your mom?"

"I think it's time," he says. But he says it with so much buried sadness that my heart twists when I hear it.

"We could still—"

"I'm done chasing shadows and ghosts," he says with a small smile, but I can see the pain hidden behind that smile.

So I decide that even if Noah is done, I'm going to do what I can to help him. I just need to figure out how.

"You have got to be kidding." Noah drops his plate to the counter.

I look around the kitchen. "What? What is it?"

Noah points to the crack in the wall. "The lobster."

Louis?

He's still alive?

"We have to save him," I say, clutching Noah's arm.

"What do you mean *we*?" he asks, giving me a sidelong glance.

Ha.

"I don't know how he's still alive. I lost hope. I thought he would've dried out and died by now. If we catch him, we can make him a salt water tank and—"

"You want him as a pet?" Noah asks incredulously.

I bite my lip and nod, eyes wide. "Mhmm."

Noah raises his eyebrows. "You want to keep your dinner as a pet?"

"Please? If we work together, we can catch him."

He stares at me for a moment, and I see it when the sadness washes away and warmth replaces it.

"*If* we save him..." he says.

"Yes?"

"You owe me."

"Why would I owe you? You should be doing this because you love me. And"—I lift a finger in the air —"out of the goodness of your heart."

He laughs. "No. Nope. If we're keeping a lobster as a pet, you owe me."

My heart melts when he says the words *we* and *pet*.

It's almost like when a couple gets a dog together. When that happens they're together *together*.

"Okay," I agree. "I owe you. What's your payment?"

He gets a happy expression on his face. "A sunny day. The rock. You. Me."

"Done," I say hurriedly. "Done deal."

Now I probably want to catch Louis more than Noah does.

"How are we going to get him?" I ask.

"With cunning," Noah says, and I laugh at his male bravado. "And tenastic tenacity."

"I thought so."

He winks, and I decide that he looks really good with his abs on full display, sprinkling scrambled eggs on the stone floor.

Cunning is right.

It only takes five minutes for Louis to decide that eggs are better than starving to death. When his claws clack over the floor, Noah and I tense, prepared.

When Louis stops to inspect the eggs, I hiss, "Go. Go! Now!"

Noah throws a large kitchen towel over Louis, and I shriek as Louis tries to buck the towel off. He scrambles across the floor, the towel over him. He darts right and left and looks for all the world, like a raging banshee.

"Grab him!" I yell.

I have the cherry red cooler that I bring home groceries in open and ready to catch him.

I thrust the cooler forward and Noah, even though I've never known him to be religious, crosses himself, looks beseechingly at heaven, and then swoops down and grabs the lumpy, flaying tyrant known as Louis.

He shouts when Louis snaps at his hands through the towel and then shoves him at the cooler. Louis rolls out from the towel and hits the cooler with a loud crack. He springs up, his baleful eyes find me, and I swear I see recognition and the thirst for vengeance.

"I'm saving you!" I shout at him.

He snaps his claws at me.

And even when this darn lobster should be dried out and dead, he still has the gumption to charge the edge of the cooler.

"Shut the lid!" Noah says.

At the last second, I do.

Louis bashes the top.

I let out a squeak of alarm and drop the cooler to the counter.

"That is one crazy lobster," Noah says.

I let out a relieved laugh. "But he's our lobster."

Noah shakes his head and then grabs me, swings me toward him, and presses a kiss to my mouth. I melt against him.

"Worth it?" I ask.

"Worth it," he says.

We drive into Annecy, Louis in his cooler between us, me giving him fresh air every now and then. We're headed to the market, to find everything we need for our new pet.

When I told Noah that Louis would appreciate us someday, he just laughed.

But I think he will.

I also think Louis showed up when he did so I'd know that hope is never dead.

So when we pass onto the narrow streets of old town, and I see Pierre walking down the sidewalk, his hand in Camille's, I know exactly what I have to do.

51

FOR AS MUCH TIME AS I'VE SPENT WITH PIERRE, I'VE NEVER been to his gallery. When I step inside and the door swings shut behind me, the din of the street fades, and I'm enveloped by quiet.

All the honking horns, the jingling bicycles, the wind through the narrow stone streets, it all disappears and is replaced by a soft, subtle reverence.

I step further into the gallery. It's bigger than I imagined it would be. The ceilings are high, soaring at least twenty feet above, which for a stone building built hundreds of years ago is really something else. But the high white ceilings take my eyes skyward, and I feel lighter, elevated. Which I'm sure is the intent. It's as if, walking into this quiet, soaring space, you're primed to love the art you find inside.

The walls are white, and throughout the gallery, there are eight-foot-high and eight-foot-long freestanding walls positioned like stones in a river. This, I realize, is so that as you view the art, you have to slow down, meander, like water flowing around stones.

I take another step in and the wood floor creaks beneath my feet.

"Hello? Bonjour?" I call, not seeing anyone inside.

The desk near the front door is vacant. On the desk there is a bouquet of white roses, their petals curling, their scent teasing. They remind me of the roses Camille had in her bike's basket, and I wonder, does Pierre know she likes roses?

No one has answered, the gallery is muffled and quiet, like an empty church. Beautiful but empty.

I frown and walk toward the first freestanding wall. It holds three paintings. I look at the plaques beneath them and find they're all by Thomas Arnout. I'm swept away and swept along. I follow the path of the art and travel through a romantic vision of the world, in blues, and oranges, and reds. Through sunsets, and chateaus, and sleepy villages.

As I walk silently through the gallery, I feel as if I've been pulled into another life. Each painting I can dive into and live an entirely new life. One where I walk down the shaded grassy path, lean down to pick the purple lavender, breathe in its scent, then push open the wooden chateau door, left slightly ajar, and greet the person waiting there for me. That's how it is with every single painting. You step close and then tumble inside, and always, just out of reach, there is someone there, waiting.

I feel short of breath.

No wonder.

No wonder Noah spent nearly a decade looking for Arnout.

How could he not?

I've never seen paintings with so much love, so much longing. They're beautiful, but also terrible. Because you don't know, is there someone waiting or isn't there?

"This was always one of my favorites."

I startle, then look over at Pierre. I was so engrossed in the painting in front of me that I didn't notice him standing next to me. He's rumpled this morning, his hair finger combed, his eyes happily tired. His hands are in his pockets and he's staring at the painting in front of us.

"I didn't hear you," I say, smiling at him.

He looks over and smiles back. In that moment I see what we both always knew. We're friends, we were always meant to be friends, and we're both very happy with that.

He nods. "I'm happy you came by. I wanted to thank you."

"There's no need." I shake my head and wave it away.

"Camille says the lightning was your idea."

"Sort of." I smile. "Although I think it was more your idea."

He shrugs happily. "We're getting married."

"Really?"

My shoulders grow tense, because the last time someone told me they were getting married after only one night together, well, that was my sister. And that doesn't seem to be going smoothly.

Pierre watches my expression and I think he can tell exactly what I'm thinking because he says, "I kept waiting for lightning. I was blinded to what had been happening for years. My feelings for Camille grew like the tiny apple seeds she loves, unnoticeable at the beginning, but now, a tree. The roots are deep. She's stuck with me now."

He grins ruefully, and I see that I was wrong. Pierre and Camille are nothing like my sister and Leo.

"Good," I say. "I'm glad."

I turn back to the painting, it's nothing like the tattoo on Noah's chest, but somehow it still reminds me of it. There isn't longing in the cottage in the tattoo, instead there's peace. But still, there's something about that little cottage, that home, that fits with the paintings in this gallery.

I turn to Pierre and take the plunge. "I came here for a reason."

52

IT TOOK AN HOUR OF LOGICAL ARGUMENT, A VISIT FROM Camille, a packed lunch of raclette, bread, and wine, and more arguments. Nothing would sway Pierre. But I knew, absolutely knew that he was in contact with Arnout.

Me telling Pierre that Noah's middle name was Lepont didn't matter.

The story of Noah's mom didn't budge him.

What finally did sway him was me taking a napkin from our lunch, a pen from the desk and drawing the cottage from Noah's tattoo.

"Do you know this place?" I'd asked.

Five minutes later I was on the back of Pierre's motorcycle, heading to the chateau. Noah was there, working in the gatehouse, with a somewhat mollified, salt-water-immersed Louis.

When I burst into the gatehouse, Pierre on my heels, Noah looked up, his brows drawn.

"What is it?" he'd asked.

Please let this work out, please let this turn out okay, I prayed. Then I said, with as much confidence as I could muster, "We're going to see Arnout."

53

THE COTTAGE IS EXACTLY LIKE THE DRAWING. IT HAS A whitewashed stone base. The entrance is a small rustic wooden door surrounded by bright orange marigolds. Above the stone, dark wooden logs make up the main part of the cottage. There are tiny square windows, and the logs reach up to a peaked roof. One side of the cottage is covered in ivy, and little blue flowers spot the green.

If I were to imagine a tiny, magical French cottage, this would be it.

Like I said, it's the same as the cottage in Noah's tattoo. Except for one thing. Behind the cottage there's a garden. A huge garden, at least five acres of flowers, grasses, fruit trees, an Eden bursting with color. In the drawing the cottage sat alone. Now I see that it's never been alone, it's in the middle of a paradise.

The air is fresh and brisk. We're higher up in altitude, having climbed the twisty roads for thirty minutes before arriving here. I can smell the flowers and the growing fruit, mixed with the wood smoke from the chimney. It's a happy, homey smell.

Noah steps beside me, his eyes taking everything in.

There's no doubt that this is the home his mom kept with her all those years.

As soon as I showed the drawing to Pierre he knew. This is the cottage where Arnout grew up. It is his family home. The place he came after he "disappeared." He never painted it and never drew it, at least that's what Pierre believed until I drew it for him.

The only thing left to do is discover the truth. If Thomas Arnout can tell us that.

In the shade of a pear tree, Thomas Arnout sits on a wooden chair, behind an easel.

Painting.

"He has good days and bad days," Pierre says, stepping beside us.

Noah nods, but doesn't say anything, his eyes on Arnout.

"I'll go tell him you're here," he says.

"Thank you," Noah says.

We stay near the house as Pierre strides through the garden to speak with Arnout.

"Are you sure you want me to come with you?" I ask.

"I'm sure." Noah squeezes my hand.

Arnout is a small figure, and what surprises me is that he's probably shorter than me. In my mind I always pictured him as a giant. Large to match his reputation. But instead he's a small man, his shoulders stooped with age. The largest part of him has to be his white hair, wildly sticking out at all angles from beneath his brown felt hat. Other than his hair though, he's tidy. He has on a pair of brown pants, a buttoned shirt, and a dark coat.

"I pictured him taller," I say to Noah, looking up. Noah's well over six feet. If Arnout is his father, he didn't inherit his stature from him. "Did you?"

Noah shakes his head. His eyes intent on the conversation currently taking place between Arnout and Pierre. It's quite animated. Pierre gestures toward us. Arnout takes his hand. Pierre shakes his head. Arnout shakes a finger at him.

"What do you think he's saying?" I ask.

Noah smiles. "We'll find out."

And sooner rather than later.

Pierre strides back toward us, an unreadable expression on his face. "He says he'll meet you."

A lump the size of a pear lodges in my throat. When I glance at Noah he seems calm.

He nods and says, "Thank you."

"I'll be in the cottage. Speaking with his nurse."

At that Pierre leaves us and all that's left is to walk the thirty feet to Arnout.

"I've imagined this for years," Noah says. "Now that it's here, it's hard to take the final steps."

I understand.

"That's why I'm here," I tell him, squeezing his hand.

He smiles at me and then says, "You're right. It's not so hard anymore if I look at it that way."

Then I wrap my arms around him and we walk across the lily-scented garden. And I wonder, when I walked down the aisle at my sister's wedding, was Noah there to help me take those final steps? Looking back on it, I think so. No. I know so.

"I'm not sure if this is a beginning or an end," Noah says, looking down at me.

"Both," I say.

Then we're coming to a stop, underneath the shade of the pear tree.

I let go of Noah's arm and he takes the final steps forward without me. He holds out his hand and says, in a firm voice, "Bonjour. Je m'appelle Noah Lepont Wright. I've wanted to meet you for a very long time."

54

"Thomas Arnout," the man says, taking Noah's palm with his left hand. His voice is rusty, like a wheelbarrow's squeaky wheel.

His eyes, I notice, are the same blue as Noah's, only a shade lighter, more washed out and faded.

I'm watching Noah, so I see his reaction to the painting before I see the painting. He stiffens, drops Arnout's hand, and takes a quick step forward. He lifts his hand, lets it hang in the air and then quickly turns back to Arnout, a stunned expression on his face.

"Aimez-vous—" Arnout begins.

But Noah steps forward and says, "Ma mère."

And although I'm not sure, I can guess what he said.

Because the painting that Arnout is working on is of a woman. She looks like Noah, the same long eyelashes and high cheekbones, the same rich black hair. The only difference is that she has laughing brown eyes instead of earnest blue. They even have the same square jaw. On Noah this feature is masculine beauty, on her, it's not the typical beauty. I'd say it's regal. And stubborn. In the painting she looks happy, but stubborn.

"Is that your mom?" I ask.

Noah turns back to me and I don't think he realizes it, but there are tears in his eyes. He nods. "It is. It's how she looked the last time I saw her."

I look more closely at the painting, and now I see that there are fine lines around her eyes and on her forehead, and threaded in her hair are light streaks of gray.

But if Arnout knows what Noah's mom looked like seven years ago, then he's seen Noah's mom.

"Impossible," Arnout says, his voice scratchy, disbelief etched on his face. "Impossible."

Ah. I know this word. And I know exactly what to say in response. "Impossible n'est pas français!"

Noah flashes me a quick smile and reaches out to take my hand.

Arnout's left hand begins to shake. I notice his knuckles are slightly swollen and he has age spots on his skin. Slowly he tugs a handkerchief from his pocket and then takes off his glasses. Lodging the glasses between his knees, with one hand he wipes them clean. When he sets them back on his nose and takes another look at Noah, he lets out a ragged breath.

I don't blame him. Noah is the spitting image of his mom.

Maybe he thought by cleaning his glasses he'd see something different. That didn't happen. The truth is there for anyone to see.

Arnout speaks then, in creaky, rapid-fire French, his hands still trembling, his eyes wide and blinking up at Noah.

"Yvette Dubois Wright," Noah says.

Arnout's hand flutters over his chest and he whispers, "La vache!"

"What's he saying?" I ask.

"He asked my mom's name, then when I told him, he said, well I guess it means, damn, or holy cow."

Noah says something back in French and Arnout nods. Then Arnout begins speaking again, his voice shaky.

And as Arnout talks, leaning forward, his eyes on Noah as if he's drinking him in, Noah translates, his voice running in time with Arnout's.

"He says," Noah begins, "that he met my mother nearly thirty years ago, in Paris. That she was the most beautiful woman he'd ever seen. He said she was visiting from Saint Martin and was supposed to fly home the next day. He doesn't know how, but somehow he convinced her to stay with him. And much to his wonder and delight, he kept convincing her for six months."

Arnout pauses. He waits until Noah finishes and then begins to speak again.

There is a brown bird on the pear tree above him, singing a piping song. It sounds a bit like a love song.

Noah leans closer to me and says in a quiet voice, "He loved my mother. More than anyone in his life. He says... more than life itself."

Arnout nods and hits his hand against his chest.

"Then why didn't he go after her?" I ask. "When your mom left?"

Noah asks him my question.

And Arnout looks back at the painting, and suddenly, the wrinkles on his face seem deeper and the weight on his shoulders seems heavier. He says something in a mournful voice.

"Because his pride stopped him. He thought my mom was right. That his work was worth much more than his love. When she left he didn't try to stop her. When she never came back he didn't try to find her. Until..."

"What?" I ask.

Noah flattens his mouth. His expression goes blank and if I wasn't holding his hand I wouldn't be able to feel the tension in him.

I can hear something in Arnout's voice, and no matter what language it is, you can always hear the sound of sorrow and apology.

"He says—" Noah's voice breaks. Then he shakes his head. He clears his throat and begins again.

"He had a stroke eight years ago. He nearly died. He lost vision in his right eye. There were other effects on his health. After that, he decided to retire. To leave the art world—no, the outside world—completely. He realized that his whole life he had created paintings. Painting after painting. And for what? Every painting was a letter to my mother, asking her to come back. But he'd never written it in words. So he did. He didn't know where she was or how to find her, so he left a postscript in his letter with Pierre. He hoped that when it was published in the papers, that she would see it and come."

I rub my thumb over the back of Noah's hand, as soft as the pear-scented breeze flowing over us, hoping to give him a modicum of strength. Or comfort.

"What about the letter your mom sent? The one where she told him about you and he painted the bridge? She said he knew about you."

Noah nods and then asks this in French.

Arnout's eyes cloud and he frowns, then shakes his head, answering.

"He says he never received a letter. He painted the bridge because it was where he and my mom first realized they loved each other. After that, he always called her his bridge. He never knew..."

"He didn't know about you?" I ask.

Noah shakes his head. "He didn't know about me."

I know Noah loves his mom, but right now, seeing the look on his face, I'd like to go back in time and have a sit down chat with her. Tell her to consider something besides Arnout's art. Except, knowing Jupiter, I can imagine what she'd say. A person's love only lasts a lifetime, but the love found in art lasts centuries. The sacrifice is worth it, she'd say.

Looking at Arnout's faded blue eyes and shaking hand, I'm not certain he agrees. Sure, once he did. He already admitted that. But now, with a lifetime behind him? At the end of your life, it's not what you did that makes you happy, it's who you loved and who loved you.

Why else would Arnout be sitting here, alone in his garden, painting the memory of the woman he loved most?

Arnout is speaking again, and I know it's painful, because his gaze is beseeching and his voice is shaky.

After a moment, Noah says quietly, "Seven years ago, shortly after he moved here, my mom answered his letter. She came here." Noah's voice is thick. "He was so happy to see her. It was his Yvette, finally home. To the cottage where he'd promised he'd escape with her. Where they were supposed to be married and raise a family. It was decades too late. But she came."

I let out a long breath and wrap my hand around his arm. "You don't have to keep telling me what he says if it hurts."

I can hear the pain in Noah's voice and it's breaking my heart. A cloud passes over the sun and the shade we're standing in grows even darker. The little bird stops singing and takes flight, leaving us behind.

"It's okay." Noah shakes his head. Arnout is speaking, and Noah continues, "After my mom came, he realized something was wrong."

Arnout's face is serious, thickly lined, and the shadow passes over him. His white hair, sticking out from under his hat, seems less full of life and more full of sorrow.

"She was cut. Bruised. He thinks she was robbed. She had no passport. No money. No purse. No suitcase."

Arnout says something and his hand cuts through the air.

Noah nods in agreement and says something in response. Then Noah says, "She wasn't coherent. She wasn't...lucid. She couldn't tell him what had happened, where she'd come from. He knew her. She was Yvette Dubois. But beyond that..."

He trails off, Arnout is watching him, a mournful expression on his face.

"He took her to the hospital. She died the next day."

Noah drops his head when he says this and keeps his gaze on the ground, on the blades of grass that are bowing gently in the wind.

"I'm sorry," I whisper, my words carried away on the wind.

Arnout speaks again and I look at him watching Noah.

"He says she is buried in a cemetery nearby. She was buried as Yvette Dubois. That's the name he knew her by. He didn't know that she had moved to the U.S. He didn't know she had a son. He didn't know he had a son."

Noah bows his head. He doesn't say any more.

Arnout struggles to stand, pushes up from his chair, but then, unable to rise, he falls back. He holds out his hand and says in a voice thick with emotion, "Mon fils."

Noah looks at him, his eyes full of a lifetime of longing, a decade of wondering, years of searching finally at their end.

"He said, my son," Noah says.

Then he drops my hand and steps forward. Arnout lets out an anguished sound and then Noah drops down before him, kneeling so that Arnout can reach out and put his hand to his face.

"Je suis navré de vous avoir fait de la peine," Arnout whispers.

Noah lets out a shuddering breath and shakes his head. "Don't be sorry," he says raggedly. He reaches for his father's hand. Takes it. "There's no need to be sorry."

As the sun comes out from behind the cloud, spilling light over Noah and his dad, I take a step back, then another, until finally I'm at the edge of the garden.

I don't think Noah needs me there anymore.

He's found what he was looking for.

55

"ARE YOU ALRIGHT?" I ASK NOAH.

It's late afternoon, the sky is a deep clear blue, like the blue you see on porcelain, and the air is tinged with that particular late afternoon smell that I love.

We're back at the chateau, the shadows from the towers stretch across the grass, and the breeze off the lake is cool and crisp.

The rumble of Pierre's motorcycle fades as he drives back to town and to Camille.

Pierre asked if Noah wanted to see his mom, but Noah said he'd rather visit her on his own. He didn't say much on the drive back and Pierre didn't prod.

But before he left us he reached out, rested his hand on Noah's arm, and said, "I'm sorry. It appears I do not know everything. Thomas always said that I have been a son to him. Now I see he has two sons."

Noah gave Pierre a firm nod and accepted his apology and his overture of friendship. I could see the misconceptions falling away for both of them. Pierre once thought Noah was a thief. Noah once thought Pierre was a liar and a cheat. Now they both see that neither was true, that they both wanted the same thing. To love and protect Thomas Arnout.

The sound of Pierre's motorcycle is replaced with the rustling of wind through tree leaves. Noah turns back to me, his blue eyes depthless as the lake below. I'd read that Lake Annecy was hundreds of feet deep in some places, and I wondered, how long would it take to reach the bottom? I have the same question now. How long will it take to find out everything inside Noah Wright?

A lifetime, I think.

"Are you?" I ask again, reaching for his hand.

He lets me thread my fingers through his. Then we walk along the path that meanders around the chateau toward the cliffside.

"I will be," he says. "For years I've painted a thousand scenarios of what could've happened. I stopped watching true crime or reading the more gruesome news stories because I didn't want to think about what might've been. Now I know, she didn't meet a horrible end. She made it to Arnout."

He gives me a sad smile that has my heart twisting. "I think she didn't realize how little time she had left. I don't believe she meant to never say goodbye."

I don't think so either. She left, but I imagine she thought she still had a month or two or six. I don't think she would've realized that in a few days, she'd be gone, her mind and her soul.

The smile fades from Noah's face and he looks out, toward the lake, and the smudges of color that make up Annecy in the distance.

"I feel as if I've spent the last seven years in the dark,

with a thousand nightmares, and only a sliver of light to hang on to. I've been searching in the dark so long."

He shakes his head and we come to a stop at the flat rocks overlooking the cliff. "But now I know my mom is okay. I knew she was gone. But now I know, she's gone and she's okay. And Arnout..." He shrugs. "It seems that Anteros had his way."

I scrunch my nose and frown. "The statue?"

"He wants to get to know me and I want to get to know him. It's good." He nods, then says again, "It's good."

"It's good" can't begin to describe the emotion in his voice, or the years of longing, but I agree, it's good.

"It is good," I say.

The edge of Noah's mouth lifts. "When I first saw you, you were the first bright thing I'd seen in years. You were the beginning of the end for me."

"Were you in unrequited love with me?"

He laughs. "No. I was just in love with you. I knew you'd love me back sooner or later."

I laugh and clasp his hand as we look over the cliffside.

"Are you certain you're going to be alright?" I finally ask.

"I don't know," he says in a serious tone.

I look over at him quickly, concerned.

"The only way I can be absolutely certain is if we..." He nods at the sun-warmed rock beneath our feet.

"Really?" I say incredulously, a hint of a smile on my lips. "That will make everything better?"

"It's worth a shot."

He reaches out and tucks a strand of hair that's

blowing in the breeze behind my ear. "You're wearing your earrings."

"I am." I reach up and thread my arms around his shoulders.

He puts his hands to my hips and brushes his mouth over my lips.

"What if this doesn't work? What if it still isn't better?" I ask.

He smiles against my mouth. "Then we'll just have to keep trying."

"For how long?"

A light enters his eyes. "For as long as it takes."

And then, my dress is off, I'm naked except for my earrings, and Noah is making love to me on the flat of the rock. The warm stone scrapes my back, but I can't be bothered to care, because I'm telling Noah I love him, and he's telling me, and everything is better.

Better than good.

I was right, he makes love slow, he makes love fast, he makes love like he's a passionate explorer and my body is a new land.

Which is why neither of us notice the taxi pull into the drive, not until the door slams and Angela steps out.

56

LET'S JUST SAY THAT WE ARE VERY LUCKY THAT THE chateau is so awe-inspiring and *distracting*. In the fifteen seconds it takes to scramble into my dress and shove my shoes on, Angela hasn't looked our way. Her mouth is slack, her expression stunned as she stares at the arched door, the climbing towers with their red roofs, and the fairy-tale beauty of it all.

Really, I can't blame her. I probably looked just as awestruck when I arrived. Except, I was meant to be here. I was expected.

"Why is your sister here?" Noah asks, tugging his shirt over his head. His hair sticks up adorably and I quickly stand on my toes and smooth it down.

"I'm not sure," I say.

Then my heart stutters. Has something happened? Is the baby okay? Has she left Leo?

"Is Leo..." I peer at the taxi, still idling in the drive, but I don't see any other passengers.

I look back at Noah, he's paused in the act of smoothing his shirt, a strange look on his face.

"What is it?" I ask.

Did Leo contact him? Does he know something is wrong?

Noah shakes his head. "Nothing. I'd just forgotten you and Leo—"

"Were friends," I say. "And if we hadn't been, I would never have met you."

He smiles at me, his eyes warm. "Exactly. And I'll be forever grateful for that."

We stand for a second, just grinning at each other, but then I jerk my head at Angela and say, "I'm going to catch up to her."

The taxi's still idling, the driver watches my sister pick her way across the drive, toward the imposing front entrance. It's unlocked and leads into the (still empty and sort of dark) great hall.

I wonder if the driver is as overprotective of Angela as mine was when I first arrived.

"Go," Noah says. "I'll be right behind you."

So I run across the lawn, hurrying across the soft grass, up the drive to the stone steps where Angela is knocking on the door.

She's using the side of her fist, thumping at the wood. In a quick second I take her in. She looks tired, her hair's messy, her clothing wrinkled, and she's definitely jetlagged.

I smile when I think about how cool cucumber slices over her eyes will fix her right up.

"Hey!" I say. "What are you doing here?"

Angela spins around, her hand flying to her chest.

"Merry. Thank goodness!" she says.

Her cheeks are red and her eyes are bloodshot. "Why haven't you returned my calls? It's been days!"

I look at her worried expression and shake my head. "I...I forgot to charge my phone?"

It's up in my suitcase, where I tossed it two days ago when the battery died. A lot has happened since then, I hadn't really thought about it. "I didn't think it was a big deal. It's only two days."

"Two days," Angela reiterates. "Forty-eight hours."

"Yes?" I say slowly. I feel like I'm missing something.

Then Angela's eyes catch on something over my shoulder.

Okay. So, my sister is one of the most beautiful people I've ever known. She just is. But when she's disapproving, she gets this pinched mouth, nostril flaring, splotchy-faced look, and it's not pretty. It's just not. She has that look right now.

So I don't know what she's staring at, but I know she disapproves. Quite strongly actually.

I look back over my shoulder and frown. It's Noah. He lifts up his hand in a wave and I wave back, throwing him a smile.

"I need you to come with me," Angela says in a measured voice.

"What?"

Angela grabs my wrist, "I need you to come. The taxi's waiting."

"You need me?" I tilt my head, looking her over. Honestly she doesn't look good.

"What's wrong?"

"I'll explain in the cab," she says.

Okay, I'm officially worried. "Let me just grab my purse and tell Noah."

Angela's mouth flattens. "Hurry."

Jeez.

I run back to Noah. "Something's up with Angela. I'm going to go with her and talk."

He frowns and looks at her standing stiffly on the steps, her arms wrapped around herself.

"Is she okay?"

I shake my head. "I don't know."

"Don't worry," he says, running a comforting hand over my arm. "I'm here. I have some things I need to do. Do what you need. Take your time. Let me know if you need anything."

I smile at him, love growing in my chest. Then I stand on my toes and kiss him. He looks sort of dazed when I drop back down.

"See you later." I smile at him.

Then before he can respond I run to grab my purse and join Angela in the taxi.

When I slide into the air-conditioned, leather-scented interior, Angela breathes what sounds like a sigh of relief.

Then she says to the driver in a no-nonsense voice, "Back to the airport please."

57

"WHAT? WHY?!" I LOOK WILDLY AROUND THE BACKSEAT OF the taxi, as if the black leather seats, the vinyl seatbelts, or the polka dot carry-on luggage at Angela's feet is going to tell me anything.

The cold dry air from the air-conditioning blows pine air-freshener over us. It's horribly fake compared to the wooded alpine scent I've grown used to.

"Because," Angela hisses, throwing a concerned look at the driver, then lowers her voice even more. "I told you Noah was a murderer and then you disappear. I thought you were dead!"

"Dead?" I cry loudly. The driver turns back and gives me a concerned look.

"Watch the road," Angela snaps.

He turns back to the curving mountain road and mutters under his breath. He's bald, but the back of his neck is covered in curling brown hair, which does nothing to hide the red flush that comes up after Angela snaps at him.

"That was rude," I tell her, then I lean forward and say to the driver, "Can you please go to Annecy? To a hotel in old town?"

"Annecy?" he asks, glancing at me in the mirror.

"Yes," then I add, "merci."

"No." Angela grips my hand, "We are leaving. I tell you that the man you are staying with is a psychopath and what do you do? You kiss him."

My cheeks grow hot and Angela's eyes widen. "Oh no. You didn't just kiss him. You...you..." Her mouth works, but no more sound comes out.

I decide to finish the sentence for her. "I love him."

She gives me a mournful look. "No. We're going to the airport. You have to leave France now. Thank goodness I got here in time. Another day and you probably never would have been heard from again. I can't believe you're so naïve as to—"

"No," I say, my voice firm.

Angela gives me a startled glance.

"No. I'm not leaving. That's enough," I say.

Then I lean closer, and in a softer voice say, "Noah is a good person. He didn't do anything wrong and I want you to stop saying he did."

Angela's eyes widen. "Oh no. All the French cheese and wine has cooked your brain."

I shake my head and take a moment to look at my sister. Really look at her. She's in a pink and blue striped dress. It's tight, so you can see that she already has a slight baby bump. Her hair is messy and her dress is wrinkled, she has purple bags under her eyes, and she looks...sad.

Under the worry and bravado and ridiculous rescue attempt, she looks really, really sad.

I reach out and take her hands between mine.

"What happened?" I ask her in a soft voice. "Is something wrong with Leo?"

At that, her face pales, her lips wobble, and tears trickle out of her eyes. Soon her mascara is running and her nose is red. She wipes at her tears.

"I'm only crying because of the hormones," she says, with a hitch in her voice.

I pull a tissue from my purse and hand it to her.

"Of course," I say as she noisily blows her nose.

"He says he made a mistake," she says into the tissue, her voice muffled.

I grip Angela's hand and she gives a small hiccupping sob.

"I'm sure he didn't mean it," I say soothingly, although, remembering how Angela was treating him, it's entirely possible that he did.

She looks at me with watery, hopeful eyes. "Do you think?"

Okay. I can't lie to her.

I shake my head. "I don't know. I'm sorry. I don't know what he's thinking."

Come to think of it, I never did. I lift a shoulder. "I mean, you told me yourself that you'd be surprised if your marriage survived this pregnancy. I don't know what things were like."

She sniffs loudly. "They were terrible."

In the front of the car, the driver grunts and then thrusts a box of tissues toward Angela.

"Don't cry," he says gruffly, his neck an even brighter red.

Poor guy.

"Merci," I tell him, handing the box to Angela.

She ignores it. "Things were terrible, Merry," she says again. "But they were also the best, the very, very best. I've never been so happy."

She wraps her arms around herself and says, "I love him."

I nod, pull a tissue from the box, and dab at the running mascara on her cheeks. "I know you do."

"But he said he thought he might have made a mistake proposing so fast. So I yelled, 'You think our marriage was a mistake?!' and then he just stood there and didn't say anything. Then I left him. Right then. I went right to the airport and flew here." She scowls at me, pushing the tissue away. "It's these hormones, Merry. They're making me a crazy person."

I wince. "I can't really argue with that," I tell her, thinking about her trying to rescue me from Noah.

She scoffs and shoves at me. Then the animation in her face fades, and she looks tired and sad again. "What do I do? How do I fix this?"

I frown and watch the flash of the sun through the trees as the road curves down the hills toward Annecy. What should she do?

"I'd start by apologizing," I tell her.

She sucks in a quick breath. "He's the one—"

"What do you care about more?" I interrupt, "Your pride or Leo?"

She drops her chin and stares down at her hands, now clenched in her lap.

"My pride," she mutters, then she looks up at me with a watery smile. "Kidding."

I sigh and then smile at her ruefully. The two of us, we really did have a terrible example of how to love. *Love is a battle* and all that. Or love is disposable. It wasn't the best thing to learn. But that doesn't mean we can't learn something new.

"Can I be honest?" I ask her, a little nervous.

"Will I like what you have to say?" she says with a sidelong glance.

"Probably not."

She sighs. "Alright then. Go ahead."

I tear at the tissue in my hand, pulling it apart. "Ever since you were little, you've had a terrible habit of wanting things and then...unwanting them."

I look up at her. Her forehead is wrinkled and her eyes are watery. I crumple the tissue in my hand. "Sometimes it seems like people are things to you and things are easily discarded. When you unwant a person, though, you can't just throw them into the bin. They're a person. It hurts."

Angela stares off to the side, looking at the buildings of Annecy getting closer. I don't know that she sees them though.

She nods, and without looking at me she says, "I can see how I might come off that way."

"But?" I ask, because I can hear the argument in her voice.

She turns back to me, takes my hand. "But I'm scared. Merry, I don't want to be unwanted first."

Ah.

I see.

"Go back to Leo," I say. "Tell him you're sorry. Tell him you love him. Tell him what you just told me."

Angela smiles, that angelic smile that had all the cashiers giving her free candy when we were kids, and she leans over and hugs me.

I'm wrapped up in her, in the warmth of her, and the

solidarity we have. She may not be perfect, but she's my sister and I love her.

When she pulls back she says, "So you're telling me that Noah Wright is actually a good guy?"

She's smiling at me, and I know that the crisis has passed. "He is. He's the kindest, most wonderful, most passionate person I've ever known."

A gleam enters Angela's eyes and I pull in a sharp breath. I know that look. It's the red bike look. She wants to red bike Noah.

I shake my head, ready to tell her that she already has a husband, but then just as quickly as the gleam came into her eyes, it's gone. She settles back in her seat.

"I'm glad for you, Merry. You deserve to be happy. But I have to argue, I think Leo is the kindest, most wonderful man in the world."

I lean back in my seat and smile back. "Good. That's the way it should be."

The taxi rattles as we pull onto a cobblestone street in old town. There's a cheery goldenrod yellow inn across the street, with bright red flowers and a red door. It's perfect.

"Why can't I stay with you?" Angela asks, peering at the inn.

"There aren't any beds. And"—I wince—"there are rats."

"Rats?!"

I nod. "And bats. And cockroaches. And there isn't electricity. Or a shower."

As I tick the list off Angela's eyes grow wider and wider. "Merry? *Why* are you staying there?"

Why?

I smile a little and tell her, "Honestly. The benefits far outweigh the detriments."

"Not for me," she says. Which is true, Angela loves thirty minute showers, blow drying her hair, and king-size beds with silk sheets.

"This inn looks nice. You can rest"—I squeeze her hand—"and then you can go home to Leo."

After getting Angela settled in and agreeing to meet for breakfast tomorrow, I walk down the street and try to find another taxi.

I'm ready, beyond ready to go back to Noah, and maybe cuddle and watch one of those gothic romance movies he keeps talking about.

But as the street I'm on spills out onto a promenade, I see that I'm at the water, and there's le Pont des Amours, the bridge of love. But this time, instead of Noah standing on the bridge, it's Leo.

58

LEO ENVELOPS ME IN A HUG. HE PICKS ME UP WITH A JOYFUL laugh and spins me around. I laugh as the dusky sky and the glowing lamps reflecting like stars glinting in the water swirl around me in a dizzy rush.

I'm so happy he's here. He must've hopped on a plane right after Angela. See. There's no doubt. He loves her.

He's slowing, and his happy spin peters out like a top tilting on its final turn. He grins at me, holding me in a hug.

I thump his shoulder. "Hi. Nice to see you. Now put me down."

"Hi Merry," he says, dropping me to the ground.

I can see right away— even though it's getting dark— that Leo has had it rough. If I thought Angela looked bad, Leo looks a thousand times worse. His hair is longer, shaggier, as if he hasn't had the time or energy to cut it. His forehead has worry lines that weren't there before. His eyes are shadowed and there's a bit of a desperate edge in the way he's looking at me.

Poor Leo.

I haven't seen him since he and Angela told me they were pregnant. Back then he was still the carefree, on-top-of-the-world Leo I always loved. Now, well, first of all, I don't love him anymore. So I can look back and see the things I missed. For instance, the carefree nature I liked, maybe it wasn't so much carefree as a disregard for hard truths he didn't want to acknowledge. And that on-top-of-the-world? Maybe there's a tiny touch of arrogance. Seeing him here, in front of me, it all hits me, quite suddenly, like a hard knock on the head.

Leo had faults. Leo wasn't perfect. Leo wasn't always kind. He didn't always do what was right.

But he was my friend.

And now he's my brother-in-law.

So secondly, I can look at him with a realistic view and want the best for him, which means sending him up to the inn, to Angela.

He has faults, but he also tries his best.

I smile at him, fondness filling me. He really does look awful. I imagine he's had a rough go of it. Maybe he and Angela should stay in France for a few days and— as Angela put it— let the wine and cheese muddle their brains.

"You got here just in time," I say, nodding back toward the street that leads to the inn. "It's perfect that you came. Absolutely perfect. I'm so glad you're here."

I grin at him and when I do, Leo steps closer, a strange expression on his face.

"How did you know I'd be here?" he asks.

"I didn't. I just saw you when I was walking. It was fate!"

I smile to myself, I can imagine Noah claiming it's Anteros at work again. Bringing lovers together.

I tug on Leo's arm and lead him back down the bridge toward the lamplit path. The sky is falling from indigo to black quickly and I want him to make it to Angela before she decides to pass out for the night.

But Leo stops, and even though I tug, he doesn't move. I may be fit, but I can't move a six-foot-tall, two-hundred-pound man who doesn't want to be moved. I turn back to him and frown.

He's in a pool of soft yellow light, cast from a glowing lamp. The bridge, the Lovers' Bridge, arches gracefully, and the water is an inky pool below us. The night is soft, the breeze gentle, and I can see why this bridge got its name.

If Noah were here with me, I'd be kissing him right now.

There's music from a nearby restaurant, and the smells of cooking—bread, wine sauce, the sweet scent of plums and charred steak—it's enough to make your mouth water.

In fact, maybe I can borrow Leo's phone and call Noah to come down and join me for dinner.

"Do you think I could borrow—"

"Merry." Leo takes another steps forward.

I take a step back. Because. Personal space.

"Why didn't we ever get together?"

Wait. What?

I frown at him. "Probably because we were friends. And then you married my sister."

I hold up my hands in a slow-down gesture—because the way Leo is looking at me? He's never looked at me that way before.

"Marriage is hard," he says, rubbing a hand over his face. "I'm tired, Merry. I was never tired with you. Why didn't I see that? Why didn't I see what was right in front of me?"

What?

He reaches out and I slap his hand away.

"You were always so fun. So nice to me."

Are you kidding me? A hysterical sort of incredulity bubbles up inside me. What an ass.

He bends close, leaning in for a kiss. *A kiss.*

I smack him. "What's wrong with you? Pull yourself together."

The crack of my palm hitting his cheek is gunshot loud. My hand stings and I shake out the needlelike pain as Leo gives me a stunned look.

"But I came to France to see you," he says imploringly, rubbing his cheek.

He...wait...what?

I take a millisecond to come to terms with this.

"You're not here for Angela?" I ask, just to make sure, backing away from him again. The cast-iron rail of the bridge digs into my back.

"Angela doesn't love me," he says in a flat voice. "She left. I did everything I could to make her happy. Everything, Merry. And she left. You never needed anything. You're easy."

I let out a choked laugh.

I want to kick him.

I'd kick a bucket of sense into him if I could.

"First of all," I say, shooting him a glare, "I'm not easy. And I do need things. Like loyalty. And compassion. And empathy. And honesty. And I don't know, how about someone who sees me and loves me? I need all of those things."

Leo sends me an incredulous look, "I know that."

"No. I don't think you do." I shrug. "And it doesn't matter. Because you're going back to my sister, and you're going to tell her you're a fool for saying proposing was a mistake—"

"You know about that?"

I raise my eyebrows.

"I didn't mean it," he says. He clenches his jaw and stares out at the lights shimmering on the lake.

"You didn't mean it," I repeat.

He nods glumly. "But once it was out there, I couldn't unsay it."

Oh jeez.

Do I have to say this again?

"Leo."

"What?" He looks back at me, and all the energy seems to have sizzled out of him, like a waterdrop evaporated on a hot stove. He just looks exhausted.

"What's more important to you? Your pride or Angela?"

He sighs and grips the iron railing. "Angela."

"Yeah." I nod. "I thought so. Look, when you think of love as a battle—not that I'm saying you do—but if you think of it as a battle, then pride is most important. But if you think of love as just that, love, then pride doesn't have any place."

He sighs. "I went at it wrong. I wanted her so much I think I smothered her. No. I know I did. She told me so."

I pat his arm sympathetically. "I get it. But Leo, there's a difference between needing love and being needy for love."

I learned that lesson the hard way.

He lets out a short, gruff laugh. "Thanks, Merry."

"You realize you've got a kid on the way?"

Leo and Angela and a baby. I really hope they figure things out.

"I know," he says. "It's terrifying. But also wonderful. I really don't want to mess this up."

I raise an eyebrow and he snorts.

"I know. I know. I basically already have."

I lean back against the railing and think about Pierre and Camille, Arnout and Yvette, me and Noah. If I've learned anything, it's that the value of loving someone can never be overestimated.

It's worth more than pride. More than art. It's worth a decade of searching. Thirty years of longing. It's worth standing in the middle of a storm. It's worth letting go of the past. It's worth forgiveness and baring your heart. And even if you're afraid, it's worth opening up and doing it anyway. Loving.

"Why did you come to Annecy?" I ask Leo, breathing in the cool air.

He sends me a rueful look. "I was panicking. I remembered how you were always able to fix things. I thought if I came, I'd feel better. I realize that was stupid."

"Very stupid," I agree.

He rubs both hands down his face and then shakes himself off, like he's shaking off water.

"I didn't mean all that about...you and me..." He waves his hands between us.

"I know."

"That's some arm you've got." He gives me a considering look and rubs his cheek. "You're great at soccer, but have you considered baseball? We could start a team. My work could sponsor—"

"Leo. Do you know what this bridge is?"

He frowns. "Yeah. That's why I was standing on it. I was contemplating the demise of my marriage in less than a hundred days."

"And?"

He leans on the railing. "I thought if Angela were here, I'd kiss her on this bridge. And that would solve everything."

I give him a quizzical smile. "Why would that solve everything?"

"Because." He elbows me good-naturedly in the side. "It's a legend. Anyone who kisses on this bridge is destined to spend the rest of their lives together. Fated love and all that. It's famous, you know?"

He turns to look at me when I'm silent for a long moment. "Merry?"

My heart turns over in my chest and I shake my head.

I think about the day Noah kissed me on this bridge. The dark passion in his eyes, the way his fingers dug into me as if he wouldn't ever let me go. How it felt as if the only way I'd keep breathing is if I kept kissing him. How the second we kissed, the only person in the world I wanted was him. I knew. I realize that it was at that kiss that—even if my mind didn't acknowledge it—my heart knew.

"Do you think Noah knows about this bridge?" I ask, my voice shaking.

Leo frowns at me. "Of course he does. He films travel shows. He knows everything about every place he visits."

A smile is growing inside me, growing so big I'm

surprised I'm not glowing bright like the lamps
positioned along the canal.

He knew.

He told me that he knew he loved me from the
minute he saw me.

But he really knew.

He kissed me on the Lovers' Bridge.

And that was him telling me that he wanted a lifetime
with me.

And I really, really want that too.

"Angela's here. In Annecy," I tell Leo, grinning at him
as I give him a quick hug. "Go and get her, bring her to
the bridge. Work things out."

I pat his arm as I pull away.

Leo, bless him, is stunned. "Wait. Angela's here? She's
in France?"

I grin and tell him the name and address of her hotel.
"I'd take you, but I have to go back to the chateau to find
Noah. I have to go."

I lift my hand in a goodbye wave and start to turn, but
Leo grabs me. "Noah's not at the chateau."

"What?"

How would Leo know?

"He's in town. I saw him when we were hugging. I
would've called out to him, but it was more important to
talk to you. Anyway, he saw us then walked away in a
hurry."

The happiness in my chest pops and leaks out,
running down toward the dark water. "He saw us
hugging?"

"Yes."

"And then he left in a hurry?"

"Yes." Leo gives a firm nod, then he perks up, "Can you take me to the hotel then? Since Noah isn't at the—"

"Bye, Leo."

I take off across the bridge at a run.

"Where are you going?" he shouts after me.

To find Noah.

I don't know what he thought when he saw Leo and me hugging on the Lovers' Bridge, but I don't want any misunderstandings. I love Noah.

And I don't want anyone else but him.

"Merry?" Leo shouts as I sprint off the bridge onto the path back toward town. "Where are you going?!"

"I'm going to start the rest of my life!" I shout as I run toward old town.

I leave Leo staring after me, standing alone on le Pont des Amours.

I don't look back, I'll only look forward from now on.

I dart through the narrow streets with their warmly lit medieval stone buildings, the outdoor cafés serving dinner, and past bicyclists and cars. My breath burns my lungs and I feel alive as I scan the street for a taxi.

Jupiter was right. I never believed I could be a swan, I never thought I could have a happy ending, or even that I deserved one. But I do.

I want to live with Noah in my fairytale chateau. Sure, the "castle" is crumbling and has kitten-sized rats. And our faithful hound is a surly lobster. And when we say I love you, the soundtrack will probably be creaky rooftiles, or groaning pipes, or the rumble of a summer thunderstorm.

My life in France hasn't been a movie with sweeping shots and orchestral music. No, it's been dirtier, messier, and more wonderful than I could have ever imagined.

But I want this.

I want this for good.

The only hitch in the plan?

I have to make sure that Noah wants it too.

But when I run out of the taxi and throw open the chateau's heavy wooden door, calling out his name, I realize, very quickly, that Noah is gone.

59

I SNIFFLE INTO THE SLEEVE OF MY SWEATER AND THEN WIPE it across my face, swiping away the tears.

"Mr. Rochester, ugh. I am not impressed."

I throw a contemptuous look at the glowing screen of my laptop, where Jane Eyre and Mr. Rochester are finally united in matrimonial bliss.

I have my arms wrapped around my knees and I'm nestled in a boat of blankets in the tower room. After a half hour of wandering around the chateau, checking every accessible room, every nook and cranny, I knew—without a doubt—that Noah wasn't here.

I charged my phone enough on the portable battery charger (swiped from Noah's suitcase) to call him. He didn't answer. I left a voicemail, just, *hey I'm at the chateau, where are you?*

Then when he didn't call back, I spent a good five minutes (okay fifteen) with my fingers hovering over the screen, debating whether or not I should send a text.

But the things I had to say, I didn't want to text.

So instead of pacing the great hall, I decided to climb up to the tower room, drag a pile of blankets and my laptop with me, and watch a gothic romance.

Now that it's over and the credits are rolling, I have to face the fact that it's late, it's dark—the moon is streaming silver crosshatches through the room—and Noah isn't back.

Which means...he isn't coming?

Or he was in an accident?

Or...?

I don't want to think that—like his mom—he'll just disappear and I'll spend the next seven years searching for him.

I glance around the tower room, silver threads of moonlight fall over me, and the glow of my laptop casts a blueish iridescence. The room is empty except for the light, my thick pile of blankets, and my computer.

The rest of the chateau is nighttime quiet. Now that the movie soundtrack has ended, there's only the wind stirring the trees, the creak of the roof, and me sniffling. Again.

"Gothic romances are terrible," I say, snapping my laptop shut and plunging the room into darkness.

"You think so?"

I look up quickly, at Noah standing in the doorway to the tower. He's bathed in darkness, and I can't read his expression. My heart trips around my chest, struggling to break through my ribs.

"You're here."

He steps into the room and when a beam of moonlight hits him I see that he's smiling.

"Where else would I be?"

I stand quickly, wiping at my eyes, smoothing my

dress. Noah walks forward and looks down at me, frowning. He touches my cheek.

"Were you crying?"

I shake my head yes then no. "I was watching *Jane Eyre*."

"Ah." He nods and brushes his fingers over my face, wiping away the salty tears.

"I was worried you were gone," I admit. "Leo said he saw you when we were hugging. I thought you figured that I still wanted Leo. When you weren't here I was scared you'd left. That you were so upset you didn't even grab your bags."

Noah drops his hands from my face and gives me a confused look. "Why would I do that?"

Good point.

"You wouldn't," I say, letting the truth sink in.

"I wouldn't," he agrees.

He reaches out and takes my hand, threading his fingers through mine. He's looking at me that way again, the way he looked at me on the bridge, right before he kissed me.

I let the last vestiges of my past fall away, breaking their hold on me. The fear that Noah would leave me was my old way of thinking, it doesn't have any place here anymore. I'm not afraid anymore.

"Can I ask you something?"

Noah tilts an eyebrow. "What?"

"Did you know when we kissed on le Pont des Amours that it meant we were destined to spend the rest of our lives together?"

His eyes flicker, but I can't read his expression. "No."

"You didn't?" I ask, surprised.

He reaches up and tucks a strand of hair behind my

ear. There's a smile, tugging at the corner of his lips. "I didn't know. I only hoped."

I step forward and wrap my arms around his waist.

"I rushed back here to tell you something," I say, looking up at him.

"What's that?" he asks, pulling me closer, running his hands down my back.

"In case I wasn't clear, I wanted you to know that I love you. You said you wanted a lifetime, and I want that too."

"That's good," he says, smiling down at me, the moon reflecting off his eyes, tinting them with warmth.

"That's good? That's all you have to say? I pour out my heart and you say, 'That's good'?" I smile at him and shake my head.

He kisses the corner of my mouth, then my jaw, then my neck. His mouth sends tingles over my skin. My body turns liquid and all it took was three kisses and the magic of moonlight spilling over us.

"That's good," Noah says, his mouth tracing along my neck and down to my collarbone, "because I called Jupiter and bought the chateau. I thought you'd want a home—"

"You what?"

"For when we're married."

I push back from Noah and look at the happy smile on his face. "For when—"

"We're married," he confirms.

He holds out a ring, one I hadn't noticed in his hands. It gleams in the moonlight, the bright stones catching and winking at me.

"Say yes," he says.

I jump into his arms, and we're kissing, his mouth

over mine, his hands holding me up, and in between kisses and breaths and love words, I say, "Yes. Yes. Yes."

LATER WHEN WE'RE LYING IN A COCOON OF BLANKETS, bathed in moonlight, Noah rubs his hands over my hips and I smile at the warmth of the ring on my finger.

"I have a question," I say, stretching back into him. "What would you have done if I said no?"

Noah chuckles and pulls me closer. He presses his mouth to the sensitive spot where my neck meets my shoulder. "I would've pulled a gothic plot twist, and locked you in my tower room."

"What a coincidence!" I say.

"Oh yeah?" His hands trail up to my breasts, his thumbs lingering on my nipples. A warm tingling rushes through me.

"Yes. Because if you were actually going to leave, I was going to lock *you* in the tower room."

"Mmm. Maybe we should just stay in the tower room then."

"For a few days?"

"At least."

Then there isn't any more talking or any more questions—because we get back to doing what you're supposed to be doing in a romantic, moonlight-filled room.

Loving.

THE NEXT MORNING I WAKE UP WHEN MY PHONE RINGS,

shrilly yanking me from a delicious dream involving Noah and a lake of French wine.

Noah groans and rolls over, throwing his arm over his eyes to keep out the noise and the burgeoning sunlight.

I don't blame him. He worked hard last night.

I turn on my phone and groan, "Hello?"

"You're welcome!" Jupiter drawls.

I scramble upright, clutching the blanket to my chest even though she (obviously) can't see me.

"What is it? What?" My mind is a bit cloudy, still stuck in that effervescent dream lake where Noah and I were skinny dipping.

"You! Merry." Her laugh is warm and rich and *so* Jupiter. "I set out to give you inspiration and I succeeded. I knew all it would take was getting you away from your family to somewhere romantic. The chateau! The man! My little duckling all grown up. Inspired!"

I blink at the sunlight, at the mess of blankets, at Noah back asleep.

"Wait. You inspired *me*? Why would you do that? I'm not an artist."

She tsks, and I can hear the censure in her voice when she says, "Because I love you, Merry. I'm your godmother. Besides, what's this about not being an artist? *Everyone* is an artist. Every day we all create our life, we create our destiny! What is more artistic than *that*?"

Jupiter is wound up, and I'm sure she's about to start waxing poetic about the Berlin Wall, or the Tate Modern, or the Marquess, and although I'm feeling really, really grateful, I have something else on my mind.

Noah's awake.

He's turned his head and he's watching me with a *particular* glint in his eyes.

"Thank you, Jupiter," I say, meaning it more than she could possibly know.

"Well, I did drive a hard bargain for the chateau. And you won't forget to let me help plan the wedding. No puce. Puce is a terrible color."

"Thank you," I say again.

And in typical Jupiter fashion, she hangs up.

I drop the phone and crawl over the warm blankets to Noah. Fresh morning air, smelling of dew and mountain lakes, drifts through the open windows.

"Who was that?" he asks, his eyes hooded as he stares at the naked line of my shoulder.

"Our fairy godmother," I answer.

He smiles and then starts to kiss down my shoulder, running his hand over my arms, down my hips.

Then, I shake my head, "Wait, I forgot. I'm supposed to meet Angela for breakfast," I cry mournfully.

Noah presses a kiss to my mouth. "I'm sure she's busy."

"What do you mean?" I fret. How much time do we have to make it into Annecy?

"Merry. I mean, Leo and Angela are in France. In Annecy. I don't think they're going to make it for breakfast."

I frown.

"And neither are we," he says.

Hmm.

"You might be right."

He grins. "Of course I am."

60

SEVENTY-THREE STEPS.

I know because I counted them.

It's only seventy-three steps through the cucumber garden, around the curving stone tower, past the gatehouse, toward the glistening sunlit rocks overlooking Lac d'Annecy. There's a wooden trellis on the flat rocks, wreathed in deep red roses, and standing in front of the trellis is Noah.

He's in a dove gray morning suit, a smile in his eyes as he scans the gathering of our friends and family.

My parents are here. And truly there must be something in the air. Because they're sitting next to each other, speaking amicably, which I don't think I've seen in nearly twenty years. My Uncle Diego and Aunt Bertie are here. They flew over, and wow, my aunt's hat is a stunner —it has a model of the Eiffel tower on top and...is that real cheese? It seems to be melting in the sun.

Oh well.

There's Noah's dad, near the front, wearing a suit,

with a blue handkerchief and a bow tie. He was, he decided, willing to come out of hiding, for his son.

Although I doubt anyone here will recognize the great Thomas Arnout.

Except maybe Jupiter. She's in a rainbow watercolor silk dress, resplendent, with her newest project—a distinguished ceramic artist fallen on hard times.

Pierre stands with Noah at the trellis. He's in the same dove gray suit, looking settled and happy. Probably because he just got back from his honeymoon with Camille.

Leo stands behind Pierre, rocking back and forth on his heels, I'm sure, trying to catch a glimpse of Angela.

She isn't here though, she had to run up to use the Louvre bathroom. She was really, really sorry, but she couldn't hold it, because as she put it, "This baby is doing jumping jacks on my bladder".

She's in the second trimester and her bump is now a ball, and I have to say, she looks cute in her bridesmaid dress.

The music starts, a single harpist, strumming the notes to let us know that it's time.

Seventy-three steps.

The best, most wonderful seventy-three steps of my life.

The sweet smell of roses drifts up from my bouquet and I smile.

"I thought you didn't like weddings," Kimmy, my second cousin, says.

I grin at her. She's putting a final layer of lipstick on. It goes perfectly with her Bordeaux colored bridesmaid dress.

"What gave you that idea? I love weddings."

"I guess so," she says, eyeing my hands, but this time I'm not clenching my bouquet in trepidation. Nope. I'm ready to walk down the aisle.

To Noah.

"Of course Meredith loves weddings!" Camille says, frowning at Kimmy. "She is the bride!"

Then, Angela hurries over, a hand on her rounded stomach.

"Sorry! Sorry! I'm back. Are you ready? Of course you're ready." She reaches out and brushes my hair back, adjusting my veil. "There. Beautiful."

I give her a wobbly smile and she wrinkles her nose. "Don't cry, Merry. Noah loves you, but even he—as nice as he is—doesn't want you to cry on your wedding day."

"I'm not crying," I tell her. "I'm just really, really happy."

She knows it's true, and so do I.

With a quick smile, she starts down the aisle.

The sounds of the harp floats on the wind, tinkling toward me.

Next, Kimmy walks down the aisle, counting her steps under her breath.

Then, Camille pats my arm and says, "Merci, Meredith."

And I know she's thanking me, again, for my help with Pierre, for our friendship, and for Pierre and Noah having a close relationship.

We're neighbors now. And friends.

"Je t'en prie," I say.

See? I'm learning. And someday, maybe I'll be able to have a full conversation in French.

At that, Camille smiles and starts down the aisle.

Then the harpist begins to play the bridal march, and it's my turn.

I step down the aisle, and when I do, the chateau, my family and friends, the music, it all disappears into the background, and all that's left is the look on Noah's face.

He loves me. There's no doubt about it.

My heart squeezes in my chest and I smile, and smile, and smile.

Seventy-three steps.

And then it's done, and I'm holding Noah's hands and he's saying I love you, and I'm saying I love you.

And when we've said our vows and promised a lifetime, we turn back toward the chateau, and we walk together, holding hands.

To home. And happiness. And a lifetime of messy, dirty, magical, *requited* love.

Because that's the best kind of love. The kind where you love someone with your whole heart and they love you with their whole heart right back.

THE END

NOTE: IF YOU'RE WONDERING WHETHER OR NOT NOAH finished his book and film on Annecy...yes. He did. It's called *Le Pont des Amours*. You can find it at your local library. Also, don't forget to watch his latest episodes, where we travel to all the most romantic locations in the world—the Amalfi Coast is next.

Love, Merry.

ACKNOWLEDGMENTS

I would like to give sincere thanks to Céline for her wonderful help in making sure my French was spot on! Thank you!!! Any and all mistakes are mine and mine alone.

Thank you to my husband, for the inspiration. Happy Birthday! If we can't fly to France, I'll write you a book that takes place in France!

Thank you to all of you who write and tell me how much you enjoy reading my stories, it always brightens my day. Thank you to all who post, write reviews, and share my books—I appreciate you so much!

And finally, thank you to my family for your endless support and love. You are the best.

JOIN SARAH READY'S NEWSLETTER

Want more Merry and Noah? Get an exclusive bonus epilogue.

When you join the Sarah Ready Newsletter you get access to sneak peaks, insider updates, exclusive bonus scenes and more.

Join today for an exclusive epilogue:

www.sarahready.com/newsletter

ABOUT THE AUTHOR

Author Sarah Ready writes contemporary romance and romantic comedy. Her books have been described as "euphoric", "heartwarming" and "laugh out loud".

Sarah writes stand-alone romcoms and romcoms in the Soul Mates in Romeo series, all of which can be found at her website: www.sarahready.com.

Stay up to date, get exclusive epilogues and bonus content. Join Sarah's newsletter at www.sarahready.com/newsletter.

ALSO BY SARAH READY

Stand Alone Romances:

The Fall in Love Checklist

Hero Ever After

Once Upon an Island

Josh and Gemma Make a Baby

Josh and Gemma the Second Time Around

French Holiday

The Space Between

Soul Mates in Romeo Romance Series:

Chasing Romeo

Love Not at First Sight

Romance by the Book

Love, Artifacts, and You

Married by Sunday

My Better Life

Scrooging Christmas

Stand Alone Novella:

Love Letters

Find these books and more by Sarah Ready at:

www.sarahready.com/romance-books